TRANSFORMATION

MORETON SCIENTIFIC INVESTIGATION SERIES
BOOK 3

ROB NESBITT

Publications

BEFORE YOU DIVE INTO THE ADVENTURE...

Rob Nesbitt

Writer, Cartoonist, Designer

If you would like to read my other books, receive free short stories and other goodies please sign up to my author mailing list here at https://rnesbitt.com

This Book is Written in American English

ONE

Jonny Clarke had done it at another museum once before without getting caught. Unplanned and plain dumb, an opportunist event, on the spur of the moment, a ridiculous whim. He hadn't known what to expect or had the slightest idea where to offload the stolen artifact. This time was different. By reverse-engineering his previous folly, he found a buyer with a specific want and a logical sequence fell into place, researched and planned, filling him with confidence.

The first visit to the museum was purely that, a visit for research and enlightenment at the hype that the newly opened Museum of Alien Life received with mixed reviews from the national press and media, some reporting a refreshing new way of exhibiting extraterrestrial evidence while others called it a scam, a Victorian-style freak show preying on the minds and pockets of those who believed there is life out there on some far-flung planet. The CEO of the museum proved that his motto, "All news is good news," was correct from the day the Museum of Alien Life opened its doors. The place, buzzing from nine in the morning till eight at night when public viewing was over, was the latest place to be in London.

On his second visit, Jonny Clarke looked as bizarre as the

mummified remains of a three-foot alien in the entrance foyer at the ticket office. Jonny's usual appearance was unremarkable, with his height of five feet six, bald head, thick gray beard and mustache, gaunt figure, and bland features. People could easily pass him in the street without a second glance. Today, clean-shaven with makeup that looked as if a plasterer had applied it with a trowel, combined with a short crimson, sequined dress, unshaved legs, curly red wig, and fox fur wrap, he attracted serious attention. The makeup made his face resemble a mechanical laughing man at a fairground with bright red lips, pink cheeks and finished off with an absurd dash of rouge on the tip of his nose. It pleased him that everyone was staring. People laughed behind his back and the lady in the ticket booth, trying to hide her disbelief at the absurd apparition, failed badly. Her eyes, still wide, after he turned on his high heels, followed him into the first exhibit hall, her mouth gaping, the tip of her glistening tongue peeping over tiny bottom teeth.

"Keep watching, folks, and you'll only remember what your eyes tell you," he whispered to himself, walking through a double-sided interactive display of *known* global alien landing sites. The large, flying saucer clock in the hall lasered seven o'clock on the far wall, giving him an hour to mingle, then change out of the outrageous disguise, while hidden till the morning.

He minced into the *Area 51* experience and clattered across the viewing platform where a gathering stood, watching and listening to the commentary. Most turned their heads as he passed. Next was the life-size alien ship in a mock hangar. Jonny swaggered around the metal walkways that spiraled around the ship, through the cockpit and living quarters, and into the stasis pod galley that alien-abducted witnesses described in the Sierra Nevada encounter over fifty years before. He strutted his stuff through every floor, landing, and exhibit, making sure almost everyone in the building had seen him walking non-stop for over forty minutes before leaning against a wall watching the door to the ladies' room. When it was clear, he entered, pulling out the two lock picks, then stopped and listened. Satisfied there was nobody in any cubicle, he slid the picks into the lock, taking less than thirty seconds to open the door, stepped inside the long narrow maintenance cupboard for the toilet cisterns, and locked the door from the inside.

After the announcement boomed through the tannoy system, the building emptied, as security herded stragglers toward the exit doors. The ticket booth cashed up, and with checks done and takings locked away, the museum fell silent.

At eight the next morning, the first members of staff arrived, and another day began. At nine o'clock, the doors opened to the public and the queue of visitors filled the entrance lobby to buy tickets and view the wonders of the Museum of Alien Life. An hour later every exhibit hall was full of chattering excited people; school trips, guided tours, and throngs of customers eager to spend money in the museum's cafe with its quirky selection of Martian mallows, Venusian vol-au-vents and little green gingerbread men.

At ten o'clock, Jonny Clarke stepped onto the sidewalk carrying a carrier bag from the museum gift shop he acquired the night before, containing a crimson dress, curly red wig, fox fur wrap, and a pair of ruby high heels. At the bottom of the bag was an envelope containing three original black and white photos and a leather drawstring pouch holding thirty pieces of stolen meteorite.

On Tavistock Road, he discarded the bag with his disguise in a trash bin, placed the envelope into his inside jacket pocket, and slipped the pouch into the concealed deep pocket. He crossed the road, taking a sharp left at Jubilee Market into Tavistock Close. As the short close opened up and the Transport Museum came into view, a voice made him pause.

"Stop right there!" He turned to see a large bald-headed man in a black suit.

"You have something that doesn't belong to you," said the man, smiling, with a flash of gold teeth.

"Sorry?" said Jonny, confused.

"I'll have the photos back, if you don't mind."

A sinking sensation dropped to the pit of his stomach and he swallowed hard. His audacious plan hadn't worked. He thought of the ridiculous disguise the day before and couldn't believe it had let him down. Enter in a disguise that nobody would recognize him in and exit in a male disguise that made him equally unrecognizable. How had they known so quickly?

Fight was not an option and not in Jonny's nature, so flight it had to be. A triumphant smirk played on Jonny's lips as he ran, confident that the man wouldn't be able to catch him.

With one well-aimed punch, a second man, positioned strategically and pretending to talk on his phone, hit him in the solar plexus. The men grabbed Jonny, lifting both his feet off the ground, and threw him into the back of an unmarked black SUV with tinted windows.

Fourteen hours later, nine miles from the Museum of Alien Life, a body surfaced in Limehouse Basin. The autopsy confirmed an alcohol level high enough to kill a man twice the size and concluded accidental death through drowning. It was assumed that Jonny Clarke had gone on a bender and fallen into the basin between the River Thames and the Commercial Road lock, the gateway into Regent's Canal.

In Jonny's concealed pocket, the scenes of crime officer discovered a leather pouch stamped with the crest logo of the Museum of Alien Life, which was the only unusual observation apart from a facial bruise of undetermined cause. The pouch, with a hole in one corner, contained two small pieces of meteorite. Along with some priceless photos that weren't recovered, it was confirmed that someone stole the pouch and its contents from the museum.

Alex Munro tapped in the six-digit code, pulled on the steel door, placed the envelope inside, and locked the safe. He would store the photos until the heat was off before shipping them to a buyer.

The missing pieces of meteorite were frustrating, as a defective camera had not caught Jonny stealing them on the museum's internal CCTV system. Thankfully, the discovery of the missing photos had been made first thing that morning. After reviewing the CCTV, Jonny was seen taking the photos but was initially thought to have escaped until his men saw him heading for the main entrance just before ten.

Alex laughed at the man's stupidity. If he had changed into his disguise after he had taken the stolen photos, he may have gotten away with it.

He examined the tear in the pouch and assumed the other pieces of the stolen meteor had fallen out between Jonny's capture in Tavistock Close and being found face down in Limehouse Basin. An annoying loss, but the insurance policy would cover it handsomely and may be good luck, making the robbery a fortuitous and profitable event that would solve his current cash flow crisis.

He smiled, locked the two meteorite pieces in a sealed container, put on his overcoat, and walked to the staff exit of the Museum of Alien Life.

TWO

Mary O'Hare carried the steaming mug of tea along the towpath, placing it next to her husband, who sprawled on his belly, squinting through the one lens left in his glasses.

"What do you think?" he said, kneeling so she could have a clear view.

"Pretty good," she said.

"Just pretty good?" he said, standing and taking a mouthful of tea.

"The gold. It doesn't look right. It's too yellowy."

"Can't do much about that, Mary. They didn't have gold paint."

"You should have waited, Connor. It's a great bit of painting, but yellow doesn't look classy like gold, and the name of the boat is the first thing people look at."

Connor O'Hare smiled and agreed with his wife as usual, but he felt more than satisfied with the new name of the sixty-foot narrowboat, the 'Pride of Skibbereen,' which proudly adorned the emerald-green hull in red and yellow ornate lettering, concealing the original name given when it was constructed fifty years before.

"Have you finished all the paperwork yet?" she said, passing him a chocolate biscuit.

"Paperwork?"

"Don't bullshit me, Connor O'Hare. You know exactly what paperwork I'm talking about. For the boat's name change."

He sighed and smiled again. She was like a dog after a bone.

"I've let the insurers know, but I haven't told the Canal and River Trust yet. I'll do it later. Let's just enjoy the new name for now and let the paint dry."

Standing as far back as he could to look at the fresh paint, Connor admired the professional finish to the lettering. Not a bad effort at all for someone who was not a signwriter. He cupped the mug in his hands to warm stiff fingers, stiff from being locked onto a brush and holding a Mahl stick for hours to steady the brush.

Limehouse Basin had many narrowboats moored up as short and long-term moorings; not much cheaper than the eye-watering rents on dry land for moorings in the basin, but he wasn't concerned. Soon on the move, they wouldn't be mooring longer than a night or two in any location, unless it took their fancy, which would be a fraction of the cost of staying at Limehouse Basin. He checked the other boat names: The Merry Pilot, Melody Rose, and Fleet of Fancy, three permanent eighty-footers. He smiled once more. His lettering was as good, if not better.

They imagined the perfect retirement summer, then planned how, where, and when they were going to do it. Saving for all those years to buy a narrowboat, and now they couldn't believe it had all come together just as they'd imagined. The fifty-year-old boat was like having a new baby all over again. The anticipation, excitement, exhilaration, then the questions and doubts. What would it look like? How would they manage to look after it? Could they afford the new addition to the family? What would they call it? A lifetime of work at the post office in their little village in southern Cork had just reached the end, both retiring on the same day to start their new adventure.

"Isn't this grand, Mary?" he said, pulling her in close. "We bloody deserve this. All those years dreaming and here we are."

"Hasn't quite sunk in. Just wish Sean and Moira could be here with us."

"Mary, we've dragged those kids on every holiday we've ever had, so chill out. Let's have a bloody break. We can always ask them to join us later. Can we just have some time together for the first time in our lives? I'm sure they would say exactly the same."

"But I miss them."

"Jeez, woman, you only said goodbye to them two days ago. And you've been FaceTiming them ever since!"

"I know you're right, but it would have been nice."

"And it will be, after we settle in and get used to our lovely little boat. Once we're all shipshape, you can invite them aboard."

She smiled, stretched up, and kissed him on the chin.

"You going to stand there all day, Connor O'Hare, or are you going to start our maiden voyage?"

"Mary, you may be the master of our house, but here, I'm the captain, and I'll decide when we set sail."

He winked at her and disappeared down into the galley, reappearing with something wrapped in colorful paper.

"A bottle of champagne smashed on the hull would damage the woodwork, so"—he pulled a chocolate-shaped bottle from the wrapping—" if you would do the honors, my good lady."

Mary shrieked with laughter.

"You silly old bugger, O'Hare!" She took the chocolate bottle in her fist. "I hereby"—she laughed again—"you do it, Connor."

"Absolutely not. The monarch always names the ship before it's launched and, as my queen, you have a duty to perform." After several false starts, Queen Mary O'Hare christened the good ship the Pride of Skibbereen and blessed all who sailed upon her. Connor slipped the moorings and started the engine.

He was about to open the throttle when something caught his eye. He took a step sideways to get the sun's reflection on the water's surface out of his eye. Bubbles weren't anything unusual on the canal, but these were different. These were bright blue and didn't pop when they reached the surface.

"Mary. Take a look at this," he said, pointing at the increasing number of blue bubbles making a large circle, building from the center outward.

"Probably some toxic crap some lazy bastard has dumped," she said, taking a bite out of the remains of the chocolate bottle in her hand.

"But there's no dead fish."

She gave a dismissive wave. "Come on, Connor, don't spoil the moment. We should be on our way. We were going to make a move today, so now's as good a time as any."

The Pride of Skibbereen was soon chugging its way across Limehouse Basin, where it could access Regent's Canal, then travel a few miles before joining the extensive Grand Union Canal for the next part of their adventure. Connor doffed his sailor's cap to his wife.

"Full speed ahead!" he shouted, waving the cap in the bright sunlight. She smiled, kissed him on the cheek, and snuggled into his shoulder. With eyes fixed on the lock gates ahead, they didn't notice the blue bubbles following in their wake.

THREE

"If they don't stop that racket, so help me, there will be a murder in this town," said Ben, looking down at two workmen digging a trench in the sidewalk outside, breaking the tarmac surface with a pneumatic drill. "I can't concentrate, and these samples have to be worked on this afternoon."

Claire peered over his shoulder. "Do you want me to work my charm on them?"

"It won't stop them."

Kath O'Brian pushed them out of the way, clutched the window frame, and peered over the edge. "I'll sort the little feckers out for you," she said, turning about-face, and marching down the stairs.

"Kath!" shouted Ben, but she ignored him.

"I can't watch," said Claire. "This could be brutal."

Ben and Claire moved away from the window, expecting a rowdy confrontation, but the drilling stopped, and all was calm. Five minutes later, Kath was back.

"Ben, get on with whatever was so urgent. Fred and Harry will be back in two hours. Is that long enough?"

"How on earth did you manage to—"

"Never you mind how. Just get on with it," she barked, winking at Claire.

"I'll make us a brew," said Claire, "while you analyze those samples. Do you need me to do some for you?"

"Thanks, but no thanks," said Ben, pulling his lab coat off the rack and shaking his head in disbelief. "I need to do this myself, but you could do a quality check for me later. I think two hours will be just about enough time to get this done."

Kath was already filling the kettle when Claire walked into the kitchen.

"Don't let on to Ben, but those two clowns digging the road up are my Patrick's cousins. I told them that if they buggered off for a couple of hours, I would let Patrick out for a few beers tonight at the Black Bear. I want Ben scratching his head for the rest of the day." She chuckled.

Claire smiled. How Ben had employed Kath O'Brian to clean for him was a complete mystery. She spoke to him like she was scolding a child and seemed to run the show, fearless of anyone who worked at Moreton Scientific Investigation or was brave enough to step over the threshold. She scared the living daylights out of everyone, but with a heart of gold, she made the place a joy to work at when the mood took her.

"I was going to let Patrick off the leash tonight anyway, so it killed two birds."

"Not like you, Kath, to let him out on a weekday. Are you going soft in your old age?"

"No. I needed the simple old bugger out of my way. Jenny Jones has some hot gossip for me concerning the landlord of the Rat and Fiddle and one of the kitchen staff. Now I don't want our Patrick earwigging, do I?"

"Eddy Tottle, having a fling? He hasn't got time to be canoodling with any of the girls in the kitchen. All the ones I can think of are ancient or happily married."

"Who said it was one of the girls?" said Kath with a sly grin, tapping the side of her nose.

"Bloody hell, Kath, not the new chef. Eddy Tottle's gay? Is that what you're saying?"

Kath burst out laughing, which developed into a hacking cough. When she stopped spluttering, she wagged her finger. "Joking, I am. All I know is that he is having a liaison with someone in the kitchen. Gender as yet unidentified. Jenny Jones will reveal all tonight."

"Will you share the gossip tomorrow?" said Claire, picking up a tray of tea and biscuits.

"Of course. Us girls must stick together," she said with a nod and another wink.

Ben didn't look up or even acknowledge the tea and biscuits. Claire left him staring down a microscope, knowing full well the tea would still be in the cup, stone cold with a thick skin in an hour.

She went through the list of current jobs, signing off the weekly water sampling for the river authority and a batch of baby food suspected of contamination. She completed both tasks: signing off the weekly water sampling for the river authority and handling a batch of baby food suspected of contamination. Now, she was faced with the job that nobody wanted: visiting Meyrick's slaughterhouse to conduct routine checks as part of their annual food safety contract. She hated this part of her work, as it included watching the slaughter of cattle, sheep, and pigs. Seeing the animals herded in alive and then stunned sickened her. She didn't mind the butchery of the carcasses, but the point at which the animals ceased to be alive left her cold and sad. As she contemplated calling the manager of Meyrick's, the office phone rang.

"Moreton Scientific Investigation, how may I help you?" said Claire, in a voice that Ben had told her reminded him of being showed how to use a life jacket on a plane.

"You didn't get this from me, right?"

"Ron. Nice to hear from you. What do you mean—didn't get what from you?"

"Got a pen?"

"Yes," said Claire, laughing. "Why the cloak and dagger?"

Ron Logan, a scientist at a rival company, The Cambridge Centre, had collaborated with them on previous occasions and was now a good friend. Claire and Ron hadn't hit it off in the early days, but Claire warmed to him after his excellent work for the team. She still loathed his personal hygiene but let it all go over her head, even though it made her feel queasy.

"Let's just say I'm hedging my bets for the future. Is that pen in your hand?"

Claire wrote a name and telephone number.

"Ben. Can I interrupt you for a second?"

He didn't answer.

"Ben."

He waved her away without taking his eye from the microscope.

"Okay, I'll tell you about Ron's strange phone call later," she said, walking back toward the lab door.

Ben swung around on his chair. "What did he say?"

She turned and took a few steps back.

"Not a lot. He told me to give you this and said you would know what to do. What's going on, Ben, and what did he mean when he said he was 'hedging his bets'?"

"Where's Kath?" whispered Ben.

"Dusting and polishing the downstairs offices. Why?"

Ben stood on tiptoe to look at the door over Claire's shoulder.

"Fancy a coffee and a sticky bun at Martha's Coffee House?" he said, taking his lab coat off.

"What's wrong with my coffee?"

"I'll explain everything when we get there, and I'm paying."

They walked together in silence to the market square. Claire struggled to keep up with him, and Ben kept looking around to make sure nobody they knew was watching them. He stopped at the cafe doorway, checked the clientele inside, made an order, and took a seat.

Ben warmed his hands on the large white latte cup, inhaled, and closed his eyes. "Nothing like the smell of fresh ground coffee, and this place makes a stunning latte."

Claire nodded, staring at him, waiting for some form of explanation.

He opened his eyes and stared into hers.

She waited, but he said nothing, just looked apprehensive, and the silence between them seemed to go on forever. She was about to prompt him when he spoke. "Do you like Ron?"

It was the last thing Claire had expected, and it was her turn not to be able to speak for a few moments. "I thought you were going to tell me my employment was about to be terminated."

Ben snorted into his coffee, spraying some of it onto the table. She mopped it up with a napkin and stared back.

"In what way? What do you mean by 'like'?"

Ben laughed. "I certainly don't mean romantically." She pulled a horrified face. "I know that would be laughable after all the names you've called him in the past."

"So, what do you mean, do I like Ron?"

A waitress arrived and placed donuts on the table. Ben glanced up at her, waiting for her to be out of earshot.

"Could you work with Ron?"

"Are you sending me on some investigation? Just me and Ron?"

Ben sipped his coffee. "No. I mean, could you work with Ron if he came to work for us?"

Claire was stunned. "Ron wants to work for you?"

"Yes, I believe he does. He's given me enough hints."

"So why don't you just ask him to join the business?"

Ben shook his head. "Miss Manson, take this as a massive compliment to your professional ability. I wouldn't take Ron on unless I had your blessing."

Claire sat back, unable to respond. She had only worked for Ben for a short while. Realistically, he should employ staff as he saw fit, not consult her, an employee hardly out of university with very little experience and still wet behind the ears.

"Ben, if you want Ron to join the business, you shouldn't have to ask for my approval. What if I said no?"

"Then he would not be asked," said Ben, taking another sip and a bite out of a donut. "You should try one of these, they're very good."

She ignored the suggestion.

"I don't like Ron's foul habits, but I think he would be an excellent asset."

Ben pointed his finger at her. "You haven't answered my question. Could you work with Ron if he came to work for us?"

"Before I answer this, what would he be doing if he worked for you?"

Ben laughed. "Don't panic, you won't be sidelined."

"But there isn't enough work for another member of staff."

"But there soon will be. Ron is feeding me leads left, right, and center, which should result in new contracts. When it reaches the point where he is viable, I will take him on, but only if you are okay with him joining. Now would you mind answering the question?"

"Just answer me one more thing."

Ben rolled his eyes.

"What have I done to deserve this?" she said.

He had never seen her looking so serious and stared back. He was being illogical and thought back to all the times she had been less than professional, taunting him during a highly embarrassing naked encounter in a decontamination tent with innuendos and hints, albeit tongue-in-cheek. By rights, he should have fired her. But she was so intuitive, clever, self-motivated, hardworking, really funny, and—beautiful. He hated to admit to himself that she was beautiful and right on his wavelength. Was it the physical attraction that made him want to keep her and risk not taking on Ron Logan, who would be a massive bonus to the business? All he knew was that he had to keep her, but he couldn't tell her why, as he didn't actually know why himself. His mind raced for an appropriate response.

"You have proved beyond doubt in the short time you have been with us you are an integral part of the team, and I would not want to jeopardize that."

They sat for a minute, staring at each other in silence. He had a distinct feeling that she was aware of his attraction to her.

She broke the long stare, took a large bite from a donut, and nodded. "Welcome Ron on board. I'm okay with it. He'll be so good for us, and don't bumble around waiting for the perfect time to take him on. Just do it. I'm certain it will work out."

Ben smiled. "Thank you, Miss Manson. I'll take it as read that you will not utter a word to the rest of the staff about this?"

"Scout's honor."

"Good. Get that coffee down you. We have work to do."

"Before we go back, could you tell me one little thing," she said, fluttering her eyelashes.

Ben blushed. His pulse quickened, anticipating an embarrassing question.

"Is Ron feeding you clients that should go to the Cambridge team?"

"I can't tell you where he's getting the information from, as I promised him I wouldn't tell a soul, and I always keep my word."

"Okay, it's just that he could get into serious trouble, and we've built a great rapport with them."

"Let's just say it's all above board and is not a conflict between us and Cambridge."

"One last request, boss."

"Go on."

"Well, two actually. When am I going to get a proper contract of employment, and, if I'm such an integral member of the team, can I expect a pay raise anytime soon?"

Ben burst out laughing.

FOUR

"Thanks for calling, Ron. Have you got something for me?" said Ben, sitting in his car, well away from the lab.

"Strange one, this. My source says there's been a weird incident on a stretch of Regent's Canal. Several fish coated in a blue slime are swimming erratically on the surface. A couple on a canal barge reported seeing blue bubbles surfacing behind their boat as they passed through the lock gates from Limehouse Basin into the canal."

"Ron, I don't know the area you're talking about. Regent's Canal, is that London?"

"I'll send you a link to the Canal Trust website, but yes, it's London, north of the River Thames. Limehouse Basin is a link between the Thames and the inland canal system in London. You'll be having a phone call to ask for your attendance. I suggest you really pull out the stops on this one; it will lead to a lot more work."

"What about your lot at Cambridge? Wouldn't they get a look in before us?"

"Just trust me on this. It pays to play golf with the right people, especially when you discuss the merits of a certain scientific investigation team from the Cotswolds that make global news."

"Nice one, Ron. Would that person just happen to work for the Home Office?"

Ron chuckled. "I really couldn't say. Let me put it this way: I've never asked for a favor, but this person seems to listen to me. I think he might like me, but I'm sure you don't want me to go into that."

"Talking of not asking for a favor, you've shown keen interest in my little enterprise down here in Moreton, and never asked me the question. I'm hoping there will be an opening in the team for an experienced investigative scientist. There wouldn't be quite the magnificent salary that Cambridge can offer, but I believe in time that it will change. If you know of anyone who might be interested, just let me know," said Ben, trying his best not to laugh.

The other end of the line went silent.

"Ron—are you still there?"

"Of course I am." Ben winced as he heard Ron blowing his nose. "When do I start?"

"That depends on how much notice you have to give your boss at Cambridge. I was going to wait longer, but something, no, someone made me change my mind."

"Thanks, Ben."

"You're very welcome Ron. I'm looking forward to you being part of the team."

As soon as Ben put the phone down, it rang. Within half an hour, Ben and Claire were on their way to London.

"Blue fish. There are no blue freshwater fish that I know of," said Claire. "Unless a few mackerel have got into the canal system. They have a blue tinge to them."

"No chance. They wouldn't last long in freshwater. They'd eventually swell up and die through osmosis."

"Oh, I knew that, but you said 'eventually.' Perhaps they hadn't been in the canal for long," said Claire. "And by the way, are we coming home tonight? I haven't brought spare clothes."

"Mmm? Would have thought so."

"Great, Ben. You mean you don't know, do you?"

"I can't see us being here for that long. It's just a few fish to collect and some water samples. The rest gets done at the lab."

"Where are we going?"

"Do me a favor. Program the satnav. I was told to meet them at Cricketers Bridge on Old Ford Road."

Claire tried the satnav, but it could only find Old Ford Road in Bethnal Green.

"That'll do," said Ben.

"You're having a laugh; you'll never find it. Hang on, I'll use What3Words."

"What the hell is that?"

"Keep up, Grandad. It's a brilliant app that you oldies wouldn't get. There we are, app downloaded, and location in the middle of the bridge located." She started laughing.

"What's so funny?"

"For every square meter on the planet, this app gives a unique three-word reference location. The location in the middle of the bridge describes Ron's job title perfectly when he joins us."

"Go on—"

"Librarian:Soon:Bless."

Ben chuckled to himself as the three words appeared on the dashboard screen.

She confirmed the location, and the satnav sprang to life.

"I've told Ron he can work for us."

"Thought you were going to wait until he drummed up more business for us?"

"Changed my mind. I'm confident he'll come up with the goods, and I don't want him to drift off somewhere else. He's given us some pretty tasty leads so far, including this one today. I think you were right about not bumbling around."

"So, when does he start?"

"I just sent him a quick text and told him he's got the job. He has to give a month's notice, but said he has time owed, so he wouldn't be working the full month out. In any case, I think they'll give him garden leave."

"Garden leave?"

"Some firms ask you to clear your desk as soon as you hand your notice in and escort you off the premises. It's called garden leave. It's supposed to stop people from collecting vital information, especially if they're about to move to a rival company."

"So, Ron could start straight away?"

"If that's the case, then yes. Officially, he's not supposed to work for us right up to his final notice date with the Cambridge team. But you know Ron, he'll do whatever he wants, and I think he wants to start with us right away."

"Where are you going to put him? We haven't got a spare office. Hang on—don't you dare put him in my office with me."

"I was, actually."

"No bloody way am I having his stinking snot rags littering my office!"

"Look, Claire—"

"Not a chance," she said, folding her arms and pursing her lips.

"I want you to move out of your office and into mine," said Ben, giving her a sideways smirk. "It's big enough for both of us, and let's be fair, we spend most of the day either in the lab or out in the field together. Bottom line is that I'll have to put him somewhere, and like you, there is no way I'm sharing my office with him."

Claire leaned across and kissed Ben on the cheek. "Sorry, I was being a bitch, and thanks."

Ben flushed, wiping away any trace of lipstick.

"I'll make sure you have your own space in the office, a brand-new desk, and whatever else you need."

She smiled. He looked across and didn't like the sly glint in her eye.

She picked her phone up and started trawling through a website. He shot a glance at the screen, displaying an office supplies website. Had he just opened Pandora's wallet?

FIVE

Redirected to Bethnal Green police station, a patrol car took them to Cricketers Bridge with blues and twos, as Old Ford Road had been closed off and traffic congestion would have made it impossible for Ben and Claire to navigate on their own.

Carrying the field kit, cameras, and an additional carryall for samples, they checked in with the duty police officer on the bridge.

"Dr. Sharman and my assistant, Miss Claire Manson."

"We've been expecting you." The police officer noted their names, signed them in, and pointed to the north side of the bridge. "They're waiting for you down there."

A gathering of police and fire officers stood a hundred yards along the towpath, looking out across the wide canal.

"I hope they don't want us to go wading in," said Claire, looking down at the murky, stagnant water. "Bet there's no end of disgusting crap at the bottom."

"Probably a few dead cats and dogs and the odd corpse wearing concrete slippers," said Ben with a smirk.

"It looks foul. I thought canals were supposed to be clean?"

"They are, but the problem is they're usually shallow, and every time a boat passes, it stirs up the muck."

They descended the walkway onto the towpath, and as they approached the emergency crews, a woman stepped out and walked toward Ben with her hand outstretched.

"Ben Sharman?"

"Yes," he said, staring at her.

"And I'm Claire Manson, Dr. Sharman's assistant."

The woman smiled and shook Ben's hand firmly, then Claire's. "Chris Williams, pleased to meet you. You were expecting a Christopher, not a Christine, by the look on your face," she said, smiling at Ben.

"No, I just..." He struggled to find the right words. The Chris Williams he spoke to on the phone earlier had what he thought was a deep male voice. This Chris Williams had the same voice but was most definitely a woman. Beautiful light -brown skin, stunning braided dreadlocks that must have taken hours to do, and a radiant smile. The other thing that threw Ben off was the hippy outfit: ankle-length cheesecloth dress, tie-dyed in a kaleidoscope of pinks, reds, and greens; a combat jacket; black Doc Martens boots; and a Stetson-style felt hat with fishing flies hooked in on one side. For some weird reason, he half expected a pin-striped Home Office official.

"I know," she laughed. "I even sound like a bloke when I sing. My mother was the same, and my nan. Just a weird quirk of genetics. Anyway, don't let my 'Old Man River' tone put you off. Shall we get down to business?"

"Please," said Claire, nudging Ben, who she could see was still deep in thought.

"Sorry," said Ben. "Could you give us as much information as possible? You don't mind if we record this?" he said, waving his micro recorder in the air.

"Please do. It's tricky trying to write notes on a dimly lit canal bank," said Chris, giving Ben another radiant smile.

"I understand that a couple on a canal barge noticed blue bubbles and blue fish swimming erratically?" said Ben.

Chris nodded. "That's correct. Mr. and Mrs. O'Hare have moored up farther along the canal if you wish to speak to them."

"That would be useful," said Ben.

"The fish were dying—roach and perch. We netted some for you to analyze, here." She walked across to a box and pulled out an assortment of fish in a large, clear evidence bag.

Ben pulled a pair of neoprene gloves from his pocket and put them on, taking the bag and holding it up to the glare from an adjacent streetlight in the estate behind the canal.

"So, the fish are not blue. They're coated in a blue gelatinous substance."

"Yes," said Chris. "Looks like some kind of weird fungal infection."

"I've seen nothing like it," said Claire as Ben passed her the bag of fish.

"Nor have I," said Chris.

"Which authority do you represent, Chris?" said Ben.

"The enforcing authority for waterways is, as you know, the Environment Agency England, the EAE. They picked this up first from the office at the local borough's water department, but it was so far off the chart for them they contacted my department. I work for the Specialist Pollution Unit. We're based in Whitehall and are the link between the Home Office and the EAE, funded by the Home Office. It isn't just waterways; it's any form of pollution that might pose a threat to national safety and security. Nobody really hears about us; we don't advertise ourselves, and we only get involved when a certain level of risk is reached. In this case, it was an unknown issue the EAE could not identify. And that's why you're involved, Dr. Sharman."

"Interesting. I must admit I haven't come across your department before. Why us in particular? There are other organizations that offer our services more local to London?"

Ben was fishing to see who Ron played golf with.

"My boss heard about you. Let's be fair, you would have to be living in a cave not to have heard of your excellent work."

"Thank you. I appreciate that. Who is your boss, and who were you using before?"

She shook her head.

"Sorry, I get it. Privileged information, I understand."

"Let's just say that you won't get any promotion for your company out of this, and we have a contract for you to sign that ensures you cannot divulge information about any part of the investigation here unless by prior approval from our department. The Home Office won't tolerate you talking to anyone outside the approved list of those involved. There was an issue with a previous company we used. The don't work for us anymore."

"Okay, now you've set out the ground rules loud and clear, how much of the canal has been affected, and where did the couple in the boat first see the unusual fish activity?"

Chris explained the O'Hares set off from Limehouse Basin in their renovated barge, cleared the lock gates to enter Regent's Canal, and noticed a trail of blue bubbles following them once they were about fifty yards clear of the lock. They stopped near Cricketers Bridge and, after a while, saw confused fish milling around the back of the boat coated in a blue substance. They rang the EAE, and by the time they arrived, most of the fish were floating upside down, dead.

Claire began taking photos and water samples at the scene and for a hundred yards north and south of the bridge. She was thankful it was the all-singing, all-dancing digital camera, which would compensate for the fading light.

"I better talk to Mr. and Mrs. O'Hare," said Ben

Ben and Chris walked farther along the canal.

"It's amazing how much wildlife there is along the canal," said Ben, "and how beautiful and peaceful it is considering it's surrounded by tower blocks."

"They call London a concrete jungle, but I can assure you there are plenty of parks and canal walks like this accessible throughout the capital. You're never far from an oasis of nature, even here."

Ben pointed to the vast green area beyond the far bank. "What's over there? It looks stunning."

"That's Victoria Park. You should visit. It's a beautiful park with boating lakes, a Chinese pagoda, and a bandstand. It's just magical on a nice day. Great to walk through in daylight, but I wouldn't venture in there after dark; that's when the human wildlife comes out to play."

"I'll bear that in mind," said Ben thoughtfully.

As the canal bent left, a barge came into view. The Pride of Skibbereen sat proudly, moored to iron rings set in concrete on the towpath.

An elderly couple in deckchairs, and drinking tea, waved to them from the towpath next to the barge.

Chris introduced Ben to the couple. Connor stood and folded their two chairs.

"Please, come on board. We can talk inside," he said and ushered Ben and Chris into the cramped galley.

Ben had never been on a canal narrowboat and was struck by how organized everything was. Every inch of wall and every corner had a purpose, without a single space wasted. He smiled, thinking that Claire could never live on a boat like this. Her office and lab workspace would make the police suspect it had been broken into and there was evidence of a struggle.

"How can I help, Dr. Sharman?" said Connor O'Hare.

"Which did you see first, the fish covered in blue slime or the blue bubbles in the water?"

Mary O'Hare jumped in. "The bubbles. Just as we cleared the lock from Limehouse into the canal. I was looking back at the lock gate and saw blue bubbles following behind."

"That's right," said Connor, "and we didn't see the fish acting weird until we got to there," he said, pointing back at Cricketers Bridge.

Mary nodded in agreement. "They look like someone has painted them blue. I've never seen fish like that," she said. "Oh, and we noticed a few of the same bubbles in the basin, right where we were moored."

Ben glanced at Chris. "Can we keep the lock gates shut until we find out what this is all about? At least from Limehouse to the next set along from here?"

"Already done. Limehouse Basin to Acton's Lock in Hackney is already sealed. We've also stopped any movement between Limehouse Basin and the Thames and sealed the entrance from the basin into Limehouse Cut."

"Sorry for my geographical incompetence. Limehouse Cut?"

Chris smiled. "No problem. There are an awful lot of nooks and crannies crammed into London, and I wouldn't expect you to know every waterway around here. Limehouse Cut is another manmade waterway that opens into Limehouse farther along on the northeast side of the basin. It links the basin to the River Lea, which runs through Central London into the Thames at Bromley-by-Bow. So we took the precaution of putting a temporary dam in place; otherwise, there would be a free passage to just about anywhere for whatever is causing this blue fish problem."

Mary looked alarmed. "How long will we be stuck here? We're supposed to be on the holiday of a lifetime."

"Sorry, Mrs. O'Hare," said Chris, "I can't answer that until we know what we're dealing with. It may be a pollutant that just affects fish, and we can deal with it. But we can't let it spread along the canal and into other watercourses. It has to be contained until we have answers."

"Are you sure you saw it in Limehouse Basin where you began your trip?" said Ben.

"Yes, and it was definitely there after we'd been through the Commercial Road lock at Limehouse," said Connor.

Ben got up to leave.

"You've both been helpful, and I promise I'll do everything I can to resolve this quickly so you can get on your way. As a precaution, don't go swimming in the canal for a while."

Mary's eyes widened.

"As if! I would never go in that filthy water, and I wouldn't let my Connor," said Mary.

"Mary, he's pulling your leg," said Connor, and they all laughed.

"Joking aside, Mrs. O'Hare, and I am deadly serious about some things..."

She clutched her hands together and bent her head sideways, taking a step closer.

"...I absolutely love your boat."

As they walked back toward Claire, Ben couldn't help wondering what might happen if this were something more serious than a few dead fish, especially as the canal ran through some of the most densely populated residential areas in the country.

SIX

The sun sparkled on the surface, making the surrounding tower blocks seem alive in the almost motionless water's reflection, only disturbed by the erratic ripples of a small carp lying on its side with one fin flailing in the air. Blue froth bubbling from its gills collected on the surface and drifted on the almost imperceptible air current blowing across the canal, colliding with and sticking to the hull of the Pride of Skibbereen.

Connor, standing on the well deck, nursing a steaming cup of coffee, watched the dying fish. The greenish-blue slime covering the head and most of the body seemed out of place, like a live piece of melting blue wax. A sad image, spoiling the serenity of the canal's awakening in the rising dawn. The carp continued to flounder, round and round. Another shape formed on the surface twenty feet from the carp, moving just below the surface at speed, and gathering pace. In a lightning strike and a sudden splash, the dying carp disappeared, taken by an unseen predator. Pike or a zander, one of the invasive species in the British Isles, thought Connor. The water stilled, and just as it resumed an almost glasslike surface, a pike erupted with the dead carp in its jaws, leaping a clear yard out of the water, landing with hardly an entry splash. Connor cursed as the shock tensed his arms, sending half his boiling hot coffee splashing over the side and scalding his thumb.

"Bloody fish," he cursed, throwing the remaining coffee over the side before stepping into the galley.

The pike swallowed the carp whole and sank to the bottom, digesting its meal among long trailing weeds. After a few minutes, it developed an involuntary twitch along the full length of its body. The twitch progressed, and the pike twisted in an uncontrollable spasm. It didn't exude the blue slime that perch, roach, and carp had done earlier. Instead, it underwent a strange transformation. The shiny blue pallor over its natural camouflage transformed the skin tone from greens and browns. Its eye sockets stretched outward, eyes bulged, and jaws expanded. Longer, more powerful teeth, stronger and sharper with extra razor incisors sprouted between the existing rows, powerful fins extended, and tail widened, muscles pumped and dorsal fins extended outward, changing shape, the tips extruding into webbed claws. When the process finished, an unfamiliar creature lay just inches above the murky silt. Blood-red eyes, powerful, lethal jaws —a super predator now over five feet long that was hungry. Very hungry.

Betty George slipped the lead over Jet's head. She smiled down at the black spaniel. The wagging started at its stubby tail, extending up its glossy back until the whole dog was moving from side to side. With his nose pressed against the front door, Jet scratched the paintwork, whining to get outside. He couldn't wait for the door to open. Betty locked the door behind her and stepped onto the pavement of Vicars Close. Jet thrust his nose to the pavement, sniffing in long sweeping arcs as he dragged Betty forward toward the entrance to the canal. She stopped when she saw the police crime scene tape blocking access to the towpath.

"Bloody kids pissing about," she muttered to Jet, yanking and snapping the tape. She unclipped Jet, who ran forward, launching himself into the water. Betty picked up a stick and threw it. Jet yelped in ecstasy, swimming expertly toward the stick. He grabbed it and paddled back to the bank with his tail guiding his body, a little black rudder.

Betty laughed and coughed at the same time, pulling the last of her knockoff cigarettes out of the packet. She flicked the lighter and inhaled deeply. The smoke wasn't the same as her brand of choice, but with a pack of twenty Embassy Gold at well over a tenner, she bought a carton of two hundred knockoffs from her best friend Ester's boyfriend, who had the uncanny knack of being able to source any fakes you could think of. Ester jokingly called him "Not on The High Street." Betty took another deep pull on the cigarette and grimaced. It tasted all right—a bit of a plastic tang to it, but for three and a half bucks for twenty, she was sure they would grow on her. Betty hurled the crumpled empty box into the canal and then shook her head as Jet swam after it.

"You're not supposed to bring it back, you daft bastard," she wheezed and coughed, spitting a large gob of phlegm into the water. A sense of intrigue filled her as they approached the bend, revealing a gathering of police officers surrounding a canal barge. So, it hadn't been kids messing about with the police tape. What was it this time? Drug bust? Yet another stabbing? Or something more serious?

One officer spotted her staring at the group and hurried toward her.

"Sorry, ma'am, but this section of the canal is closed. How did you get onto it?"

She glared at him. "What do you mean it's closed? I walk down here every day. What's it closed for anyway?" she said, evading the question.

"Something polluting the canal. We're trying to identify what it is. Until we do, this stretch of the canal is supposed to be out of bounds to the public."

She glanced at the old couple standing next to the barge. "What are they doing here then if I can't walk my bleedin' dog? They don't look out of bounds."

"They own the barge and are marooned here till we complete our investigations."

"Investigations, my arse. You lot are all standing around drinking tea, doing sod all!"

The officer changed tack. "Look, ma'am, I won't ask again. Please leave the canal footpath immediately."

He stepped toward her. She was about to take a step toward him in a standoff when there was a large splash behind her. They turned to see Jet yelping in pain, trying to get back to the bank. Swimming much slower and more upright than usual, the water around the distressed dog was turning a deep crimson. It took several painful minutes of coaxing before the officer could reach Jet's collar and pull him out. Betty, the officer, and several of his colleagues who ran along the towpath to assist watched in horror as they lifted the howling dog clear. One of its front paws was missing.

A thin ripple darted across the surface of the canal on the opposite bank and a huge head surfaced with a vivid red eye looking across at them.

"What the hell!" said one of the officers, pointing at the fish.

The grotesquely transformed pike swallowed the small black paw before diving. The last thing the police officers and Betty saw was the flash of its huge silver-blue flank and a blood-red tail.

SEVEN

"I feel pretty disgusting sitting here in the same clothes I wore last night," complained Claire. "Good thing I brought my hairbrush with me, otherwise, you'd be sitting opposite the wild woman of Borneo for breakfast."

Ben raised his hands. "I didn't think we'd be so hands-on at this stage. My apologies for the tenth time," he said, laughing. "Don't forget, I've seen you looking like a wild woman before first thing in the morning. Not such a terrible sight."

"When was that? I never look that bad at work."

"Remember when you fell asleep on the lab bench in the middle of the night and got a chocolate biscuit stuck to the side of your face?"

She put a hand to her cheek, recalling the all-night lab session on a previous case, and sniggered. "A bit more forward planning in the future, Ben. It's fine for you men to slum it in your sweaty rags, but I like to look presentable."

"Yes, boss," said Ben, throwing up a salute. He was about to spread marmalade onto a second slice of toast when his phone pinged.

"Shit," he muttered, scrolling through the message. "There's been an incident early this morning in the canal near the O'Hares' barge."

"What is it?"

"Huge, weird-looking fish sighted immediately after a dog was attacked in the water, right by the barge. Chris says the fish was blue and wants us back there in half an hour. She's sending a car."

Claire shook her head. "I'm having my breakfast and then a shower first, and I don't care if she has to wait."

"Fair enough," he said. "Just don't be long."

She forced a smile, then tucked into her full English breakfast.

It was the second time in twenty-four hours that they found themselves in the back of a police patrol car.

"Do you think you'll have this wrapped up soon?" said the driver, looking at Ben in the rearview mirror. "Only this bridge closure is causing absolute havoc."

"I wish I could tell you," said Ben. "But it's not up to me. The Environment Agency has jurisdiction. I'm just a lowly scientist they called in to assist, and I'm hoping we can get back to base later this morning. As for the bridge closure, you're asking the wrong person."

"Moreton-in-Marsh, you're from there?" said the driver.

"Not originally," said Ben. "I just work out of there."

"Nice place, my old man said. He was a fire officer back in the early eighties. Used to go to college there."

"Just a mile up the road from us," said Claire. "It's not just for the fire service anymore. I think it's for anyone willing to pay."

"My old man said it's not the same as it was, but I think that's just him looking through rose-colored glasses. Used to be a great place to train back in the day, he reckoned. I was going to join up, but he put me off. Said the job wasn't what it used to be. Either that, or he didn't want me to discover any of his past exploits. Bit of a boy in his day, my old fella," he said with a grin.

Ben recalled a conversation with an old lecturer at the college who liked Moreton so much he stayed. He said there were a few officers like him who met their future wives in the town and stayed.

After passing a long queue of traffic, the patrol car pulled up at Cricketers Bridge, where Chris was waiting for them.

"Dog had its paw bitten off while swimming in the canal, and I think its attacker is a fish not native to these waters," she said, scrolling through grisly photos of a small black dog minus a front paw.

"Is the dog still here?" asked Ben, looking at the photos.

"No, we rushed it to a local vet to be patched up. I told the vet to be extremely careful when dealing with the wound, and I have officers down there impounding every glove, swab, and instrument he uses to treat the poor animal. I'll make sure you get it all for testing."

"This fish. Do you have a description?"

"Large, five or six feet long—"

"In a canal? You don't get fish that big in a canal. That has to have come in from the sea through the Thames and Limehouse Basin."

"I thought that too. The witnesses, including the dog's owner and police officers who were on the bank at dawn when it happened, said it looked like a huge pike with bright red eyes and fins, and the body was a bluish silver. Perhaps it was just blue, but with the sunlight reflecting off it, it could appear silver."

"You're thinking of the color of the dead fish?"

"Well, yes. Seems like too much of a coincidence. But I'm keeping an open mind," said Chris. "Could it be a small shark that has got through the lock system?"

"Unlikely. Bull sharks can tolerate freshwater for long periods, but never this far north. About as far as the Moroccan coastline, at a stretch."

"Any other sightings of Jaws?" said Claire.

"An hour before the incident, Mr. O'Hare was standing at the back of his boat when he saw a large pike take a dying carp, which was covered in blue slime."

Her phone rang.

"Betty George just arrived home. Her dog didn't make it."

"Oh, the poor woman, that's awful," said Claire.

"I may sound callous," said Ben, "but I need to talk to her. Where are the dog's remains?"

"Still at the vet. We insisted on quarantining the body. She's not a happy bunny."

"I can't say I blame her," said Claire. "I'll talk to her and see if I can get anything more from her. See what she remembers about this rogue fish."

"Best of luck," said one of the police officers. "She was giving me some tasty verbal just before it happened.

"I'll try my best to charm her," said Claire. "Would you show me the lady's house?" she said to the officer with one of her sultry smiles. Ben rolled his eyes, and she scowled, catching him in the act.

Betty George was in floods of tears when they reached the house, and Claire's heart melted. She explained she was a scientist, not a police officer, and had come to help.

"Can I come in?" said Claire. She put her arm around the sobbing woman. "I just need to have a chat about what happened." Claire waved the police officer away with her other hand. "Shall I put the kettle on for you? It must have been a nasty shock," she said as she followed Betty into the house.

The living room was as neat as a pin and not what Claire had expected after listening to the officer's description and assumptions about Betty George.

"He was just a puppy, really," she said, burying her head in a large handkerchief.

"I never wanted a dog, but when my husband passed away..." She coughed, pulled out a cigarette, and lit up. "When my Alf died, I was lonely, and my friend Alice, she breeds dogs, see. She said I could have Jet to keep me company." I don't know what I'll do..."

Claire sat on the arm of the sofa and put her arm around her. "I'm sure he had a wonderful time with you, Mrs. George. Did you go to the canal to walk him often?"

"Every day, unless it was tipping down. He didn't mind the rain.

Loved the water, but I can't stand getting cold and wet. I caught pneumonia once, and I don't bloody want it again."

"Did you see anything unusual in the water this morning before it happened?"

She stared at the floor in thought for a moment. "No, nothing. Just the same as any morning, apart from the police tape. I thought it was those little bastards off the estate who vandalize the place and play hell with the old folks. The little sods that spray disgusting things on the brick walls along the canal."

"Where was the police tape?"

"Across the entrance to the canal from Vicars Row, you know, this street."

"I know where you mean. I just walked through the gap myself," said Claire.

"When you saw that Jet was in trouble, was there any other sign of movement in the water?"

She didn't answer and began to cry again.

"I'm so sorry, Mrs. George. I hate to have to ask these questions, but we need to stop this from happening again. It could be a little child next time, so it's really important."

Betty nodded and took another pull on the cigarette. Claire screwed her nose up at the smell of the tobacco. She thought she could smell a hint of burned rubber.

"Could you describe the large fish that everyone saw after Jet was pulled out?"

She tapped ash into her palm and stared at the window. "It had a massive head. Like a pike but much more vicious looking. Lots of teeth. Bloody great red eye. About as long as a grown man—six feet, I reckon."

"Could it have been a shark?"

"Not a shark, I'm certain. It was nothing like I've ever seen."

"Are you sure it wasn't a shark?"

"My dad was a fishmonger for fifty years. I used to go with him to buy fish at Billingsgate Market. I know my bleeding fish, and I am telling you this one is nothing I have ever seen before, and I thought I knew everyone under the sun."

"Okay, Betty, I'm sorry to have to tell you we will need to look at Jet before you can have him back. Due to the recent strange incidents on the canal in the last twenty-four hours, we must make sure people are kept away from danger."

Betty George gave a little sob and nodded.

"My fault," she sobbed. "I should have paid attention to that police tape. Thought it was those little bastards on the estate messing about."

"It isn't your fault, Mrs. George, and I promise I will personally look after Jet and return him to you as soon as I can. Here's my card. I'm not going to feed you any cock-and-bull story. If you need to talk to me or think of anything else you remember about that fish, just call me. Okay?"

Claire made Betty a cup of tea and left the house, closing the door quietly behind her.

"Well?" said Ben.

"This is getting weirder by the minute," said Claire. "Betty George has a really good knowledge of fish and has never seen a fish like it before. Her father was a fish buyer at Billingsgate Market, so she knows more than a bit about fish."

"What would you recommend, Dr. Sharman?" said Chris. "Keep this section of the canal under quarantine?"

"Until I've done some tests, keep the towpath off limits to the public and boat users, and keep the lock gates closed you have already earmarked. I think it would be okay to open Cricketers Bridge to traffic as long as there are no pedestrians trying to access the towpath. Warn any barges marooned along this stretch and any households whose gardens back onto the canal. I've seen access gates from several gardens."

"Take that as read. What about Moby Dick?" said Chris.

"Moby who?" said Claire.

Ben shook his head. "You should read proper books and get your head out of TikTok and Facebook! Moby Dick was a fictitious rogue whale. It would solve a lot of issues if someone could catch the red-eyed monster."

"I'll see what I can do," said Chris.

"And I don't like the idea of the O'Hare's being left here. They've seen blue bubbles follow them through the lock gates. It would be wise to move their boat back into the basin. At least they can be away from this stretch of canal where the problem seems to be."

"Agreed," said Chris. "I'll get them to move back into the basin and I'll look into putting them in temporary accommodation as soon while this is going on."

A hundred yards away, a swan stretched up, flapping its wings, starting its takeoff. Gaining momentum, webbed feet paddling, splashing, and rising slowly, the swan had clear air between it and the water until savage jaws tore it out of the sky and dragged it under the surface in a huge swirl of brown water.

EIGHT

A large male toad pushed upward, forcing the long, dew-soaked grass aside, hopping across the towpath, slipping under the iron-railed fence into the undergrowth of Victoria Park. After enjoying a feast on the far side of the canal bank where the water was always still, it needed a place to rest. In just a few minutes, the instinctive draw to the boating lake, where it had hatched two seasons before, was complete as it dove in and rose into a dense patch of weeds. Now dormant, the toad digested its banquet of tadpoles and froglets that had been feasting on the body of a dead stickleback, swathed in a bright blue slime, deep in the mud and mire of the canal bed.

Small ripples ran up and down the warty amphibian skin as internal changes stirred. The toad's eyes dipped back into their sockets, then popped back out, and its whole body vibrated, webbed feet splayed, then contracted. Limbs grew. Eyes lightened to a deep crimson bulging in their sockets. Convulsing, it thrashed around the tangles of broad-leafed pondweed. Growing, stretching. Teeth developed where there should be none. Brown mottled skin morphed to a deep blue spotted hide, sprouting bristles and spikes along the spinal ridge. The convulsions stopped. Hunger set in, and now something very un-toad-like, dove deep into the depths of the pond, voraciously seeking food.

Ben and Claire stared at the sealed box on the lab bench.

"Shall I do the honors?" said Claire.

"Certainly not, if you were about to offer to open it," said Ben. "We treat this as we would any biohazard and open and examine it using decontamination protocols."

"Does that mean we have to get our kit off together in a shower when we're finished?" said Claire with a wry smile.

Ben reddened, remembering the embarrassing moment on a previous case when they'd been forced to disrobe and shower naked together in a decontamination tent. He blushed again as he recalled that it had happened not once, but twice. It was equally humiliating the second time.

"No, we won't be doing that," said Ben. "We'll use the inflatable lab with airlocks as a precaution, but not the full decontamination suits. I don't think this is anywhere near as serious as our previous alien encounter."

"Pity," she said, with a feigned pout.

Ben shook his head and had to look away as he smiled. He knew she loved to tease him. Although it had been disturbing for him during those naked encounters, he remembered how stunning she looked without a stitch on. He dwelled a little too long on the memory.

"A penny for your thoughts," she said, making him go scarlet. She left, laughing loudly, to set up the equipment they needed. He could still hear her laughing as she reached reception for the keys.

"I could wring that girl's neck," he said to himself, with a smile.

The fish netted close to the 'Pride of Skibbereen,' measured five feet, ten inches from nose to tail and weighed eighty-four pounds, almost forty pounds heavier than the largest pike ever caught on rod and line in the UK. But this was no pike.

"It's bloody monstrous," said Claire, using a reverse clamp to pry the enormous jaws open. "Imagine that taking a bite out of your leg."

"It shredded the first net they used, went through it with ease," said Ben. "Chris Williams said they had to use a special metal mesh net, similar to medieval chain mail, and it still had a bloody good go at that before they dragged it out."

Each of the hundreds of razor-sharp teeth was a good inch long, inward sloping, designed to grip its prey before swallowing it whole. Once trapped in those jaws, there would be no escape.

"A giant, extremely deformed pike should be the logical conclusion," said Ben, staring into its cavernous mouth, "as it has many similar features."

"Or?"

"Not sure, but the other dead fish, the O'Hares' account of the blue bubbles following them, the attack on the dog, and this behemoth all in the space of a few hours, is too much of a coincidence.

"I can understand toxic waste," said Claire, passing a scalpel, "but to have an effect like this would suggest that it has been going on for a very long time, and as you say, it all seems to have been reported and happening in one day."

"I don't like coincidences, but the only way to find out is to do what we do best and put our scientific heads on."

She nodded in agreement.

"Right then, let's get to it. Can I have another dozen sample bags?" he said, extending his hand.

Ben made the first incision in front of the rear fin, slicing all the way through to the head, exposing the inner organs.

"Strange doing this," he said. "Never done an autopsy on a fish before. Gutted plenty with my old man mackerel fishing. Normally just pull its guts out."

Claire winced.

"This is odd," said Ben, pointing at the lining of the fish's inner body cavity. Claire took a couple of close-up photos. "The inner layer is blue. In fact, you can see from the incision that all layers under the scales have a blue pallor."

They removed the internal organs and spilled the stomach contents into a large steel dish. Claire pulled apart the various kills with tweezers and forceps.

"Perch, minnow, and some kind of bird," she said, lifting the contents out piece by piece.

"Breastbone and part of a long neck," said Ben.

Claire, teasing slime from the remains of the bird's neck, exposed white feathers.

"Part of a swan?" said Ben. "Hell of a catch for a canal fish!"

She placed it back in the steel bowl and started to laugh.

"What's so amusing?" said Ben.

"A punctual fish," she said, lifting a man's watch on a steel strap with the tweezers, "and it's still working!"

"Let me see," said Ben. "Wow! I thought you were pulling my leg." He stared in amazement as the second hand swept around the dial. Ben reached for his phone. "No wonder it's still working!"

"What do you mean?"

Ben pointed at the watch face and started scrolling and typing.

"And?"

"The brand."

"Rolex? Wow!" she said, wiping the watch face with a tissue.

"The best, but read what it says underneath."

Claire held the watch up and leaned in. "Print size is small but hang on. It says Submariner, 1000ft 300m, Superlative Chronometer Officially Certified."

"One of the most expensive watches in the world," said Ben.

Claire sneered. "Probably a fake, and I don't like the strap," she said and placed it in another steel dish.

"I'll have to let Chris know about this. If it is the genuine article, it would cost just under thirty grand to buy new."

"Shut up!" She picked up the watch and stared at it.

He pushed the phone to her face. Her eyes widened at the retail price on the screen.

"Jeez! Perhaps the strap isn't that bad after all."

After two hours of performing an autopsy on the fish and taking many samples for analysis, Ben pulled off his neoprene gloves.

"I'm starving. Fancy a spot of lunch in Chipping Norton? I think we've earned it."

Claire looked down at the grisly array of aquatic body parts and rubbed her stomach.

"I was hungry, but—"

"By the time we get there, you'll have gotten your appetite back. Fish guts are enough to put anyone off their food. Come on, before the rush starts."

NINE

Ben's phone pinged just as cod, chips, and mushy peas arrived at their table in the Plough Inn.

"I really don't know how you can eat that after slicing up that abomination this morning," she said, nibbling a ham baguette.

He ignored her, sprinkling salt and vinegar over the chips, then squeezed a lemon slice over the cod. Claire winced as she caught the mixture of vinegar and lemon fumes rising off Ben's plate.

"I might agree if it were battered pike," he said as his phone pinged again.

"Why does everyone want a piece of me when I want food?" He pointed to his plate as he stood. "Don't steal my chips. I have to make a call out of everyone's earshot."

He returned twenty minutes later.

"Where's my food?" he said, looking down at the space on the table. "You didn't—"

"Eat it? Is that what you think?" said Claire.

"Well, where is it then?"

"I asked the waitress to keep it warm as you had a very important life-or-death phone call to make. She was very understanding—unlike you, Dr. Sharman."

He put both palms up to her. "I knew I could count on you," he said and patted her head.

Claire waved to the waitress, who quickly returned Ben's slightly dried up fish and chips.

"What was so urgent?" said Claire.

"Chris Williams. More blue fish floating in the canal, farther than the next lock gates in both directions. It's definitely in Limehouse Basin, but we always suspected that, so no surprise. It has also spread into a boating lake in Victoria Park, which she said has no water channel or pipework connected to the canal."

"So, has something crawled, walked, slithered, or been carried from the canal to the lake?" said Claire.

"Or the other way around. It could have originated in the lake. Perhaps it's spread by air currents," said Ben, wolfing down the battered fish. "Can you and your favorite person go back to Bethnal Green and take a look? We need to find the origin of this problem and see if you can find the extent of the spread."

"You mean Ron?"

"Yes. See what he's doing and ask him to meet you there. No offense, but another pair of eyes and ears might see something we've missed."

"None taken," said Claire. "By the way, does your current hospitality extend to coffee?"

He looked at her with a mouthful of mushy peas, trying to swallow.

Claire waved again at the waitress before he could speak. "Two lattes, please."

"Regular or large?"

Claire grinned at Ben; he rolled his eyes.

"Large."

Ron Logan jumped at the chance to take part in the investigation as he was at a loose end. The boss of the Cambridge team had indeed had him escorted off the premises on a month's garden leave.

"Before you go," said Ben, "can I see you in our office, Claire?"

For a second, she looked perplexed, then remembered Ben's kind offer to move her into his office away from Ron.

"Close the door and take a seat." Ben looked out into the main office. Kath O'Brian had accosted Ron. "I'll say this quick before Kath releases her grip on him and she comes snooping in here. Until Ron has served out his employment with the Cambridge lot, don't give too much away about our business, just in case he changes his mind and goes back to them or somewhere else."

"Do you think he would?"

"No, I don't, but I'm taking no chances. And keep any sensitive documents away from prying eyes until he officially works for us. I'm almost certain he won't do anything like that, but there's too much at stake for any confidential information to go sailing into the arms of a rival company."

"Understood, boss," she said, and was about to go.

"I'll have your things moved in here by the time you get back, okay?"

"Can I sit by the window, where your desk is?" she said with a winning smile.

"Out! Before I put you at a desk in the boiler room."

Although Claire didn't like Ron at all when they first met, he had won her respect through his canny way of getting things done and the ability to pull strings from the most unlikely sources to move investigations forward. He was a great team player, and she slowly defrosted to him as time went by. The one thing that still made her shudder was his 'nose management,' as she called it. Ron was constantly blowing his nose and leaving a trail of tissues wherever he went. It made her feel ill just thinking about it.

As she pulled into Bethnal Green police station, Ron, as if on cue, sat on the wing of his car blowing his nose. He leaped up and offered his empty hand. Claire put her hands up instantly.

"Hello, Ron, nice to see you. Sorry, but I'm not shaking hands with you after you've had your paws all over that snout of yours. No offense and all that."

Ron shrugged his shoulders, rammed the used tissue into the breast pocket of his jacket, and followed her into the station.

Chris Williams was waiting for them in a large meeting room set up specifically for the incident on the canal. "An update," she said, pointing at the incident board, which had a blown-up map of Regent's Canal, Limehouse Basin, and part of the River Thames, plus various notes and photos pinned at points of interest.

"Since the attack on Betty George's dog, there have been one hundred and twenty-one dead fish retrieved from the canal and a further thirty-six from Limehouse Basin. I have them on ice for you to take back to the lab, Claire."

Claire smiled and nodded, inwardly groaning at the thought of a car boot full of blue slimy fish, even if they were in sealed containers.

"As a precaution, I've moved everyone using canal barges in the affected areas and temporarily re-housed them in hotels."

"There have been more incidents." Chris pointed to the top of the map. "The first here, at Victoria Park in the boating lake." A child using a fishing net to catch tiddlers said he saw a giant frog. When his mother looked, she said she saw a frog about the size of a football. She said it had red eyes and teeth protruding from its mouth."

"Frogs have tiny maxillary and vomerine teeth on their upper jaw," said Claire. "For gripping prey before swallowing them whole."

"Same for toads? I'm asking because we have a photo of this 'frog' that the mother took on her phone. It's not a brilliant quality, but after we enlarged the image, it looked more toadlike to me." Chris pointed to a photo on a separate board.

Claire walked over to the photo. "Good God, it's a horror version! I think you're right. Unlike a frog, a toad doesn't have teeth, but this beast does—on both jaws, and they're vicious looking. What the hell is going on?"

"You're the scientist. You tell us," said Chris abruptly.

"We're still running tests on the previous samples. We took the large fish apart, and Ben and the rest of the team back at Moreton are working flat out to get you some answers."

"Sorry," said Chris, "I wasn't having a go at you. It's just that this is way off-piste from our normal investigations, and it's unsettling."

"No need to apologize," said Claire. "Until we know what's causing this, we can't give you much except to proceed with caution and keep the area restricted."

"Any idea on timescale? Only the bloody press and the local councillors are starting to ramp it up."

"I'll get you an update from the lab within the hour," said Claire, looking at her watch. "Could you take me to the boating lake, and is it possible to talk to the kid and his mother who saw the toad-frog thing? We need to track down the source."

Chris pinned a newspaper article to the board. "This happened just before it all kicked off. Probably unrelated, but I thought you should see it. I've emailed you and Ben copies just now," said Chris, handing Claire a copied sheet.

It was the *Evening Standard*'s report of the robbery at the Museum of Alien Life and the subsequent drowning of the suspect in Limehouse Basin.

"Interesting," said Claire. "Did they ever retrieve the missing meteorite sample?"

"Not to my knowledge, but I thought anything that's ended up in the basin may be of interest, especially this. There are no other reports of any recent pollution in the basin and haven't been for at least six months. The last notified incident was at the end of last year. Several gallons of diesel leaked from a barge, but the authorities dealt with it swiftly, and I don't see how it could have caused what's happening at the moment. That's not to say there haven't been other unreported incidents."

"I'll look into the drowning," said Claire, placing the newspaper report into her briefcase. "Where is this Museum of Alien Life?"

Chris sighed. "It's a bloody circus show if you ask me, but you know what the public loves these days. Bullshit, conspiracy theories, and the bizarre. That place has it all. It's the other side of Hyde Park from the real museums," she said and laughed. "Tavistock Road, near Portobello Road Market, close to Paddington. One of my drivers will take you there if you want to look."

"No, that will be fine," said Claire. "I'll find it; it's on the way back."

After a coffee in the staff canteen, they were escorted to Victoria Park. It was a fine sunny day, and the park was a welcome break from the surrounding bustle and endless noise.

"Don't know about you, Ron," said Claire, "but I couldn't stick it up here for long."

"I could get quite used to being in a busy place. So vibrant. More action in a dead stoat than Moreton."

"I'll give you that, but I like space and green fields. There's not much of it up here, and it smells."

Ron sniffed the air. "Of what? All I can smell is fresh air."

Claire looked at his red bulbous nose in disbelief. A hooter that size—surely he could pick up the underlying stale tarmac-infused air?" She decided not to pursue it.

They walked through the park from the canal towpath. It was a welcome change, and Claire could see the appeal of escaping from city life in such a lovely oasis.

The boating lake was still and quiet, with a couple of police officers seated on one of the park's ornate metal benches. They stood bolt upright when they saw Chris, Ron, and Claire approaching.

"Morning, Ma'am," said the older constable.

"Any more sign of Godzilla?" said Chris.

The younger man smirked. "No, Ma'am. Nothing at all. It's strange. The lake is normally full of ducks and geese, but I haven't seen a single one since we got here."

"Why so strange? If there are no people allowed in the park, then there's no one feeding the ducks, so wouldn't they go somewhere else?"

"You would think," said the constable. "But I've lived here all my life, and I've never seen the pond empty of birds. Even when there's been nobody about. Have a listen; what can you hear?"

They all stood still and listened.

"Cars, traffic, sounds of the city in the background," said Chris. "Am I missing something?"

"Have another listen and see if you can hear any birdsong."

They all strained their ears.

"Nothing," said Claire. "That is odd. You would expect some birds singing in such a large and beautiful park."

The constable nodded. "There are no birds in the park, miss. I've been looking. Not so much as a pigeon. You can't find anywhere in London without a pigeon. Something's spooked them."

TEN

Alex Munro paced the plush red carpet in his austere office, deep in thought. The last phone call rattled him. An official from a Home Office department was sending two scientists to interview him, and he didn't like it. He thought the problem with Jonny Clarke was done and dusted. He just wanted the insurance to pay up. The client buying the photos needed to pay up, and that should be the end of the matter. Sixty thousand pounds richer from the sale and the matter forgotten. Jonny Clarke's cause of death was officially declared as suicide and just collateral damage in a business deal, with a twist.

So why were two scientists so interested in the meteorite fragments he didn't retrieve? Chris Williams had provided scant details, and several scenarios were going through his mind. Had someone grassed him up? No, that couldn't be the case; otherwise, the police would have shown up, not a couple of lab geeks.

A thought struck him. Had they found the missing fragments? If they had, he would have to declare it to the insurance company, and they wouldn't pay up for that. Fingers crossed it would just be a general inquiry. Could the big story in the press be linked to it?

Reports of giant meat-eating fish in the canal near Limehouse Basin? What if there was a link? Would they attribute weird stuff to his museum? It had the potential to bring positive attention. Even negative press had a silver lining, didn't it? His overactive mind snapped back to reality when his intercom buzzed.

A well-spoken voice filled the room from the speaker.

"Your three o'clock appointment has arrived, Mr. Munro. Shall I send them both in?"

"Please, Jenny, and could you prepare some tea and coffee for our guests," he said, lining up pens and a leather-bound desk diary. Sitting behind the enormous oak desk, he straightened his tie and then swept one hand through his thinning, mousy hair. He folded and unfolded his arms before pulling the desk diary across and lifting a pen, then pushed them away and gripped his knees. The door knocked. He half spoke, half coughed.

"Come in," he said, folding and unfolding his arms once more. As the door opened, he sprang out of the chair and walked across the room with his hand outstretched. He shook Ron's hand, then Claire's, and gestured for them to be seated on two chairs facing the desk. They were a lot lower than him in his captain's office chair, and even though Ron towered over the man when they entered the office, he looked quite lofty, sitting bolt upright behind his imposing desk.

"How can I help you both today?" he said, looking at Ron.

Claire spoke. "You had several items stolen, including pieces of meteorite. I believe you had only two fragments returned after they were found on the body of Mr. Jonny Clarke, who allegedly stole them from the museum."

"Not quite correct, Miss Manson. There was no 'allegedly' about it. Jonny Clarke stole them."

"Okay," said Claire, taken aback by the resentment in his voice. "The two pieces that were retrieved from Mr. Clarke's body—were they from the same source as the missing pieces?"

"Oh, that's easy. They were all from the same impact site. A recent discovery by pure chance. Two travelers witnessed the impact near Teakettle Junction in Death Valley, Nevada. They were exploring the area; God only knows why, as there's nothing there apart from dirt and rocks. They searched the impact site and found many fragments scattered over a vast area and collected them. They sold off most pieces, and I was fortunate enough to buy several using money from the museum's trust foundation. The number of large donors we get still amazes me. What we do here seems to fascinate people."

"Have you any images of the missing pieces, just so we know what we're looking for?"

"Do you have a card?" he inquired.

She passed her business card across the table.

"I'll get my secretary to send you the images. They have scale references, so you get a sense of the size, but they range from a quarter of an inch to an inch in diameter. You would waste your time trying to find them in Limehouse Basin."

"I didn't assume they were in the basin. Have you had more information, Mr. Munro?" She saw his neck flush, but his face remained impassive.

"No, just my assumption. That's where the body was found."

"Well, if we find them, I'm sure you'd be glad to get them back."

Alex Munro said nothing. He thought of the insurance money covering the missing meteorite fragments and prayed they would not discover their location. They had cost him nothing. The idea of using the museum trust fund money was a spontaneous thought that crossed his mind. The small collection was, in fact, stolen from the finders, who had mysteriously disappeared a few weeks after their discovery became public knowledge.

"Would it be possible for us to see the two remaining pieces of meteorite, Mr. Munro?" said Ron.

"Of course. I'll get them out of the safe. We haven't put them back on display yet." He pressed a button under his desk, and a panel on the wall next to his desk slid upward into a wall recess, revealing a huge steel safe door. He had the door open in seconds and pulled out a small cloth-covered dish. In the dish were two pieces of what looked like rough reddish stones, each about half an inch wide, flecked with green and orange.

"Would it be possible for us to take one piece back to the lab for analysis?" she said and smiled.

"Oh, I couldn't let you do that," he said, his stern voice returning for a moment.

"I understand," said Claire. "Do you mind if I quickly examine them here, with protective gloves on, of course—a close-up look under a magnifying glass?"

He was about to refuse but paused and thought better of it and smiled. "If it will help, be my guest, Miss Manson. More coffee or tea?" he said.

"That would be lovely," said Claire, who didn't want another cup but wanted more time to study the two samples. She picked up the larger piece and looked carefully through the folding magnifying glass. She had a quick look at the surface, which gave very little away —a lump of sparkly rock—then focused her attention on Alex Munro with a sideways glance. He was staring at the intercom, ordering more refreshments. She moved the metal eyepiece closer, keeping a watchful eye on Munro, then slowly scraped the outer hood of the lens across the sample. She looked back at him, then looked the other way to Ron, and winked.

"Is that a genuine photo?" said Ron, pointing at the large reproduction on the wall of a clearly defined dish shape hovering a few hundred yards from a commercial airline's wing. "Only I can see machine marks on its surface. Every fake photo I have ever seen of a UFO appears blurred and ambiguous. This image is so pin sharp it doesn't seem real."

Alex beamed. "Everyone who's seen this photo has said more or less the same." Alex stood and walked over to the photo, pointing to an opening on top of the UFO.

Claire looked sideways. Alex had most of his back to her and was looking at the photo on the wall. She dug into the sample as hard as she dared, praying it wouldn't make a noise. She checked her palm and, with a satisfied smile, placed both samples back on the dish, pulled the neoprene gloves off inside out, and replaced them in her pocket.

"Interesting, but not much being given away, Mr. Munro. Are you sure we couldn't borrow one to do some basic tests? I can assure you that we—"

"Quite sure," he said.

More tea and coffee arrived, and they took a few sips before she looked at her watch.

"My goodness is that the time?" said Claire, wide-eyed. "My apologies, Mr. Munro. We really must be going." She shook his hand, thanked him, and walked out, followed by Ron.

"That man's a real piece of work," said Claire as they walked to the car park.

"So are you," said Ron, sniggering. "Queen of espionage, and that look of surprise when you realized how late it was." He sniggered again. "Worthy of a bloody Oscar!"

"You were pretty good yourself, Ron. You actually looked interested in that creepy fake photo."

"Don't me and you make a great team?" he said, pulling a large hanky from his sleeve.

"Goodnight, Ron," she said, and scurried away before he got it halfway to his nose. As they pulled out of the car park in their separate cars and drove down Tavistock Road, the heavily-built man in the long gray trench coat checked his phone, replayed the short video, and confirmed that both car registration plates were clear. He took a screenshot of each and messaged them to his contact, who immediately responded with an instruction.

ELEVEN

"Well, if it isn't the devil himself," said Kath O'Brian, opening the door to Ron with one hand while still using the floor polisher with the other. "You may as well ask Ben for a job; you've practically lived here all week," she said, pushing the door shut.

Ron looked at her, shaking his head. "Will you stop that contraption before you kill someone?"

She gave him her usual death stare and turned off the cleaner.

"Kath, you are a sight for sore eyes."

"Ah, you're just saying that," she said with a coy smile.

"No, really," he said with a straight face. "It makes my bloody eyes sore just looking at you."

"Cheeky bastard," she said and began laughing hysterically, which morphed into a chesty wheeze and then a hacking cough.

Ron rushed up the stairs before she could recover and start one of her endless yarns.

"Just in time, Ron," said Ben, in the middle of creating a huge incident board, busily drawing a timeline. "What time did you get back from London last night? Did you go home?"

"The Black Bear," said Ron.

"You stayed here—in Moreton?"

"I couldn't stick getting up at the crack of dawn to drive across from Cambridge, and I wanted to have a good look at the local housing stock on offer in the estate agents' windows. I'm moving down this way, and it may as well be in the town where I work. Don't fancy some cozy thatched place in the middle of nowhere."

"You realize I can't afford to pay for accommodation while you're looking?"

"Ben, I'm not exactly short in the wallet department, so no worries there, mate," said Ron, standing close to the incident board, taking it all in. "By the way, Ben, it's Bethnal, not *Benthal* Green."

"Thanks," said Ben, correcting the board with an attempt at a smile. "What about your other half?"

"What about him?"

"How does Graham feel about relocating to this charming backwater?""

"Haven't broached the subject yet and won't until I start working for you."

Ben pulled a face, contemplating what his Amy would have to say if he changed jobs and was thinking of moving to the other side of the country without so much as a mention. He banished the inevitable and horrific outcome from his mind. "So, what have you and Claire found out?"

"Where is she?" said Ron.

Ben stretched to the far corner of the board and listed common wildlife in the Regent's Canal area. "Getting us coffees, I hope. The kettle's broken, so I sent her to the cafe and hopefully she'll get some stickies."

"Stickies?"

"Sticky buns—keep up, Ron. Probably donuts knowing Claire."

"Actually, it's Danish pastries," said Claire, placing the tray of coffee and box of pastries on the lab bench. She hurled her jacket at the coat rack, where it landed and clung on for dear life. "Let's eat and chat," said Claire.

She and Ron updated Ben on their trip to London. Ben laughed at Claire's audacious sample strategy in Alex Munro's office.

"You are a sneaky little madam," said Ben. "I bet you think you're clever, don't you?"

"Pretty much," she said.

"Did you check for CCTV in his office while you were busy desecrating his priceless artifacts?"

"Shit," she said. She looked at Ron, who shrugged his shoulders. "I didn't think to look. Mind you, even if there was a camera, he wouldn't see what I was doing. What do you think, Ron?"

Ron said nothing, shrugging his shoulders once more.

"Okay," said Ben, "let's assume he won't find out you stole a sample from under his nose. What was your aim, and what tests are you going to perform?"

Claire chewed the last bite of her pastry and screwed up the bag. "I haven't really thought about it yet. I just want to determine the composition and see if there are any strange substances in the meteorite's makeup."

"Okay, what else today?" said Ben.

"A kid saw a giant toad in Victoria Park near the canal."

"How giant?" said Ben.

Claire passed him the enlarged photo. "Chris Williams said it was the size of a football."

Ben stared at the image, then pinned it to the incident board. "Frankenstein would have been proud of it. I think it backs up my theory."

"What theory?" said Ron.

"I'll come to that in a minute. What other news from London?"

"A pile of dead fish to process, some from the canal and a few found dead in Limehouse Basin," said Claire.

"How many?"

"A couple of hundred."

"Can I suggest you just sample one of each species from each location? We need to move quickly with this investigation."

"A weird thing to report," said Ron, wiping crumbs off his chin.

"Go ahead," said Ben. "Surely it can't get much weirder?"

"We were in Victoria Park, and there were absolutely no birds, which according to a local cop who lives in the area, is unheard of. There are usually ducks, geese, and pigeons by the score in the park, but nothing since the weird blue fish thing. Not so much as a chirp."

"Any logical explanation?"

"Nope. The young cop made us listen, and apart from the background traffic noise, there was nothing. Something has driven them away," said Ron.

"Or kept them away," said Claire.

"Okay. If there's nothing else to report, I've run several tests on some of the smaller fish, and our monster pike, and it *is* a pike."

"Really?" said Claire.

"Yes, most definitely a pike, but it has morphed into something else. From the chemical analysis results and some visual evidence of the smaller fish being partway through a transformation process themselves, I've come up with a theory. It's unbelievable, but just bear with me."

"Before you do that, I have a theory of my own," said Claire. "Want to hear it?"

Ben nodded.

"I think this monster pike is just a giant deformity, as are other aquatic creatures in that section of the canal. I think someone tipped something into the water some time ago, severely interfering with either the reproductive cycle of some creatures and resulting in abnormal young or polluting specific areas and causing these animals to grow abnormally.

"Could be possible," said Ben. "What about you, Ron, have you got any other slant on this?"

"Alien interference," he said with a smile. "No, seriously, not a bloody clue at the moment."

Ben walked to his new incident board. "A creature in Limehouse Basin, let's say a water snail, has ingested something that has caused a fundamental change in its genetic makeup. This is where I agree with you to a certain extent. The dragonfly larva eats the snail, and then the fish eats the dragonfly larva, continuing up the food chain until we reach the pike."

Ben picked up a board marker and drew the outline of a fish.

"I've noticed similarities in the smaller fish to the life cycle of flies, butterflies, and moths."

Claire looked puzzled and was about to speak. Ben put up a hand.

"Hear me out. As we know, a caterpillar forms into a chrysalis before emerging as a butterfly, which bears no resemblance to its younger, caterpillar state. During the earlier stage, the caterpillar digests itself into a soup while in the chrysalis state, and from the soup's ingredients reassembles itself as a butterfly. An amazing process. I have detected evidence of the same process in the fish samples, but not on the total body scale you would find within a butterfly chrysalis. It is more localized and very rapid."

"So I was right?" said Claire with an air of triumph.

"Not so fast, Miss Manson. The abnormalities that you have suggested, arising from the initial pollution in your case, are random. I'm suggesting a radical genetic change that results in orchestrated changes to the animals' physical and mental state. If I am right, we have to stop this before it reaches the top of the food chain."

"Us!" said Ron. "Bloody hell, my nose is big enough without it morphing into something else."

Claire snorted. "You'd look quite fetching with a trunk, Ron."

Ben stopped laughing. "Seriously, if there's any merit in my theory, we have to sort this out fast. Break the chain and find the source. If there is some toxic waste out there that could cause this effect, I have yet to see it. Claire, can you work on the meteorite sample as priority? Ron, I want you to contact Chris Williams and get her to step up the security on Limehouse Basin, the section of Regent's Canal affected, and Victoria Park. If this theory proves correct, we will need to conduct a thorough search of the entire section of that waterway to find the source.

"Police divers?" said Ron.

"Last resort. There are other ways putting no one in contact and at risk. Ron, I would like you to stay at the site until we work this out and eliminate the risk. Claire, book him accommodation, and this time I'm not worried about the cost, within reason. The Home Office is paying for this, without a budget limit."

Claire whistled. "Sure you don't want me to be the person on site?"

"Nice try, but no. I want you here running tests and other important tasks. Can't do it all here myself, and I don't want you booking yourself into Claridge's and swanning off to Oxford Street with the firm's credit card, do I?"

"As if!" she said.

"Right, folks, let's get to it. Ron, keep in contact. Any new info, ring it through and liaise with Roger to update the board."

"Claire, can you call in our IT wizard, and I don't care how much she costs, we're not paying. Chris Williams has given me a blank check for this investigation."

Claire relished the thought of having every resource at their disposal without having to agonize over the budget. It would be great to have Kerry Bailey around for more than just a few hours to help with IT. Ben only used self-employed Kerry when required, just a couple of hours a week. With the purse strings loosened, Kerry could work and socialize a little.

Claire decided she needed fresh air and met Kerry at the coffee shop.

Her face said it all. Kerry's beaming smile was all Claire needed.

"I'll take that as a yes then," said Claire.

"Of course. You know how much I enjoy working with you and Ben."

"Can you afford to drop everything? We need you straight away."

"I have a couple of projects on the go for long-standing clients, but I can work around them. They're not time-critical."

"Great, can you start, say, in an hour?"

"I'll do better than that. Let me grab my stuff from the flat, and I'll come back with you now."

They walked through the short alleyway that connected to Kerry's street, chattering excitedly. He followed them to Kerry's front door. Confident in their clarity, he sent the video and photo to Alex. He smiled, satisfied that he had captured Kerry Bailey face-on and in high definition. He inwardly marveled at how technology had advanced since the days of phone boxes and cameras with film that needed to be developed. A few seconds later, a message appeared acknowledging receipt of the video clip and photo.

TWELVE

Kerry Bailey was, in Ben's opinion, worth her weight in gold. She could find things on the internet and delve into darker and more depraved places in cyberspace that nobody else he knew could reach. Although Kerry was only twenty-four, she had the air of a much older woman, unless she was with Claire, and then they both regressed into teenagers. He liked her because she was logical and methodical to the point of obsession. Once given a task, Kerry pursued it like a terrier after a rat.

On the downside, there was something scary about her that was both ridiculous and completely out of sync with his logical scientific mind. She had a thin, gaunt look with gray eyes that reminded him of his mother's cat Baxter. It had cold gray eyes, with matching gray fur, a cat that slept with one eye open, so Ben could never escape its ice-cold stare. Baxter had always given Ben the creeps, but they tolerated each other with a mutual contempt.

Kerry had the same gray eyes and just to unsettle Ben even more, she recently dyed her hair gray. He thought it ridiculous that women with natural-colored hair, with no gray showing, dyed their hair gray. Claire said it was trendy. It seemed to be the "in" thing. But it wasn't his thing. It made Kerry look ten years older, a look that repelled him. Not in a creepy way but in a monotone, bland, he didn't quite know what way. Whatever it was, he felt slightly threatened by it, or was it fear? He didn't quite know. What he did know was that she was an expert in computing and had an exceptional and inquisitive mind that was right on the money for his scientific, investigative business. Absolutely perfect, apart from the eyes with that unnerving stare framed in a thin face and gray hair.

He looked up into her Baxter eyes on the other side of the desk as he brought her up to speed with the current investigation.

"I need you to research and gather information about the section of Regent's Canal and Limehouse Basin. Find out what cargo the barges carried when it was in industrial use. Also, investigate the full history of anything introduced into the water, including spillages, leaks, dumping, and boats sinking. In fact, please find anything you can from when it was constructed. Was there any pre-existing infrastructure on the site? I want a list of all marine and aquatic life and all terrestrial animals that live near to or in the water. Can you also do some research on the meteor sample that may have found its way into Limehouse Basin and anything and everything you can find about Jonny Clarke, the man who recently drowned there? I also need a global sweep of any similar instances of rapid deformity in fish and amphibians." Ben paused as their eyes locked.

"Is that everything?" she said.

He kept staring. The image of Baxter taunting him flashed through his mind. "I... I think so, for now."

She looked at him curiously.

Baxter vanished from his thoughts. "Yes, that should keep you occupied. I'll have a lot more for you to do and don't worry if there are gaps between any tasks that Claire or I give you. You're being paid your hourly rate regardless of whether you're researching on the computer or watching the back of your eyelids."

She laughed. "Thanks, Ben, I really appreciate this opportunity."

He smiled. "Good, now get out of my office and get to work.

Sorry there's no office for you but as you're using all your own kit just slum it wherever you want."

He watched her walk away toward the kitchen. Good job she didn't decide to use Claire's desk in his room. He tried to banish the thought of a gray cat sleeping on Claire's desk with one eye open.

The half-mile walk from the Travelodge Hotel to Cricketers Bridge was just enough for Ron to enjoy two cigarettes. His guilty pleasure would put him in a wooden overcoat, six feet under just like his father and elder brother. But he smoked since he was eight years old and it was part of him. Ron thought about what life would be like without a cigarette and it felt totally alien. He would never give it up, so what was the point of worrying about his future health?

Halfway through the first smoke of the day, he sensed he was being followed. The reflection of a thickset man came and went in the windows opposite. Ron sped up. The man sped up. Ron slowed, so did the man. Who was this stalker? He stopped, bent down, fiddled with his shoelaces and looked behind. The man strolled leisurely toward him barely twenty yards behind. Was he imagining it or was he being tailed, and if so why?

Only one way to find out. Ron stood, turned and crossed the road, doubling back the way he had come, watching the man. As they passed on opposite sides of the road Ron stared across. The man didn't look back, fixing his eyes straight ahead. Ron watched and waited. Sure enough, the man looked over his shoulder a few seconds later and glanced away again. Was it just some nosy sod? The press? One of those London footpads about to relieve him of his wallet? The man crossed the road and turned into a side street. Ron gave it a couple of minutes, crossed the road again, and briskly walked until he reached the turning. He stared across, down the side street. No sign of the man. He settled to a steady pace and lit up a second Marlboro Light.

In the distance he was glad to see Chris Williams' outstretched arm waving to him. He looked behind and the street was empty, apart from a postman delivering a parcel to one of the houses. The man had gone.

"Glad you could make it," said Chris. "Save me having to ask Ben to send someone. There's been another development."

Ron nipped the glowing end off the Marlboro Light and pushed the butt into his pocket.

"Follow me," she said. "I have already signed you in at the scene access control point. Not exactly following protocol as you should do it in person, but time is of the essence."

"What's the development, Chris?"

"A sewage inspection the other side of Victoria Park where two workers using remote cameras have seen something unusual, which frightened them both to death. Best if you look yourself."

They strode through the park onto Gore Road where several police officers congregated around a large white van.

"This is Bob French, from Hackney Borough Council," said Chris. Ron shook hands with the man who did not look at all well. "Bob and his teammate have a mobile, robotic camera inspecting the walls of rainwater culverts under the street. Basically, they drive a remote mini vehicle carrying a camera along the culverts checking for any collapse, blockage, anything that will impede the flow of water. It's a routine check. Show Ron what you saw, Bob."

Bob beckoned Ron into the back of the van where a series of monitors sat in a row on a bench. He pressed several buttons and a monochrome picture appeared of an arched stone culvert with a small stream of water flowing through. The small vehicle propelling the camera moved forward and the view remained constant with the same stone-lined arch. A rat suddenly ran from behind the vehicle, its back end coming into view. It stopped, turned and looked back then ran off into the distance. The view jolted and distorted as another rat ran past. It was a lot bigger than the first. Bob stopped the video.

Ron was puzzled, wondering if he had missed something.

"I thought the same when I first watched this," said Chris. "The problem is scale. We didn't tell you what size the culvert is. Run it again, Bob."

Bob manipulated the controls and the video re-ran from the original position.

"The culvert arch is four feet high from the base to the midpoint of the arched roof."

Ron's mouth fell open as the first and then the second larger rat ran past. Bob froze the image of the second rat.

Ron stared, mentally calculating.

"We think the bigger rat is at least twice the size of the biggest rat we have ever seen down there. Show Ron the still shot you took after that, Bob."

Bob swiveled to a different monitor and opened a photo file.

"Bloody hell," said Ron.

"Almost what I said when I first saw that grotesque face, except I was a bit more colorful than that."

The photo showed three king-sized rats moving toward the camera. Almost bulging out of its head, the middle rat's eyes looked directly at the lens. Its front two teeth were elongated, giving it a sinister goofy look, but it was the other teeth protruding from its jaw that made the entire head look like some fantasy furry horror from hell. Ron stared at the rat's eyes shining back at him. Although it was a monochrome photo, the eyes were a consistent color. No distinction between the pupil, iris, and surrounding membranes. He would bet his life that the eyes were blood red.

THIRTEEN

Horace Clancy almost face-planted on the pavement outside the Grapes public house. Eight pints of Fisherman's Folly and several tots of rum were playing havoc with the signal between his brain and legs, and it looked very much as if the alcohol was winning. He didn't want to go outside to relieve himself, but try as he might, he could not negotiate the stairs to the toilets.

The blast of cold air outside had him reeling, and a wooden bollard outside the main entrance helped keep him upright. The bar had been so cozy and warm, and he was on top of the world for the first few pints, with all his woes washed away in an amber sea of pleasant thoughts. He knew his limit and was about to leave when an old work colleague and drinking partner showed up.

Teddy Carver insisted Horace stay for a catch-up drink, which turned into two, then three. By the fourth pint, he'd lost count. He remembered Teddy having hollow legs, drinking day and night with no ill effect, but Horace did not have the same cast-iron constitution, and the visits to the gents became more frequent. On his last attempt to climb the stairs, Teddy pushed past and suggested that he would be better off going to the toilet in some dark corner outside. Horace tried the stairs a few more times before admitting defeat and took his old friend's advice.

After releasing his grip on the wooden bollard, Horace lurched sideways and started a loping gait in the direction of home, one leg working perfectly, the other slewing sideways with a slight drag on the pavement. Now on inebriated autopilot, a shred of sensibility broke the surface, telling him to get home and sleep it off, and there was a good place to take a leak just a few hundred yards along the street. It took fifteen minutes to reach the start of the walkway alongside the east side of Limehouse Basin. Horace faced the high wall separating the path from Northey Street, fumbling with his zip. He staggered backward, nearly falling into the inlet from the Thames, then fell forward, bracing himself with one hand against the cool London bricks, and smiled as he relieved himself, soaking his boots in urine. Zipping himself up, Horace felt much better and almost decided to return to the Grapes but thought better of it. Only a hundred yards to his narrowboat. He could feel his bed calling to him, like a beckoning siren dressed in a duvet cover.

He took a step forward when a firm hand gripped his shoulder.

"Where do you think you're going, Horace?"

He turned and looked up at a police officer, a good foot taller than himself.

"Constanoon afterble," said Horace, and burst out laughing. The officer smiled and shook his head.

"Old ones are the best, Horace. Now, what are you doing here?"

"Going to me bed," he said, swaying from side to side.

"You're not supposed to be staying here, Horace. I thought you were going to stay with your sister until this incident is all over?"

"Was, Officer, but she's buggered off without telling me. I've got nowhere to go." The policeman cupped his hands together and blew into them while looking around. The other officer on duty with him had gone for a break but would be back soon.

"Look, Horace, I'll help you get back to your boat, and once you're on it and tucked up, you stay there, and I didn't see you, right?"

"Thanks, Jim," said Horace, winking at him. "You're not like those other cops. You're alright, you are. Not so much of a wanker as the rest."

Jim laughed. "I'll take that as a compliment. Now, shift your arse," he said, locking arms with Horace, and frog-marching him along the dark path. They reached the dingy narrowboat, and Jim helped Horace inside. "Keep your lights out, otherwise you'll be seen by my boss and chucked out. Oh, and if I catch you pissing on the pavement again, you'll have a bed for the night down the nick. Goodnight, Horace, and get some shut-eye."

Jim hurried to the road junction just as his sergeant appeared.

"Anything going on?" said the sergeant, handing him a welcome cup of coffee.

"No, Sarge. All quiet at the moment."

"Bleedin' waste of time if you ask me." They stood chatting for a few minutes when the sergeant stopped mid-sentence and pointed.

Jim turned and looked into the almost black water of the basin.

"There!" said the sergeant, pointing at circling lights glowing deep below the surface. Jim pulled out his phone and began to video the strange phenomenon. The cluster of around twenty pinprick lights, moved together in a continuous circle. They stopped suddenly and then headed in a straight line toward the middle of the basin at great speed before they disappeared from sight. The two policemen stood in silence for a minute, trying to process what they had just witnessed.

"I know this seems ridiculous," said the sergeant, "but I think I better call this in."

Jim nodded. "That scientist said anything unusual, and he needs to know about it straight away."

The sergeant laughed. "What the hell am I supposed to tell our control, that we've just watched a herd of underwater fairy lights swim across Limehouse Basin? They'll be taking the piss till I retire!"

"True, but that's what we just saw."

The sergeant reluctantly called it in, grateful that Jim could back it up with video evidence. Ron Logan was glad of the call, and a patrol car picked him up from the hotel. When he arrived at the lock gates between the Thames and the basin, there were dozens of officers scanning the water for the strange lights.

FOURTEEN

"Keep staring down that thing and you'll go blind," said Kath O'Brian as she passed with the vacuum cleaner.

Claire sat up from the microscope and yawned. "You know what, Kath, I think you're right. My head's pounding. Do we have any pills in the medical cupboard?"

"Not my department, young lady. That's the one place I don't clean, apart from the lab stores. Ben won't let me step foot in there in case I break something and cause an explosion. Rich coming from that clumsy little sod. Remember that tray of drinks last year? The Christmas party. Ended up all over the table and us. I rest my case."

Claire chuckled. Ben, flailing in midair with a full tray of drinks after he tripped over a handbag sticking out from under the table, was the highlight of the evening. The fact it was Kath's handbag didn't seem to enter Kath's memory.

"Drink lots of water and take time out from that contraption. That's what you need. Pills just cover things up."

Claire gathered her notes, did as she was told, and found Ben in the kitchen on the phone. She pointed to the new kettle, and he gave her the thumbs-up.

"So how many oversized rats are down there?" said Ben.

Claire couldn't hear who was on the other end of the call but guessed it was Ron or Chris Williams.

"This is getting serious. The authorities need to cull them before any more get infected with whatever this is. Keep me in the loop, Ron."

"What oversized rats?" said Claire, passing him his mug of coffee.

"Looks like this mutation is spreading. They've seen rats in the sewers, double the size of what they should be, with distorted features like the giant pike. I'm guessing that rats have been feeding on an affected fish or some other creature. The problem is no longer confined to water."

"Shit!"

"Exactly, and getting pretty deep at that," said Ben. "The only saving grace is that apart from large dogs, there won't be many predators that can take them out and get the mutation passed to them."

"You mean you hope."

"Pray more like. We need to find the source, and I think Ron may have found it," said Ben.

"Really?"

"Has anything unusual come out of your meteorite sample?"

"Something I wouldn't expect. There are small particles that I need to investigate further."

"Explain?"

"The makeup of the samples is as you would expect, with known Earth elements, but there are small particles that I can't identify. They don't appear to be pure mineral."

"Are you telling me there may be the remains of a life form?"

"Fossils? No. I can't say at the moment as I haven't had conclusive results. It could be an unknown element or compound. It just seems off that they are not responding to basic test procedures."

"Have you re-run the tests to cover any mistakes? I'm not criticizing, just covering that aspect."

"Yes, I've run the tests three times, but there are no results so far."

"Interesting. So if these particles are not mineral, that only leaves—"

"Animal or vegetable," said Claire, and laughed. "Don't you think you're jumping the gun here?"

"I know some meteorites found have contained the five bases for RNA and DNA. Is it possible that there could be something groundbreaking here?"

"Are you suggesting some extraterrestrial form of life? I think I need to do some different tests. I'm sure there'll be a logical explanation. A life form on a piece of meteorite traveling, for God only knows how long, through space? Come off it, Ben."

He winked at her. "Just playing devil's advocate. Just supposing it is animal and it has had some effect on our own terrestrial wildlife?"

"Let's do what you preach and stick to proven facts."

He liked it when Claire argued with him. She was very perceptive and had put him in his place a few times since she began working for him. He turned to leave.

"Hang on, Ben," said Claire, tapping him on the shoulder. "You were about to tell me about Ron's discovery?"

He explained the strange underwater lights in Limehouse Basin the previous night, witnessed by police officers. After he had relayed the new information, she sat for an entire minute, staring at the wall covering her eyes with both hands.

"It'll come to me soon," she said pulling her hands away. "It's ringing a bell. I've heard of this phenomenon before, but I can't think where."

"Are you thinking of GloFish?"

"GloFish?"

"Genetically modified fish used to detect pollution. They absorb a specific wavelength of sunlight and can re-emit it to give a glowing appearance. People keep them as pets now."

She shook her head. "No, not GloFish. Hang on. I've got it! My friend Daisy in uni was researching some sort of weird unexplained sighting in fresh water. I'll call her later and let you know."

"I'm going to take a trip to Bethnal Green later today," said Ben. "I think I need to catch up with Ron and see these alien lights for myself!"

She rolled her eyes as he left and returned to the lab. Thumbing through her address book, she found Daisy Rogers' number and rang.

"Hi, Daisy, it's Claire Manson."

"That's weird. I was just thinking about you! How strange is that?" said Daisy.

"How come?"

"I just bumped into an old flame of yours in the pub."

"Oh dear, which one?"

Daisy laughed. "Bloody hell, Claire, the one that you should never have let go."

"Give me a clue?"

"Nigel."

"Patterson?"

"Yep. Got it in one. He's only made a few million playing the stock market since we finished our course. Ironic, really. He was always scrounging a drink or helping himself to our food at the flat."

"So he's really made a fortune, then?"

"Bloody loaded."

"And how do you know that? Let me guess—he told you? He always was a liar."

"He did, and he bought all the drinks and lunch, dressed in the most expensive designer clobber, and had all his teeth sorted."

"Not the tooth at the front that I always said looked like it was signaling to turn left?"

"Straight as an arrow now, and he gave me a lift in his Aston Martin. I think for once he was telling the truth—bloody minted!"

"Good luck to him, but as you just said, he was an old flame and for a very good reason."

"What was it? You never told me why you two split."

"Because he was batting for both sides. I didn't want a relationship where my partner wasn't sure if he wanted me or another fella."

"Nigel was bent?"

"Not completely, just bending a bit. Daisy, there are some people that like both genders. Are you living in the Victorian age?"

"Well, I would never have guessed."

"Same here until I caught him snogging one of the lecturers in the car park of the Grovers Arms."

"Grovers Arms? Was that the trendy pub near our flat? I only went there once."

"You were with me, and that was the night I saw Nigel and Professor Lewis in the car park."

"Lewis! You're kidding me? You never said a thing?"

"If you remember, we went there to celebrate you passing one of your final exams, and I didn't want to spoil it with my relationship woes. Anyway, the reason I was calling was to ask you about your dissertation. Are you still living in London?"

"No, my parents moved to Cirencester six months ago to retire. I went with them."

Claire smiled. "Just a stone's throw from here."

"I know. Sorry I haven't rung you to let you know, but I had a problem with my phone and lost all my contacts, and my address book is buried in one of the boxes we still haven't unpacked from the move."

"No excuse now, is there?" said Claire. "Can we meet up and I'll come to you? I love Cirencester. The sooner the better."

"I usually go to Keith's Coffee Shop, near the marketplace. The soup's delicious and the coffee's to die for. It's just off the market square in Black Jack Street and I'm at a loose end tomorrow if that's okay, say ten in the morning?"

"Perfect. Do you have a copy of your dissertation you could bring?"

"It's somewhere on my laptop. You have me intrigued."

Claire ended the call and felt a rush of nostalgia. Although university was a tough academic gig, she really enjoyed the experience, greatly enhanced by Daisy Rogers, a vivacious redhead she'd taken to immediately. They both shared a wacky sense of humor and seemed to know what each other was thinking, even ending sentences for each other or saying exactly the same thing at the same time. Claire said that although they looked nothing alike, they were identical twins by different parents. In their second year, they had not taken the usual route of a shabby shared student house but went upmarket with an upper-floor flat and remained in it until they graduated. It suited both, as they spent most of their student days working obsessively hard; Claire in chemistry and Daisy studying geography and environmental management. Both liked the assurance that they understood the importance of work and quiet to study, and both enjoyed occasional riotous nights out together to let off steam, relieving the pressure of constant study and exams. Claire hoped the next day would rekindle their relationship and provide some insight into the strange aquatic lights in Limehouse Basin.

FIFTEEN

The alarm went off for the second time and kept beeping for a full minute before Ron's arm appeared from under the duvet, extended, and tried to grab the phone, knocking it off the bedside table. He cursed, pulling himself to the side of the bed, rubbing the sleep from his eyes before dropping to his knees, searching for the phone. His fumbling fingers silenced the alarm and he crawled back under the sheets.

The previous night's excitement dragged on until three, when the strange lights in Limehouse Basin made a brief reappearance before disappearing into the murky depths once more. Ron was so wound up from the sighting that he couldn't get back to sleep until seven. After such a short but deep sleep, every muscle in Ron's body ached for a couple more hours. He would have done just that if the need for the bathroom and a cigarette weren't so strong. He glared at the smoke detector above, remembering more hospitable times when you could have a smoke in bed. Since the windows were fitted with child-proof safety catches and couldn't be opened enough to hang out into fresh air, Ron got dressed and dragged himself outside into the glaring sunshine.

With uncombed hair and shoes but no socks, he looked a real mess and, in the eyes of anyone passing, looked as if he had just crawled home after a night of wild debauchery. Ron didn't care what he looked like, only interested in getting a nicotine fix to set him up for the day. Satisfied after the second Marlboro Light, Ron showered, made himself look respectable, ordered a full English breakfast in the hotel restaurant, and after several cups of strong black coffee, began to feel part of the human race once more. His phone rang.

"Ron Logan?" said a Cockney voice.

"Speaking," said Ron, checking the caller ID, which was withheld.

"It would be good for your health and well-being if you left the area immediately, particularly the canal and Limehouse Basin. Tell your boss Sharman and his charming sidekick Miss Manson, the same applies to them."

"I don't understand. Who is this?"

"Someone who could alter your good looks. Leave, and you won't have your face rearranged—got it?"

Ron didn't respond. He was stunned. The call ended.

Ron stared into the dregs of his coffee, his thoughts spinning. A prank? He thought of Roger back in Moreton, who was very good at putting on accents, but surely, he wouldn't pull a stunt like this? He wondered who to call first. He rang Ben.

"Probably a local resident or boat owner that can't go on the canal," said Ben. "I can see no benefit to anyone else if we left the investigation, and even then, Chris would get some other organization to take over from us. What do you think, Ron?"

"I don't know who it could be. I thought of the Cambridge team being annoyed at me jumping ship and joining you, but they have far more integrity. If it's genuine, I suggest you and Claire stay well away. I think you should anyway until I've spoken to Chris Williams and the local cops."

"Can't keep me away, Logan, and don't forget, I'm your boss."

"Not yet, you're not. Don't you think there would be safety in fewer numbers here?"

"I am not being scared off by some idiot, and the two of us are a better match for any would-be thug trying to get us off the case. I think my initial thoughts were right. Empty threats from a stranded barge owner or a local resident who can't ride his bicycle to work along the towpath and has to go the long way around."

"I suppose that makes sense, but this guy sounded nasty."

"Stay in your hotel till I get there. I'll get Claire to book me a room for a couple of nights. Won't hurt her to hold the fort here at Moreton for a while and do me a favor. Let Chris Williams know straight away, and I'll see you later."

Ben met Ron in the hotel bar just as it was getting dark.

"Been here all day, Ron?" said Ben, pulling up a chair. "Let me get you a drink."

"Slept most of the afternoon. I'll have a whiskey and pep, please. Make it a double."

Ben whistled. "Phone call that bad, eh?"

"No, I've been holding off having a drink all day until you got here. I didn't want to be half-cut when the boss arrived, now did I?"

"Quite agree, Ron. Oh, by the way, did you get hold of Chris Williams?"

"Can't get hold of her, been trying all day. I rang the local cops, and they said the same. She's gone off grid."

"Wish you'd told me earlier. I could have contacted her head of department."

"Done that, but they refused to comment. Bloody civil service weirdos. I bet they said that because they weren't even aware she'd disappeared."

Ben ordered drinks and sat back down, nursing a large glass of merlot in cupped hands.

"Have you had anyone contact you from the police?"

"Just the sergeant that I met last night. Wanted to know if I would be down there again tonight. Looks like we'll have plenty of company."

"Oh?"

"Press has got wind of the lights. The sergeant reckons everyone, and his dog will be there tonight. He's had to call reinforcements to cope with any nosy buggers trying to gatecrash the basin."

Ben took a large swig of the wine and leaned back in the chair. What had started off as a simple pollution investigation was rapidly turning into a major incident that could make national or even international news. Was it good fortune to be under the spotlight yet again? The last two cases that put Moreton Scientific Investigation under the media spotlight had proved fortuitous, and work had flooded in. Third time lucky again, Ben wondered?

His phone rang.

"Hi, it's Kerry, can you talk?"

"Fire away, Kerry," said Ben, signaling to Ron for pen and paper.

"I've emailed you a potted history of Regent's Canal and Limehouse Basin, plus a list of known cargo hauled between the internal canal network and the Thames through the basin. Nothing untoward. No recent pollution of note."

"Okay, I'll take a look," he said, putting the pen down, disappointed. He was hoping Kerry was going to come up with some gold nugget.

"That's the boring bit," said Kerry brightly.

Ben sat up and took another mouthful of merlot.

"You asked me to do a trawl on any similar incidents, and there was an unsubstantiated sighting of mysterious lights in a freshwater lake in Nevada a couple of years back."

"Nevada? That's one hell of a coincidence. The meteorite fragments from the Museum of Alien Life in London were sourced just over the state border from Nevada in California."

"Yes, Teakettle Junction, which is roughly two hundred miles south of Pyramid Lake, where the sighting occurred. Here's the clincher. I tracked down the witnesses of the meteor impact and narrowed it down precisely by hacking into some useful data. The trajectory before impact was one hundred and ninety-two degrees south heading twelve degrees north, and guess what?"

"Teakettle Junction and Pyramid Lake are on exactly the same trajectory?"

"Spot on. Cosmic coincidence or what?"

Ben put the empty glass in the air, waving it at Ron for a refill.

"I've said it before. I don't believe in coincidences, especially when the odds are stacking against it. What happened at Lake—"

"Lake Pyramid, it's on a Native American reservation just north of Reno. They had an enormous problem a couple of years back when an unprecedented algae bloom made the lake toxic and off limits to humans. It was just after that time that some campers who weren't aware of the ban saw strange lights near the south shores of the lake. They said they watched them for a few nights. I've just texted you the link to YouTube."

"They filmed it?"

"And posted a few videos. It looks very similar to the one Ron sent me."

Ben followed the link and watched glowing lights moving deep in bright green water.

"Is that the algae bloom you mentioned turning the water a strange green color?"

"Yes, it was harmless to animal life, but not good for us. That's why they prohibited any visitors for a while until they cleared it up.

"Any other similarities, dead fish, blue slime, giant rats?"

"No, nothing confirmed. The authorities kept everyone away, so there was hardly anyone around to report anything unusual. So, something could have happened, and nobody was there to witness it."

Ben re-ran several videos. They all displayed the same pattern as Limehouse Basin. A formation of deep lights turning in circles, then moving away and diving at speed.

"I think we can safely say that there is a definite link." Ben was struck with a sudden thought.

"Did the algae bloom start before or after the meteor impact?"

"Well before." He could hear Kerry rustling through notes. "Three months before."

"Okay, so the meteor didn't cause the algae bloom. So, I wonder?"

"Wonder what?" said Kerry.

"Can you do some more sniffing around for water samples at the time of the sightings, if there are any?"

"Will do. A hunch?"

"Yes. Let me know if you find anything, and thanks, Kerry. Fantastic work."

Ron stared over a large whiskey and pep. "Your Merlot's getting warm, boss."

"Mmm," he said, taking a sip. "Things are knitting together, Ron. I believe we have yet another alien encounter."

SIXTEEN

"You're looking very pleased with yourself," said Claire.

"Just had my first bit of praise from Ben."

"Bloody hell, Kerry, you're privileged. What did you do to deserve that?"

"Bit of research, that's all," she said with a smug grin.

"Come on, spill the beans."

"It's what I came in to tell you," said Kerry, still grinning. "He's bloody hard to please. I've been here from the start, and I don't think he's ever said anything, good or bad, about my IT work."

"Just his way. Most of the time he's on a different planet, totally absorbed with whatever's the latest shiny thing," said Claire, who felt guilty. "I'm being harsh. He just works so hard he's oblivious. He's said on many occasions how important you are to us all, and I know he means it. Anyway, what were you going to tell me?"

Kerry sat at the front lab bench and explained the link between Teakettle Junction and Pyramid Lake.

"There has to be something in the meteorite that's causing this," said Claire as soon as Kerry finished. "The sample I have has some anomalies that so far I can't explain. I'll have to get my thinking cap on for different tests."

"Let's finish this conversation over a cuppa," said Kerry. "Coffee always sharpens my mind, and there's something we're missing, but I can't quite put my finger on it."

They sat together for an hour discussing the differences between Limehouse Basin and Pyramid Lake, and although Claire came up with a few more ideas for tests, she still wasn't happy.

"I've a feeling we will analyze this forever without coming close. If this is an extraterrestrial phenomenon, we may not even have a test capable of determining what the issue is. So bloody frustrating, Kerry. I've been strapped to that microscope for over a day now and still nothing concrete."

Kerry picked up their mugs and walked to the sink. "I'm sure we'll crack it, eventually. Either here or the other two down in London." She pulled the handle on the cold water too quickly, and a jet of water hit the cup and sprayed in her face.

Claire recoiled but caught the brunt of it, soaking her hair.

"I'll bloody kill Ben. I've asked him to fix that at least a dozen times. My hair will be like a frizz-bomb, and I'm supposed to be meeting Dave for a drink straight after work."

"Dry your hair. I'll get my straighteners and hairdryer from home. Only take a couple of minutes, and who's going to stop us? While the cat's away!"

Kerry threw her coat on and was gone. Claire stared at her bedraggled hair in the mirror of the ladies' room.

"Bloody men." She brushed it and watched it curl before her eyes. Her hair doubled in volume in just a couple of minutes. All her hard work straightening that morning vanished. She winced, noticing how much she was looking like her mother, who never straightened her hair. A sudden glint in her reflection made her lean right up to the mirror's surface. "Out you come, you little sod," she said, addressing a solitary gray hair. With a swift yank, it came out. She held it up in front of her, examining the almost white strand. How long would it be before she would need to dye her hair? How old had her mother been? Thirty, thirty-five? Shit, it was only a few years away.

She kept brushing, hoping there would be no more sudden flashes of gray in the glare of the mirror strip light. She stood back and stared at herself staring back, not happy with the accidental look.

"Bloody water." She kept brushing furiously, then paused. She stood bolt upright thinking, grinned, and shouted, "Water!" at the top of her voice. Throwing the brush into the sink, Claire rushed back to the lab.

Kerry returned to find Claire setting up several pieces of lab equipment, condensers, test tubes, and an array of glass containers.

"You're eager. Do you still want me to fix your hair? I've brought shampoo. Hope you like it. It was one of those 'value' brands, but it smells pretty good."

Claire swiveled on her stool. "Sod my hair for now. You're a bloody genius, Kerry Bailey, do you know that?"

"Me?"

"Yes, you. That drenching got me thinking about how it completely altered my look. Just a bit of water."

"So?"

"Part of the meteor landed in Death Valley, one of the driest places on the planet. Nothing happened we know of there. No wildlife morphing into something horrific, no weird lights. That didn't happen till fragments found their way into Limehouse Basin and Regent's Canal. I bet that more of the meteorite or meteorite shower ended up in Pyramid Lake. Water is the common denominator. There is none where it landed in Death Valley, and it was in an area where the little rain there is simply runs off or evaporates quickly."

"You think water activated something in the fragments?"

"It's a strong possibility. No, I'm being illogical. Come on, Claire, put your scientist's head on. Facts, girl, facts!"

Kerry stifled a laugh. "You sound like a nutty professor."

Claire laughed back. "Well, perhaps I am. What do you reckon? Good theory?"

"You can but try. What's all this crap you've set up? All you need to do to prove it is to plonk a sample in water, stand back, and watch."

Claire looked at the bench strewn with equipment.

"You're right. Tell you what, Kerry, sort my hair out and we can both come back and watch."

With perfectly coiffed hair, Claire sat chatting to Kerry for over an hour with no reaction from either of the four king-sized round-bottomed flasks. Each one had different water—pure, salt, acidic, and alkaline.

Kath appeared at the door. "Claire, your fella's at the bloody door. I told him he can't come in."

"Why not, Kath?"

"He looks stinking dirty, and I've just polished the floor in reception, that's why. Anyway, I'm off home. Will you be locking up?"

"Dirty? We're supposed to be going to the Black Bear for some food," said Claire, but Kath was already on her way.

"Do me a favor, Kerry. If that old dragon's out of sight, let him in. I need to set up surveillance and some other bits and pieces. And tell Dave to take his shoes off if they are mucky."

She looked at the four glass flasks, willing for something to prove her theory. But all she could see was clear water in each.

"Sorry, Claire, I just popped in to say I'll have to shower quickly and get a change of clothes," said Dave. She walked up to him and kissed him passionately. He arched backward, trying not to touch her with his filthy overalls.

"Think I'll join you, then we can go out," she said, raising an eyebrow. Claire looked over her shoulder at the four lifeless flasks, turned on the surveillance camera, and switched the lab lights off.

At the side of the River Thames, Ben and Ron contemplated the night ahead. Chris Williams reappeared and apologized for her unannounced absence. The powers that be summoned her for an update, which turned into an all-day grilling with several departments. She was put so much under the spotlight that she didn't have a chance to let everyone know where she was. She joined them and gladly agreed with the consensus to have a pre-vigil meeting at the Grapes.

The tiny pub was packed, but a couple was just leaving, and they managed to squeeze into a corner alcove. Ben bought them a double round to save another trip to the crowded bar.

"So, you've been busy all day?" said Ron.

Chris downed a whole pint of lager in one, astonishing the other two.

"Must have been one hell of a day then?" said Ben.

"You could say that," said Chris, putting the empty glass down and lifting her next pint off the tray. "This incident has gone international."

"The media, I suppose?" said Ben.

"No, Homeland Security and NASA want to speak to you in person," she said, then downed half of her next drink.

"Slow down, Chris, you'll be drinking us under the table," said Ron.

She laughed and took another mouthful. "Sorry, guys, force of habit. I always start quick. Don't panic, after the first six pints, I slow down." Ron's eyes widened. She laughed again. "God, it's so good to be out of that bloody office. I'm taking the piss, Ron. This will be my last."

"The Americans are onto this?" said Ben.

"Sure are. They were in contact as soon as they found out about the robbery at the Museum of Alien Life. There are two officials flying in as we speak, so don't drink too many, as they want to meet you at our headquarters first thing in the morning."

"What are they so interested in us for?" said Ben. "Is it anything to do with the meteor landing site in California?"

"No, Pyramid Lake. They've had some similar strange experiences at the lake and the surrounding area in the last twelve months."

"What similarities?" asked Ben.

"Fish and local wildlife developing unnatural features. Nothing much to go on, that's why I'm keen for your input in the morning. I'll have a car at the hotel for seven thirty. Any more from the threat you received, Ron?"

"Not a dicky bird. Ben was probably right, just some idle threat."

The three stayed till the pub closed, and none of them had the appetite to stay up all night to watch the aquatic illuminations at Limehouse Basin, now that there was an early start in the morning.

Claire snuggled up to Dave, stroking his warm muscular back, listening to his breathing while he slumbered. It had been a long day and an interesting evening. After nearly breaking their necks during a passionate romp in the shower, the couple spent a quiet evening in the Black Bear. She forgave him for turning up at the lab looking like a hobo. Dave was covered in mortar dust because he had been helping a friend demolish a wall. It took her ages to get the grit out of his hair in the shower. She smiled; nothing like sharing a shower to get a man's undivided attention. Her thoughts drifted back to her water theory, and she had nearly dozed off when a tune heard earlier on the pub's old-fashioned jukebox kept ear-worming her awake. Noddy Holder's distinctive gravel voice filled her head. Someone chose her all-time favorite song, 'Everyday' by Slade, and she made Dave play it another five times, much to the annoyance of other customers, and now her mind wouldn't let it rest. She slipped out of the bedroom, pulling on her robe as she tiptoed down the stairs.

Unclipping her phone from the charger, she pressed the video link app to the lab. The four glass flasks were just about visible but blurred as arcing light seared across the screen. She adjusted the settings, but they remained out of focus and distorted.

"Bloody signal," she muttered.

She made a cup of tea and settled down on the sofa with her laptop, pulling a large tartan throw around her shoulders, and logged into the video link. The lab bench flickered into view. This time the image was pin sharp. Claire almost tipped tea over the laptop when she saw the cause of the earlier distortion on her phone.

SEVENTEEN

"Hell, Ron, you're one scary man first thing in the morning," said Ben, pulling his chair out and placing a plate of toast and marmalade on the table.

"Love you too," said Ron. "You don't look so hot yourself, mate. Did you sleep alright?"

"Like the proverbial log. That Fisherman's Folly is a mean pint and rendered me unconscious before my head hit the pillow. Best night's sleep I've had for weeks, and you know what, Ron?"

"What?"

"Not so much as an inkling of a headache. Think I've just found my drink."

"Mate, don't be fooled. By dinnertime you'll feel like shite. You had five of them last night and a glass of red."

"Don't put the curse on me. I actually feel great."

"Didn't have your phone on, did you?" said Ron.

"Why?"

"Claire's been ringing you since the early hours. She got me up instead, but I thought I'd let you have your beauty sleep."

"What did she want?"

"You better look at this." Ron adjusted his phone and passed it over the table.

"What am I looking at, Ron?"

"Video clip from our lab, pointing at four flasks full of water."

"I can see that, but what are the flashing lights? Why has she set up flashing lights in or behind two of the flasks?"

"She didn't. The lights are inside the flasks. She put a sample of meteorite dust in each, and whatever is in the dust reacted in two of the tests."

"Bloody hell—the lights in Limehouse Basin!" exclaimed Ben.

"Could be. She wants you to ring her as soon as possible," said Ron, tucking into his breakfast.

Ben pushed the toast away and went outside.

"Was she worth it?" said Claire sarcastically when she answered his call.

"Sorry, Claire, didn't realize I'd knocked my phone off last night," he lied.

"Sure it wasn't that Chris Williams that kept you away from my calls? She was giving you the eye, and you were obviously enjoying the attention."

Ben laughed. "Manson, if I were any other boss, you would have been looking for another employer a long time ago."

"You're not denying it then?" she countered.

"Okay, okay, banter time over. What the hell was going on in the lab? I've seen the video clip on Ron's phone, but it doesn't make much sense. Is it the meteor particles causing the light?"

"Yes, but only in two flasks: pure distilled water and water with a pH value of six point five to replicate the slight acidity in the canal. Saltwater and water with a pH value above seven did not react."

"Interesting, and could be very significant," said Ben. "Tell me about the lights. When did they appear, how do they move, how many—"

"Whoa! I still haven't got my head around it myself yet. The reaction started at three fifty-one this morning. The video I set up picked up a slight bubbling in the pure water flask. Within three minutes, that had progressed to a pinprick of light, and the light began slowly moving within the flask at four oh six. The pH value of six point five reaction had the same sequence of events but was much slower, with the reaction beginning at four twenty-seven and taking thirty-two minutes for the lights to appear and a further fifteen minutes for the lights to show movement. Since then, both samples have increased in brightness so much that it's quite painful to look at them without eye protection. This must be how the lights can be seen in Limehouse Basin, as the water is quite thick with a silt suspension. They are so intense that they can cut through deep, murky water."

"Is it a single light in each flask?" said Ben, fascinated by the video clip he kept watching again and again.

"No. In the acidic water, there are two, and the pure water has at least five, maybe six. It's hard to tell, as they're so bright."

"Thoughts?"

"I've tested the atmosphere in the flasks and there's no change to the air in each container. The water composition has also not changed in any chemical or physical way. The water temperature has remained constant, which is unbelievable, considering the intense light. I was expecting it to boil over!" said Claire.

"Light without heat?"

"No discernible rise in temperature since either sample began emitting light," said Claire, "so the particles must be generating photons to produce visible UV wavelengths as opposed to heat-generating infrared wavelengths."

"Yes," agreed Ben, smiling at her conclusion.

"It's the intensity of the light that's throwing me," said Claire. "It is literally arc light brightness."

"Have you tried removing particles from the flask?"

"That's my next move," said Claire. "Just setting up some additional eye protection."

"I want you to do this under full decontamination conditions. Just remember that something turned those fish blue and transformed the pike and the toad. Too much of a coincidence, and I don't want you to turn from Dr. Jekyll into Miss Hyde."

He smiled as he listened to her laughing and telling Roger.

"Don't worry, that's already set up. Pity you're not here for the decontamination."

"Don't you dare mention what I think you were thinking!"

She giggled. "I don't have a clue what you mean, Dr. Sharman."

He ended the call and went back to tell Ron.

The man sat behind Ben and listened to the conversation. When they got up to leave, he wiped his mouth with his napkin, stood, and walked out of the hotel.

Alex Munro listened as the man repeated the content of the conversation between Ben and Ron. He frowned, wondering how Sharman had got hold of the meteorite fragments. He thought back to the visit from the two scientists, closing his eyes to re-run the meeting in his mind. Claire Manson asked to see the remaining fragments and handled them with neoprene gloves. He heard her asking if they could take the samples for tests. He refused. No way was he having a lab ruining his precious meteorite fragments. Tests would always do something or destroy something. She examined the fragments with a magnifying eyepiece. He remembered admiring her stunning black shining hair and a glimpse of her neck. Most men seemed to be attracted by other female features, but Alex always had a thing for a woman's neck and beautiful, natural hair. Even the ugliest woman could turn his head if she had a perfect slender neck and stunning hair. Claire had both, and he found it difficult not to stare during the meeting. He focused on the man, Ron Logan, who asked him if the large photo on the wall was a fake. Of course, it was a fake, but he would never admit that it was. It must have been obvious to a scientist that the picture was phony, so why ask? Was it a simple distraction? He thought harder, trying to view the meeting in his mind's eye from different angles. Ron Logan stood to his side, pointing at the metallic surface of the UFO in the photograph. She was sitting behind, but still in his peripheral vision. What was she doing? No sudden movements? No. She had continued to look at both fragments, then stopped, placed them back on the dish, and peeled off the gloves one by one. Nothing untoward that he could remember. He re-ran the scene again with the same conclusion. Was it sleight of hand? Had she substituted one or both fragments to remove for lab tests? He was certain that she hadn't, but that they were doing tests on the meteorite fragments could mean only one of two things. Either she had made a switch during the meeting, or they had found some or all the fragments at the bottom of Limehouse Basin. He checked the safe and stared at the two fragments. In his mind, there was no question that these were the original pieces, and she hadn't made the switch. When the call was answered, he picked up the desk phone and wasted no time giving orders.

EIGHTEEN

Herbie Lomax had to bend as he offered Ben a hand. Ben took it and felt the very firm grip of the enormous man in a black suit, who reminded him of one of the Addams family from the cult TV show. Ben looked down at the hand engulfing his own and was glad it was a friendly meeting.

"And this is Vince King, a representative from NASA," said Chris Williams.

King stepped forward with his hand out. "Let me correct you there. I am an advisor who used to work for NASA. I am assisting Mr. Lomax in his investigations in an advisory capacity. NASA has no direct interest in this at the moment, but I am sure they will, eventually."

"Pleased to meet you both," said Ben.

Claire Williams switched on a large monitor at the end of the table, and Claire and Roger appeared on screen in the lab at Moreton for a live meeting link.

After further introductions, Ben said, "I believe we have a common interest?"

Herbie Lomax said nothing and leaned back in his chair, which groaned under his immense bulk. Ben took a second look, wondering if he deliberately made himself look like Lurch. Or was it Herman Munster? Perhaps he had imagined the wrong character. He half expected to see bolts bulging out of the giant's neck.

Vince King leaned forward, his bald head gleaming in the bright LED lights of the conference room. Something familiar registered in Ben's memory. The man's scalp, mottled with bright pink, brown, and bright blotches, was quite bizarre. Then it came to him. When he was very young, he loved tinned meat, particularly a brand called Spam. The color of Vince King's head matched the slices of Spam that five-year-old Ben Sharman was passionate about. He suppressed a snigger. The names 'Spam Head' and 'Lurch' were now etched into his mind.

"We have a common interest," said Vince, "and I believe it is to our mutual benefit to collaborate. We are greatly impressed by your previous investigations across the pond here in England," said Vince.

"Actually," interrupted Ron, "the last case originated in Wales."

"My apologies. Is Wales not part of England? My geographical knowledge outside the US is, I'm ashamed to say, sometimes a little rusty."

Ben smiled. "The UK is a union of four countries: England, Scotland, Wales, and Northern Ireland. Although technically, Southern Ireland is not part of the UK, it is part of the British Isles. I can see why our American friends sometimes get confused. I would be in your shoes!"

Vince smiled and held up a hand, acknowledging his error. Herbie Lomax remained impassive.

"We have been in close contact with your government and have tracked the incident in London since the robbery at the Museum of Alien Life," said Vince, pulling some aerial photos out of a leather carryall. He laid them out on the table. Chris Williams also displayed them on the split screen for Claire and Roger's benefit.

"This is Pyramid Lake two years ago. As you can see, large areas are bright green, almost fluorescent green, from an unusual algae bloom that poisoned the water."

"But only to humans?" said Ben.

"You are well-informed. Yes, it wasn't good for human consumption or exposure, and we stopped anyone from using the lake. Just after that event, we believe fragments of meteorite entered the lake; the same found at the impact site two hundred and seventy miles south at Teakettle Junction, which I understand you are well aware of." He spread the images out, showing the initial impact site.

"You say you believe it to be from the same source at both sites?" said Ron.

"I'll clarify. They are from the same meteorite source, which we believe broke up during entry into Earth's atmosphere. We assume that during the breakup, some pieces 'bounced' during their descent through the atmosphere, which is the best way I can describe it, separating from the main source and traveling farther to Pyramid Lake."

Ben pointed to the two-hundred-and-seventy-mile expanse between the two sites. "Are you saying that these are the only two areas where particles impacted?"

"That is unknown. Logically, there must be more traces that have touched down either before Teakettle Junction, between the two sites or north of Pyramid Lake. The only reason we've identified the two sites is because of eyewitnesses at Teakettle Junction and subsequent evidence at the point of impact and through our own investigations at Pyramid Lake, which I will come onto."

Claire raised her hand on the link monitor.

"Have you any conclusions from the mysterious lights in the lake?"

"We haven't. Only speculation, which I never rely on. Hard facts always trump someone's unfounded theories, although it is significant that the lights in Pyramid Lake were only seen after the arrival of the meteor."

Claire nodded. "I'm not sure if Ben has informed you yet, but I've conducted an experiment here at our lab and I can confirm that particles from a fragment sample react in certain water conditions to produce dazzling UV wavelength light, which is mobile."

Herbie Lomax shook his head. "Why weren't we told, Dr. Sharman?" he said sharply.

"My apologies. I just received the information, so my apologies. Claire conducted the tests in the early hours of this morning. I was about to tell you."

Herbie nodded once. Ben looked sideways at him, hoping his answer had satisfied his obvious displeasure, but his face was again unreadable.

"Sorry, Ben," said Claire. He smiled and waved the blame away.

"Go on, Claire," said Ben. "Please tell everyone what you observed and found."

She described her reasoning behind the four separate water tests and the timeline of the results in great detail. Ben cupped his hand over his mouth so that she could not see him smiling.

"You have been very thorough, Miss Manson," said Vince. "You know I just said I don't like speculation?"

"Yes."

"Well, I'm going to make an exception here. I'd like to hear what you think is going on in Limehouse Basin."

Claire's eyes widened. She looked across at Ben.

"Go on, Claire," said Ben. "Tell them what you think. It's just speculation. I'm sure these two gentlemen aren't going to ridicule you if it doesn't turn out to be correct."

Ben felt for her as he saw her neck and cheeks redden on the screen. He made a note to apologize to her later for not taking the lead himself.

Claire coughed and cleared her throat. "I've a couple of theories. Either each of the glowing particles is a living alien being that has been brought out of some incredible stasis by the addition of water or, more worryingly, bacteria or a virus also re-animated by water."

The conference room fell silent for a minute.

"I know they are unbelievable theories, and as you've pointed out, they are mere speculation, as I have yet to get any proof," said Claire, who fell silent, hoping someone would comment and fill the deafening silence.

Vince stared at Herbie. "Shall I?" he said. Herbie nodded back.

"I can tell you that one of your speculations is correct, and I have to congratulate Ben and your team for coming to that conclusion in such a short time. Even though you have not yet any definitive proof. We reached the same conclusion, but it took us two years. We believe the particles emitting light are alien life forms. A complete entity, not bacteria or viruses."

"How did you come to that conclusion?" said Claire.

Vince looked across at Herbie, who nodded again and said, "Spill your guts, Vince."

"When the lights first appeared in Pyramid Lake, they were observed by members of the Paiute Tribe who govern the federally recognized reservation surrounding the lake and, of course, the lake itself. As the area was under scrutiny because of the algae problem, an individual reported it back to Homeland Security. I have taken a particular interest in the case for two reasons. The first reason is obvious, as it may have had a connection to the flight path of the meteor strike at Teakettle Junction. We had plenty of data to suggest that more fragments could have landed as far as four hundred miles away than the first impact site. The second is a personal interest. My ancestors on my maternal grandmother's side were all from the Paiute Tribe, and I spent a lot of my childhood in that area visiting relatives. I love the area. Not very scientific, I know, but relevant in my case."

Herbie's eyes rolled.

"Okay, Herb, I'll cut to the chase."

"The sightings stopped soon after they started, but there were more a month ago. We discovered a new sighting in the Truckee River that feeds the lake and have not released this information to the media to keep folks out of our way while we investigated. The light sources emit a powerful UV light. How this is done, we are yet to find out. We believe the lights are some sort of alien entity, but that is an assumption. Most faded out after a week, but some appear to have either adapted to the saline conditions or moved into the Truckee River with its own water chemical composition."

"I couldn't get any reaction from a saline solution," said Claire.

"What strength was the salinity?" said Vince.

"I replicated seawater."

"Pyramid Lake is one-sixth the salt content of the oceans," said Vince. "I think that allowed the alien entities to be revived from stasis. I would suggest that seawater is too saline for that to happen. I suspect that eventually, many entities were overcome even in the lower strength of lake salt, and entities near or in the Truckee inlet benefited from a far lower salt content."

Ben interrupted. "How does this fit in with our fish turning blue and changing physical shape?"

"We think these entities have a parasitic or symbiotic relationship with other living animals. We placed one of the light sources in a tank containing six Lahontan cutthroat trout, a species found in the river and lake. Parts of the fish changed shape, dissolving then reconstructing into a different anatomical format."

"Yes!" shouted Claire and blushed again. "Sorry. You just confirmed something."

Vince pulled another image. It was an image of a grotesque fish which had some remaining characteristics of the original cutthroat trout.

"We saw the same type of transformation in a pike, a British species," said Ben. "Was this cutthroat trout much larger after transformation?"

Vince nodded. "About forty pounds heavier than the record forty-one pounder pulled out of the lake way back in 1925. We repeated the experiment, and the process repeated, with another monster cutthroat trout developing, but this time we left it to see what would happen. It killed and ate two of the other trout, and the remaining two trout suffered attacks but were not killed and developed the blue gelatinous coating and died. It passed a yet-to-be-identified toxin, venom, or fungus, we're not sure yet, through its bite, which caused its victims to become blue and die."

"Have there been any other types of wildlife affected?" said Ben.

"This is where it gets interesting and why we think we could help each other. A few months after local tribesmen saw the first lights in Pyramid Lake, a teenager went missing. He was a loner who often disappeared for days at a time with his fishing rod and backpack. His widowed mother had given up on him many years ago, as he was constantly disappearing. At first, everyone would be out searching, but after a few years, it became the accepted thing. He would be back in a few days, and life went on as normal. When he went AWOL the last time, he never returned, and there has been no trace of him since."

"Could this be connected?" said Ben.

"Speculation," said Vince. "There are rumors of a man-bear, around the southern section of the lake close to the Truckee River inlet. At least a half-dozen men and women have claimed to have seen this man-bear. One hunter claimed that after shooting a small deer, the man-bear came out of the undergrowth, picked up the carcass, and was gone in a flash."

"You think the man-bear is the teenager affected by this alien entity?"

"I don't think anything, just hear me out. I have interviewed the six people, including the hunter with the hijacked deer carcass, and the description in each case is almost identical. You have to keep in mind that each sighting was different. Some at a distance, some closer. They describe a man's shape covered in long hair, upright but in three cases upright and also very swift on all fours. The one thing that they all agree on, and to me is strange, is the color of the hair—a distinct dark blue. Facially, only one person could give details. The nose resembled a small bear snout with human-type eyes, which were vivid red."

"The blue fur and red eyes seem consistent," said Ben.

"From a non-scientific perspective, this sounds bloody absurd," said Chris Williams. "A grizzly man-bear running around the forest would get the same ridicule as the Yeti or Bigfoot."

Herbie Lomax smiled. Ben couldn't believe the change in the big man's face. The friendly look transformed his dour face.

"I agree with you, Miss Williams, but the game changer in this case is that Vince has obtained video footage of the man-bear climbing a telegraph pole like the wind."

"Come off it. It's got to be a bear," said Chris Williams.

Vince turned his palms upright. "Ever met a bear that can talk?"

NINETEEN

The Virgin Atlantic flight to Reno with a connection at San Francisco International seemed like a dream come true. Claire had never been to America before, and now here she was, with the flight and all expenses paid. At thirty-three thousand feet above the Atlantic, it was her first long-haul flight, having never ventured beyond Europe. Unknown to her or Ben before they said they would go, the arrangements had already been made even before the meeting with Vince King and Herbie Lomax took place. She thought it arrogant of the Americans to assume they would fall in line, but Ben agreed straight away after a quick word with Chris Williams, who told him it would be in his best interest to cooperate at the wishes of the Home Secretary, no less. At first, Claire didn't think they could go, as obtaining a visa to enter the States took weeks, but when she raised the point, Herbie Lomax laughed. Chris Williams winked at her, and Ben told her to stop worrying.

She smiled as she stretched out next to Ben in Business Class, enjoying the high life. It only seemed like yesterday when she applied for the temporary position with Moreton Scientific Investigation.

After an amazing sequence of events, she'd been made permanent and now felt like an integral part of the team, at the cutting edge of the discovery of alien life in not one but two investigations that had the global media buzzing like nothing before. The media frenzy of both cases spirited away the dire state of the lab's economy. Her continued good fortune, now saw her at the sharp end of another possible alien encounter. She smiled, sipping a cocktail filled with orange juice, vodka, ice, and another spirit she'd never heard of, and nibbling on some posh snack food that she also didn't have a clue about. Life was good! She'd even bagged a handsome, kind, and funny fella in Dave Kelly, who had been a special forces sergeant in their first alien encounter. The perfect job, the perfect partner, and now off to the US of A. Okay, it was work, but she couldn't complain. She wondered what it would have been like if Ben had been single, without Amy, his dragon of a partner. Would he have made a move on her? She knew he liked her, and not just professionally or as a friend; it was blatantly obvious by the way he sometimes looked at her. Then again, if she was going out with him, it could taint their work relationship, or it might enhance it. She would never know. Or would she? Her mind drifted. She tried to picture herself standing at the altar in St. David's Church with Ben, but every time she imagined him smiling down at her, his face changed to Dave's. She laughed and took another sip of the Harvey Wallbanger. It was going down far too easily, and she knew it had to be the last.

"What's tickled you?" said Ben, sitting up.

"Oh, nothing," she said. "Just my imagination running riot as usual."

He looked at the plasma screen with the flight map displayed. "Another thirty minutes and we'll be landing. Seems like we've been flying over America for hours!"

"Two and a half, to be precise."

"It's vast," said Ben, leaning over her to look out of the window. She caught a waft of his aftershave.

"Why did you pick me to come with you? Why not Ron?"

He sat back in his seat. "I didn't."

"What do you mean you didn't?"

"The Yanks had already sorted it. Chris Williams asked me what the hierarchy was. I told her I was CEO, and the rest were staff. She pressed me for a designated deputy. I told her it was you."

"And?"

"She was fishing. She already knew what the Americans were after. They wanted me and the second-in-command to be flown over to Pyramid Lake to assist."

"I'm deputy CEO?" she said, grinning.

"In the eyes of our American friends."

"And in yours?"

"Miss Claire Manson, lab assistant," he said, grinning back.

She punched him playfully on the shoulder. "Thanks for nothing. Just out of curiosity, if you had the choice, would you have picked me over, Ron?"

"I considered Ron, but he's still not officially employed by us yet, and I'm sure they would have checked that out. No, if I had the choice, I would definitely have asked Kath O'Brian."

"Kath?!"

"Amy wouldn't have minded if it was Kath."

"Oh shit, I forgot. I'm in her bad books again, aren't I?"

"She thinks I'm going on my own. I didn't bother to tell her you were coming. I couldn't stick the grief."

"Sorry."

"Nothing to be sorry about. Not your fault. To be honest, she isn't the most pleasant person to be around at the moment. Nothing I do seems to be right." He clasped his hands together in his lap and looked down. "Sorry, I shouldn't be talking about this."

"Is she still suffering?"

"The alien abduction? I suppose so. No, it's more than that. I think it's partly work and a lot to do with me. We used to have a laugh, discuss work a lot, and go out and have fun. But lately, all she wants to do is read a book. I'm thinking she should join a silent order of nuns. She hardly speaks, and when she does, it always has an underlying abrasive tone."

"Bloody hell, Ben, perhaps she has depression?"

"I've tried to get her to go to the doctors to discuss it, but you know what she's like. Won't listen to reason."

He fell silent. Claire was amazed. Ben never talked out of turn about Amy. Things must have really gotten to him.

"Perhaps this break away from her will smooth things out?"

"We'll see. But if things don't get any better and she won't do anything about it, I can't see us lasting."

The connection went without a hitch at San Francisco International, and after a brief break, enough for coffee and donuts, they were soon aboard the Airbus A-320, which would take just over an hour to travel the hundred and ninety-two miles in not so luxurious seats.

"Claire, I'm sorry I offloaded my problems earlier. I shouldn't have. It's just that..." He fell silent for a moment. "You're the only person I can talk to about it."

Claire was dumbstruck and couldn't think of anything to say.

"Claire. I really like you."

Her eyes widened, wondering where this was going. She'd fantasized about her and Ben, but it was just that—fantasy. Or was it?

"I haven't said this before, but you really are a good friend, and I need one at the moment."

She felt a cold chill run up her spine.

"Thank goodness for that. For one minute, I thought you were about to—"

"Thought I was about to what?"

She went scarlet and turned to look out the window.

"Sorry, Claire. I can see I'm embarrassing you. I just wanted to say how much I appreciate you."

She nodded and said nothing. They sat in silence for a while. She wanted to make sure she still didn't look like a beetroot when she faced forward. Her heart was pounding. Was he trying to say something that he couldn't come right out with, or had he said what he meant? Just good friends? She looked at him and tried desperately to reel her feelings in. What was she thinking? Dave was a wonderful boyfriend; she couldn't fault him. So why was she peering over the fence looking for greener grass? She breathed in deeply, caught hold of his hand, and squeezed.

"Ben, if you want to talk about anything, anytime, I'm a great listener. Don't sit there all glum, broiling away in your own negative thoughts, right?"

He leaned across and kissed her cheek. She could feel the heat rushing to her face once more.

"Thanks, Claire. Sometimes I just need someone as a sounding board, and I know you'll tell me straight. Another reason that I'm glad you're coming. I want to have a chat about the future of the business."

Claire felt relieved that they were heading away from cringe street.

He went on. "First, I know I was ribbing you about being my second-in-command, but I'd like to make that position official to the rest of the team. Ron is a very good investigative scientist. In fact, he can be quite brilliant at ferreting out and finding leads in places that the rest of us seem unable to reach. But, he isn't someone who I'd want to step into my position if I were absent."

"Because he leaves his stinking snot rags everywhere?" said Claire.

"Well, there is that, but no. It's his abrupt nature. You need to have the inherent knack to wing it diplomatically, in a friendly and accommodating way. Unfortunately, Ron doesn't quite cut the mustard in that department."

"But I do?" she said smugly.

"You know you do," he said and laughed. "You can charm the bloody birds from the trees when you want something. You only have to flash those eyes at Dave, and he does your every bidding."

"Does it work on you?" she said, fluttering her eyelashes. It was his turn to blush. She felt bad but at the same time sensed electricity between them. He looked her in the eyes and held the gaze for just a fraction longer than she thought necessary. It was at that moment she knew she could have him if she wanted to.

He looked forward, still slightly flushed in the face. "So, would you accept the position of Managing Director of Moreton Scientific Investigation?"

Claire grinned, leaned across, pulled him by the ears, and kissed him on the lips.

He managed to extricate himself, by which time they were both laughing. "I'll take that as a yes, then?"

She nodded vigorously.

"Not a word to anyone till I announce it to everyone when we get back. I'm going to give Ron an official title as well, but you're above him in the pecking order."

"I wonder how he's doing in London?" said Claire.

"Last report from him was that they've almost completed raising the pH level in both the basin, the canal, and the boating lake in Victoria Park, and it seems to have had the desired effect. The lights in the basin have stopped, and they've netted a substantial number of blue fish. They're concentrating on the giant rat issue, baiting every sewer in the area. I'm hopeful the problem will soon be over."

"The thing I don't get," said Claire, "is why the Americans want us involved. They seem to know just as much as we do. We could've collaborated via video link."

"I've been thinking the same. There's something big that they haven't told us. Something different they can't deal with and need us to do it for them."

"How do you know that?" said Claire.

"Intuition, my gut feeling. You don't get the US and British Governments almost ordering you to go to the States based on a flimsy reason that, you rightly said, could have been sorted out on a conference call. I'm just wondering what the hell we've let ourselves in for. I wonder if they'll still pull out all the stops when we reach our hotel."

TWENTY

The chauffeur-driven sedan arrived at their 'hotel' at three in the afternoon. Claire stared in wonder at the eight-bedroom detached villa on Serenade Drive, twenty miles north of the center of Reno, just off Pyramid Lake Road, the main highway between the lake and the city.

"Wow, it's huge!" she said, stepping out of the air-conditioned car into the furnace outside.

"The door's open; I'll bring your luggage," said the driver.

Ben expected a hotel and wasn't sure what to make of the ultra-modern slate-gray house backing onto a parched scrubland hill. The house reeked of opulence as he opened the gigantic oak front door into a hallway the size of his lab back in the Cotswolds. Claire pushed past him, wanting to see every room all at once.

"Ben, you won't believe this! Come here!" she shouted.

He walked through a barn of a kitchen, which had a long concertina door opening onto a full-size swimming pool and patio, complete with its own thatched poolside bar. Claire, already sat on a stool at the bar, her mouth wide open, took in the vast piece of real estate.

A girl in a crisp white blouse and navy skirt appeared behind them.

"Welcome to Reno. I am Dorothy. I am house manager."

Ben turned and stared at the girl, who he assumed was around the same age as Claire, but much shorter, with tan skin and very dark eyes. "House manager? I don't understand."

"Mr. Lomax told me to welcome you and explain. House is yours for duration of trip. I run house for you, and other staff will cook and clean. We here to serve you day and night. Can I fix drink for you?"

Ben continued to stare at her.

"Yes, that would be lovely, Dorothy. I'm Claire, and this dumbstruck man is my boss, Ben."

"My apologies," said Ben. "It's just that I thought we would be staying in a hotel, not a stunning house like this, with staff looking after us."

"Mr. Lomax hire house because it near lake and short drive from city center. Not much around lake unless you like rocks and dust," said Dorothy, passing them ice-cold beers. "Best hotels in middle of Reno. Mr. Lomax said more pleasant with nice house, pool, and us to look after you. Much closer to where you work."

"And where would that be?" asked Ben, enjoying the cool, crisp beer.

"Not sure. Mr. Lomax said near lake. He left this for you with directions." She pulled a small envelope from her pocketbook and handed it to Ben. He slid his finger under the flap and peeled it back. Inside was a single sheet of paper and a set of house and car keys. He read it slowly, then passed it to Claire.

"You enjoy drinks. I prepare food; you must be hungry. I told you have no allergies and eat all foods." Ben looked at Claire and shrugged his shoulders.

"Mr. Lomax has been doing his homework, Dorothy. We'll eat whatever you give us."

Dorothy smiled sweetly and disappeared into the house.

"This is plain weird," said Ben. "They seem to know the ins and outs of everything and give us a luxury house, and I still don't know how this is justifiable."

"Enjoy it, Ben. It's not often we get treated like VIPs. Fancy a dip in the pool?"

"No, I'm going to chill for five minutes, then unpack."

Claire returned in a red bikini and placed a thick, white towel over the back of a sun lounger.

"No need to unpack; Dorothy's already done it."

She lowered herself slowly down the wide semi-circular pool steps into the water.

Ben tried not to stare at her curvaceous figure. He could feel his eyes winning and turned his back on her, taking in the vast arid view surrounding the back of the house. They were on a new estate on the very limits of northern Reno. He could tell there would be more development, with several advertising hoardings detailing building plots as they approached the house. He wondered why they built such a large city in what was basically desert land.

Only the hardiest plants grew sporadically beyond the perimeter fence throughout the gently sloping rock-strewn hills. The garden, spread out beyond the pool, was orderly and functional, with colored gravel, palm trees, and succulents, filling the plot right up to the boundary fence. All very pleasant, but once the novelty wore off, totally uninspiring. It made him realize how much he took Moreton-in-Marsh and the surrounding Cotswold countryside for granted. The colors were different, wall-to-wall lush greens back home and here, desiccated browns and grays with minimal patches of green scrub. The light seemed different, bright and harsh. Shadows were dark and sharp. He wasn't looking in the sun's direction and still had to squint from the painful light reflected off the light brown and sandy-colored soil.

"Come in, Ben, the water is lovely and warm. It's beautiful in here," she pleaded.

Five minutes later, he dove into the cold water, surfaced, and gasped for air. Claire was in hysterics.

"Lying cow," he said and began splashing her. She retreated to the far end of the pool and pulled two inflatable loungers across for them. They floated next to each other, chatting about the events that had brought them to Reno.

"Lomax said he's giving us a full day to get over jetlag. We won't be doing much till tomorrow night," said Ben. "What do you want to do during the day?"

"Visit Reno, I guess. It'd be stupid to come all this way and not take a look."

"We'll go to the lake first. I want to get used to driving on the other side of the road with whatever lurks in the garage, unless you want to drive?"

"I'll pass on that," said Claire, peering at him through one eye.

"The road to the lake should be a good practice run, and we can see what it's like up there without Lomax hovering. Then we can head into Reno."

"Sounds good to me," she said, and was promptly upturned off her lounger. Ben was out of the pool before she could retaliate.

Supper was a full-blown Sunday roast. Dorothy had even made Yorkshire puddings to perfection.

"Thought you miss home," she said. "Enjoy."

"How did you learn to cook Yorkshire puddings?" asked Claire.

"My mother. She live in London as housemaid for few years. She show me. You like?"

Ben nodded his approval with a mouthful of beef and Yorkshire pudding.

"It looks fantastic, Dorothy."

"Thank you so much," she said, gave a bow, and disappeared.

"Nice girl," said Ben.

"Cracking cook. This is one of the best roast dinners I've ever tasted. The gravy is stunning. I'll have to get her to teach me," said Claire.

"What for? Dave cooks in your house," said Ben.

"Perhaps he won't be the chef for much longer," she said and got stuck into the roast potatoes.

Ben was puzzled at her remark but enjoying his meal too much to delve into Claire's mysterious love life.

TWENTY-ONE

Gently rising hills and the same harsh, sun-bleached scenery as the scrubland at the back of the house lined either side of 445 Pyramid Way, obscuring any first sighting of the lake. They passed a remote store and then nothing for a mile or two before the road bent and dipped, revealing a patch of distant blue water.

"There's a pull-in just up ahead on the right, with a name I can't quite pronounce." She paused and mouthed the name twice before saying, "Kooyooe Panunadu Overlook. I think I just about got it right." Ben laughed at the overemphasized vowels.

"It says here it's a park and garden."

"Overlook? Sounds like we should be able to see the lake from here," said Ben.

"Here," she said, pointing to a huge gravel pull-in with a craggy hill behind.

Ben brought the Lincoln Navigator to a halt. "What a car," he exclaimed.

"Feels like a bus compared with my little runaround back home. Bloody huge."

"Very nice to drive, smooth as silk, and look at this," he said, pulling the sun visor down. "A fuel card, courtesy of Uncle Sam."

"Good job too," said Claire. "I bet it does plenty of gallons to the mile."

"This trip just keeps giving." Ben laughed. "Shall we climb that hill and take a look at the Pyramid?"

Claire peered out of the window, looking down at the ground.

"Are you getting out, or do I have to go up there on my own?" said Ben.

"Just checking first."

"Checking for what?" said Ben, climbing out.

"Snakes."

Ben shot her a wicked smile. "Don't panic, there are only a few."

"Like what?"

"Six types of rattlesnakes. Three venomous spiders including the black widow, a few scorpions, and just for good measure, there are bugs and caterpillars that would love to dine on you, maim or sting you. Any other local inside information you require, Miss Manson?"

Claire walked cautiously to the back of the SUV and pulled out a pair of leather boots. "I'd like to see those suckers bite through these," she said, leaning against the tailgate, and pulling them on.

Ben started laughing. "There's no grass, no moss, so I think you'd spot rattlers a mile off."

"I'm taking no chances, and in any case, I look the part in my cowgirl boots."

They climbed to the top of the overlook crag where the elevated hill provided an uninterrupted view of Pyramid Lake. Claire started taking photos.

"One of two remaining true lakes from the original Lake Lahontan, a Pleistocene lake which covered a larger area twelve thousand seven hundred years ago."

"Quite spectacular but barren," said Claire. "How big did it used to be?"

"The original Lake Lahontan fanned out through northern

Nevada, eastern California, and southern Oregon, covering an area of eight and a half thousand square miles."

"Shrunk quite a lot then?" said Claire. "How do you know all this crap?"

"I'm a scientist. I like to know these things."

"Okay, clever clogs, what's that over there sticking out of the water?"

She pointed to a distant outcrop, on the other side of the lake.

"If I'm not mistaken, that's Anaho Island, a national wildlife refuge. Protection designated by President Woodrow Wilson in 1913. There you go, another useless fact for you."

"The man-bear would be easy to spot around here," said Claire, looking through binoculars. "There's nothing here, no buildings that I can see, no trees, just desert."

"We're in Nevada," Ben quipped. "It is pretty dry here all year. I have my doubts about this man-bear. The weird fish we've seen is one thing, but half-man, half-bear just seems unbelievable. I don't know why, but I get this nagging feeling and my gut is still telling me that the Americans have a hidden agenda."

"Well, we won't know till we work with them," said Claire. "So, we may as well chill out. Let's hit the town."

They walked back down the slope of the overlook to the SUV, with Claire's eyes firmly fixed on the ground in front of her, on high alert for snakes.

It took half an hour to reach the center of Reno, the GPS guiding them through the grid of streets until they reached the Riverside area near St. Thomas Aquinas Cathedral. They spent the rest of the morning and early afternoon exploring. A pleasant stroll along the Truckee Riverwalk, then a welcome visit to the cool interior of the cathedral, and, drawn like a magnet, Claire got her way and Ben tried to keep up with her through the many shops in central Reno. After she tried on dozens of shoes, dresses, and blouses and bought nothing, they took a short cab ride to Shanty Dolan's Irish Bar.

"This is great. I adore American football," said Claire, admiring the gigantic screens all around the bar.

"You adore it?"

"Who wouldn't? Just look at all those hunks," she said, with a huge grin.

"It has nothing to do with skill, tactics, and game plans, then? Just the sight of men's butts as they're bent double?"

She nodded, still grinning.

"I don't get the attraction," said Ben. "They run around jostling, knocking each other over for ten seconds and then the commentators spend hours analyzing the last move. What is it with Americans and stats?"

"Who cares? They're gorgeous."

"Take a seat. I'll get us some drinks."

Ben got to the bar, was handed a menu, and told that table service would arrive any minute. It did, just before he sat.

A red-haired waitress, with a pretty face full of freckles, and mischievous green eyes, greeted them.

"Hi, I'm Erin, glad to see you at Shanty Dolan's. What can I get you folks to drink?"

"Two large glasses of Guinness," said Claire, before Ben could open his mouth. "Do you do the shamrock thing in the froth?"

"Every time," said Erin. "I see you have menus. I'll be back with your drinks and take your order. If there's anything I can do for you folks, just wave and I'll be over."

"Where did you hear about this place, Ben?" said Claire.

"Like I said, I'm a scientist and I like scientific research. Been open since St. Patrick's Day 2022 and has great reviews. Besides that, I have Irish blood coursing through my veins. My maternal great-grandfather, Jack Kirby, was from a tiny village called Buttevant in County Cork. The Kirbys have lived there for generations. I keep meaning to visit one day, to do some family tree research."

Erin returned, and they ordered food.

"Looks like the Kirby genetic code is alive and well," said Claire.

"What do you mean?"

"You practically made love to that Guinness. It went down the hatch in one."

"Smooth as a Kashmir codpiece," said Ben, waving at Erin for another round. "Good choice that, but I forgot I'm driving. You have mine. I'll order a Coke."

"You carry on, Ben, I'll drive back." She could see the internal battle written all over his face. He loved driving the car, but as his second Guinness arrived, he lost interest in being behind the wheel for the return leg.

"So, you're almost a leprechaun?"

"I wish. If I was, I could magically find out what the real story is over here."

"Remind me again. Why are you so convinced they've a hidden agenda?"

Ben finished the second Guinness and picked up Claire's. "Just look at the facts. Lomax and King represent two organizations with massive resources."

"Vince King said he used to work for NASA."

"Maybe King isn't in NASA anymore, but he'll still have contacts. We're a two-bit outfit in the middle of nowhere back home. What could we bring to the table that they haven't got or know already?"

"Experience with extraterrestrial beings? British intuition, with a bit of Irish thrown in for good measure? Don't undersell yourself, Ben. Big doesn't always mean better. What's the old saying? Good things come in small packages."

Erin returned, face full of smiles. "Can I get you folks anything else?"

Ben downed the third Guinness and handed her the glass.

"I'll just have a Coke," said Claire. "Oh, and Erin, what's the lake like?"

"Which one? There are a few."

"Pyramid Lake."

"It's big. Great fishing, my brother tells me. We used to go up there a lot until they stopped visitors. Algae poisoned the water a couple of years back. There's not much up there unless you go off-road into the mountains."

"Anything weird up there? Back home we have a prehistoric monster in a loch in Scotland."

"There's total hooey about a man who's supposed to look like a bear, if that's what you mean?"

"Man looks like a bear?" said Claire.

"Started just after the ban. I think it was a rumor spread by the cops and security to keep people away from the lake. They said that people have gone missing since the man-bear turned up. I don't know anyone gone missing at the lake."

"Interesting," said Ben.

"Yeah. Hogwash, if you ask me."

"Anyone you know who's seen it?" said Claire.

"My uncle Joe. He's a keen fisherman. He reckons he's seen it twice."

"Wow. Does your uncle live in Reno?"

"No, Nixon, just south of the lake. He likes the whiskey, so I wouldn't rely on him." She rolled her eyes. "Told me once he saw a UFO hovering above his house." A man waved at her from the bar. "Sorry. Have to go. Boss giving me the evil eye."

They finished up, paid the bill, and walked out into the harsh Nevada sunshine.

"Really enjoyed that," said Ben.

"You look a bit sparkly eyed. Must be the old black gold you were pouring down your throat," said Claire. "Won't be a minute," she said and disappeared back into the bar, returning quickly.

"What was that about?" said Ben, puzzled.

She finished typing a note on her phone. "Joe Westing, Erin's uncle. I have his details."

"What?"

"Some investigator you are. He's a witness to this bear thing. Might be worth a chat with him."

Claire drove back along the 445 and within a mile, Ben's snores filled the car. Jetlag and alcohol, she thought.

She pulled the big car into the drive, clicked the fob, and the garage door opened. Once inside, she killed the engine and looked across at Ben, who had stopped snoring. His content and peaceful expression tempted her to leave him sleeping in the car, but he woke when Dorothy opened the car door.

"Mr. Lomax coming for dinner. He here in an hour."

TWENTY-TWO

Herbie Lomax was a completely different animal from the surly giant they met in London. When he smiled, his entire face lit up.

"So, how do you like the house?" said Lomax.

"Pretty impressive," said Ben. "Makes my house look like a matchbox."

"It may be bigger, but I know where I would rather live," said Lomax. "Just rocks and prickly bushes out here."

"You've visited Moreton-in-Marsh?" said Ben, digging into a succulent ribeye steak.

"I spent some time in the Cotswolds when I was a teenager. I have relatives in Wotton-under-Edge. It was a very happy time in my life. A summer I'll never forget."

"It is beautiful," said Claire. "I have an aunt who lives in Wotton. She owns a cake shop on the main road on a hill, where all the shops are."

"You're kidding me?"

"No, I still see her from time to time."

"Well, I'll be darned. Are you talking about Betty's Pantry?"

Claire looked at him, open-mouthed.

"Small world, eh?" said Ben.

"Your aunt is Betty?" said Lomax, grinning and shaking his head in disbelief.

"Why, yes."

"Lovely lady and bakes the best cakes I ever had."

"This is unbelievable," said Claire. "Where were you staying?"

"Can't remember the name of the street. It was on the outskirts, in a row of houses, with fields out back. Stayed with my mother's second or third cousin. Dead now, but I think there's still family in the area."

"If you come over the pond again, I'll take you there," said Claire. "A trip down memory lane."

"Bet it's changed a lot since I was there. It was years ago."

"Maybe on the outskirts, but the town center has stayed unchanged; most buildings are listed."

"Listed?"

"Historical buildings are graded and protected so that they can't be demolished or altered. There are strict heritage rules."

"Of course, we have similar laws."

"When are we able to get our hands dirty over here?" said Ben, trying to steer the conversation away from the Cotswolds.

"Tomorrow afternoon. Vince King has a local building for you to work out of. It's a fully functional lab with a couple of technicians at your disposal. We'll give you the introductions, a guided tour of the facility, and a briefing on the mission."

"Mission?" said Ben.

"Sorry. Vince's NASA terminology. He may not work for them anymore, but they've brainwashed him with their speak. We'll fill you in on the details of why we've asked you to come all this way and what we'd like you to do for the mission." He laughed.

Lomax left just after the meal. Dorothy ushered them out to the patio where there were drinks waiting on the bar.

"Just one Harvey Wallbanger for me," said Claire, with eyes closed, savoring the drink. "Clear head required tomorrow."

"They must have found something significant to lay all this on for us, plus a fully equipped lab with staff," said Ben. "But there's something not quite ringing true."

"I don't care. This beats a pint in the Black Bear."

"For a while. I think the novelty will soon wear off. Don't you think it's a hell of a coincidence that Herbie Lomax knew your aunt?"

"Stranger things have happened. When I was in uni, one of my housemates turned out to be a second cousin. And don't forget, most Yanks are of European descent."

"I suppose. But something's still niggling me."

"Ben, can't you enjoy this experience? It's not often you get a free working trip. And besides, if you play your cards right, it could lead to more international jollies!"

Ben downed the beer and cracked open a second bottle.

"I'm going to have an early night and check in with Ron."

"And leave me all on my lonesome?" she said, pouting.

"Sorry, but I'm knackered. Just make sure the coyotes don't get you out here," he said, picking up his beer, and strolling inside.

Claire watched the sun dip behind the barren hills beyond the garden. It was still very warm, and the cocktail had given her a warm fuzzy feeling, but it didn't last. Did Ben's misgivings about the 'mission' have any substance, or was he just being paranoid?

Ron didn't appreciate being woken up so early. Ben listened for a minute to grunts, groans, and nose-blowing on the other end of the phone. "Sorry, Ron. Forgot about the eight-hour time difference. I'll call you later."

"I'm wide awake now, and would have been up in an hour, anyway."

"How's everything? Any developments?"

"I think it's all contained. All weird fish and other wildlife seem to be captured, and the lights in the basin disappeared. They netted the basin and the canal from top to bottom. You ought to have seen some of the shit they pulled out!"

"Any stiffs?"

"No, but there's enough scrap metal to build a bloody cruise liner. A right dumping ground."

"Chris Williams happy?"

"Yes, she sends her best and will be on the blower to you later today. Or is it still yesterday where you are? My brain can't function this early."

"It's today here, Ron. You're in the future." Ben laughed. "Listen, I'm glad the heat's off. I need you to do some ferreting for me."

"Fire away, boss."

"Can you check out Herbie Lomax, Homeland Security, and Vince King, ex-NASA? See what you can find out about them, and for now, don't discuss this with anyone else."

"Why the cloak and dagger, Ben?"

"Gut feeling. Can't put my finger on it. We're being treated like royalty over here. You wouldn't believe the place they have put us in. House, pool, car, staff, the works. But something isn't sitting right with me."

"Anything else you want me to do?"

"That'll do for now. Just keep me updated with progress in London."

Ben ended the call and began to roll down the blinds. Claire looked up from the bar below, raised her glass, and blew him a kiss.

"That damned girl will be the ruin of me," he said to himself, and slid between the sheets.

TWENTY-THREE

Barngate Holdings, an impressive lakeside building just north of Nixon, looked totally alien against the harsh, barren slopes.

"Impressive!" said Ben, as they approached the only building in sight. The two-story giant of polished metal and glass, set in verdant grounds of grasses, palms, and giant cacti, gleamed across the vast surface of Pyramid Lake.

Ben approached the gatehouse and lowered the window of the Lincoln. A security guard saluted.

"Welcome to Barngate Holdings, Dr. Sharman." He rested his arm on the roof of the car, dipped his head, and looked across at Claire. "And welcome to you too, Miss Manson."

"How do you know who we are?" she said.

He laughed. "Been expecting you. You're sitting in a company car."

Ben shook his head. Claire blushed.

"If you go to the far right of the building and drive around the side. You can't miss the offices and lab, it's the only single-story part on the whole site. There's a small parking lot out front and they're waiting for you there. Have a nice day." He saluted again and raised the barrier.

Ben maneuvered the Lincoln around a circular water feature with an ostentatious statue of a water nymph spraying jets of water from its mouth.

"Bloody weird and tasteless," muttered Claire. They drove along the frontage and turned toward the back of the building.

Halfway down, Herbie Lomax waved and pointed to a space in the parking lot.

"Nice day for it," said Ben, shaking hands with Herbie.

"Nearly always fine here. Only ever rains a couple of times a month, if that. Follow me."

He led them through a door that opened as they approached. Inside the cool, marble-floored entrance hall was Vince King.

"Hope you're enjoying the house," said Vince.

"Absolutely love it," said Claire, placing her hand on his forearm. "You've been a wonderful host."

Ben cringed, watching Claire's eyes flutter as she smiled sweetly at Vince King, who smiled back. Did he actually look doe-eyed?

"You are so welcome, Miss Manson."

"Please call me Claire," she insisted.

As they walked into a large office, Ben poked Claire in the back.

In the room was a very short bald man about fifty, who reminded Ben of Danny DeVito, and an older woman, with steel-gray curly hair and a steely gray stare. The man offered his hand to Ben.

"Kelvin Staples, pleased to meet you, Dr. Sharman. I'm so impressed with the work you've done over in England, and I'm so excited to work with you."

Ben grinned as the handshake continued. Kelvin Staples was bouncing on his heels, an excitable puppy with a star-struck smile.

"I look forward to it," said Ben, withdrawing his hand and offering it to the woman.

Her hand, cold and clammy, made the briefest contact.

"Elsa Smyth," she said curtly.

"Pleased to meet you, Elsa."

Vince King stepped forward. "Kelvin and Elsa are highly qualified technicians at your complete disposal day and night. Now, if you would be so good as to step into the next room, you'll see why we've flown you halfway across the world."

The other room was a screening room-come-lecture hall. The big difference was the seating: tiered, luxurious leather chairs, more like double sofas than single seats.

Ben and Claire sat, sinking into the soft leather. The auditorium lights dimmed.

"Where's the popcorn?" whispered Claire into Ben's ear.

"Shut it," he hissed.

An aerial view of the lake appeared on the screen, accompanied by a male commentator's voice that would have done Hollywood proud.

"Pyramid Lake. March twelve, 2020."

Several small lights streaked down from a starlit sky, making huge splashing entries into the lake's dark water.

"March seventeen, 2020. A week later."

Lights appeared under the surface of the water. A fisherman on the bank pointed them out to a companion. The screen switched to phone footage.

"Members of the Paiute Tribe fishing for cutthroat trout took this on a phone on that fishing trip on January seventeenth. Another six sightings of the strange phenomenon took place for a further four weeks."

The commentary continued, detailing what they had already been told, and then it got interesting.

The view of a hillside at the side of the lake.

"A fixed camera was set up to monitor the area around the lake after reports of a man-bear, allegedly seen by the Paiute Tribe."

The view switched to a map just north of where the Truckee River entered the lake, then switched back to the fixed camera view. Several stills appeared in quick succession. The head and arm of a hairy, stooping 'something' came into shot on the left. The next was a full human shape striding from left to right. In the next frame, the human shape had stopped and turned to face the camera. The next, it is walking directly at the camera. The final is the upper torso and lower half of the head. After this came a series of enhanced images. The presentation ended, and the auditorium lights came on.

"That was bloody underwhelming," whispered Ben.

Vince King appeared at the front of the room.

"As you can see, we have strong evidence for the existence of an alien life form in the water, which you already knew from our discussions back in London. The hairy man-bear is why we have brought you here."

"Herbie told us back at that meeting that this man-bear can talk?" said Ben.

"I'll come to that," said Vince, taking a seat next to them. "The images you just witnessed are the only images we have of this so-called man-bear. I can see by your faces that you're not convinced."

"We've discounted nothing," said Ben. "But I have to say they are inconclusive. Have you any other tangible evidence? Those photos are no better proof than the classic Bigfoot and Yeti images which never rang true."

"Agreed. They are inconclusive. As you hinted, they could be a complete fake. Man in a bear suit or AI-generated. I totally agree. It was a witness from the Paiute Tribe who claimed he chased this man-bear up a telegraph pole. He said it shouted obscenities at him in English. It remained there until he left. When the witness returned with a companion, they found it gone and no one has seen it since."

"You still haven't told us why you asked us here and what you expect us to do," said Ben.

"Quite simple, Dr. Sharman. I want you to either prove or disprove the existence of this man-bear."

"What?"

"You are the recognized authority in alien investigation. We have the resources to do it ourselves, but there are factions in the Paiute

Tribe and conspiracy theorists everywhere that would disregard any conclusion we come up with."

"Seriously?"

"Seriously, Dr. Sharman. Just think of Area Fifty-one. There are millions out there who believe in the garbage spun by conspiracy theorists. We just want this put to bed by a recognized authority from outside the US."

"So, what's your professional view?"

"That the man-bear is a total hoax. I think individuals in the Paiutes invented it just to scare people away. Obviously, if you can prove otherwise, that's fine."

"Or promote the area?" said Claire.

"No, the hard-liners want people to leave the area alone."

Claire laughed. "It doesn't matter what they want or don't want, it would attract more people wanting to catch sight of the man-bear."

"Whatever your view, we just need this to be investigated to a definitive conclusion."

Herbie Lomax interrupted. "From a national security perspective, it's not good to have another unproven non-human wandering the countryside. It makes a mockery of our department, makes us look stupid if we can't deal with a home-based threat of this nature. Either it exists or, as we suspect, it doesn't, and the United States of America would greatly appreciate your help."

Ben considered the request. "Do you mind if I have a moment with Claire?"

Herbie glanced at Vince and nodded. It was not the immediate "yes" the two men had expected. They left the auditorium.

"What's your take on this, Claire?"

"I think your hunch was right."

"Hidden agenda?"

"Yes. I was expecting some revelation, like they'd discovered a hidden alien ship or found a commune of aliens. This seems too simple. There's definitely something they're not telling us."

"Let's go with it," said Ben. "What have we got to lose?"

"A free holiday in absolute luxury if we refuse!"

"I was never going to refuse. I just wanted your thoughts."

"Thanks, Ben," she said and squeezed his hand.

"One thing, Claire, before we accept."

"What?"

"Keep your touchy-feely tactics away from Vince King. It's a bit sickly and totally unprofessional."

"Jealous?"

He turned and looked her in the eye. "You are a terrible woman. Do you know that?"

She nodded. "I do."

TWENTY-FOUR

The drive from the lab to the spot where the man-bear had been captured on camera lasted barely ten minutes but seemed longer as the monotonous view dragged on. Ben drifted from the endless barren hills to watching Kelvin Staples at the wheel of the giant pickup. The driver's seat, raised to the maximum, had an added sponge cushion so Kelvin could see over the steering wheel. It was worth letting him drive just to watch. Hard braking might be a problem. Would the little man be able to press down enough on the pedal which he could barely reach in an emergency? Being short wasn't the issue here, thought Ben. The length of his legs caused the greatest concern. A long body and short legs on an average-sized man wasn't a problem. A long body and short legs on a really short man gave Ben bad premonitions. Did he want to die in America? Running off the road, drowning in an icy lake at the hands of a man barely taller than an eight-year-old? Ben was grateful when they reached their destination, a parking lot next to the lake.

"How did you get roped into this investigation, Kelvin?" said Claire.

"I'm freelance. Had the call from Mr. King six months ago."

"Six months?" said Ben, giving Claire a quizzical look.

"Yes. He asked me to set up the lab and begin investigating the sightings of the mysterious man-bear."

"But that was well before we were involved."

"I believe the problems you've experienced in London triggered him to get you on board. Just a coincidence. Stars aligning and all that. Just glad you're over here."

"You said freelance. What's your background?"

"I majored in Biological Sciences at Cornell, worked full time as a lab tech for fifteen years at New York Medical College. I got bored and joined the NYPD." He laughed at the look on Claire's face. "Not as a cop. Far too old, and as you can see, I'm not exactly built for it. After another ten years, I got bored with testing evidence and bureaucratic bullshit and went on my own."

He guided them away from the lakeside parking lot across the adjoining boulder-strewn ground toward a lone wooden post.

"What about Elsa Smyth?" said Claire. "What's her background?"

"She was drafted in recently. More admin than scientist. She doesn't say much, so I can't say much about her. To be honest, I'm made up that you're working with us. Elsa's not much of a conversationalist, and I like to talk. She doesn't."

"What can you tell us about this sighting?" said Ben, removing his sunglasses to look at the plain wooden post.

"Vince told you everything I know."

"Did you investigate the claim?"

"No. It was Elsa and Vince who came here to check it out."

"Don't you think that was a little odd? You just said she's not a scientist."

"She's not, but I do what I'm told to do by the man who pays me."

"Apart from the images, did they discover any physical evidence?"

"Nothing. They found no footprints, no fibers, fur, nothing whatsoever."

Ben looked at the screenshots of the man-bear on his phone, judging where it had stood in relation to the still camera mounted on the wooden post.

"Claire, take some photos of me from that post at the same height as the still camera mounting."

He moved through the various poses and positions, copying the movements of the man-bear. Ben scanned the ground in the area but could see nothing apart from rock, soil, and the occasional desiccated leaves.

"It was moving in that direction," said Ben, pointing south. "Is there anything of interest that way? All I can see is more barren land."

"If it was following the Truckee River, it would take it through Marble Bluff Fish Passage, then on to Nixon."

"Can we take a look at Nixon and Marble Bluff?" said Ben. "There's nothing here. No trees, no cover. I just don't get why a half-man, half-bear would be wandering around this wasteland."

"Don't forget it's supposed to be half-human," said Claire. "Therefore, half-stupid."

They passed through Nixon and turned left onto a narrow blacktop, taking them down to Marble Bluff.

The road ended opposite a small concrete dam across the river.

"Is that it?" said Ben, staring at the twenty-foot-high sloping structure spanning the river.

"You mean the dam?" asked Kelvin.

"I'd call that a weir, not a dam."

"Don't forget, the Truckee isn't a vast river. It only needed a small construction to contain the dam water behind it."

"There's not much here either," said Ben. "Why the dam?"

"Built to control soil erosion."

"So, what's that other waterway over there?" said Ben, pointing at a narrow passage of water bypassing the dam.

"The dam is a barrier for migrating trout traveling upstream to spawn. There were big issues with different dams along the Truckee.

Some bottom-feeders couldn't traverse the dams at all and had their feeding grounds restricted, so they constructed this fish-way to allow the fish free access to move up and downstream.

"Where does the Truckee go from here?" said Claire.

Kelvin pointed upstream. "The river originates at Lake Tahoe and flows through Reno and Nixon, ending up here, feeding into Lake Pyramid; one hundred and twenty miles of river."

"Interesting," said Claire, "but I agree with Ben. If this man-bear exists, there's nothing here for it in terms of food, apart from fish, and this is not typical bear habitat. Unless, of course, the human aspect of it is keeping it local. But if that were the case, someone else would have seen it."

"Kelvin, can we meet the man who chased the man-bear up a telegraph pole?" said Ben.

"Sure, I'll set it up, but it will take time to track him down. If we go back to the lab, I'll go through the files and arrange contact. Shall we stop for a bite to eat first?"

"Sounds just the ticket," said Ben.

"I think you'll like this. A bit of good cooking with a dash of Native American culture."

He took them to a diner on Main Street, Fernley, twenty miles south of Nixon.

"What a combination," said Claire as she walked into Mary and Moe's Wigwam Diner and Indian Museum.

"Said you'd like it," said Kelvin with a toothy grin. "Let's order; we can look at the artifacts later. I don't know about you, but I'm famished," he said, rubbing his stomach hanging over his trouser belt.

They ordered Big Mo burgers on Kelvin's recommendation, which turned out to be a big hit, but far too much for Claire.

"How on earth did you two manage to put all that food away?" she said, as the two men cleared their plates.

"You're not going to finish that?" said Kelvin.

"I'd burst," said Claire, watching Kelvin pull her plate across the table.

"Waste not, want not, as my ma used to preach," he said, taking a bite out of the remains of Claire's burger. "Take a look at the museum stuff. I'll catch up," he said, cramming his mouth full of fries and slaw.

Claire quickly left the table, heading for the displays on offer.

"Quite an appetite," said Ben, laughing.

"I could have eaten more, but he kept looking at my plate like a starved dog as he was finishing his own. Put me right off."

"His table etiquette is different, but he's alright. I like Kelvin."

"Oh, I didn't say I don't like him. Just a bit of a beast at the table. Don't look back; he's picking his teeth with a fork!"

Ben couldn't help himself. Kelvin smiled and waved. Ben pulled a smile and waved back.

The Native American museum section of the diner was interesting, with displays of the Nevada Northern Paiute Tribe's artifacts. A line of glass cases was filled with arrowheads, stone tools, highly intricate beadwork, and woven baskets. The kachina dolls caught Claire's eye.

"Wow, I didn't think these were real. I thought they were made-up cartoon characters. Look at these, Ben. Wouldn't want to meet a life-size kachina doll in a dark alley."

Ben looked into the cabinet and nodded.

"Almost as scary as that alien back in Moreton."

As Claire stared into the glass, a man stepped into view on the other side. He was old and dark-skinned, with piercing black eyes, crowned with thick, black eyebrows. Of Native American heritage. He stared right at her and Ben.

"What is Sitting Bull looking at?" whispered Claire, without moving her lips.

"Us, by the look of it," he whispered back.

The man's intense stare faltered and morphed into a smile. He beckoned them to the other side of the cabinet.

"You must be the famous doctor?" he said quietly.

"Doctor, yes," said Ben. "Famous, probably not in these parts."

"And you must be Miss Claire Manson?" he said.

"I am," she replied, intrigued. "And you are?"

"Egan."

"Pleased to meet you, Egan," said Ben, offering a hand, which the old man shook with a firm grip. He released his hand and pointed a gnarled finger at the cabinet.

"They're carved from cottonwood, painted in bright colors to represent mythological figures. Not made by my tribe, but they are beautiful, don't you think?"

"A bit on the scary side," said Claire, "but yes, they are beautiful in a menacing sort of way. I take it you are of the Paiute Tribe?"

"You guessed correctly, Miss Manson. So, have you found your man-bear yet?"

Claire looked at Ben and raised her eyebrows.

"You're well-informed, Egan. I can't discuss anything with you as I am working for someone over here, and please forgive me, but I don't know who you are."

The old man nodded. "I think you'll find most folks around here are well-informed. It's in all the papers. Even on the local news channel this morning."

"Really?" said Ben. "Where can I get a copy of a local paper?"

"Ask the waitress; they keep them for the customers."

Ben swung around, looking for the waitress.

"Can I offer you some advice, Dr. Sharman?"

"Please do," said Ben, half expecting to be told to butt out and get the next plane home.

"You're looking in the wrong place," he said, tapping the side of his forehead. "Bears in a desert? Think about it."

"You enjoying the display?" boomed Kelvin's voice across the diner as he walked toward them.

"Yes, very interesting. We were just talking to this gentleman who—"

Ben turned to introduce Egan, but he was gone.

"Where'd he go?" said Ben.

"Search me," said Claire.

Ben walked across to the waitress, who had just finished taking an order. "Have you got a local newspaper I could look at?" he said with a smile. She grinned back. "Of course. Do you want to keep it? You're on page six. Nice photo."

Ben was stunned.

She returned with a copy of the *Reno Gazette*. He slipped her five bucks and rolled up the paper. She winked at him. "Any time, Dr. Sharman, and you're far better looking in the flesh." She winked again, turned, and headed for the kitchen door.

"I'll get the check," said Kelvin, who walked back to the table, peeling off a couple of bills.

"What was all that about?" said Claire.

"Nothing. Just following up on our mysterious man's advice. Seems like we're newsworthy around here."

TWENTY-FIVE

That evening, after another superb dinner from Dorothy, Ben retrieved a map and the newspaper and sat at the patio bar.

"You know that gut feeling?" said Ben, laying the paper on the countertop and opening it up to page six. "Well, it's getting stronger by the hour. I had a quick look at this upstairs. Read it. Tell me what you think."

Claire pulled the open paper in front of her with one hand and steadied the straw from her Harvey Wallbanger with the other. She studied the photo of Ben standing outside the lab in Moreton after the dramatic conclusion of the alien investigation the year before. It had appeared everywhere after confirmation proved alien life existed in the cave systems below the town and surrounding area of the Cotswolds. She was thrilled when *National Geographic* magazine used the same photo on the front page and she was elated to discover her photo inside, along with several references to her contribution to the investigation. This was different. It didn't sit right with her, and an uneasy sensation gripped her stomach.

She folded the paper and stared at the rocky skyline.

Ben paused, waiting for her reaction. "Well? Do you have an opinion?"

"Whoever wrote this was given far too much information for it not to be from Vince, Herbie, or someone close to them. It spells out when we got here, where we're staying, and, more worryingly, exactly why we are here. It's so crass. 'The world's elite alien hunters flown in to capture the Pyramid Lake man-bear.' It's like some cheesy line out of those old *Marvel* comics my dad used to have when he was a kid."

"Spot on, my dear girl. If that mysterious chap today hadn't disappeared, he might have given us a bit more."

"You think?"

"He told me to look in the paper and said, 'You're looking in the wrong place,' and then he said, 'Bears in the desert?' which I already thought was implausible."

"So?"

"Let's just say that our man-bear exists. Where would it live?"

"Bears stick to forest and only venture out of that habitat for food and maybe during the breeding season."

"Exactly. They don't like open desert."

"Hypothetically, if this thing has both bear and human traits, then the human element could keep it near civilization."

She took a large sip of her cocktail. "This is so good. You should have one."

"I'll stick to beer, thanks. The sun out here is giving me a headache without adding mixing drinks into the equation. I think that man, what's his name?"

"Egan. It's that beer. Makes you forgetful."

"Egan. Reading between the lines, he's telling us that our man-bear exists but isn't living on the shores of Pyramid Lake, which makes perfect sense."

"So?"

"So," he said, opening a local area map, "logically, the man-bear lives in forest, which is quite a hike to the west." He pointed at a mass of green on the map, covering a vast area.

"All well and good," said Claire, "but even if Egan was correct, where the hell would we start to look? We're being paid to carry out our investigation around Pyramid Lake, not trying to find a bear freak in a massive green haystack, part of which is also in a different state," she said, jabbing a finger at 'California' printed on the left side of the dotted state line.

"And Vince and his team don't give me a nice warm feeling either."

"I agree with that one hundred percent."

"So, what's your gut feeling?"

She drained the last of her cocktail. "Vince wants us here for another purpose."

Ben grinned. "How come you always seem to know what I'm thinking?"

"Because we align perfectly."

"And what do you think his purpose is?"

"I'm not sure yet."

"We need to find that old man again. If he's telling me to look somewhere else, then I'll bet a buck gets ten that he knows where."

"And if we can't find him or he doesn't know?"

"Then we enjoy the free trip, then high-tail it back home. But tomorrow, Vince is going to be disappointed."

"Why?"

"Because we're going to do our own thing without a chaperone."

"Meaning what?"

"Kelvin has been with us like a leech all day. He's been told to keep us under observation. I can tell. Tomorrow we lose him."

"How?"

"Nobody's told us we have to report for duty at the lab, have they?"

"No, but—"

"No buts. We won't turn up at the lab. I'll send Vince a text to say we're following up a lead and I'll switch my damned phone off."

"Sounds like a plan. Where do we start?"

"Fernley, at Mary and Moe's Wigwam Diner. My guess is that someone there will know where we can find Egan."

"Sure you're not going back just to see that waitress? I saw your little dalliance with her. I can lip-read, you know, even from the other side of the diner."

She raised an eyebrow and gave him the mischievous look that he found irresistible.

"I can't help it if women find me interesting. She was hitting on me. It wasn't the other way around."

"Found you interesting! She looked as if she'd have put you on her menu right there and then."

"Seriously, I bet she knows this Egan, and we'll find him tomorrow."

"Why don't we skip breakfast in the morning and have it at the diner? I'm sure Dorothy wouldn't mind a lie-in for a change. You can run a charm offensive on your waitress, and I can watch you squirm."

"Deal. It will also be interesting to see how our hosts react when their experts go AWOL."

TWENTY-SIX

Only a trucker and a thin, purple-faced man in a suit and Stetson occupied the diner. The same waitress appeared from the kitchen. As soon as she saw Ben, her face lit up.

"Well, hello, Dr. Sharman." Claire tried to stifle a snigger, failed, and pretended it was a sneeze.

"Please take a seat. Coffee?"

"Please," said Ben, shaking his head at Claire as the waitress twirled around.

"I think she might eat you all up on her own," said Claire.

"You're loving this, aren't you?" he hissed under his breath.

"As long as you just flirt."

"What's that supposed to mean?"

Claire burst out laughing.

"Here you are," said the waitress, placing cups and the coffeepot on the table, her eyes on Ben.

"What's your name?" he said.

Her smile widened. Claire stared at her teeth. The girl seemed to have far too many in a grin that went from ear to ear. More than the usual thirty-two? Claire decided she would try to count them. When the girl laughed, her mouth opened so wide they were all there to see.

"Zinnia Charleston at your service, Dr. Sharman." She giggled, touched his arm, and tilted her head.

"Wow, that's a great name. Zinnias are such beautiful flowers. I have them in my garden back in the UK," lied Ben.

"You got a piece of me back home then," she said, laughing. Claire started to count.

"Now, what can I get you folks?"

Ben looked at the breakfast menu and laughed. "I'll have the Running Bear."

"Eggs?"

"Poached, please."

"And you, ma'am?" she said, still not taking her eyes off Ben.

"French toast, please."

As they sat drinking coffee and waiting for the food to arrive, Claire pulled a face.

"What's up?" said Ben.

"Look who just showed up," said Claire, pointing at the car lot.

Kelvin waved to them from the front seat of the giant pickup.

"Shit," said Ben, "he's like a bad smell. Do me a favor, when he comes in and sits with us, which I have no doubt he will, I'll go to the toilet and hopefully chat to Zinnia out of earshot."

Sure enough, Kelvin bustled in and pulled himself alongside Claire.

"Liked this place that much?" he said with a cheery smile. He waved at Zinnia, pointing at Ben's cup, then at himself, and stuck three fingers in the air. She gave him the thumbs-up.

"What did you just order?"

"Walking Hungry."

Ben checked the menu. "Steak at this time of day?"

"Gotta start the day well, my friend. Nothing like ground sirloin to set you up."

"Do you normally have breakfast in here, Kelvin?" asked Claire, "or are you stalking us?"

Ben smiled and got up. "Bathroom calls." He winked at Claire.

Kelvin tried to respond but remained silent.

"So, are you stalking us," she said, "or just a coincidence?"

"No, I saw the car as I was passing and thought I would join you."

She thought he sounded embarrassed and no wonder. She watched his car approaching the diner and he signaled to turn into the diner's car park well before he could have seen their car. He already knew they were there. But how? Had he been tipped off by the man-eating waitress?

Claire placed her hand on his. "Just teasing. It's lovely to see you. What are you up to today?"

"There's been another sighting. Close to the lab, so we'll need to investigate."

"Another sighting of the man-bear?"

"Yes, and there are better photos, by all accounts, but I haven't seen them yet."

"Who's the witness?"

"Guy from Reno. He was driving from Sutcliffe on the four four six when the darn thing ran across the road."

"Sutcliffe?"

"Just up the road from the lab."

"You mean a town?"

"Not exactly. There's a lodge where you can buy fishing gear, get accommodation, beer, and food. Population about three hundred, right on the side of the lake."

Claire took a quick look across the diner. Ben, leaning against the bar, was in deep conversation with Zinnia, who had her hand on his upper arm. Claire felt a jolt of negative energy in her stomach. She used the hand-on-arm trick many times and knew how effective it could be to win a man over.

"So, what did this guy from Reno see?" she said, turning back to face Kelvin.

"The man-bear. He said it ran from the lakeside right in front of him and carried on running until he lost sight. He said he nearly ran it over."

"And he took photos?"

"No."

"You said there were better photos?"

"Sorry, I meant video. The guy's truck has a dashboard camera."

Ben sat back down opposite, and Zinnia followed with a tray of food.

"One Running Bear for Ben and French toast for you, miss," said Zinnia with a huge smile. "And yours won't be long, Kelvin. Jessie's cooking today." Kelvin nodded in approval.

"Best cook this side of the state line is Jessie Baker," said Kelvin.

Ben looked down at his plate. "Why does America have such huge portions? I'll never be able to eat all this."

"Just push it my way if you can't," said Kelvin. "I love pancakes."

"Kelvin was telling me that there's been another sighting, and it's captured on video."

Kelvin brought Ben up to speed on the latest sighting.

"Any physical evidence? Have you looked for tracks?"

"No, we received the information only late last night. The guy sat on this for two weeks before telling us."

"Two weeks?"

"We only found out when Elsa overheard it mentioned in a conversation at a bar in Reno."

"She doesn't look the type for bars," said Claire.

"She works there," said Kelvin, lifting a pancake from Ben's abandoned plate.

"Are we talking about the same Elsa?" said Ben.

Claire nudged Ben's foot. Kelvin was looking down at the table again and stopped talking.

"What did she hear in the bar?" said Ben.

"Two guys were laughing about what their buddy saw. Didn't

believe a word of it. She started talking to them, and when they said where he saw it, she got his name and followed it up."

Ben took a last mouthful of coffee and shook his head. "Hell, I've left my notes at the house," said Ben. "Catch up with you later, Kelvin."

"But—"

Before he could protest further, they left him with half of Ben's breakfast and half his own.

"I've already paid the bill and given Zinnia a hefty tip to keep him there as long as possible," said Ben. "Let's get well away before he follows us."

As they pulled out of the diner and headed toward Reno, Kelvin opened the app on his phone, kept a watchful eye on the screen, and leaned forward to enjoy the rest of his and Ben's breakfast.

TWENTY-SEVEN

A mile outside Nixon, Ben pulled off the highway onto a dusty track that snaked up an incline, seemingly going nowhere.

"Where are we going?" asked Claire, who was being thrown about between the door and Ben on the uneven, rock-strewn track.

"Not far, and we'll be there."

"Where's there?"

The track took a sharp turn between two giant boulders.

"Egan?" said Claire.

Ben nodded, drove through the gap, and pulled up outside an immaculate silver trailer.

"He's expecting us," said Ben. "Zinnia set it up."

"Hell's teeth. That trailer's like a mirror," said Claire, putting on her sunglasses. The morning sun blazed off the sixty-foot trailer's highly polished surface, making them both squint. "It must be bloody roasting inside that tin box."

They could hear a man laughing. Egan stepped from one side of the trailer carrying a loaded shotgun. Claire, wide-eyed, raised her hands.

"Can't be too sure these days," he said, removing the cartridges from the shotgun. "Come inside the oven," he said, opening the door to the trailer.

The interior, as immaculate as the outside, had air conditioning that kept the air fresh and cool.

"Wow," said Claire. "This is amazing. How can you keep the sun from baking you in here?"

"I've got enough solar panels out back to freeze you to death. Please, sit down. Can I fix you a cold drink or a cup of coffee?"

Ben looked around the trailer as his eyes adjusted from the harsh sunlight outside. He anticipated walls and surfaces filled with Native American memorabilia but was taken aback to find interior decor of a minimalist design—no sign of Egan's heritage. Very simple, modern, and functional.

Egan placed a tray of coffee in front of them. "Did you expect my home to be a museum, Dr. Sharman?"

Ben smiled. "You're very perceptive. I must admit, I anticipated some reference to your cultural heritage."

"While I'm a strong advocate for our heritage, I have to admit that sitting in a room surrounded by Native American history would be incredibly dull for me. I like simplicity, clean lines, and modern technology. So no, I don't immerse myself in my heritage." He smiled again and raised his cup of coffee. "I like you, Dr. Sharman. You say it as it is, and I can tell you have come here, unfortunately, under false pretenses."

"Sorry?"

"The people who brought here misled you."

Ben glanced at Claire.

"Why do you think that?" said Claire.

Egan started to pace the small area in the middle of the room. He turned and stared at Claire.

"Let's start with why you came here."

"We were asked to," said Ben.

"But why?" said Egan, turning to face Ben, who suddenly felt as if he was in a courtroom witness box, being grilled by a barrister.

"To help the American side of the investigation."

Egan laughed. "But you don't believe that now, do you?"

"I'm not sure what you're getting at," said Ben, feeling uncomfortable with the man's intuitive interrogation.

"You sat in my trailer says it all," said Egan, still smiling. "Vince King brought you over to work for him to prove or disprove the existence of this so-called man-bear. Correct, Dr. Sharman?"

Ben said nothing.

"And now you're asking yourselves why."

A wave of wonder washed over Claire's face as she listened to the man's remarkable insight. She couldn't help herself. Her mouth was half open, and her eyes were wide in awe. Ben started laughing.

"Sorry, Egan. I have an assistant, sorry, a partner, who can never hide her feelings. Her face paints a picture and a thousand words. You are quite correct. I came here thinking I was going to collaborate with someone in a joint crusade, but I do suspect that Vince King wants something else."

"In a nutshell, Dr. Sharman, Mr. King wants you for one thing only: publicity."

Ben considered the accusation. There was only one question. "Why?"

"Let me give you some background. Vince King is a very ambitious man. He owns the waterfront complex farther up the lake from Barngate Holdings. He wants to expand it, develop it, call it what you will, into a huge, thriving holiday and leisure resort on the lake. Personally, I think he could turn Pyramid Lake into another Las Vegas because, no doubt, the wrong type of leisure would soon follow."

Claire sat, brows furrowed, listening and thinking. "What you're saying is that with us here and the buzz that surrounds the sightings of the man-bear, it will help him achieve his goal?"

"Yes."

"But what if we prove there is no man-bear?"

Egan leaned back against the kitchen worktop and pointed at Claire. "How are you going to prove that it doesn't exist?"

She nodded, realizing that it wasn't possible. "We can't," said Claire. "We can only prove that it does exist. If we can't prove it, then it's just like the Loch Ness Monster back home in Scotland. Nobody has proved conclusively that it exists, but thousands of tourists go there every year to see if they can spot it in Loch Ness. I can see where you're taking this, Egan, and I think you may be right. He's using Ben's name to get this to go viral. People will flock here to see if they can sight the man-bear."

Egan raised his coffee cup to Claire. "Exactly. Now to turn this discussion on its head: what if I told you that the man-bear does exist?"

"Say that again," said Ben.

"The bear-man does exist, but not at Pyramid Lake."

"Are you serious?" said Ben, thinking Egan was joking.

"Absolutely. It exists, but you're looking in the wrong place."

"Sorry, you have me at a loss."

"The photos that were taken of a person who looked like a bear being chased up a telegraph pole were fakes, for sure, but a man resembling a bear is real and lives in the forests around the lake."

"Hang on," said Claire. "There are no forests around Pyramid Lake."

"I didn't mention Pyramid Lake. I'm talking about Lake Tahoe, which has plenty of forest and is bear country."

"Can you prove this?"

"Of course. I can take you to the man-bear's lair if you'd like to see him."

"Are we talking about a man who's evolved into a bear-like creature from the effects of the meteor particles in Pyramid Lake?"

"Indirectly, yes. Cutthroat trout from Pyramid Lake, contaminated by pollutants, migrated to Lake Tahoe, where local people caught and ate them. Several locals died, but one man, who was trying to catch trout migrating up the Truckee River, survived but got infected. He lives near the lake, and I'm prepared to take you to him for your research to prevent this from happening to others."

Ben and Claire sat in silence.

Egan stepped outside to smoke a pipe.

Ben looked over his shoulder and could see Egan standing away from the trailer, then turned to Claire. "Either this old fella is as nutty as a fruitcake, and we head back to Vince King's office, or we run with this and let him take us to meet Yogi Bear."

"The whole thing seems like bullshit," said Claire, still trying to compute the last few minutes' conversation. "But I think Egan's bullshit is giving off less stink than Vince King's, and we should follow it up and meet the talking bear."

TWENTY-EIGHT

Cathy La Rue blew Ron a kiss from the stage of the Old Ship Inn and smiled. He smiled back and raised his glass to her as she burst into a deep baritone version of Abba's "Gimme, Gimme, Gimme." It was a welcome distraction from the unusual case he was working on for Ben Sharman, which left him mentally drained. Ron eased back in his chair, enjoying the glow of the bar lights and the absurdity of what he was watching on stage. He took another sip of a large gin and tonic, contemplating his new job at Moreton Scientific Investigation, a momentous move that his partner Graham was not yet aware of. Ron wondered when he should broach the subject, which would be tricky, as it meant relocating more than a hundred miles from their rented house near Cambridge to the Cotswolds. Graham didn't work, which created less upheaval, but they had settled in their small cottage close to the unusual St. Mary's Church with its round spire, and it would be hard to leave the idyllic village of Swaffham Prior they both loved. Cathy La Rue finished the song to rapturous applause, a big favorite with the customers apart from one man standing in a corner of the bar.

"Do we have to be inside this place?" said a bald-headed man.

His companion laughed, revealing two gold teeth. "It's a gay pub. What did you expect? They even advertise on their website as LGBT with cabaret. Are you that homophobic, Zak?"

"No, no, each to his own, mate. It's just that I'm straight and quite a few men are eyeing me up and down like a piece of meat since we walked in. It's bloody unnerving. Can't we wait for our target outside?"

"The boss said we have to keep eyes on him at all times and we can't do that from outside, so man up and stop whinging. You never know, a big handsome brute like you should have no problem hooking up with any of the clientele in here." He laughed again as Zak pulled a face.

"Shut up, Wayne."

"I reckon that tall bloke with the dyed black hair would be right up your street," Wayne said, his grin so wide that it revealed even more gold teeth.

"Ha, Bloody ha."

Wayne began laughing hysterically, then stopped abruptly, put his pint on the counter, and pointed toward the stage. "Look out. Our target's leaving."

Ron knocked back the rest of his G and T and made for the front door. The two men followed, expecting to see Ron walking away from the pub, which was on the corner of a crossroads. Wayne stepped out first, almost colliding with the back of Ron, who had stopped dead to light up a Marlboro. Wayne apologized and then stood next to him, pulling his own cigarettes out and offering one to Zak. The three men stood smoking in companionable silence. Ron took two long drags on the cigarette before turning to take a good look at the two men. The bald-headed man looked familiar, but he couldn't figure out where he'd seen the face before. He dropped the dying embers of the cigarette onto the floor and lit another.

"You're enjoying the show?" said Wayne. "Cathy's a real tease, isn't she?"

Ron smiled. "She certainly is."

"You from around here, my friend? Your accent doesn't sound local," said Wayne, with several teeth glinting in the dim glow from the illuminated pub sign, swinging lazily in the breeze above.

"No, just working here a few days and thought I'd take a look at the show. Seems to have a friendly atmosphere." Ron noticed the bald-headed man looking away but caught the look on his face. Disapproval.

Something in Ron's subconscious began to surface. Unease, a sense of danger. He shrugged it off as just being stood in a dark street outside an unfamiliar pub with a couple of strangers, but as he continued to smoke, the unease grew. A shiver went up his back. He turned and went back inside. Some primeval message from deep in his mind was saying "safety in numbers," so instead of going back to the hotel, he ordered another drink and was going to sit back in his seat, but it was now occupied. He stood by the bar, listening to the compere introducing another drag act.

"And now, what you've all been waiting for. She's here tonight for one night only. Our one and only Mary Lyn Monroe." A dazzling apparition appeared from behind the stage curtain, complete with a peroxide blonde wig, beauty spot, and a five o'clock shadow. Unfortunately, Mary Lyn, wearing the same iconic, billowing white dress that the real Monroe wore in the film *The Seven Year Itch*, didn't quite pull it off, with hairy legs stark against the white satin, size eighteen garment. The voice wasn't the same cute style either; a lifetime of smoking forty a day made her sing like a bull elephant seal on some far-off South Atlantic shoreline. Everyone in the audience appreciated the diversion from reality and enjoyed the show, shouting and hooting approval at every wink, flounce of the ample hips, and gravelly out-of-tune line emitting from Mary Lyn's blood-red lips. Ron soon forgot about the man outside and got back into the party atmosphere. After Mary Lyn's encore, he scanned the bar, glad to find the two men were no longer there.

With another G and T down the hatch, Ron looked at his watch and left the pub, heading back to the hotel, deciding to take a slight detour for another look at Limehouse Basin. The same police officer was on duty that escorted Horace Clancy back to his canal boat.

"Evening, Mr. Logan."

"Sergeant. Any sign of the lights in the basin since clearing out the junk?"

"Not a flicker, sir, and I hope it stays that way. Less paperwork for me."

Ron smiled, imagining having to write reports every time he found something significant, and was glad a secretary was at his disposal who could do all the typing.

"Thank you. I'll leave you in peace and hope you have a quiet night."

Ron walked on, past the Grapes' public house, looking out at the River Thames skyline through gaps in the wharf buildings. He shook his head, wondering how many people were crammed into such a small area and glad he was about to move to real countryside with space and clean air where you could walk for miles without seeing a soul. He was so engrossed in his future idyllic life that Ron didn't notice the man in the shadows as he passed the arch into Duke Shore Wharf but he heard footsteps twenty yards behind as the man began to follow. The same shiver he experienced earlier outside the Old Ship Inn was back, and he crossed the road, walking faster, trying to tread lightly so he could hear the person behind. The footsteps behind quickened to keep up, and Ron looked over his shoulder as the bald-headed man darted across the road to be on the same side. Ron kept up the pace, not wanting the man to shorten the gap, and inwardly prayed a taxi would appear, but Narrow Street was empty, with only the noise of televisions and music pulsing out of flat windows. A footpath appeared, running at right angles to the road. Ron took it and started jogging. The path, almost pitch dark, and lined with trees, was a mistake. He should have kept to the road where there were people, albeit in their flats, who might hear if he needed to call out for help. The footsteps behind were also jogging as the man closed in. Should he hide in the trees? What if the man caught up with him in this lonely, dark park? No one would hear. Ron cursed his chest, which wheezed as he tried to pick up the pace, and then his heart sank. Beneath a dim street lamp just twenty yards ahead stood a grinning second man, who Ron recognized from the light reflecting off gold teeth.

TWENTY-NINE

Five thousand miles away, driving south on Highway 50, close to the shore of Lake Tahoe, Ben followed the red pickup. Thick pine forests blocked most of the lake view to the right and were even denser on the left. Perfect bear country. It had been an interesting drive through Reno, then south, skirting the old Wild West town of Carson City, the state capital, with arid mountainous views almost all the way.

"He's slowing down," said Claire. "I think we've arrived."

The red pickup signaled right and pulled off the highway into what Ben assumed was a holiday park until he read the wooden sign at the side of the stone-walled entrance: "Zephyr Cove Private Community."

"Must be using this to park up before we head into the forest," said Claire, taking in some of the luxurious New England-style houses, each one custom-built with a hefty price tag on the real estate market.

"Nice place," said Ben, and laughed. "One day I might be able to afford to rent one for a week!"

Egan's car took a left-hand fork on the gravel road and pulled up in front of a wood-fronted house with a multi-pitched roof. Ben parked between the pickup and a red Ferrari, stopped the engine, and whistled. "Wowser. Either he has some very rich friends, or we're taking a hell of a risk using this drive to park in."

"Don't be ridiculous, Ben. He must know the owner. He wouldn't just park here. I wonder if he has a rifle?"

"Rifle?" said Ben.

"Bears," said Claire, staring up the mountain at the dense forest. "I bet those trees are full of them. Watching us."

Ben smiled. "I'm sure Egan hasn't reached his threescore years and ten by sheer luck, wandering around bear-infested forests without a gun or two."

They stepped out of the car's air-conditioned interior into a wall of heat, which seemed to have got much hotter since they left Egan's trailer.

"Jeez, this is making my eyeballs sweat," said Claire. "I don't fancy trekking up mountains in this."

"You won't have to," said Egan, chuckling. "Please. Follow me into the house."

"Who lives here, Egan?" said Ben. "It's one hell of a nice place."

"Thank you. I can't agree more. That's why I bought it."

Claire and Ben stopped walking. "You live here?" said Claire. "But I thought—"

Egan laughed again. "The trailer?"

"Well, yes, I thought you lived there."

"Only when I feel the need to get back to nature. I couldn't live there throughout the year. Would you?"

The smile disappeared from Egan's face, and he stood staring at Claire, waiting for an answer.

"Well, I suppose... I think it's a very nice trailer... but..."

He slapped both knees and roared with laughter. "The trailer's in the middle of nowhere in a rocky desert. Of course, you wouldn't want to spend time there. Let me explain. I'm one guardian of the tribal assets, and the trailer is my office, or should I say the tribe's mobile office, which we can move around the reservation. I don't stay there apart from meeting up with other elders to discuss our affairs and to meet eminent scientists from over the pond on a crusade to discover the mysterious man-bear. No, this is my home, and please let's step inside and get out of the heat before we all melt."

Ben stretched his arm across to Claire and with one finger under her chin, pushed her mouth shut.

The cool entrance hall was enormous, lined with duck-egg blue wood paneling and a multitude of family photos and paintings charting the family history back into the nineteenth century. The display of family portraits wound up the staircase, disappearing on the landing as the oak banisters swept in a large arc to the landing above.

"I love this, Egan," said Claire. "Do you mind if I take a closer look at the pictures?"

He extended his arm, offering her access to the staircase. "Meet my family and ancestors. They all lived in this house for well over a hundred years, and I thought it fitting that they should still be here watching over us. I hope my children will keep up the tradition and make sure I'll be watching whoever steps through our front door."

"This house doesn't look that old," said Ben. "I thought this private settlement was more recent."

"The land has been in my family for generations, and it was just this house until about twenty years ago. I needed the money, so I developed it into what you see now."

"Lovely properties and what a view of the lake," said Claire as they walked into a huge kitchen diner with floor-to-ceiling glazing looking down over Lake Tahoe. "It's amazing!"

"Step out back onto the veranda. You'll get the full view from out there, and it's cooler in the shade. Coffee, everyone?"

Ben nodded in approval.

A wide, elevated veranda, shaded with a huge canvas canopy extending out twenty feet from the exterior wall, provided an exceptional view of the lake, and Claire could not resist taking photos.

"Egan, is that the top of the lake in the distance?" she said, pointing straight out to the hazy far bank.

"You're pointing due east. The top of the lake is north of here."

"What's that shoreline I can see?"

"California, about twelve miles away. You're lucky it's a clear day and you can see it."

"Twelve miles across. Wow, it's huge."

"One of the largest freshwater lakes in the US. About twenty-two miles long and twelve miles wide in parts, and it's deep."

"How deep?"

"Over sixteen hundred feet at the deepest point and has some of the clearest water you'll see for an inland lake, as it's not warm enough for algae blooms to form."

"Very impressive," said Ben. "Can we get back to why we've come here? You were going to show us the man-bear, and we've already spent too much time away from our hosts, who will be wondering why the hell they invested a heap of money to fly us over and wine and dine us in a luxury villa."

"Of course. I'll take you to him now."

Claire frowned. "Is it far to walk? Only it's absolutely boiling today."

Egan laughed. "No, we can be there in a couple of minutes. Follow me; we'll have coffee when we get back."

Egan took them out onto the road, and Claire felt herself begin to sweat.

"Nice car," said Ben, pointing at the Ferrari. "Had it long?"

"Not mine. It's my son's. I'm not a car person, and I only have the pickup. I've had it years, as you can tell. A sporty car like that's no good to me, especially on a lot of the tracks I use to get to tribal members' homes."

"Your son lives with you?"

"No, but you'll meet him shortly. He only lives a hundred yards away."

The road sloped down to the shoreline of the lake, where the view widened to reveal the expanse of the immense body of water in both directions as the trees thinned out.

"Wow, this is stunning," said Claire, raising her phone for more photos.

"It is, isn't it?" said Egan, nodding in agreement. "I can see why my forebears settled here. Beautiful scenery with good hunting in the forests and plentiful fish in the lake. Clean, endless water supply, fertile soil. They made the perfect choice."

"One thing I don't understand," said Ben. "You work with the Paiute tribal elders, but I didn't think Lake Tahoe was part of their reservation."

"You are quite correct, Dr. Sharman. In the past, the area around the lake stretching up to Reno and Carson City were the tribal lands of the Washoe. After my parents died in a road accident just after I was born, my uncle, who married a descendant of the Washoe tribe, adopted me. But I haven't forgotten my own heritage."

Egan stopped outside another large, detached house, as grand as his own, with the same multi-pitched roof and wooden-paneled New England-style walls. He pushed open the large oak door and ushered them in.

Egan shouted, "Jacy, you have visitors," and walked into the kitchen diner, where a man sat reading a book at the table. He closed it, smiled, and walked toward Ben with his hand out.

Ben shook the offered hand, and Jacy shook hands with Claire.

"Pleased to meet you both. I trust your visit to Nevada has been enjoyable so far?"

There was no mistaking that Jacy was Egan's son. He was how Egan must have looked twenty-five years before, less rugged, without the gray hair.

"Can I fix you a coffee, cold drink, or something stronger?" he said. "And please, sit down."

"Do we have time, Egan?" said Ben. "Only I need to meet the person we came to see and get back before Vince King sends out a search party."

"I'll have a coffee, Jacy, in my usual cup and go easy on the sugar," said Egan, beginning to laugh. "Depends on how long you wish to speak to him."

"What's so funny?" said Ben.

"You've already started talking to the man-bear," he replied. "My son Jacy is the man you wished to speak to."

THIRTY

Ben stared at Egan, waiting for him to reveal where the real man-bear was, but Egan continued to smile and nod.

"What's going on?" said Ben.

"Dad. Stop messing with them. Sorry, Dr. Sharman. My father has a weird sense of humor; let me explain."

"I can't wait to hear this," said Claire, gawking at Jacy, who looked like a normal human being without a hint of bear.

"I'll start from the beginning."

"Good a place as any," said Ben, raising his eyebrows at Claire.

"I think you'll change your viewpoint after you listen to what he has to say. Now, while he tells you, I'll make the coffee," said Egan, opening several cupboards before finding the mugs.

They turned to Jacy.

"I know all about the man-bear hype, and I can see what you're thinking when you look at me," he said, looking directly at Claire. "One of the best spots to catch great trout is where the lake discharges into the Truckee River, and since I do a lot of fishing on the lake, I've lots of success there. I go very early in the morning to avoid kayakers and small sailboats. One trip, I caught a monster. It was just after sunrise, and I hooked my first fish of the day, a decent-sized cutthroat trout. As I reeled it in, something much bigger decided the trout I hooked was going to be its breakfast. It hit the smaller trout like a steam train and gave me one hell of a fight, nearly pulling me in off the bank when it struck. I don't use a line with a big breaking strain, as the biggest I catch on the lake is normally less than ten pounds. But that morning, I'd forgotten to pack my freshwater reel and had to use a spare. I do a bit of fishing at Catalina Island, so I often have bits and pieces of sea fishing kit with me, which is built for much bigger fish."

"Where's Catalina Island?" said Ben. "We're miles from any coast here."

"Sorry," said Jacy. "I'm not making this clear. Santa Catalina Island is off the coast of Los Angeles. Beautiful place, well away from the busy coastal areas. I stay at a hotel on the island, do a spot of spearfishing, and charter a boat when I go there for some deep sea fishing, which is some of the best in the US. I love it because you never know what you'll catch, but I normally go for the great barracuda, which is one hell of a scrapper."

Egan placed mugs and a coffee pot on the table. "Went there once on a family holiday when he was a kid and can't keep him away from there," said Egan, pouring coffee.

"When the bigger fish grabbed the first trout, it took almost an hour to reel it in. I've never experienced a fight like it, and I've caught some big ones out on the ocean in my time, but this one was something else. When I saw it, I couldn't believe what I was looking at." He passed Ben a photo.

Ben laid it on the table for Claire to see. He took a quick look at her face and smiled at her horrified reaction. Straddled across Jacy's outstretched arms, the monster fish was indeed a monster, which Ben estimated at over five feet long. Resembling a giant trout, the fish had a distinct blue pallor to the scales, blood-red eyes, tail, and fins. The head provided the monstrous appearance with a set of serrated, vicious teeth on upper and lower jaws and an extended bottom jawline. The beast's head was the size of the head of a fully-grown Rottweiler.

"After I got over the fish's weird appearance, assuming it was just a giant deformed trout, I took it home, gutted, filleted, and stored most of it in the freezer. I love sushi and got through a few fillets of raw fish before I got the first signs of the reaction."

"Reaction?" said Ben, suspecting where this was going, but not quite convinced.

"I've never been a hairy specimen," said Jacy, "but I began sprouting thick black hair everywhere apart from the palms of my hands and soles of my feet. I tried to shave it off, but it grew back within a couple of days, so I tried hair removal cream. Hell, I was almost bathing in the damned stuff daily, and the hair still kept growing."

"How did you stop it?" said Claire, with the same wide-eyed look she had at seeing the photo.

"I'll come to that in a minute. I didn't realize the connection between the hair thing and that fish and kept on eating it. Then things got far worse, and my body shape changed. I bulked up with no diet, steroids, or exercise. It was just plain weird." He placed another photo on the table. The face, more chiseled, crowned an amazing body befitting a Mr. Universe bodybuilding competitor. Claire looked at the photo, then Jacy, then back to the photo.

"Is this really you?" she said.

"Yes, it's no fake, I can assure you of that. Listen, I wouldn't believe this either if I were you, but I'm just telling you what happened. Up to you how you take it."

"And how long did this change take?" said Claire.

"This is even more unbelievable," said Jacy, shaking his head and smiling. "I caught the fish on a Sunday morning. The hair started sprouting like wildfire about two days later, and I looked like that by the following weekend." He tapped the photo. "So, in less than a week, I went from this"—he pointed to his present physique, then at the photo of himself standing in shorts—"to that, in just under a week, and put on over a hundred pounds of pure muscle."

Ben picked up both photos and stared at them for a minute. Claire sipped her coffee with eyes also locked on the two strange images.

"You were going to tell us how you stopped the reaction," said Ben. "My apologies for sounding skeptical, but this is, well, I'm sure you can appreciate, unbelievable. If this is all true, and your story is very convincing, how is it you look normal now?"

"I'm not."

"Sorry, I don't follow."

"It comes and goes. After that first week, I just wanted to get away from everyone I know. I didn't want people talking, so I took a vacation to Catalina Island. It was difficult with the hair thing going on, but the people I know on the island just thought I was into some extreme bodybuilding regime, pumping steroids. After a few days, the effects reversed, and I was almost back to normal."

Ben looked puzzled. "Almost?"

Jacy unbuttoned his shirt, exposing an extremely hairy chest with patches of blue skin visible underneath.

"You see, from the neck up, I look normal. Below the neckline, there are several areas of my body with patches of blue skin covered in hair. If you look at the hair, it isn't a true black but has a blue tinge. The same color as that damned monster fish's scales."

"Do you mind if I take a closer look? I can't believe it!" exclaimed Ben, his eyes wide with astonishment.

Jacy took his shirt off, revealing several large patches of hair on his chest, back, and one upper arm. Ben moved closer, observing the thick, coarse hair, which had a blue sheen, but from a distance looked black. The skin below looked normal, apart from the blue sheen.

"Would you mind if I took samples? And don't worry, I don't want to cut chunks of flesh off you."

Jacy laughed. "Be my guest. If you can find out what's causing this and help me put it right, I don't care if you start hacking bits off me."

"Did you go for medical advice when it happened?" said Ben.

"No, perhaps I should have done. It was such a shock, and I didn't want people to see me covered in hair like that. The only time I went out that first week was after dark, and for those first few days, I took the keys to Dad's trailer over at Pyramid Lake and stayed there."

"Did anyone see you?"

"One of Dad's friends when I woke up the on last morning I stayed in the trailer. I just got up and went outside and hadn't gotten dressed. As naked as the day I was born and covered in hair when he pulled up in a Jeep. Scared the crap out of me and almost gave the poor man a heart attack. Dad told me the old guy doesn't see too well, forgot to put his glasses on that morning. Pity, if he had, he would have recognized my face as he's known me since I was a kid, but he didn't. He looked at me through the Jeep's side window for a few seconds. I heard him scream before he swung around and was gone."

"And the legend of the man-bear was born!" said Ben.

"Yep. He told a few friends, reported back to Dad, who obviously knew who the man had seen covered in hair, but didn't own up. The friends told more friends, and the stories, like Chinese whispers, got more ridiculous. There's one tale about the man-bear being chased and running straight up a telegraph pole. It's amazing how people embellish stories until they become ridiculous."

"I've been shown photos of this man-bear," said Ben. "Allegedly taken where the Truckee enters Pyramid Lake."

"Wasn't me, that's for sure," said Jacy. "I heard about those photos. Either there's another poor soul who has been eating weird blue fish, or they're fakes, and my money's on the latter."

"I'm going to take a sample of body hair, a swab of your skin, and a mouth swab, if that's okay? said Claire."

"No problem."

"Could I also take a blood sample?"

Jacy winced. "Yes, he will," said Egan. "He hates needles. Just be gentle with him."

Claire was already pulling a pair of nitrile gloves on. "Don't worry, Jacy. I'm pretty good with a syringe and it's pain free."

Jacy pulled his shirt back on after they completed collecting samples.

"One last thing before we go," said Ben. "Do you have any of the fish left in the freezer?"

"As a matter of fact, I do. Once the physical changes started, I realized it could be something to do with the blue monster, so I kept it. Please take it; I'll pack it in ice and put it in a cooler bag. I filleted it, so there's no head or bones.

"That's great. And can I take a copy of your photos with my phone?"

"You're welcome to them. I have copies you can have."

An hour later, they pulled up to the gatehouse barrier at Barngate Holdings.

"Glad you're here," said the security guard. "Mr. King was getting worried about you. I'll let him know you're here."

Vince King did not look pleased when he ushered them into his office. "Can I ask why you went to Zephyr Cove this morning and not here?"

Ben was surprised. "How did you know we went to Zephyr Cove, Mr. King? Were we being followed like we were to the diner this morning?"

"Nobody's been following you, Dr. Sharman. When you didn't show, I thought you might have gotten lost. When you didn't check in after four hours, I checked the car tracker. We fit all our vehicles with car trackers. It showed me where you went, and I could see you were heading back, so I didn't send the cavalry out to look for you."

"My apologies, Mr. King. I should have called."

"Why Zephyr Cove?"

Ben raised his hands. "We heard that this man-bear had been seen in that area and received advice to look there rather than the land around Pyramid Lake. I took the initiative and scoped out the area to get a feel for it. You've asked us to look into this, and that's what we did."

Herbie Lomax stepped into the room. "Vince, I'd have done the same and followed up on that information. Dr. Sharman and Miss Manson are doing what we've asked them to do." Vince, red-faced, slumped into his chair.

"You're right, Herb'. My apologies. I was just worried something happened to you."

"I'm sure Dr. Sharman will inform us in the future if they are going on a field trip." He smiled and winked at Ben and Claire, and mouthed, "Come with me," to them.

They followed him into the lab.

"Sorry about that. He gets wound up when things don't go to plan. He assumed you would be coming straight here. I'll speak to him about his manners, Dr. Sharman. Now, if you'll excuse me." He turned and walked out of the lab.

"This is turning into a bloody farce," said Claire.

Ben put a finger to his lips and moved his eyes to the right. Kelvin Staples was working on the next bench, unpacking test tubes, hidden behind a mound of supply boxes.

Ben's phone rang, and he disappeared to take it out of earshot, returning five minutes later, looking worried.

"That was Roger. Ron hasn't checked in since yesterday afternoon. Nobody knows where he is. He's not answering his phone, and it goes straight to voicemail every time."

THIRTY-ONE

Alex Munro smiled at the text as he walked down the granite steps and allowed himself a reward in the wine cellar. He selected a magnum of his latest acquisition, a 2016 Pluribus Cabernet Sauvignon, a steal at fourteen hundred pounds a bottle, one of twenty-four magnums he sourced from Harrods months before. Finally, there was some good news now that Sharman and his assistant were in America, and Ron Logan had been removed from Moreton Scientific Investigation's meddling.

Sitting back in the plush red leather, he lifted the crystal glass to his lips and closed his eyes, appreciating the smooth, dark, and juicy flavors of fig and blackberry. He had dealt with the thorn in his side and could now relax for a while, knowing the problem had gone away. Sharman was on the other side of the Atlantic, and his most trusted men had taken Logan off the case. The only fly in the ointment was the insurance company, dragging their heels, looking for a way not to pay out for the photos and missing meteor fragments. Munro had been very astute in his dealings with the representative from Malik Elite Underwriters, negotiating a terrific deal that paid big even for small-ticket items. He ran his index finger around the rim of the glass and sighed. Insurers were all the same, smiling, and promising the earth while they took your money but evasive and reluctant when a claim came across their desk, especially a claim as large as he was covered for.

He took another sip of the exquisite wine and smiled again, knowing he would buy many more cases on the strength of the payout. Malik Elite Underwriters could balk and wriggle as much as they liked, but the priceless photos would never see the light of day again, other than in the buyer's private collection, which would never be revealed. And what were the odds of anyone finding tiny meteor fragments if they were at the bottom of Limehouse Basin? The inevitable cash settlement would clear several outstanding loans that interfered with his lifestyle. Cutting back and tightening his belt on luxuries, such as the recent purchase of a five-bedroom Italian villa on the Amalfi Coast, was not in Alex Munro's nature. It had taken years of criminal activity and careful money laundering to reach his current wealthy status, and no tin-pot outfit like Sharman's Moreton Scientific Investigation was going to spoil his hard-earned lifestyle.

He poured himself another measure, lifted the glass, and stared into the deep ruby liquid, mesmerized by the color and the sharp glints of light from the cut glass, casting his mind back to a world where no luxuries existed in a tumble-down rented house with battered second-hand furniture, hand-me-down clothes, perpetual hunger, and constant beatings from an alcoholic mother. The day school finished, he left home, working for a local business selling second-hand cars, which turned out to be only a front for another less-than-reputable business selling stolen goods and knockoff designer gear.

Lionel Cooke was the father Alex Munro never had. His biological father, a local drug dealer, disappeared as soon as his mother announced she was pregnant. Cooke, from the East End of London, was a small-time crook with big ambitions, far exceeding his capability. Fifteen years later, he took the lad under his wing after a brief affair with Alex's mother when he saw how badly she treated her son.

Not that gratuitous brutality bothered him, but it mirrored his own violent upbringing, and he saw himself in the young lad. When Alex left home, Cooke found him living rough on the streets and took him in, igniting the spark of a long and successful career in crime.

Munro proved to be his benefactor's biggest asset. Although Cooke, deluded with his own ego, took all the credit for the expansion of his empire, it was Munro who found the contacts in India and the Far East to produce fake designer clothes and create the intricate web of shipments to get the contraband into the UK. Munro also masterminded the targeted robberies of high-value goods with an undetectable network of buyers.

Ironically, Munro was Cooke's eventual downfall. Never acknowledging the lad's amazing capabilities and the wealth he created, Cooke gave him a meager allowance, a roof over his head, food, and the bare necessities for carrying out his role in the business, while Cooke spent lavishly on expensive cars, clothes, and holidays.

The crunch came when Munro asked for a brand-new car. Cooke flew into an inexplicable rage and flatly refused to replace the ten-year-old Ford Mondeo, taking exception to the lad for having the audacity to ask for a BMW. Alex watched in amazement as Cooke's face grew bright red, almost purple. He never saw him lose it like that. He stared at Cooke's face, wincing at the contorted rage of bared teeth and spittle, then glanced down at a line of coke on the leather-topped desk. The abuse was loud, obscene, and so out of place. Cooke became erratic, often hyper, making no sense, but never shouted at him like that. It became white noise as Alex floated back in time to the cold, filthy council house. When he looked back up at Cooke, he could see his mother's face in his mind. He was sure Cooke would calm down, which is why he wasn't prepared for the first blow. Cooke had never laid a finger on him before or even raised his voice.

A full-force punch in the face broke Alex's nose, sending a gush of blood down the front of his crisp white shirt. In a split second, a second punch was coming straight for his face from Cooke's weaker arm, but Alex ducked at the last second, and the man's enormous fist passed over his head, brushing his hair. While Cooke's body was still in motion, Alex braced both feet against the floor and fired an uppercut, burying it under Cooke's chin with great power as he swung and rose on his feet at the same time. The impact was colossal, despite the lad's apparent slight stature, as the momentum he created drove his fist against the underside of the jaw so hard that several implants snapped, spraying an arc of blood and teeth across the desk. Cooke staggered backward, enraged even more. He balled his fists and charged at Alex, hoping to grasp him in a bear hug and wrestle him to the ground with his superior bulk. But Alex read it all the way, crouched, slid his hand to his sock, and pulled out the switchblade he always carried, pressing the release button as his arm stretched upward and forward to meet Cooke. They collided as Cooke's barrel chest struck Alex in the forehead, carrying them both clean over the desk.

Alex, lying flat on his back, saw the knife spiraling into the air, out of reach, and waited for the inevitable beating as the bigger man landed on top of him, pinning him to the floor. But Cooke sprang up instead and stepped back. Alex didn't hesitate and vaulted over the desk, heading for the door. The fight was over, as far as he was concerned, and not worth continuing to get beaten half to death.

As his hand turned the door handle, a gargled scream stopped him in his tracks. He glanced back at Lionel Cooke, eyes bulging, staggering from behind the desk, trying to put pressure on his throat, gushing with blood with one hand while the other stretched out, reaching for Alex. It seemed an eternity before the big man stopped shuffling forward, dropped to his knees with a look of absolute hatred, then hit the wooden floor. Blood continued to pump out of his convulsing body until he stopped moving, rigid and still.

Alex continued to stare at the scene. What was once a pristine office now resembled an artist's studio where the artist had gone berserk, flicking brushes loaded with crimson paint at a huge canvas, producing stains and splatters on every surface of the room: walls, ceiling, floor, furniture, and himself. Not only was he drenched in blood down the front of his shirt from Cooke's initial punch, but blood spatter covered him from head to foot. He slumped on the leather sofa used for guest meetings and continued to stare at the bloodbath for another hour, trying to come to terms with what had just happened and wondering how he was going to take advantage of the situation.

He smiled once more and took another sip of the crimson wine, remembering how he meticulously cleaned up the crime scene, faked a different murder scene with Cooke's body in a burned-out car, and months later, to his surprise and delight, was informed by Cooke's solicitor that he, at the tender age of twenty-one, was the sole heir to everything Lionel Cooke had possessed.

THIRTY-TWO

The dashcam footage was so blurred it made Ben laugh.

"Something amusing, Dr. Sharman?" asked Vince King, who still had an air of resentment in his voice after ranting at Ben minutes earlier.

"Sorry, Vince," said Ben. "But these images are, frankly, worthless. How much did the guy pay for the dashcam that took this? The 'man-bear' could be anything from a man or woman dressed in black to a trick of the light. I can't believe you've taken this seriously."

Herbie could see Vince starting to boil again and stepped in.

"The evidence is from the verbal description when Vince interviewed the driver. Yes, the footage is awful, but the witness account backs up witnesses from other sightings."

"And where is the current witness now?" said Ben. "Can I interview him?"

Herbie shook his head. "The witness doesn't want to get involved. Worried if it gets into the press he'll be ridiculed by local folk."

"You mean, leaked to the press, like our involvement in this case has been?"

Herbie looked puzzled. "Sorry, Ben, I don't follow."

Ben walked out of the conference room, returned a minute later, and threw the *Reno Gazette* onto the conference table.

"Page six," said Ben.

Herbie stretched to pick up the paper, sat, opened it to the offending page, and read.

"Someone seems to have inside information," said Herbie.

"Well, it wasn't from us," said Ben, glaring at Vince.

"How dare you look at me like that!" shouted Vince, getting out of his seat. "What do you take me for? Some kind of attention seeker? I had nothing to do with that article." He threw the projector remote control across the room and stormed out.

Herbie followed him. Ben and Claire said nothing and just sat listening to a muffled argument farther down the corridor. Ben sent a text to Roger for an update on Ron and got an almost immediate response: '`still missing.`' He raised the screen for Claire to see.

"I think we ought to get out of here and go home," whispered Claire.

Ben shook his head. "The police will be all over this. I'll give it till the morning, and if Ron hasn't surfaced by then, we'll make our excuses and go, even if I have to pay for the flights myself."

Herbie's low voice made them both jump. "Vince is sorry he lost his cool. He's left the building. I told him to go home before he says something he'll regret."

"You can see why I think someone has been talking to the press, though, can't you?" said Ben. "Far too much detail to be anything a reporter could dig up without inside information. Wouldn't you agree, Herbie?"

"I agree. But don't jump to conclusions yet. I'll do some digging and find out who's been shooting their mouth off. Okay?"

"Fair enough."

"Anyway, you'll be glad to hear I have some good news for you."

"They found Ron?"

"Sorry?"

"Ron Logan. Our investigator in London. He's been missing since last night."

"I wasn't aware of that," said Herbie.

"I should have told you. He's been out of contact since last night UK time, which is totally out of character. I'm worried because someone who doesn't want him investigating in London made a direct threat to him.

"Sorry to hear that. Anything I can do to help with my London contacts?"

"No. Chris Williams has rattled the police commissioner's cage, and they've thrown everything at it. I'm sure he'll turn up soon. What was the good news you had for us, Herbie?"

"Some time ago, one sighting of the man-bear was the talk of Nixon. We investigated, and it led to a dead end as nobody was willing to talk until today. I received a message that the witness who saw the man-bear was a local Paiute elder, who lives in Nixon."

"Would this elder have seen this man-bear near the Paiute's trailer on a trail just off Pyramid Lake?"

"How on earth did you know that?"

"Just call it intuition. Sorry, please go on," said Ben, giving Claire a knowing look.

Herbie described what the elder had seen, which tallied up with Jacy's account of being seen at the trailer with a full body of hair.

"All well and good, Herbie, but we need physical evidence. Blood or hair samples so we can get down to the bare—sorry, excuse the pun—the bare facts. Not second-hand witness accounts or another dodgy video. It has to be rock-solid evidence, and just to be clear, I don't want to see any photos or videos unless they're crystal clear. I apologize if I sound rude and ungrateful, Vince has shown us amazing hospitality, but I take my scientific research business seriously, and at the moment, I feel there's some hidden agenda in progress."

Herbie laughed. "You certainly hold nothing back. I'll make sure Vince understands that. He won't bother you again for a couple of days, so you'll have peace to get on with your work without him snapping at your heels. Anyway, I have another appointment. You should both get back to the house as most of the day has gone."

"Herbie, we don't work office hours. We've made progress through our investigations today, but I appreciate we need to get back on the scientific saddle and start looking for tangible evidence and some answers. I think we'll stay longer and catch up on some tests I want to carry out."

After Herbie Lomax had gone, Claire announced she was starving. "Can't the tests wait till tomorrow?"

He winked at her, walked to the door, and peered up and down the corridor before coming back in. "We've samples to test, don't forget, and I've a feeling they won't appreciate us testing samples that aren't from Pyramid Lake. There's a vending machine in the canteen to keep us going with a few snacks. I'll ring Dorothy and let her know we won't be dining tonight."

THIRTY-THREE

Was the overpowering smell grease or oil? A bit of both, thought Ron. He eased his tongue, stuck to the roof of his mouth, tried to swallow but couldn't, and screwed his eyes shut with the pain that came and went, pulsing in agonizing waves, interrupted only by extreme nausea. Sitting in pitch darkness, where was he, and how had he got there? As his thoughts came back into focus, he battled to think against the unrelenting jolts of pain. The image of the man with the gold teeth came back to him, then the other man grabbing him from behind, powerful arms locked around his chest so tight he struggled to breathe, before the syringe, glinting in the dim light of the street lamp, plunged into his arm.

He was definitely drugged, and he had no memory of the rest of the journey to this place. Bundled into a van or car and brought to... where? How long had he been here? A few hours? A day, or more? He listened to the virtual silence, just the sound of his breath wheezing through the cloth gag. He held his breath and listened again. Distant traffic and voices. He tried to call out for help, but the shout, dry mouthed and through the gag, came out as a garbled rasp. The smell could be coming from the gag, an oily, greasy rag, but it felt pretty dry, so it must be the general smell in the space he was in. A garage or workshop, part of a factory unit? Wherever it was, he sensed the space he was in wasn't large. Maybe a room inside a larger building, or was it just a compact unit on an industrial estate?

Worried that he might vomit into the rag and choke, he focused on keeping the bile down and slowed his breathing as he edged toward sheer panic, and tried to manipulate the gag with his teeth and tongue, which was near impossible with the tight rag cutting into both sides of his mouth. He tried to bite his tongue to make his mouth water, but all he could do was bite on the gag, and he was so thirsty and dry that nothing would happen anyway. His shoulders ached from being pulled backward with both hands secured behind the uncomfortable cold metal chair. He twisted his hands together with very little give but stopped when the plastic cable ties cut into his flesh. His legs, shackled to the chair so tightly that the circulation had almost stopped, only had feeling in them to just below his knees. He couldn't feel his feet. Gagged and stuck fast, like a rat in a trap, Ron wondered what the men wanted and what would happen next. He shuddered as the voice from the phone call that woke him up in the hotel came back to him: "Leave, and you won't have your face rearranged."

As his eyes became accustomed to the dark, chinks of light appeared. A long faint strip of light, ten feet long at ground level, must be the bottom of a roller shutter door, thought Ron. Above him, pinpricks of urban light spiked through wire mesh. A roof light with a fly screen? At the opposite end of the dark space blinked a small red light, on and off every thirty seconds, quite high on a far wall, or was it the ceiling? He couldn't tell. The blinking light reminded him of something he saw before. Familiar, but where? Similar lights flashed on and off in Ben's building back at Moreton-in-Marsh. Smoke detectors with indicator lights flicking on and off to show they were operational and able to detect a fire?

He tried to rock the chair, and it moved. If he could guide it inch by inch to the roller shutter door, perhaps he could make enough noise hitting the door with his shoulder that a passerby might hear, if there was anyone out there. He shuffled up and down in the chair, using limited mobility to push with his feet, while rocking and forcing his torso up and down. The pain jolted through his wrists like needles with every movement, but Ron pushed the chair sideways toward the door, inch by painful inch. He felt encouraged as the light under the roller shutter door got closer. All went well until the room filled with flashing light and the deafening sound of a wailing alarm, so loud it made Ron's ears hurt. He was locked in an engineering workshop lockup, under a railway arch, evidenced by the arched brick roof, benches filled with electric sanders, belt grinders, drills, and racks of tools, along with drums of oil, car parts, and piles of scrap metal, and the earlier rumbling coming from above. His ears started buzzing with a high-pitched whine due to the ear-splitting sirens.

With the siren blaring for another five minutes before ceasing, the intense white strobe light continued to flash, making his eyes water. He continued shuffling the chair, eventually reaching the roller shutter door, and rocked back and forth, striking the door with his shoulder. There were voices outside. He stopped moving and tried to listen above the high-pitched buzzing that wouldn't stop.

"Check around the back. I'm pretty sure there's only this way in," said a man. "It's solid; there's no other way in," said a woman.

"What's the score with the keyholder?"

"I'll get on the radio, Sarge."

As soon as Ron heard that, he began banging furiously on the metal door with the side of his head.

"Someone's in there, Sarge."

"Hello," boomed the sergeant. "Anyone in there?"

Ron stopped and tried to shout through the gag.

"Can you hear that?" said the police constable. "That doesn't sound right."

"Get onto control and see where the damned keyholder is. Failing that, ask for the fire service to attend. In fact, get the fire service to attend, anyway."

Ten minutes later, blue flashing lights filled the street and there was movement as the fire service pried open the roller shutter. They untied Ron and carried him to the back of the patrol car. Once the sergeant had reported back, a lengthy call came through on his phone.

"You're Ron Logan of Moreton Scientific Investigation?"

Ron nodded, rose to his feet, groaned, and hobbled out, trying to light a Marlboro, but his hands shook so badly he couldn't grip and flick the Zippo lighter into action.

"Here, let me," said the sergeant, taking the lighter from Ron's wavering fingers. "You're a wanted man, Mr. Logan. Every cop has been on the lookout for you this evening."

"Where are we?" croaked Ron. The officer passed him a bottle of water and Ron gulped it down greedily.

"Mentmore Terrace."

"Where's that?"

"Hackney. Someone locked you in a private machine shop. It's an archway unit under the train line. London Fields station is just a few yards up the road from here. Bloody good job you set the intruder alarm off; otherwise, you'd have been in there all night."

"I wondered what that racket was. Those thugs must be bloody stupid resetting the alarm." Ron laughed, then coughed and couldn't stop coughing for a minute. "Nothing like a good old smoke," said Ron.

"We'll get you to the hospital to be checked out, Mr. Logan. Orders from my gaffer."

"No chance," said Ron. "Hospitals make me feel terrible, and I feel bad enough as it is. Just want to get back to the Travelodge and get some shut-eye. Besides, your gaffer isn't my gaffer, so respectfully I have to decline."

"Your choice, but we have to escort you from here, and you have the pleasure of a patrol car keeping watch on the hotel for the night."

"Glad to hear about the ride. The price of a taxi cab from here would be extortionate," said Ron. "Any idea who owns this place?"

"It's supposed to be empty, according to the owner, but you can never tell around here. It's bullshit and he'll sublet. Either tax avoidance or criminal activity. You must be pretty important, Mr. Logan. We were told from the highest level that every resource is to be put into finding out who abducted you. When we get you back to the hotel, Detective Inspector Mercer will meet you. Unfortunately, you won't be getting much sleep just yet."

THIRTY-FOUR

Detective Inspector Steve Stone, seated in the hotel bedroom watching TV, almost gave Ron a heart attack as he entered the room. Stone leaped to his feet and offered a hand. "Sorry, I should have waited in reception, but I wasn't sure when you'd get here, so I took the liberty of getting a pass key. DI Stone. I've come to ask you a few questions about your unfortunate incident."

Ron shook his hand and gave the DI the once over. Middle-aged, going thin on top, not a local accent. Welsh or Irish? And quite a mischievous look about him. He didn't look like a cop.

"ID, please," said Ron, backing up to the door.

Stone pulled out a wallet, opened it, and passed it to him. Ron took a good, hard look at the photo on the warrant card. "Stone, you said?"

"That's right. Steve Stone, Metropolitan Police."

"Only the sergeant told me I would meet a Detective Inspector Mercer?"

"Sorry about that. She's been delayed at another incident. They assigned me to meet you instead."

Ron raised his hand as Stone reached for the wallet. "Mind if I confirm that?"

"Be my guest. Do you want my boss's number?"

"No," said Ron. "I have someone much higher up the tree to confirm it. Besides, if you aren't who you say you are, you could give me a bogus number."

Stone smiled. "Not a problem, Mr. Logan."

After confirming DI Stone was genuine, Ron took off his coat and sat at the small desk.

"I understand there was a verbal threat telling you, Dr. Sharman, and Miss Claire Manson to stop investigating the incident at Limehouse Basin and go back to your base in Moreton-in-Marsh."

"That's right," said Ron, fumbling for his pack of Marlboro before remembering he was inside a no-smoking building and not at home.

"The man who threatened you. Would you say he sounded like either of the men that abducted you?"

Ron considered this but shook his head. "Could have been, but I only heard the men talking outside the pub for a short time. Hearing a voice on a phone sounds different. The accent was the same, but it's the same as millions of men in London."

"My colleague said you had a good look at the men in and outside the Old Ship Inn?"

"I did."

"And it was the same men who followed you later?"

"One of them, definitely. The one with the gold teeth, but I'm not sure about the one following behind. I assume they were the same pair of characters I saw at the pub."

Ron provided a detailed description and a step-by-step account up to the point when he was released from the workshop in Hackney.

DI Stone gave him a card and left, but Ron's head was spinning with the events of the last eight hours and having to relive them with the detective, meant no chance of sleep. He put his coat on and stepped out to the front of the Travelodge and lit up a Marlboro. A police officer got out of the patrol car parked outside.

"Everything okay, Mr. Logan?"

"Nothing a few hours kip couldn't put right," said Ron.

"What time would you like to be taken to the police station at Bethnal Green? Chris Williams wants to meet you there."

"I'm wide awake, so I'll have breakfast at seven. Seven thirty okay with you?"

The officer gave him the thumbs-up and walked back to the car. Ron stepped into the hotel reception, and his phone rang.

It was the same voice as on the previous anonymous call.

"You got lucky, Logan. Watch your back, mate. Not even that copper you just spoke to outside will be able to help you and your team if you don't all back off. Do I make myself clear? Just pack your little scientific instruments up, get in your car, and head west. Otherwise, you might get soaked, just like that arsehole Jonny Clarke."

The call ended. Ron scanned the hotel corridor. His heart was thumping, and his skin cold and clammy. He pulled a crumpled handkerchief from his shirt sleeve and dabbed at his forehead. Was the caller inside the hotel? He avoided the lift and took the stairs where he could see anyone ahead and behind. A lift door would open blind to the floors above, and if someone was waiting in the hotel, he wanted to see them first.

Ron switched his bedroom light on and pulled the curtain back, looking down at the street below, wondering if the caller had been watching him from some dark doorway. The thought of sitting in the hotel and having breakfast now seemed unappealing. He retraced his steps down the staircase, eyes darting left and right, and peered out of the front door, feeling safe now that he had the patrol car in sight. He crossed the road, and his phone rang again. Ron let it ring and climbed into the rear seat.

"I'd like to go to Bethnal Green police station now," he said, staring at 'number withheld' on the screen.

THIRTY-FIVE

Claire stood in front of the vending machine, frowning. "Hope you like bagels, Ben. It's all that's left, and I bet they're like bricks."

"Tell you what, why don't we talk to the security man at the gatehouse and see where we can get a carry-out? I don't fancy anything on display. King may have a fantastic building, but his catering sucks here," said Ben, looking through the glass panel at mostly empty food carousels.

The security guard recommended Mary and Moe's Wigwam Diner, which made Claire laugh out loud, much to Ben's annoyance.

The drive to Nixon was slow, with a broken-down truck just outside the town keeping the local cops busy and the traffic heading into town backing up.

"What are the chances she'll be there?" said Claire with a sly grin as they approached the diner. "Perhaps we should eat in rather than get a carry-out, or you'll upset her?"

Ben leaned across and flicked the end of her nose with a finger.

"Ow! That hurt."

"Just a reminder that you should keep your hooter out. We can eat in if you like, as long as it doesn't take forever."

As Ben pulled into the diner car park, his phone beeped.

"Who wants me now?" he said, swinging into the only space left. He killed the engine and checked his phone. Claire was about to let him know his admirer was watching them from the diner window when Ben let out a whoop and fist-pumped the air.

"What the hell?" she said, leaning over to read the screen.

"Ron is safe and well. Someone had kidnapped him. Order us food, and I'll join you in a minute. I'm going to see what's happening back home."

By the time Ben walked into the diner, their order was on the table. Several other customers were giving them angry looks, and some pointed in their direction.

"What's going on?" said Ben, glancing left and right at some stern faces.

"Your admirer just allowed us to jump to the head of the queue. We waltzed in and got fed straightaway in front of all of them. Never mind them, what's the score with Ron? Is he alright?"

Ben brought her up to speed with the kidnapping and his lucky escape from the lockup in Hackney.

"I don't want to think what might have happened if Ron hadn't set the intruder alarm off," said Ben, shoveling a mouthful of fries into his mouth. "You have to admit, whoever did this must be as thick as two short planks to re-set the bloody intruder alarm with a prisoner inside. How stupid could they be?"

"Why do they want Ron and us off the investigation?"

Ben looked thoughtfully at her.

"What?" she said.

"It's not why. It's what."

She put her knife and fork down and wiped her mouth. "You think they want something?"

"No. I think it's a 'what' they are trying to stop us from finding, and my money's on that weird museum."

"Alex Munro?"

"He's the only one I can think of with a solid connection to our investigation. A burglary at the museum with fragments of meteor stolen by a man who ends up drowned in Limehouse Basin. Meteor fragments that are connected directly to Pyramid Lake with similar fish and wildlife problems. As I've said before, I don't believe in coincidences. Can you think of anyone else who's connected?"

"What if someone doesn't want something discovered in Limehouse Basin, or Regent's Canal, like a dead body?"

"The police have already searched the canal and the basin and found nothing suspicious, and I can't think why anyone else would want us out of there."

Claire drummed her fingers on the table. "Let's think through this logically and wind back to the start. Why are we investigating in London?"

"Oh, come on," said Ben, sitting back and raising his arms in the air.

"Just humor me."

"Because the Home Office wanted us to?"

"What are we trying to find out?"

"Why and how fish and other creatures are being infected and morphing into weird variations."

Claire nudged his leg under the table. "Hang on. Lover girl is heading our way with that doe-eyed look, and I'm damned sure it's not meant for me."

"Well, hi there, Dr. Sharman," she said with her trademark grin. Claire subconsciously started counting teeth.

"Please call me Ben."

"If we were somewhere else, I would," she said and winked. "But my boss would give me a roasting if he heard me call customers by their first names. Can I get you another drink, and would you like the dessert menu? We have a stunning special tonight—peach pie and cream. It's our new chef's signature dish. He just started tonight, and it's mouth-watering."

"Why not? How could I possibly say no to that?"

After Claire declined and the waitress walked away, Claire

locked both hands together and lowered her chin onto them, looking up at Ben with her best doe-eyed look. "If we were somewhere else, I would," she said in a high-pitched drawl.

Ben laughed and shook his head. "Can we get back to what we were talking about?"

Claire straightened up. "Sorry, boss, I couldn't resist it. Just one last thing about the waitress."

"Go on?" he said, still smiling, enjoying the banter.

"I can always call a cab, and you can pick me up from the lab later."

Ben laughed so loud people stopped eating and turned to look.

"Enough," hissed Ben. "We've just had a colleague kidnapped, and you're being frivolous."

"Okay. Why would someone or an organization want us to fail?"

"Mmm... good point. It might not be an individual. The only organization I can think of that might benefit is the Cambridge Scientific Team, but I really don't think that's likely."

"Agreed, but they're on my suspects list, and it might be someone in the Cambridge team and not the boss."

"Keep the conspiracy theories coming, Claire," said Ben, enjoying watching her cogs turning.

A huge, bearded man in dirty overalls wearing an oil-stained baseball cap shouted across the diner at the waitress. "Any chance of food over here? Or do I have to sit with those two Brits to get served straight away?" he said, pointing at Claire and Ben. There were murmurs of approval from several diners who still hadn't been served.

Ben's neck reddened, and he looked sheepishly down at the tablecloth, while Claire turned in her seat and glared at the man. Their eyes locked for a few seconds before he looked away. She smiled, nodded, and swept a stony look across the onlooking customers before returning to the conversation.

"Friendly bunch in here," she said, loud enough for others to hear.

Ben clasped his hands together under the table. "Let's get out of here."

"Not yet," said Claire. "Don't give the weirdo with the beardo the satisfaction. Stay another five minutes."

"Okay," said Ben, still feeling the hot prickles on his neck and face. "Where were we?"

Claire pointed at him. "What would be the net gain for someone if the infection spread? Could this be some terrorist organization out to cause mayhem in the capital?"

"That's more likely than the Cambridge team trying to stitch us up, but terrorists would have disposed of Ron."

"You would think so, but perhaps they wanted to keep him alive and ask for a ransom, just to throw the police off the terrorist scent, while back at the ranch the bacteria or virus, or whatever it is, spreads."

"Peach pie," said the waitress, arriving behind Claire. "Enjoy, Dr. Sharman." There were more murmurs of disapproval around them. The waitress turned and gave the bearded man a caustic look as she strutted back to the kitchen.

Ben didn't register how the chef's signature dish tasted as he wolfed it down, eager to leave. After paying the check, Claire followed Ben out, but stopped at the big, bearded man's table and lifted the baseball cap off his head, turning it to look at the motif on the front.

"What's the big red 'A' on the front for, then, sweetie?" she said.

"Don't you Brits know nothing about baseball?" he said with a snarl. "The best goddamn team in the state of Nevada. The Reno Aces."

She placed the cap back on his head, straightened it, gently patted the top, and, as she walked away, turned and said, "Nice. And there was me thinking it stood for arsehole!"

Hoots of laughter erupted as she swung the door open.

THIRTY-SIX

A man stepped out of the shadows into the middle of the road with his arm out, twenty yards before they reached the security gatehouse. Ben pulled up and the man walked to the driver's door.

"Dr. Sharman?"

Ben wound the window down.

"Who's asking," said Claire leaning across Ben before he could answer.

The man offered a hand to her. "Jeff West, *New York Times*, pleased to meet you... Miss Manson?"

"Correct, and likewise. What do you want Dr. Sharman for?"

Ben sat back, smiled, and let Claire do the talking.

"We've picked up on the story that the local paper featured this morning, and it's interesting." He pulled out a voice recorder and pushed it close to Ben. Claire calmly took it off him, switched it off and handed it back.

"You don't do that to Dr. Sharman. If you want an interview you need to apply for an appointment." She stared at him long and hard.

The security guard stepped out of the gatehouse.

"Everything okay, Dr. Sharman?"

"This man was just about to apply for an interview with the doctor," said Claire.

"Do I get one?" said Jeff West smiling at Claire.

"Do I get a say in this?" said Ben.

"Meet us in Nixon at Mary and Moe's Wigwam Diner. Eight thirty in the morning for breakfast and you're paying," said Claire. "Drive on Ben."

Ben laughed. "Yes, m'lady," he said, and pulled forward.

"Didn't want to get involved off the cuff. It gives us time to think and a chance to put the record straight. Your reputation is worth a lot more than King's bullshit."

"You seriously think we should give him the interview?"

"Yes, and there are two other benefits."

"Such as?"

"A free breakfast and you get to see your cutie pie again."

"I think you're right. Getting the press on side might upset Vince but if I don't they'll only have his twist. I'll give it some thought. Now we need to work!"

Claire laid out the plastic ziplock evidence bags used at Zephyr Cove on the main work bench and divided the bags in two, working through each one, making notes, preparing slides, creating high magnification images and running several tests.

"DNA identification will be tricky," said Claire. "Whatever we send off will be picked up by Vince King."

"True, if we label it clearly."

"Sorry, I don't follow?"

"Label the samples for test by coded numbers and letters rather than by actual name and location, so he won't know what they are or where we've taken them from. I don't trust him to keep what we find confidential. Let's focus on what we need to know to solve this mystery and hopefully find a cure for the infection to stop it spreading. Yes, we're being paid to assist with the investigation here but finding a way to stop the mutations here and back home is paramount."

Okay. What if we code each sample such as J for Jacy, RUA for right upper arm and so on?"

"Great idea. You work out a key for all the information we need when they come back while I create a batch of identical samples to take back home."

"Can we do that? How the hell will we get them through US and UK customs? They'll think we're carrying drugs. And if they start opening them up they'll contaminate the samples."

Ben tapped the side of his forehead.

"How?" said Claire.

"Already discussed before we flew over here. Chris Williams will arrange a courier to collect them and they'll be flown back to the UK in a sealed diplomatic case, free from inspection by customs and taken straight to Cambridge for further analysis.

"Hang on. Cambridge? They're on my list of suspects."

"Rubbish. Where else would we get it done so quickly, and who could we trust with such a high-profile incident in London?"

Claire considered this and eventually nodded in agreement. "I suppose you're right. When are you sending the samples off?"

Ben looked at his watch. "Already mobilized. The courier will be here in an hour, so I better make sure everything is prepared and packed."

Forty minutes later, to their amazement and annoyance, Vince King walked into the lab.

"I'm afraid I'm going to have to ask you both to leave immediately as we have a situation."

"Situation? What situation," said Ben.

"Intruder alert in another part of the building. For your own safety, I need you to leave the site while security do a thorough search."

Ben looked at Claire and shrugged his shoulders.

"Okay," said Ben picking up his briefcase and a sealed box containing the samples.

Claire pulled their coats from the rack and followed Ben to the car park. At the gatehouse a motorcyclist approached them.

"Dr. Sharman?"

"Yes?"

"You have a package for me?"

Ben checked his watch. The courier was twenty minutes early.

"Pretty good going from Vegas?"

"I get paid to be on time, Dr. Sharman, and I was told this is of the utmost urgency."

Ben handed over the sealed box, which the courier locked into a large side pannier, then he mounted the Harley Davidson and roared off heading north into the night.

Ben turned right out of the entrance, keeping his eye on the rearview mirror.

"What's wrong, Ben?" said Claire.

"Everything. I'm so stupid."

"What are you talking about?"

"King, who isn't supposed to bother us for a few days, shows up with some cock-and-bull story about an intruder alarm, just before our courier was about to arrive. Strange don't you think? And the courier turned up twenty minutes before they were scheduled."

"I think you're overreacting. If there was a security breach on the site, Vince King has every right to turn up and ask us to evacuate. If it were me I'd do the same if there was any risk to staff. Imagine if a gun-toting burglar caught us in the lab. Vince owns the place after all and so what if the courier was early?"

"If that were all true I would agree, but think, Claire."

As they were about to turn off onto the road to Reno a motorbike passed them at speed.

"I believe that confirms it," said Ben, watching the bike's red tail light getting smaller in the mirror. He checked his watch. "Yep, bang on schedule."

"Confirms what?" said Claire impatiently.

"That the lab is bugged. Vince King's been listening to every conversation we've had in there. I wouldn't be surprised if there are hidden cameras in the lab."

"Ben. What's the problem?"

"The courier came from Las Vegas and is going straight back there with our samples, right?"

"And?"

"Think of the geography and the journey back."

Claire frowned, then her eyes widened, and her mouth dropped open. "Oh, shit you're right. The dispatch rider turned left out of the site heading north and Vegas is south. Are you sure he was taking the samples to Vegas?"

"Harry Reid International in Paradise, Las Vegas. One hundred percent. If Chris Williams made other arrangements she would have warned me. I think the motorbike that just passed us is the real dispatch rider. I'm going to wait here and see if he comes back this way."

Ten minutes later the same bike and rider passed them heading south.

"King's taken our samples," said Ben. "Step outside the car," said Ben with his finger to his lips.

They both got out, shut the doors and moved away from the car.

"King might have the car bugged," said Ben.

"I guessed that's why we're stood on the roadside in the middle of nowhere," said Claire. "So what's so urgent that it couldn't wait until we get back to the house?"

"Two things. First, I kept another set of samples back as insurance."

"Why?"

"In case they got lost or damaged in transit."

"Please don't tell me they're in the lab?"

"You were sat on them, under your seat in the car. I took them out when I went out for fresh air when I took a break in the lab."

Claire laughed. "I wondered where you'd got to. And the other thing?"

"King's bugged the lab and I suspect the car, so be careful what you say in the house, okay?"

Claire nodded then her face changed to horror. "Perhaps he's got cameras in the bedrooms and... please God no, cameras in the bathrooms!"

Ben shrugged his shoulders. "Perhaps I'm going over the top. Just be careful when we discuss anything okay?"

They drove off in silence and all Claire could think of was King leering at a screen while she lay in the bathtub.

THIRTY-SEVEN

Watching the monitor during his late morning break, Bob French hoped a giant rat would appear, so he wouldn't have to go down the vertical shaft into the maintenance tunnel. Ironically, Bob suffered from musophobia, and although it wasn't the ideal occupation for someone with a fear of rats, Bob kept his extreme aversion hidden from his colleagues. He'd managed the phobia all his life, but the size of the new strain discovered in the sewers had him considering the unthinkable. After thirty-five years in the same job, Bob had never taken a day's sick leave, but he was giving it serious thought, especially if one of the oversized rodents appeared on the monitor.

The remote sewer camera under Gore Road, just around the corner from where he was about to start, had recorded footage of giant rats. It made him go cold thinking about it, and after Ron Logan saw Bob's video evidence, a full-scale cull had been carried out with bait laid throughout the local sewer network, killing several hundred normal-sized rats over the last couple of days. What if hideous mutations were still scurrying through the network, and what if the poison bait didn't affect them as no large rat corpses had been found? Bob tried to stop thinking about rats crawling over him as it wasn't doing his blood pressure any favors, imagining their large, pink-clawed feet digging in, razor-sharp teeth gnawing flesh, and worst of all, the tickling sensation of whiskers brushing against his skin. He shuddered from head to toe.

"Are you going to stare at that screen all day, Bob?" said Katie, one of the inspection crew, pulling on a set of waders. "If we're going to get this finished before the rush hour, we need to get our skates on," she said.

Bob sighed, opened his locker, and pulled out the sliding rack of kit hangers.

"You sure you don't want me to come down?" said Ginger, a tall, thin lad with a shock of red hair who joined the department straight from college.

"I'd love to swap places with you, my old son," said Bob with a grunt as he wrestled to get his feet into the waders, "but you know the score. Off limits to rookies. They'd have my guts for garters if you so much as put a toe down that access shaft. You've got the most important job, our surface man today, so no sloping off to have a sneaky smoke while we're down there. Understood?"

Ginger nodded and took the chair in front of the monitor, pulling on the comms headphones.

With the body cams set to record and transmit and the remote sewer camera vehicle already lowered to the bottom of the shaft, they began the slow descent down the metal ladder linking the surface on Victoria Park Road to the large maintenance tunnel eighty feet below.

Two-thirds of the way down, Bob looked up.

"You okay, Katie? Why have you stopped?"

"I'm fine. Just turning my cap lamp on. Seems darker than normal down here."

Bob looked down at the concrete platform at the shaft's bottom twenty feet below. The tunnel was usually lit up like a football stadium by the automatic system when anyone descended the shaft, but for some reason, there was hardly any light reflecting up from below.

He slowed down and stopped. "Katie, can you stop and keep still a second?"

"Why?"

"Just need to listen out for something."

She stopped and held her breath.

Bob turned his head so that his good ear was pointing down the shaft, and listened. Above the normal stream of flowing water, a distinct splashing sound could be heard. He strained to hear as noise from a passing bus on the street above reverberated down the shaft. Then all was still apart from the gentle rippling of running water.

"Okay, Katie. You can move again."

When they reached the base of the shaft, Bob turned his cap lamp off and detached the high-powered torch from his kit belt, lighting up the tunnel, and revealing huge circular ribs of concrete supports. The stream was in a narrow channel with two wide concrete walkways on either side. The twelve-foot concrete tunnel sections had metal brackets hanging down a couple of inches from the roof at every junction to support the string of overhead lights and power cables that stretched away in both directions. They were flickering on and off.

"Must be some electrical fault on the system," said Bob, whose voice created a slight echo in the tunnel. "The circuit board is fifty yards ahead. I'll get the RVC set up and we'll take a look."

Bob lifted the small remote vehicle with three wheels on either side, checked the camera once more, and set it running with the handheld remote. The RVC's LED lamps produced a bright circular band of light ahead of the vehicle as it moved slowly forward along the tunnel, automatically adjusting with invisible sensors, so it followed the base of the tunnel, perfectly aligned in the middle with wheels on either side of the flowing water in the channel below. Bob watched the screen for any sign of a rat but also for any faults in the wall lining, which was what they were being paid to look for. He also laid the high-powered torch down so the beam of light shone up the tunnel in the opposite direction.

"Bit of a waste of the juice in those expensive lithium batteries?" said Katie with her hand on Bob's shoulder.

"Force of habit. I like to know what's behind us."

"Are we going to follow the RVC?"

"Yes. Give it a minute or two and we'll catch it up. Pointless going yet, as it's so bloody slow. Pointless exercise anyway. This tunnel is new and unless there's been a bloody earthquake, I can't see any deterioration of the internal lining happening anytime soon. It keeps us gainfully employed, so we'll go through the motions and keep the powers that be happy."

"Did you hear that, Bob?"

"You can stop calling me Bob now we're out of Ginger's earshot. What am I supposed to be listening to? I can't hear anything."

"Yes, Dad. Splashing. It's coming from behind us."

Bob spun around and picked the high-powered torch off the concrete walkway. He shone it up the tunnel and checked the waterway all the way to the first bend, a hundred yards away. A small shiver ran across his shoulders.

"No, I can't hear a thing."

She put a gloved finger just in front of her lips. "There it was again. You must be able to hear that."

Bob turned his head to one side and caught the faint noise. "Must be round the next bend. I'll get the RVC back and we'll send it to scout out the source."

"Why don't we just walk down there and look and let the RVC do its work on the west section?"

Bob thought about it and nodded. "As you're the nearest, you lead the way," he said and laughed. "Ladies first."

"Dad just admit you're scared. It's me you're talking to," she said, taking the torch from him and moving steadily along the narrow concrete walkway. "Probably a piece of debris flapping around or a couple of rats playing."

Katie laughed, imagining the look on his face. As they approached the bend, the splashing noises stopped. All was silent apart from the stream flowing beneath their feet. She gestured for them to stop and strained to detect any movement. A cool breeze ruffled her fringe, and she picked up the hint of something unpleasant.

"Can you smell that, Dad?" she whispered.

"You know I can't smell sod all since I had Covid. What is it?"

"Not sure. You know. That disgusting bin juice smell, like gone-off chicken."

"It's just sewage."

"Dad, I know what sewage smells like."

"That smell could be coming from miles away. Shall we get going?"

"Weird," said Katie, moving forward again.

There was a sudden rush of movement and the unmistakable sound of tiny feet against concrete. Rats on the move.

Bob inhaled sharply and could feel beads of sweat forming on his forehead as the sound of fleeing rodents scratching into the distance filled the tunnel. As they rounded the bend, there was nothing moving.

"They're gone," said Katie, "so relax, big brave Bob!"

Bob exhaled, glad that his daughter had chosen the same profession, allowing him to work with someone who understood his phobia and who he could trust to keep it secret.

"Hang on, there's something in the water channel. What the hell—"

She worked the powerful beam along the middle water trench until it illuminated something dark and shaking. She moved closer, trying to make out the shape.

"Let me see, Katie," said Bob, easing past her.

The torch revealed something covered in wet fur the size of a small dog. It was moving. Bob drew back. A head appeared from the furry mass in the trench. Red eyes glared up at Bob from a huge, distorted rat's face. It hissed, with ears pinned back, spraying out blue spittle, revealing rows of razor-sharp serrated teeth as it snarled and growled, arching its back, preparing to attack.

Bob let out a blood-curdling scream and passed out, falling backward onto Katie, almost knocking her into the trench as the giant rat turned and disappeared into the blackness. Katie struggled against her father's bulk and lay him flat on the concrete walkway. She lifted the torch, scanning the receding walkway, making sure it had gone. As she lowered the beam from the far distant tunnel and worked it back along the trench, a man's lower arm, mutilated by rat bites, illuminated in the shallow water, with fingers curled inward like a claw, broke the surface.

THIRTY-EIGHT

"You're keeping me busy, Mr. Logan," said DI Stone. "How are you feeling?"

Ron stubbed out the Marlboro with his heel and then, remembering his littering habit of a lifetime, picked it up and put it in his shirt pocket, feeling Steve Stone's watchful presence. "I'm good. Feet and wrists still ache a bit, but I'll live."

"Good. I have some news for you. We've identified the rest of the body that was attached to the man's arm in the sewer.

"Identified? I don't follow. Do you mean found?"

"Well, yes, it was discovered four days ago before this rat problem became apparent.

"Please enlighten me," said Ron, offering the detective a Marlboro.

"Thanks, but no. Gave up years ago."

"Mind if I do?"

"It's a free world, Mr. Logan, and we're outside in fresh air."

Ron lit up, checked the wind's direction, and moved so Steve Stone didn't end up in a cloud of smoke.

"A body with a missing arm was discovered in a block of flats in

Bethnal Green, just the other side of Cricketers Bridge. If you like, I can walk you over there through the park. It's a few hundred yards the other side of the bridge."

Ron nodded in agreement. "Any idea who the deceased was?"

"Sammy Abara, a local drug dealer. Murdered with a machete and dumped in one of the block's garbage chutes where the body got wedged between the second and third floors. As more garbage accumulated in the chute, it caused a blockage until one resident called the council to clear it, and they discovered a body missing its right arm. At first we suspected the murderer took it and sent it to the victim's gang leader as a warning."

"Post-mortem carried out?"

Stone shook his head. "No date yet. Things don't move that fast around here, even though it's a murder. It's scheduled for the day after tomorrow. I expect you'll want to attend?"

Ron's eyes screwed shut at the thought. He knew someone from Moreton Scientific Investigation would have to attend, but he was damned if it would be him. "One of my colleagues will attend the PM. If you give me the details when you know, I'll pass it on."

"Oh, I thought you'd like to keep the continuity going, Mr. Logan, and attend yourself?"

"No, we've a dedicated member of the team who attends post-mortems," lied Ron, picturing Roger's face at being told to watch a body being carved up.

"Any idea how the man's arm went AWOL?"

"Pretty certain a machete sliced right through it, but how it found its way into the sewer is a mystery. We're revisiting house-to-house inquiries to see if anyone remembers anything they saw, but don't hold your breath. Most folk clam up, especially if the crime is part of a turf war. Gangs don't appreciate witnesses that talk."

"Any CCTV?"

"There are a few cameras in the area, and we are going over them again. If anything comes up, I'll let you know straight away."

"The two sewage workers that discovered the arm. Where can I contact them?"

"Both of them are at home since the father was discharged from the hospital after a checkup. He collapsed in the sewer; luckily, she was with him to raise the alarm straight away. He had to be rescued by the fire service. If you remember, you met him before when he showed you the video of the giant rats in the sewer under Gore Road."

Ron pulled out a moleskin notebook and flicked through several pages. "Bob French?"

"Yes, and his daughter Katie."

"Why on earth would he take his daughter down a sewer?" said Ron, lighting another Marlboro and stepping on the one he'd just put out at the same time, while Stone wasn't looking.

"It may seem odd to you, but not unusual around here. Katie French followed in her father's footsteps. She's a sewage worker and works with him. A lot of trades in London carry on through the generations, and even though it may seem strange, it isn't uncommon."

"I have his contact details, and you say she's at the same address?"

"Yes, she's staying with him at the moment. You could walk that from here as well. Just a few blocks away on Tudor Road, behind the petrol station just off Mare Street. Shall we take a stroll to the murder scene, and I'll talk you through it?"

As they walked through Victoria Park, Ron called Roger and gave him the 'good news.' To his surprise, Roger appeared delighted with his gruesome task, which Ron thought was just plain weird. A sense of relief washed over Ron as he realized he'd managed to escape a situation that he truly despised, and he couldn't help but feel pleased about it.

Having focused on the canal and Limehouse Basin, Ron found it interesting to immerse himself in the brick and concrete world of London suburbia. Once a series of small villages before World War II, the view from the bridge seemed to Ron to be organized chaos, crammed with small to medium blocks of the post-war era and increasing numbers of ultra-modern blocks. Perpetual development meant tower cranes were never absent, forever moving the London outline upward toward the heavens.

Fernleigh House spanned half the length of one side of a small cul-de-sac, with four floors and all flat entrance doors opening onto open communal balconies.

"The lift's out of order, so we'll have to take the stairs," said Stone as they entered the south entrance. When they reached the fourth-floor balcony, Ron struggled to breathe.

"You okay, Mr. Logan?" said Stone.

"Fine," gasped Ron.

"Good," Stone said as he pulled back the iron handle of the counterbalanced chute hopper lid to reveal the filthy steel chute lining where the body had been discovered ten feet below them. Ron gagged, took a step backward, and pulled a handkerchief from his sleeve to cover his nose and mouth.

"Pretty rank, isn't it, Mr. Logan? But I suppose it's better than having to walk up and down those stairs to empty your bin."

Ron took several photos and peered down the chute, which faded to blackness several feet below. "Where does this go?" he said, stepping well away from the chute now he had seen and taken photos of every detail.

"Let's go back down, and I'll show you."

"What are you two doing?" said a gravelly woman's voice behind them.

They both turned to see a tiny, wizened old lady peering around the side of her flat entrance door.

"Just inspecting the disposal hatch, madam."

"You from the council? Only my sink's leaking again, and I've rung your so-called helpline, but no bugger ever answers it."

Ron stepped toward her. "Sorry, but no, we're not. What seems to be the matter with your sink?"

"Don't," whispered Stone, but it was too late. The old lady went into a monologue of her own personal history, about how it had been such a nice place to live before 'all them foreigners' moved in. She eventually explained how the sink took ages to empty, and after her son Nigel fixed it, the sink started leaking into the cupboard underneath. Ron listened and smoked another Marlboro until she stopped talking.

"You need a new washer in the U-bend by the sound of it," said Ron.

"You reckon?"

"I do. Now that I've diagnosed the problem of your sink and I'm sure Nigel can install a new washer, could you help me out?"

"Depends on what you want. I haven't got owt to give you, if that's what you're thinking."

"No, nothing physical. Just your obvious expert knowledge on this block of flats."

The old lady smiled and seemed to stand a little taller. "What I don't know about this place 'ain't worth knowing," she said and nodded to herself.

"The man that was found in the chute."

"You 'ain't police, are you?"

"Certainly not," said Ron, looking quite shocked. He could hear a snigger behind him as Stone tried to keep a straight face.

"Okay. What do you want to know?"

"Did you see anything out of the ordinary around the time before the chute got blocked?"

"No, but I heard them fighting out here. I didn't go out to look or look out of the window. Don't pay to be nosey anymore."

"So, what did you hear?"

"Three men. Arguing about money. Then there was a fight, and it stopped. I heard the chute open, and something went down it. You can hear it plain as day from my kitchen window." She pointed to the window next to the door. "With the air vent open, I can hear everything. I didn't think anything of it other than there was a fair bit of blood on the balcony and I threw a bucket of water with bleach over it and swept it into the drain over there." They turned and saw an opening with a small domed mesh cover on the floor just beyond the chute. "Couldn't leave it to congeal and stink the place out, now could I?. There would be a million flies and maggots in no time."

Ron blew his nose. "Anything else you can think of, Mrs....?"

"Miss Crowley. No, nothing unusual apart from coppers banging on my door ever since they pulled that poor sod out of the chute. I can't use it anymore. I chuck my crap down the chute at the other end of the balcony out of respect."

"Respect?" said Ron.

"Respect for the dead. It would be like emptying your bin into someone's grave."

"Oh, I see," said Ron. "Well, you've been really helpful, Miss Crowley, and I hope your son fixes your sink soon." She disappeared as quickly as she'd appeared.

Stone patted Ron on the back. "You have a way with the ladies. You got more out of her than our boys got out of the entire block!"

"Pity she destroyed vital evidence," said Ron.

Stone beckoned him away toward the stairs and whispered, "She didn't do a brilliant job cleaning up the blood as we got plenty of evidence. Before we go down, I'll just explain the waste system. The chute runs from this floor and serves the residents on this floor and the first and second floors. The third-floor chute hatch had a problem six months ago, and the council put a temporary seal on the hatch. Otherwise, someone would have spotted the man's body earlier since he was stuck at third-floor level, just a few feet below the sealed hopper. The chute drops to a refuse store accessed from street level. Follow me and I'll show you."

They walked down to the ground floor, stepped out of the main entrance, and turned to face a heavy set of black cast-iron doors. Stone pulled them open, revealing the opening to the round metal chute above and a huge rectangular metal bin on wheels directly below it.

"Not exactly rocket science after all," said Ron, who'd imagined some complex waste disposal system.

"Nope. The rubbish drops into the bins, and a waste disposal truck comes around once a week to empty them."

Ron reached for his handkerchief once more, covered his face, and stepped inside, activating his phone flashlight. He pulled a second empty wheeled bin out onto the pavement and stepped back inside. He crouched near the back wall and searched the floor.

"Rat feces," he said, pointing them out to Stone. "And some are much larger than usual," he said, pulling out an evidence bag.

"What are you saying, Mr. Logan?"

"I think whoever murdered your victim cut off his lower arm with the machete, threw it down the chute where it landed on a pretty full bin, and maybe bounced off, landing on the floor behind the bin out of sight. You might want to check for blood traces in here."

"We did," said Stone, smiling. "And there was a lot of blood spatter."

"Just in the bin or on the floor as well?"

"Both, but there must have been a fair amount from the corpse as he may not have been dead before someone pushed him into the chute."

"And bled out?"

"Possibly."

"I think our king-sized rat found the arm sometime after and took it back to its lair. What worries me the most is it has the run of a large, densely populated area. The only saving grace is it scavenged the man's lower arm, but how long before these giant rats' attack humans or, worse still, the infection spreads to the human population?"

THIRTY-NINE

When they arrived at the diner, Zinnia Charleston was standing outside the door waiting for them.

"There's a man inside who says he's meeting you. He's at the far table in the corner," she said, pointing through the door to Jeff West, who was reading a newspaper and drinking coffee in a corner alcove seat. "Before you go in, Dr. Sharman." She looked around to see if anyone else was listening from inside. "Could I have a word?" She looked at Claire. "In private?"

Claire smiled, dying to laugh, as Ben's neck began to redden. She stepped inside and walked over to the corner alcove. Jeff West stood and offered a hand. Claire took it and gave it a firm shake.

"Please take a seat, Miss Manson, and have whatever you like from the menu. As you pointed out yesterday, it's on me."

He grinned, revealing perfect teeth that looked natural, unlike so many men she saw who seemed to think veneers and teeth whitening made them more attractive. To Claire, they just made her feel like she was conversing with a shark. It seemed like a genuine smile, but she had learned never to trust a reporter. A tune came into her head as she studied his grinning face: "Never Smile at a Crocodile." She smiled back.

She estimated him to be in his late twenties, just starting to develop a few lines and creases that made his face interesting. Claire had a thing about eyes and took a closer look at his deep blue eyes, seeing the telltale dark outline of the irises that made his eyes stand out. Nature was amazing with its little tricks and foibles that could turn someone's eyes and face from just pleasant to amazingly attractive. The face she looked at was at least a nine out of ten, from the mesmerizing eyes alone.

"Is Dr. Sharman going to join us?" he said, peering over her shoulder. "He seems deep in conversation with that pretty waitress."

She turned to see Ben leaning in close to Zinnia, who had her hand resting on his arm. She felt pangs of irrational jealousy and tried to brush them aside.

"Yes, he does seem preoccupied." Too preoccupied, she thought.

"Zinnia!" came a shout from the kitchen door. "Service!" The owner had both hands in the air, eyes loaded with daggers. Zinnia left Ben at the door and scuttled off to the kitchen.

Claire decided to save the banter with Ben for later as the reporter, from one of the most prominent newspapers in the US, was paying close attention.

Ben shook hands with Jeff and sat next to Claire.

"Before we say a word," said Claire, "can you show me some proof that you actually work for the *New York Times*?"

Jeff West smiled and nodded, pulling out his driver's license.

"I'm not a cop, so I don't carry any official newspaper ID, but here's my driver's license and"—he pulled out a copy of the *New York Times*—"if you look on page three, today's edition, you'll see I wrote the main article on that page."

"Just double-checking," said Claire. "I already know you worked with the Times. Just making sure you still work for them."

"Miss Manson, if you ever get bored with scientific investigation, please call me. I believe you'd make a great investigative journalist," he said and winked at Ben.

Zinnia, still in a fluster after the boss chewed her ear off, took their order, and Ben settled back with his coffee. "What do you want to ask me, Mr. West?"

"I read the report in the *Reno Gazette* about Vince King asking you to assist in the investigation of the so-called man-bear that some folks claimed to have seen around Pyramid Lake. I've also followed your previous two cases involving extraterrestrial investigations and am not only very impressed with your amazing encounters, but curious."

"Curious why?" said Ben.

"Curious why you have left a hot investigation back in London, England, to come all the way here on the hearsay of a few locals. To put it bluntly, it's either money..." Ben felt Claire tense up next to him. "...or, there's more than hearsay to this story, and I can tell you, before you rip me to shreds, Miss Manson..." Ben laughed out loud at West's reading of Claire's expression. Although Ben couldn't see her face, he knew exactly what it would look like at this point. "I believe it's the latter because your professional and personal ethics, I'm told by a professor in Cardiff, England, are—"

"Wales," corrected Claire.

"Sorry. Your professional and personal ethics, I'm told by a professor in Cardiff, Wales, are beyond reproach."

"That doesn't mean I wouldn't come to the US for commercial reasons," said Ben. "I have a business to run, after all."

West nodded. "Even so, I don't think you would have left the UK while you were involved in such a high-profile case, and remain here even though one of your team was kidnapped."

Ben cast his eye over the article in the newspaper, read a few lines, and looked up at West. "You can write, that's for sure. So, what did my old professor, Don Gladwell, say about me? All good, I hope."

"Hell of a nice guy. Met him in a lecture he gave at Rockefeller University, New York, and yes, he gave you a glowing report."

Ben smiled. Professor Don Gladwell had been instrumental in getting him the job at Moreton-in-Marsh, and Ben went on to become the CEO. Don Gladwell was, as West had put it, 'one hell of a guy' and a great friend.

"My partner Claire just asked you for ID, but I'm more interested in the angle you'll take when reporting anything we discuss."

"Fear not, Dr. Sharman. I'll treat you fairly and openly and will be seen to be doing so."

"That sounds formal and robotic," said Ben.

"Without fear or favor, in the words of your newspaper's patriarch Adolph Ochs," said Claire.

Ben turned to her. "What are you talking about?"

West was now grinning even wider. "You are very lucky to have such an astute partner, Dr. Sharman. Miss Manson has obviously looked at the *Times* handbook of values and practices, which is there for all to see. Look, I'm not here to undermine or derail your very fine career. I'm simply doing my job, finding the truth behind the story. The report in the *Reno Gazette* was well written, but it lacked substance and sensationalized reports of this elusive man-bear without any hard facts."

Ben and Claire nodded together. West knew at that point he had their cooperation in the bag.

"The article says that several witnesses have seen the man-bear, and one even spoke to it while the creature was at the top of a telegraph pole. Sounds ridiculous, like something out of some fifties low-budget horror movie: 'Godzilla vs The Man-Bear.'" They all laughed.

"Okay," said Ben. "You ask, and I'll tell you what I can."

"Do you mind if I record this?"

"No," interrupted Claire. "Make notes. Dr. Sharman can refute things said in your notes, but not when you've recorded his voice."

"She's as sharp as this knife," said West, tapping the side of a plate piled with pancakes, bacon, and maple syrup that had just arrived with a serrated knife. He pulled out a notepad from his leather shoulder bag and unscrewed a fountain pen.

"How did you get involved in the investigation this side of the pond?"

Ben explained the connection between the incident at Limehouse Basin and Regent's Canal and a meteor strike at Teakettle Junction, which then revealed a link to Pyramid Lake. After Vince King and an official from Homeland Security requested their help with the sightings of the man-bear, it was a logical move to accept the request to gather evidence from the source of the problem. Vince wanted them to prove or disprove the existence of the man-bear at Pyramid Lake. Ben outlined his thoughts on bear territory and why he believed it unlikely that a man-bear would inhabit the barren hills around Pyramid Lake but would be more likely to favor forested areas, of which there were plenty to the west around Lake Tahoe.

"Do you believe the man-bear exists?"

"I can neither prove nor disprove its existence at this point," said Ben, glancing at Claire. The unsaid interaction did not go unnoticed by Jeff West.

"You think there may be, or is it just that you don't want to admit that it exists?"

Ben shuffled in his seat. "What I'm saying is that although several sightings have occurred, the visual and verbal encounters of these witnesses do not provide conclusive evidence. Photographic and video evidence has been very poor, and we have no physical evidence such as footprints, skin, blood, or hair samples we can test to determine what this phantom beast is."

"So, you don't believe it exists?"

"I have an open mind, but logic is leading me to believe that it doesn't exist, based on the lack of evidence and the assumed habitat."

"But you have discovered abnormalities in other animals?"

"Correct."

"Specifically?"

"Are you referring to London?"

"Of course."

"Sorry, but I cannot divulge anything relating to the UK investigation."

"Why?" said West, while writing quickly then looked up again without waiting for an answer, he continued, "I heard it was rats. That doesn't sound good. How does it spread?"

"If you're referring to London, I cannot comment. I'm restricted to the information I can divulge."

"Likewise for the amphibians, I guess?"

Ben just smiled.

"Is that happening over here?"

"There are anomalies we have seen in fish. The development here seems slower. It's as if there's some kind of inhibitor here at Pyramid Lake, and that's what I want to focus on."

"So that must mean the development in London is rapid? Has it affected the human population in the UK?"

Ben said nothing.

"How long do you think you'll be here, Dr. Sharman?"

"Until I've exhausted all avenues of investigation. It's a long way to backtrack if I haven't got all the information I need, but I will have to fly back soon, as our situation is more advanced." Ben checked himself from saying "serious," or "critical."

West asked several more questions about the tests they were carrying out and some background on Moreton Scientific Investigation, which pleased Ben. He also drove with Ben and Claire to the south shore of Pyramid Lake for a mini photo shoot before dropping the bombshell.

FORTY

They watched West's Chevy disappear in a cloud of dust and grit as it accelerated from the pullout heading north, passing the entrance to Barngate Holdings and driving onward toward Vince King's new development farther up Pyramid Lake's shoreline.

"I hope he keeps his word," said Ben. "Otherwise, we might have to do a moonlight flit."

"When can we get a copy of tomorrow's *New York Times*?" asked Claire.

"I believe it's midnight if you subscribe online, which I want you to do right now. If West doesn't stick to his ethical mantra, we need to know as early as possible. Then it's off to the nearest hotel until we can book a flight home."

"Do you trust him, Ben?"

"I can see why he didn't tell us at first, and to be honest, I would have done the same in his shoes. I'm confident he'll not let us down, even though he's a journalist. After all, he didn't have to tell us why he really traveled two thousand miles."

"It makes the puzzle clearer now he's confirmed King's real motivation."

"Just remember, not a word out of place in that building, the car, or the house. Who knows what King's capable of? He may seem okay on the surface, but if Jeff West's informer is right, we could be in trouble if he thinks we know what he's up to. We'll act dumb, get our job done, and get the hell out. Let Jeff West expose him. "

They were about to get into the car when Claire beckoned him back to the lakeside.

"What about the samples under my car seat you were going to send to Chris Williams?"

Ben gave her the thumbs-up. "Already sorted. I rang Chris, and she got the dispatch rider to turn around. The poor man had almost got to Vegas when he got redirected. He picked the new samples up from me at the end of the street from the house. I went for a stroll in the early hours this morning. I was so tired and wound up with what West was going to ask that I clean forgot to tell you. Shall we take a peek at what's inside Vince King's switched package that was on the way to Vegas?"

Ben lifted it out from under the seat and began tearing open the wrapper, revealing a locked zipper case. Inside were several bagged sample cases with identical labels to the real parcel King hijacked.

Ben scratched his head. "How the hell did he do that?"

"He's a piece of work," said Claire. "You were right. He's been watching us all the time. There must be cameras in the lab, and if I find a camera in my en suite at the house, he'll have very painful pieces missing from his body by the time I'm finished with him."

"It just adds weight to West's theory. And there's one thing you can't do when you get back to the lab."

"Don't worry, I'll be as nice as pie to the scumbag."

"Yes. Keep him sweet. Be nice and don't forget to tell your face. No, I was talking about the cameras. He must know that we know it's bugged, but don't start looking for hidden cameras when we get back. Let's just keep things on an even keel till West blows the lid off Barngate Holdings. I'll get these fake samples of King's sent to the UK. That dispatch rider will be thanking me for the overtime."

"Just one other teensy-weensy thing," she said. Ben looked at her, wary of the predatory look in her eyes.

"Let me guess. You want to know what I discussed with Zinnia, don't you?"

Claire said nothing and kept staring expectantly.

"God, you are so transparent. She had a message for me from Egan."

"Oh," said Claire, looking disappointed.

"He wants to meet up with us later tonight. He has more news."

"Why didn't he just call you?"

"I'm taking precautions. If Vince has everything bugged, why not the phones?"

"Is that possible? I thought you had to have a warrant or one of those court order things and be a cop to do stuff like that?"

"You're right, unless you work for Homeland Security."

"Herbie Lomax?"

"Exactly. Why do you think he's hanging out with King?"

Claire didn't have an answer.

"I reckon he's on King's payroll, so getting the phones bugged might not be so difficult."

Claire changed the subject. "She was just passing a message?"

"And she asked me out."

"I knew it," said Claire, and immediately softened her tone. "I mean, it was obvious she was going to."

"I'm taking her to a drive-in movie tonight in Reno."

Ben stared at Claire's animated face, then burst out laughing. "She asked, and I politely informed her that I was already in a relationship and declined. Did you think for one minute I would be making out with her in the back of the car at the cinema parking lot?"

Claire laughed, more out of relief. "So, you broke her heart?"

"She was okay when I turned her down, except for her doe eyes. I nearly changed my mind and said yes."

Claire looked at her watch. "Let's shift. It's gone ten, and the voyeur will be wondering where we are."

Elsa Smyth was the only other person in the lab when they arrived.

"Morning, both," she said with a smile.

Claire looked stunned.

"Morning, Elsa," said Ben. "On your own this morning?"

"Yes. Kelvin called in sick, which makes it a far happier place," she said, still with a smile on her face.

"No Herbie Lomax or Vince King?" said Claire.

"Thankfully, no, which makes it even better."

"Has she been drinking?" said Claire under her breath as they pulled their lab coats off the cloak stand.

"If she has, I want some of the same stuff," whispered Ben.

Elsa caught them both staring at her, put the manual she was reading down, and walked over. "Something bothering you?" she said, still smiling.

Claire looked at Ben and said, "To be honest, and don't take this the wrong way, but when we first came here, you were... how can I put it?"

"Frosty?" she said.

Ben's neck reddened as he inwardly cringed.

There were a few moments of awkward silence.

"My apologies," said Elsa. "I was rather prickly. I'd just had a run-in with Vince King before you got here, and it was very unprofessional to show my feelings to you, especially at our first meeting."

"Apologies accepted," said Ben.

She smiled again. Ben couldn't help noticing how the smile transformed Elsa's face from a sour-faced, middle-aged woman into quite a beautiful person who looked so much younger when her mouth curved upward.

"Vince can be a real pain in the arse when he doesn't get his own way or things aren't going quite to plan, as I'm sure you realize after his tantrum yesterday."

"You heard about it then?" said Claire.

Elsa pointed to the ceiling.

"I was in the stockroom, just about to leave, where the CCTV monitors are."

Ben and Claire looked up.

"It's a camera disguised as a smoke detector," whispered Elsa. "Vince is paranoid about being burgled."

"Picks up sound as well?" said Claire.

"Yes. I could hear the conversation, clear as a bell. There are cameras in almost every room," said Elsa. "Except the restrooms."

"Sure about that?" said Claire.

Elsa laughed. "Of course, that would be illegal and highly distasteful."

Claire made a mental note to check the house when they got back.

Elsa opened a cupboard, lifted out an aluminum briefcase, and opened it on the lab bench, revealing several compartments filled with sealed evidence bags, photos, papers, and a spiral notebook.

"There are a range of samples prepared for you. Vince asked me to give you full access to the work we've already done." She typed on a keyboard, and a spreadsheet opened on the monitor. "I have listed everything in the case with all the details, dates, and locations the samples were taken from."

"Impressive," said Ben, scanning the spreadsheet.

"Thank you, Dr. Sharman. I like to keep things in order. Now, if you'll excuse me, I have to get some work done. If you need me for anything, just ask."

Claire took a closer look at the hidden camera, and Ben shook his head. "I've left some notes in the car. Could you fetch them for me?"

Claire took the hint, and Ben followed a minute later, meeting her in the car park.

"Just remember to keep the conversation to a minimum and stop looking at the damned smoke detectors. I think the monitors in the stockroom aren't the only system he has to watch and listen. So think very carefully before saying anything, and just because Elsa seems to be much more friendly and is making out she doesn't like Vince or

Kelvin, doesn't mean she's on our side. So just beware of her. For now, I don't trust her."

They spent the rest of the morning evaluating, discussing, and testing water samples from various locations around Pyramid Lake and the dam area where the Truckee River entered the lake, plus samples taken of the annual algae bloom. There were fish samples with dates before and after the meteor strike at Teakettle Junction.

"This algae bloom is an interesting phenomenon," said Ben, "which doesn't occur on this scale in Limehouse Basin or Regent's Canal. It's a factor we should look at as a significant variable between the two sites."

Claire nodded. "The great thing is that researchers have been taking these fish and water samples every month, sometimes weekly, since the meteor strike, and they have clearly documented the dates and extent of the annual algae blooms. This is going to be an interesting task."

"Nodularia spumigena is the most prolific blue-green algae that forms in certain conditions when light, nutrients, and temperature are optimal," said Claire, reading off a website she had found on her phone. "There's a warning report issued by tribal elders. The result can produce huge floating blooms in the right conditions that affect the water toxicity. People are advised not to swim, use the lake for water sports, or consume fish as it can cause vomiting and other unpleasant effects. The aerial photos of the last major bloom are amazing. Look at this, Ben."

The image on the screen showed vast swathes of the floating bright green bloom hugging part of the lake's western coastline.

"Not exactly a tourist mecca when that's going on," said Ben. "What's intriguing is there doesn't seem to be much mutation of fish and wildlife considering the size of both lakes and the linking Truckee River between them. You would have thought there would be more spread and evidence of the infection. I believe that difference, when compared to the small body of water back home with its high instance of transformed fish and wildlife, will unlock this mystery."

Ben's phone rang. He looked for the caller ID and cut it off. "I'm going to take this outside," mouthed Ben, winking.

In the car park, Ben eyed the external walls for CCTV and chose a spot near the chain-link fence at the front of the car park, well away from the building.

"Sorry I cut you off, Ron. We have a privacy issue over here. We're being watched and listened to remotely, so from now on, while I'm at the Barngate building, I will cut your calls and ring back."

"Understood," said Ron. "A quick update. Another giant rat incident in a sewer service tunnel under Victoria Park Road."

"On the other side of Victoria Park from the canal?"

"Correct. A sewer worker and his daughter came across a giant rat tucking into a severed man's arm."

"Bloody hell, Ron. Did the rat kill the man? Who was he? This is awful!"

"Hold your horses, Ben. No, the man was attacked on the fourth-floor balcony of a block of flats not far from the canal during a local drug turf war. Looks like they cut his arm off with a machete and dumped him, still alive, into the waste chute, where he got wedged on the floor below and bled to death."

"He was still inside the chute?"

"Yes."

"God. Just hope he was out of it. I can't think of a worse way to go. In agony, pinned inside a stinking waste chute, knowing you are going to die."

"In my opinion, his arm went into the chute first and ended up on the floor in the bin store. I found evidence that rats had been there, including at least one very large one and I believe it carried the severed lower arm to the sewer. Still trying to work out how it got there. What worries me the most is it was about to attack the sewage worker but got scared off when he screamed."

"Is the man okay?"

"Yes, shaken up, but no harm done apart from being half scared to death."

"Why did you mention his daughter? You made it sound as if she was with him down the sewer?"

"She was. I thought it weird at first but found out since that she also works in the same department, part time." Ron started laughing.

"What's so funny," said Ben.

"Something to tell Claire, then stand back and watch her face."

"What?"

"The daughter also has a sandwich round and often gets asked to attend the emergency services larger incidents to supply the troops with grub. Claire had a couple of sandwiches from her catering van while she was at the canal with you. What a combo—sewage and sarnies!"

Ben listened to Ron cackling, then coughing.

"Did you check out Herbie Logan and Vince King for me?"

"Yes," said Ron, still coughing. "Both check out, but although King did work for NASA, he was just a technician, on a low grade. Has he said he was one of the higher-ups?"

"No, Ron. We just assumed he was." Thanks for that. It just makes this seem even weirder. You've confirmed Herbie Lomax is a Homeland Security official?"

"Absolutely. Chris Williams confirmed that he's been an agent with them for over ten years. Sorry, Ben, got to go. Meeting with Chris Williams to widen the rat extermination program. I'll keep you updated."

Ben told Claire about the sandwiches she had bought on Cricketers Bridge a few days earlier, stood back, and enjoyed the contorted expressions.

FORTY-ONE

Ben made a detour on the way back to the house, turning onto the familiar track leading up to Egan's trailer. With the sun still well above the distant hills, they were glad Egan ushered them quickly inside his air-conditioned haven.

"Nice of you folks to drop by," he said, pointing to the sofa and a chair for them to sit down. "Coffee or a cold beer?"

Claire looked at Ben, whose forehead glistened with sweat. "I'll have a coffee, and I think he'll have a beer." Ben shook his head. "He'll have an ice-cold beer, and I'll drive home."

Ben didn't protest and sank back in his chair, taking the glass Egan pulled from the freezer. Frost formed on the outside as Ben poured the beer. The first mouthful was like paradise; it hit the spot, and he sat back, closing his eyes before taking another large mouthful. "That's so good," he said, wiping froth from his top lip.

"Nothing like the first cold beer on a hot day," said Egan, holding up his own glass in a toast. "Here's to your research and a cure for bear syndrome." Ben raised his glass and drank the beer down in one.

"Another?" said Egan, opening the refrigerator.

Ben glanced at Claire.

"I'm not your wife. You don't need my permission."

"In that case, it would be rude not to," said Ben, taking a second bottle from Egan. "Now, why did you ask us to come?"

"There's another case of someone being affected by fish."

"God, no! Hang on. This isn't the one seen by a motorist at Pyramid Lake? We watched a so-called video of the sighting, supplied by Vince King."

Egan looked puzzled. "No, this is a definite. Take my word for it. I saw this person, and it was at Lake Tahoe in the forest."

"Like your son?"

"This guy is far more advanced. Covered in hair, walks with a stoop, and massive when he straightens up. To be honest, he frightened the crap out of me."

"How did you know where to find this man?" said Ben. "Was it far from where you live?"

"Miles from us. The other side of the lake at Meeks Bay. I have a friend over there who heard reports of a Sasquatch-type man seen by hunters along Meeks Creek, which runs off the hills behind Meeks Bay into Lake Tahoe. There's a forest trail up into the hills which comes to a dead end. I traveled up there with Jacy and didn't expect to find anything, but a weird thing happened. Jacy could feel a presence, and I believe the guy up there could feel Jacy's presence as well. We hiked up to the creek and almost got there when the damned thing stepped out in front of us, bold as brass."

"How near did you get?"

"As close as you are to me."

"Go on," said Ben, turning on the recording app on his phone. "Don't mind if I record this, Egan? Only any information like this could be critical, and I don't want to commit this discussion to memory. Too important."

"Not a problem. If you want photos of me as well, just make sure you get me on my best side," he said, his eyes twinkling. "The guy, or whatever you want to call him, was around seven feet tall and broad. I mean really broad, and I could tell there were some formidable muscles under that layer of thick black hair, which has that same iridescent blue sheen that Jacy has."

"Seven feet tall?"

"Yep, there or thereabout, and that was with the stoop, like he was bowing his head slightly. I'd say he was seven-six straightened up. The face has slightly less hair than the rest of his body, and the skin underneath has a slight blue pallor. A bit like that fish Jacy caught. His eyes were human. It was the way he looked at me, sort of summing me up, like you would when you first meet someone. Sort of weighing up if you're friend or foe, if you see what I mean."

Ben nodded. "Did he speak?"

"No, he didn't say a word for the whole couple of minutes he faced us, but he communicated with Jacy."

"How?" said Ben.

"Telepathy, I guess. Best you ask Jacy about that. He'll be able to give you a better account than me. He said this guy didn't speak through telepathy but shared thoughts. Like giving a picture of what he was thinking without a voice."

"So this encounter lasted just a few minutes?"

"After he shared thoughts with Jacy, he turned and moved away at great speed. There was no way I could keep up. But I have this," he said, passing Ben his phone.

It was a head-to-toe photo, perfectly in focus, of the giant man they had met .

"Wow," said Ben, passing the phone to Claire. "That was quick thinking, Egan, and how on earth did you get such an excellent picture? I would have been shaking like a leaf with that beast of a man ten feet away."

"That was the strangest thing. He only scared the wits out of me when he stepped out of the trees. As soon as we faced him, the fear drained away. It was like we were in an envelope of serene calmness."

"Wish I'd been with you," said Ben.

"You can be. When can you come to my place again? Jacy wants to speak to you. He thinks he might find our human Sasquatch again."

"We could do tomorrow afternoon. The problem is we're being stalked by a tracking device fitted to the car King gave us. Vince King probably knows I'm here now. I'm not bothered, as we're in an area he wants us to be, but tomorrow, if he knows we're over at Tahoe, it'll be trouble for us."

Ben stopped talking and started drawing an imaginary map in midair. "This Meeks Bay. You said it's directly opposite your place on the other shoreline?"

"That's right."

"California?"

"You're correct. The state line runs north to south through Lake Tahoe. My house is on the east coast in Nevada, and Meeks Bay is on the west coast in California."

"How long would it take us to get there from your place?"

"It's about forty-five miles, just under an hour's drive, but we won't be doing that."

"No?"

"I have a pretty decent motorboat to take us straight across. Much more pleasant, and my friend at Meeks Bay will take us up the forest trail. Leave your car in Reno tomorrow, and I'll pick you up, save Mr. King getting all hot and bothered about you being over at my place. What he doesn't know, he can't complain about, right?"

"Are you sure?"

"Of course. Anything to help Jacy and this other poor guy in the mountains. There's a parking lot on Elm Street; shall we say twelve thirty?"

"That's great, Egan, and thanks for the beers. We'll see you tomorrow."

After a short drive without speaking, they pulled back into the driveway of the house, waiting for the garage doors to open. Claire tapped Ben on the shoulder and winked.

"I know what I forgot to ask."

"What?" said Ben, wondering what she was up to.

"My bikini is old and getting uncomfortable. Do you think we could slope off to Reno at some point for me to get another one? I saw a store in the middle of town that sells them, and I need a few other bits and pieces while we're there."

Ben winked back. "I don't want to take too many liberties. Tell you what, let's take a couple of hours off tomorrow to get your stuff from Reno and work late when we get back. It's only fair."

"Okay."

"Don't sulk," he said, raising his voice. "We're here to do a job, right?"

"Okay, okay, I get it. No need to shout at me."

They got out of the car, and Ben slammed the door as hard as he could and stormed up to his room, muttering to himself.

"What matter with him?" said Dorothy, after Ben had almost knocked her flying.

"Nothing to do with you. He's mad at me," said Claire, tilting her head and pushing her hair back while having a good look at the ceiling. There were three smoke detectors in the small room.

FORTY-TWO

Ben's heart raced as he tried to walk without making a sound, but it was almost impossible with a million bone dry pine needles crackling under every step. He'd glimpsed an enormous shadow in the trees. At first there appeared to be nothing but the ghostly trunks of the evergreen monsters until, out of the corner of his eye, something moved. A slight shadowy moving blur. Enough to make him turn his head toward where his peripheral vision had picked it up. He stood, stock still, staring at the spot thirty feet away, but whatever had been moving was still and hiding behind one of the massive trunks or blending in so well that he couldn't pick it out. He stopped breathing for a few seconds and listened, but all he could hear was the sound of the creek, now barely a trickle, and the thumping of his heart working overtime. The steep climb from the track and sudden realization that he was no longer alone stepped up the thudding pulse filling his ears. He stared without blinking till both eyes began to sting, then saw the eyes open. It wasn't hiding. It was there, right in front of him, in plain sight. Two piercing eyes staring back. He looked up as clouds thinned, allowing moonlight to cascade into the clearing. When he looked back at the eyes, he could assess its massive figure as over seven feet tall. It raised a fist and tapped the tree twice, not taking its eyes off him. Ben wondered how fast he could run but remembered Egan's words, 'He turned and moved away at great speed. There was no way I could keep up.' Ben knew that if the huge man attacked, he wouldn't get far. He looked around for a weapon, a branch or rock, but there was none in sight, just a thick blanket of pine needles. The beast knocked on the tree again.

Ben stirred and sat bolt upright in bed, bathed in a cold, clinging sweat.

The double tap sounded again. Ben pulled himself out of bed, still shaking, and opened the door a crack. The door hit his face as Claire pushed her way in.

"What's going on?" said Ben, facing her in his boxer shorts.

She held a finger to her lips and pushed him back against the bed, making him sit on the edge.

"Claire?"

She waved a finger at him, put her hand on his neck, pulled him close, and whispered, "Do you want to see what Jeff West said about you or not?"

Ben rubbed his eyes. "Let me get my dressing gown."

"Don't bother," she whispered. "I've seen every inch of you before, remember? And I'm not staying long. Don't want to give anyone in this house any funny ideas!"

Ben sat back on the bed.

Claire found the page on her phone and passed it to Ben.

Jeff West had been as good as his word and described Ben's account of why he was investigating in Nevada as accurately as if Ben had written it himself.

Ben leaned over and whispered, "Great, we don't have to run away to a hotel. So, get your butt back in your own bedroom, Miss Manson."

"Sure you want me to go, Dr. Sharman?" she said, kissing him on the cheek and laughing.

"Out," he said, and she got up. He could hear her sniggering until the door closed behind her.

He climbed back into bed and considered the implications of what West had written. Yes, it was an expertly crafted piece of journalism, but he considered the title "Eminent British Scientist Joins Hunt for the Nevada Sasquatch" a little tacky. Apart from that, he liked the way West reported his skepticism that the mysterious man-bear actually existed. It would be interesting to see what Vince King thought of the article, and thankfully, there wasn't so much as a hint of West's real motive for visiting the area. He hoped that when West did start to stir the pot and rake some muck on whatever Vince King was up to, he and Claire would be safely back in Moreton-in-Marsh.

He had almost dozed off again when his phone rang. It was Ron.

"Sorry to call so late, but I need to update you on this."

"No problem, I hadn't gone to sleep. What's up?"

"That sewer worker, Bob French."

"What about him? You said he was okay?"

"He was, but I got a call from the hospital. His daughter called an ambulance in the early hours this morning. He's having some weird side effects, which I don't understand because he didn't come into direct contact with that giant rat he encountered under Victoria Park Road."

"What weird effects?"

"His face has erupted with blue spots. Like he's got severe chickenpox, but the spots are bright blue."

"He must have been in some sort of contact for that to happen."

"I told the hospital to move him into an isolation ward, and Chris Williams is going to have him transferred to a remote treatment facility they have. She's taking no risks with this, and it's probably for the best since we still don't really know what we're dealing with here."

"Do some more digging, Ron. I just wish Claire and I were back with you."

"It's all under control, so don't worry. I've got Roger coming down here to help for a day or two. He's going to attend the PM on the murdered man with the hacked-off arm. Sorry, but you know how I am with hospitals and anything medical. I had to get him to do it for me, or I'd be lying on a gurney next to the corpse!"

Ben laughed out loud.

"How's it going at your end?" said Ron.

"Okay." Ben glanced up at the two smoke detectors above the bed. "I had a bit of a bust-up with Claire earlier tonight. She got a bit shirty with me. I just hope it'll smooth itself out in the morning."

"What's up with her?"

"I gave her a few home truths and shouted at her when she sulked. Nothing serious. Saw her about half an hour ago, and she'd calmed down, so all looks good. We're doing a lot of tests." He lowered his voice to a whisper and cupped his hand around his mouth and the phone. "I sent some samples that should be on their way to the lab at Moreton. Sent them through a diplomatic route, thanks to Chris Williams. Excellent courier service—they were here on time and picked it up from the gatehouse at the Barngate building."

"We've received both packages. I understand there was a hitch?"

"No, only one went. I gave it personally to the dispatch rider when he collected it at the gatehouse. Anyway, I'll call you later for an update," Ben said, cutting the call before Ron could say any more about the second real batch of samples they had received. Ben wasn't sure if his phone had been tapped and decided to get a new burner phone on their trip to Reno. He lay back in bed, his head whirling, filled with giant rats, sewers, and a giant hairy man. Eventually, sleep overcame him without another visit to the dark forest.

FORTY-THREE

Katie and Angela waved through the observation window, giving Bob warm smiles, both women trying their best not to cry. He smiled, waved back, and pointed at the clock on the wall, followed by a hand gesture for Katie to go. She shook her head. The sandwich round could wait. The mysterious blue blotches peppering his face scared her and her mother more than anything they had ever known, and Katie vowed not to leave the hospital until the medical staff identified the cause of this weird skin condition and how to treat it.

She was sure it was the hideous creature they witnessed in the sewer trench but couldn't understand how he had become infected by it or why. If it was something contagious from the rat, she had shown none of the strange symptoms.

During her training to work in the water and sewage department, there had been a lengthy session on Weil's disease, a severe form of leptospirosis, a blood infection caused by the bacteria Leptospira. The infection, transmitted via the urine of rats or contaminated water, could cause a variety of symptoms ranging from headaches and vomiting to more severe effects such as kidney failure, pulmonary bleeding syndrome, and, in the worst cases, death. Bob French displayed none of these symptoms, and to her relief, he'd devoured every meal that was served, even asking for double helpings of desserts. He had a healthy appetite, and so far, all tests—blood, urine, and cardiac—were normal.

"There's someone to see you," said the duty nurse. "Ron Logan, from Moreton Scientific Investigation."

Katie nodded, waved, and mouthed to her father through the observation window that she would be back soon, then followed the nurse to an empty office.

"I won't be long, Mum," she said. "Just got to have a word with the scientist. Hopefully, he'll have good news about how to treat Dad."

"Sorry to disturb you," said Ron, shaking her hand.

Katie looked at him, puzzled, as he appeared more ill than her father. Sweat beaded on Ron's forehead, and she thought she could detect a slight tremble in his voice.

"Are you okay, Mr. Logan?"

"Sorry. Do I look that bad? I have a thing about hospitals. I wouldn't normally step inside the door of this place, but needs must, and I have to ask you a few questions."

"Shall we go outside to talk?" she said, concerned that Ron might keel over at any moment.

The look of relief on Ron's face said it all, and they found a bench in a small open courtyard attached to the isolation ward. Ron fumbled in his pocket and pulled out a packet of Marlboros, offering one to Katie.

She pointed at a large "no smoking" sign on the wall opposite. "Thank you, but I don't smoke."

Ron pushed the packet back into his coat pocket, pulled out a handkerchief, and wiped his steamed-up glasses.

"Sorry," he said. "Can you tell me everything you did and saw when you went down the sewer at Victoria Park Road?"

Katie relived the event in great detail, describing the giant rat as rodent-shaped but with a more muscular body and a distorted head, bulging red eyes, a red tail, and rows of razor-sharp teeth, more akin to a carnivore such as a dog or fox.

"You said neither you nor your father physically came into contact with the rat?"

"No. After Dad screamed, it ran off. Dad fell backward onto me, and the torch rolled into the trench. By the time I pulled it back out of the trench and looked up the tunnel, it had gone. I think Dad scared it off. A good thing he screamed. It was squaring up to attack him."

"Were you wearing protective gear?"

"Yes, all the time we were down there."

"Gloves?"

"Of course. That's something we're most careful about. Weil's disease and exposed hands aren't a good idea."

"Quite," said Ron. "You said the rat was in the water at the bottom of the trench. Which way was the water flowing?"

"Away from us. The tunnel slopes away from the entry point toward Hackney Wick a couple of miles farther up Victoria Park Road."

"What about the flow? Was there any chance of it pooling in that area and not moving?"

"No, a constant flow. I think you're looking at whether infected water could have come our way?"

"Exactly, and that may be the case, as we don't know where the enormous rat or rats, if there are more of them, were before you entered the sewer. Possibly upstream."

Katie shuddered, imagining several of the creatures running along the sewer.

"How did you realize it was about to attack Bob?"

"After it looked up at us, it hunkered down, lowering the front of its body with its hindquarters raised higher than the front. I saw its muscles tense up. You know, like a lion does just before it charges at a zebra or antelope. It flattened back its ears, and its ghastly red tail flicked in and out of the trench. I'm convinced it would have attacked Dad if he hadn't scared it off by screaming."

"Did it do anything else before it ran off, or make a noise?"

"It hissed at him like a cat would. It was the most horrible thing I've ever heard."

"Interesting. When it hissed at him, how far was it from your father?"

"Three feet. Maybe four. When it started doing that, he fell backward onto me."

"Could you see it when it was making this noise?"

"No. Dad was backing into me and blocked my view. To be honest, I'm glad I couldn't see it when it made that noise. Dad said its face was pure evil."

"You were lucky you couldn't see it. I believe it breathed out contaminated vapor and spat water droplets as it was threatening your father, and that, I believe, is the cause of his current condition."

She held her hand over her mouth for a few seconds, then drew it away. "What will happen to him?"

"We're looking for ways to slow down, halt, and reverse any effects."

Ron left the hospital with skin swabs, blood, and urine samples taken from Bob French and was about to get into his car when he spotted a note lodged under the windscreen wiper. He sat in the car and read it.

'Shouldn't you be at home making sure Graham is safe?'

FORTY-FOUR

Getting away from the lab hadn't been a problem as Kelvin had been called away by Vince King, who hadn't appeared since he asked them to vacate the building after the so-called security breach, and Elsa Smyth didn't seem interested in whether they were there or not. Ben casually informed her they were taking a couple of hours off to buy some essentials and would be working late to make up the time. It was more to corroborate what he and Claire had discussed before, for the benefit of anyone who'd been listening in on their conversation.

"Time's up, Claire. Egan's just sent me a text. He's waiting outside."

"Just a minute," she said from inside the booth. "I can't decide whether to buy the red or the green bikini. What do you think?"

"Just grab one and let's go," he said, looking at his watch again. "We've got important business; it's not a shopping trip!"

The curtain flew back, and she stood with a radiant smile. "Red it is," she grinned, standing in one of the skimpiest bikinis Ben had ever seen. "To go with the color of your face."

Ben marched off and shouted back, "I'll be in the car with Egan. Be there in two minutes, or we're going without you."

He stepped into the baking heat on the sidewalk and vowed never to go shopping with her again. Arriving an hour before Egan was due, Ben spent most of the hour outside the same changing booth as Claire seemed to try on half the contents of the store. How Dave, her boyfriend, ever put up with her was a mystery, he thought. The man must have the patience of Job.

Ben breathed a sigh of relief as he sank into the cool embrace of the car's air conditioning, grateful to escape the scorching sun and the suffocating atmosphere of the store.

"Claire will be here any second," said Ben.

Egan pointed at the shop. "You sure about that?" he said.

Ben looked in and past the window displays. He could just make out Claire, laden with bags, browsing through a rack of blouses.

"Sorry about this, Egan. Two minutes, and I'll be back with her," he said, stepping back out. A minute later, Claire was almost thrown into the back seat. Egan sat bemused, shaking his head.

"You didn't have to push me out like that. It was so embarrassing," she protested.

Ben buckled himself into the seat belt, turned, and said, "Ever seen *A Bug's Life*, Egan?"

"The Pixar film for kids?"

"That's the one," said Ben. "Claire is like that moth at the porch light—when she sees a clothes shop, 'I can't help myself!'"

Egan roared with laughter, and even Claire had to smile.

Ben remained stony-faced. "Can we get going?" he said. "She's wasted enough time already."

After they cleared the bustle of Reno, Highway 580 was quiet.

"We've decided to go back to the UK in the next couple of days, and I need a favor," said Ben.

"What can I do for you?" said Egan.

"My staff member Ron, who's working on the London part of this investigation, has received another threat, and I've instructed him to step back from the case. Extract himself from London, to be precise.

He'll still be working on it back at our headquarters at Moreton-in-Marsh."

"So you need to go back and take his place?"

"Not exactly. I need to work at my own facility without being watched and spied on by Vince King, and yes, I need to take up the slack in London as well."

"Let me guess, you need a ride to the airport?"

"I won't use Vince's company car for obvious reasons. I don't want to book a cab or hire a car, as it could be traceable, and his sidekick Herbie Lomax is more than capable of tracking us."

"Not a problem, Ben. Just let me know when. Which airport?"

"Vegas. I can book a direct flight when we get there and hopefully, that won't give them any time to stop us leaving. I'm being paranoid, but King has gone to great lengths to get us here, and after seeing him lose it in the lab after we visited you at your home, I don't feel I can trust him not to do something stupid if we decide to leave before he's achieved his aim."

"Which is publicity."

"I believe you were right. His motive is publicity linked to corruption. Getting back home will benefit Jacy, and I'll be able to work faster to find a cure, antidote, or some other way of counteracting the infection. If there's anything I need, or you have more information, then we can always arrange a conference call or a dispatch rider to pick anything up."

At Egan's house, they made their way straight to the jetty at the bottom of a steep track through the garden.

"Isn't Jacy coming with us?" asked Ben.

"He's already at Meeks Bay on the other side. He's gone ahead to set up the gear we'll need."

"Wow," said Claire, pulling out her phone for photos. "You really do live in paradise. It makes you wonder."

"About what?" said Ben, lowering the field kit and a backpack into the motorboat, which was also what he hadn't expected. He stepped back, admiring the sleek blue and white sixteen-foot hull with "The Skimmer" emblazoned in silver and red on the side. A veritable monster of a powerboat that wouldn't look out of place, heading out to sea from a coast guard station, responding to a mayday call.

"Makes me realize how little of this planet we get to see in our lives," said Claire.

"Just enjoy the experience while you're here and make the most of it," said Egan. "Wait till we get farther out on the water; you can look back and appreciate what can't be seen from the house."

He held his hand out for Claire and helped her into the boat. She would have shrugged it off but accepted, as the last time she refused help like this, she ended up half-submerged in a freezing cold Welsh reservoir, and she liked Egan. It would be rude to refuse his gentlemanly help.

"One heck of a boat, Egan," said Ben, admiring the plush seats and large twin outboard motors. "She's a beauty."

"She is, but don't get too excited. We won't be at full throttle all the way across." Egan saw the disappointed look on Ben's face. "There are rules on Tahoe. Five miles an hour max in the 'no wake zone' which extends six hundred feet from the shoreline, and there are regular patrol boats watching. There's no limit after that but you have to be sensible," he said with a mischievous grin. He opened a large locker and passed them a life jacket each. "Not compulsory unless you're under the age of twelve, but it's my boat, and the captain says you must wear one. Plenty have drowned over the years. The water's freezing compared to the air temperature, and many drownings are caused by cold water shock, which is the reason you're putting on those life jackets."

Claire groaned; she was hot enough without a bulky life jacket clinging like a thermal blanket.

"Don't you fret, Miss Manson. There'll be a nice cooling breeze as we make our way over. You'll be glad you've got that jacket on."

The boat pulled away from the jetty, and just a few hundred

yards out, they looked back at the vast expanse of forest climbing away from the shore into the rising hills and distant peaks.

"I said you'd like the view out here. I'm so grateful my family had the sense to put a stake in the ground here."

Egan throttled up, and the engines roared into action. Claire sat back smiling, her dark hair streaming back like a fluttering flag in the wind, and she was glad of the life jacket.

When they reached the midpoint, Egan reduced speed.

"What's up?" said Ben, who had been enjoying the exhilarating ride.

Egan pointed north at a fast-approaching boat. "Just being cautious," he said, opening a locker and pulling out a pair of binoculars. "Not the coastguard but looks official. Don't often see boat crews in combat gear holding assault rifles and one with a bullhorn. Think we may be in a spot of bother, although I may be wrong and it's a false alarm and they're going to sail straight past. Any funny business, and I'm going to get the hell away from them. This baby can outrun their tin can—I hope. Both of you better sit down, as I may have to floor it, and I don't want one of you going over the side."

"Stop your boat," came the order from the approaching boat.

Ben saw rifles being raised. "Better do as they say, Egan," said Ben. "Can't see you outrunning bullets."

The boat with five crew members was now only a hundred yards away.

Ben shouted, "Egan. It's Herbie Lomax. How the hell did he know we were here?"

FORTY-FIVE

"I don't like this," said Claire.

Egan pushed the throttle to maximum, and the twin Mercury Verado engines screamed into life, lifting the front end out of the water and slamming Ben and Claire back into their seats.

"Hold on to your sunglasses, folks!" shouted Egan over the roar of the engines.

Ben glanced over his shoulder. The other boat was in pursuit and keeping up with them.

"I don't think we're going to lose them, Egan. They've got some beef under the hood."

Egan raised a hand with his thumb pointing up. "I haven't reached full speed yet."

Ben took another look behind. They were pulling away from their pursuers, with Egan's boat skimming across the lake at full speed. Out of the corner of his eye, he saw Claire's hair streaming out behind like a mass of writhing snakes.

"I'm going to call ahead," shouted Egan. "Someone will pick us up and drive us away to a place where they won't find us, so be prepared to make a swift exit from the boat when we reach there. I'll land us on the beach near the jetty. No time to mess around tying up. Friends will sort that out for me later."

Ben looked again over the twin outboard motors. Through the wake and spray, the chasing boat receded far behind, no longer within touching distance but still chasing. Egan's powerful craft would give them valuable seconds to jump out and make a run for it to whoever was waiting on the other side. Why was Herbie Lomax chasing them? Was there any point in running? He would catch up eventually, even if they eluded him today. Ben had visions of being arrested, facing trumped-up charges, and federal agencies framing him and Claire. Prison, never to see home again.

The negativity swirled around for five minutes as the boat bounced and bucked across the waves.

"Get ready," said Egan, swinging the boat to the right and pointing it at a small gravel beach. He cut the motors and raised the twin engines clear of the water as they glided in, wedging the boat on the sandy shore.

They leaped out and ran up the beach, trying to get purchase on the soft sand. It leveled out onto a dirt road.

"There," shouted Egan, pointing at a dusty pickup fifty yards ahead. Ben looked out at the lake; the second boat had almost reached the jetty up ahead. Would they be able to get in the back of the pickup and get past the jetty in time?

With the tailgate left down, Egan and Ben leaped onto the flatbed and hauled Claire up with them.

"Go!" screamed Egan to the driver. The pickup lurched forward. Ben watched three of the men jump onto the jetty and start running.

"Keep your heads down," shouted Ben.

The pickup passed the jetty before the three men reached the road, leaving them choking in a cloud of dust.

"That was too damned close for my liking," said Claire, lifting her head above the boarded side of the flatbed.

The pickup suddenly braked hard. Claire tumbled over, banging her head on the back of the cab. The vehicle came to a halt, and for a few seconds, dust caught up with them, blinding everyone.

"What are you stopping for?" shouted Egan, hammering a fist on the driver's cab roof. There was no answer. When the dust cleared, Ben looked to the front of the pickup. The driver and Jacy were standing with their hands in the air. Two armed men had their rifles trained on them.

"All of you, get out," came an order from the front.

Reluctantly, they climbed down, and Ben and Egan stood with their hands up.

"Miss Manson. Hands in the air, please," said one man, as she was busily rubbing her head where she had collided with the back of the cab.

The armed men marched them back to the jetty, where Herbie Lomax sat at a picnic table.

"You can put your hands down now and please take a seat."

He gave a signal to the five men surrounding them, and they walked back to the jetty, taking Egan, Jacy and the driver with them.

"Sorry, it had to be like this," said Herbie.

"Had to be like what?" said Claire, still rubbing the lump on her head.

"Cloak and dagger. Chasing you across the lake."

"You make it sound like a joke," said Claire, glaring at him.

"What's this all about, Herbie? Is Vince paying you enough?" said Ben.

Herbie laughed and didn't stop for quite some time. He removed his sunglasses and wiped both eyes.

"I'm not on Vince King's payroll."

"Sure about that?" said Ben. "It sure looks that way to me."

"And I understand why you think that. I'm working with Vince King, not for him."

"What's this all about?" said Ben.

"What I am about to tell you is classified, so it stays between us, right?" Herbie looked hard at both of them in turn.

"I think you can take that as read, Herbie," said Ben.

"I asked my men to take Egan, Jacy and the other fella to the jetty. This discussion is not for their ears."

"Understood," said Ben. Egan and the pickup driver were escorted away. Herbie watched them go, took off his sunglasses, and turned to Ben.

"Okay. My initial investigation was into the sightings of the elusive man-bear and the problems associated with the deformities centered on Pyramid Lake following the meteor strike at Teakettle Junction. At the same time I looked into this for the department, another different investigation was being carried out by colleagues covering this state that I cannot discuss."

Ben nodded and asked, "When you say this state, do you mean Nevada or California?"

"Sorry, Nevada. I forgot we're sitting here in the Golden State. But that's as far as I can reveal for the other investigation. While working with Vince, I discovered something unrelated to my investigation, reported it back to my superiors, and they immediately sent me to our headquarters in DC to be briefed on the other secret investigation. From that point on, I was working on both investigations."

"I can hazard a guess what the other investigation entailed," said Ben.

Herbie shook his head. "Guess all you like, but you'll not get a confirmation from me. As part of my original mission, I went along with Vince's idea to bring you across to investigate, which turned out to be the right decision as Vince's team was getting nowhere fast."

"I don't think he wanted us for our investigative skills," said Ben.

"And what makes you think that, Dr. Sharman?"

"Just my sixth sense yelling loud and clear, Herbie. So loud it makes my ears ache."

Herbie just smiled.

"So why have you chased us across the lake, armed to the teeth?"

"I've been keeping a close eye on you to see if you come up with any tangible evidence that may indicate a threat to American citizens, and for your own protection."

"Protection? Protection from what?"

"Nothing specific, but if you were to discover or even disrupt the second investigation, there may be a risk to you."

"In what way?"

"I am not at liberty to discuss that, but rest assured you have had considerable protection while you are here. I know you are considering going back to the UK as soon as possible, in the next couple of days, once you have gathered more samples and any other information you can glean, right?"

"What if we do?"

"I would ask, sorry, strongly request that you stay a little longer and help me out. And when I say 'me,' I'm talking about the United States of America."

"Help you out how?" said Ben, realizing the request coming from an official of Homeland Security meant he had no choice.

"By continuing the work you came here to do."

"Nothing else?"

Herbie laughed. "No, I don't want you doing a James Bond on Vince or anyone else. Just try to keep the peace with him. Play along, do your tests, and as soon as I give you the nod, you can go home. Do we have an agreement?"

"Do we have a choice?"

Herbie said nothing.

"I'll take that as a no, then," said Ben. "Do we both have to stay, or can Claire go home? I don't like the idea that she may be in danger."

"No way, José! You're not getting rid of me," said Claire. "Herbie, don't bother answering because I'm not leaving anytime soon."

Herbie shrugged his shoulders.

Ben laughed. "I can never get rid of her. Herbie, you still haven't answered my question. Why did you chase us across the lake?"

"Two things, well, three actually. The first I have already done, to get you to hang around a while longer. The second, to accompany you into the hills," he said, pointing at the rising forest behind the bay, "to see if there's anything in this man-bear myth. And thirdly, to protect you as you are woefully under-prepared if there is such an entity lurking up there."

"You want to come with us?"

"We are coming with you, or should I say, you're coming with us. Just waiting for transport to arrive. We're going on a bear hunt, Dr. Sharman."

FORTY-SIX

Omar Malik surveyed London from his sixtieth-floor apartment in The Shard, not taking in the fabulous view from the tallest building in Western Europe, but deep in troubled thought. Through twenty-five years of hard work and trust-building, Omar transformed his business from humble beginnings to blue-chip status, which resulted in unstinting loyalty from his high-profile clients. He demanded the very best from anyone employed by his company and also expected all his clients to act honorably. The news his personal assistant had just delivered broke that expectation, annoying him more than he ever thought possible.

He treated his clients with utmost respect and courtesy, ensuring they received a service that was almost impossible for his rivals to replicate, going the extra mile at every stage. When one of his major clients had a serious kitchen fire, he immediately had them taken to an upmarket hotel and restored the family home to its former glory, even though the house was not part of the insurance package for the client's multi-million-pound restaurant chain. He would often invite clients to spend time at one of his luxury villas in the South of France and Italy, and every client received high-quality, seasonal gifts.

"Believe in fate, but always lean forward to allow fate to see you," was the saying his father, Tariq, always quoted when Omar first ventured into the insurance business.

He saw every act of *kindness* as leaning forward to catch fate's eye, an investment that invoked the power of reciprocity, where human beings instinctively strive to repay any favor bestowed upon them. His repayment was their continued loyalty and support, and one of his latest customers had just broken that trust in the worst possible way.

The note, delivered to the office from his cousin Azra, inviting him to lunch at The Savoy, resulted in some interesting but disturbing news. Azra's expertise as an auctioneer of high-quality antiques and memorabilia was requested by one of her regular clients to give her expert opinion on sale items for auction. During her evaluation of several antiques and curios, the client mentioned rumors of some unique photos that had appeared on the black market. She was aware of Omar's connection with the Museum of Alien Life and thought the information would be useful to him, even though she couldn't corroborate whether the rumor had any substance.

Omar thanked her for lunch and the information and made some phone calls, confirming his worst fears after the identity of the person offering the photos for sale was revealed.

He continued to stare across Central London, processing the facts. The flagrant breach of trust was unforgivable, and he soon reached a conclusion, then a decision. After making another phone call, he unlocked the drinks cabinet, poured himself a large measure of Macallan Oscuro single malt, took a sip and smiled, satisfied that the balance of honor would be restored.

FORTY-SEVEN

Two hours after the meeting at Meeks Bay, three black Terrain Crossover SUVs pulled into the car lot next to the jetty.

"You and Miss Manson in the middle vehicle, Egan and Jacy in the rear vehicle. I'll be in the lead car," said Herbie, handing each of them a headset radio mic and a stab vest.

"Really?" said Ben, holding up the vest.

"Absolutely. When we go into unknown territory, it's a requirement. Don't waste time; just get it on, and we can go."

Ben saw it was useless to argue and pulled the straps tight, feeling slightly claustrophobic.

"Okay," said Herbie. "Questions before we head up into the forest?"

"How do you know where to go?" asked Egan.

"We've been tracking you for days, Egan. We know exactly where you've been, what you've discussed, and, more to the point, where you were heading today."

Egan laughed. "What happened to the land of the free?"

Herbie smiled. "It's because of the likes of us you are free. Now, anything else?"

"Do we have weapons in case we're attacked?" asked Claire, still trying to figure out how to put the vest on.

Ben took it off her, turned it inside out, and put it over her head, tightening the straps one by one.

"How embarrassing," whispered Claire. "I feel like a kid being dressed for school."

Ben smiled and patted the top of her head.

"My team is armed. Egan and Jacy are licensed to carry weapons, but not you, Dr. Sharman, or Miss Manson. I think we have enough firepower between us. Now, if you have any more questions, please use the headsets I just gave you. We're moving out."

Ben loaded the field kit retrieved from Egan's boat and climbed into the back of the middle SUV with Claire.

"Jeff Easter," said the driver, arching his hand backward. They both shook it. "And my co-pilot is Penny Walters. Hold on to your hats, guys, this is going to be a rough ride."

Claire was about to protest, as she hadn't put her seatbelt on, when the SUV took off, slamming her back into the seat.

The forest track up the hillside behind Meeks Bay was as Jeff Easter had predicted: rough. They rocked and rolled their way along the track, barely wide enough for the SUVs, and at one point Ben and Claire left their seats, hitting their heads on the roof lining. They eventually reached an open patch of waste ground where the track ended. All three vehicles peeled off and parked in scrub grass surrounded by thick forest.

"Bloody hell, Jeff," said Claire, rubbing the top of her head. "Was there any need to drive like a lunatic to get here? I feel ill, and I whacked my head."

"Sorry, Miss Manson, but you would have felt much worse if we took our time," said Jeff. "Do you feel well enough to walk?"

"Fresh air will sort me out," said Claire, swinging her legs out of the door.

"Enjoy that?" said Herbie Lomax with a wide grin, which soon disappeared when Claire gave him a look that could curdle milk. "I'll take that as a no, then," he said. "My apologies. My fault. I told the drivers to get up here as quickly as possible, and they did. The next stage will be at a more sedate pace, provided Egan doesn't decide to take it at a gallop."

"You want me to lead?" asked Egan.

"Of course, my friend. You and your son know the terrain and the spot where you met our man-bear. Makes perfect sense to me."

Egan nodded.

The three drivers opened the roof boxes on the SUVs and started unloading various bags and boxes. Everyone was given backpacks and something to carry.

"We won't be coming back to the vehicles until we conclude this search," said Herbie. "So we may be up in the hills overnight if needed."

Claire was about to protest when Ben shook his head.

"Problem, Miss Manson?" asked Herbie.

"No problem," said Ben, ignoring Claire's furious glare.

"Good. We've wasted enough time. Egan, please lead the way."

"One last question," said Ben. "What about Vince King? He went apeshit when we went missing for a couple of hours before."

"Don't you worry about King. I asked you to carry out some field work, and he won't argue with me. Now, can we get a move on?"

There was a definite track for the first half mile through scrubland, rocks, and pine debris before it petered out, but Egan didn't falter and continued up the thirty-degree slope, skirting around fallen trees and ravines that scarred the hillside. The group of eight climbed steadily upward through dense ancient forest for over an hour, then the terrain leveled out and a clearing appeared.

"How far to go?" asked Herbie.

"We've come about halfway," said Egan. "Shall we take a break?"

Claire decided for them, throwing her backpack down and almost collapsing on the ground.

Herbie laughed. "Ten minutes, then we move on. Make sure you drink plenty of water."

Ben watched Egan and Jacy huddled together in deep conversation, then Jacy walked over to him and sat down.

"He's watching us," said Jacy, "from the trees ahead. He's been watching us ever since we started trekking through deeper forest."

"The man-bear?"

"No bear, just a man, and yes, he's watching us. I can sense it and something else."

"What?"

"There are three of them, and I don't want Herbie or his men to know."

"Three? Are you sure?"

"Certain. Two males and a female. The one me and Dad met before, a female, and another male who's not so friendly and has a more advanced infection. Could be dangerous."

"Shouldn't we tell Herbie? He needs to know if we're in danger."

"The friendlier one will keep the unstable one in check for now, and I don't want Herbie's men shooting first and asking questions later. Don't forget, these are not monsters; they are people who need treating. But Herbie's men have killer man-bears in their heads, and I'm sure somebody will end up dead if they know where they are."

"They'll have to find out at some point."

"I'm going to give Herbie the slip and talk to the three people watching us and make them realize how dangerous it is for them. Hopefully, you can reverse the infection and get them back to normal before something bad happens."

"Meaning?"

"One of them gets shot by Herbie's crew, or the man with the advanced symptoms becomes uncontrollable."

Ben glanced across at Herbie and his men.

"How do you propose to get away, Jacy?"

"Gotta take a leak at some point," he said with a smile. "I might just get choosy about how far away from this clearing I need to go for privacy."

Jacy walked across to Herbie and spoke briefly. Herbie nodded, and Jacy stepped through a gap in the trees and was gone.

FORTY-EIGHT

The shrill cries of a dark-eyed Junco and the constant chirping of the colorful western tanager filled the garden of the log cabin high above Rubicon Bay. With every table filled with seeds and nuts, she waited for the birds to arrive and bring her little patch of paradise alive.

The log cabin, perched on a prominent ridge, came as a complete surprise to Amanda Dooley when a distant relative, who emigrated to California five decades before, left the cabin and a considerable sum to Amanda, her nearest surviving relative.

Her initial thought, after discovering her inheritance, was to sell the property and benefit from a sizable amount of cash. While considering her options, curiosity got the better of her, and she took the long flight from the UK to look at her new property. It was love at first sight, and she decided on the spot to keep the cabin for a couple of years before selling it. That love affair started in the fall of 2005, and it had been Amanda Dooley's holiday destination ever since, where she spent the maximum ninety days a year allowed without a visa at her second home.

She slid back in the rocker on the veranda, cracked open a second can of ice-cold beer, looked down the long garden, and cursed, remembering she'd left her glasses on the kitchen table. She sat for a while, enjoying the beer, and taking in the sounds from the surrounding pines, with woodpeckers drumming in their constant search for grubs hiding under bark, and the high-pitched cries of tiny chickadees that would soon take advantage of the nets filled with nuts hanging from her bird tables.

Amanda smiled at her good fortune and thought back to the tiny, terraced cottage where she spent her early years in the Welsh Valleys before moving to the hustle and bustle of London. Now, she was in her own log cabin high above Lake Tahoe, knocking back a few beers and enjoying the abundant wildlife. Who would have thought it?

The slight pine-laced breeze in the shadow cast by the deep veranda's canopy made the temperature perfect. Her eyelids closed, and she was snoring gently within minutes, still gripping the half-full can of beer.

As she drifted and daydreamed, her mind wandered to her garden, which was adorned with flowers and birds, and now boasted a fountain in the midst of the grass. Rising from her seat, she gazed at the fountain and gently inserted her hand into the refreshing water. She awoke with a start. Silently cursing, she tilted the almost empty can upright and let her wet sleeve drip dry in the heat, dropping it to the side. She'd change it when she went in for her glasses. With her other hand, she swept most of the pool of beer off the table and laughed to herself. Fountain of beer in the garden, she mused.

Lifting the third can, she was about to pull the ring when a noise from the farthest bird table caught her ear. She squinted down the garden and saw a large brown blur.

"Damned bears," she whispered and reached under the table.

With her eyes almost screwed shut she could make out the hazy figure with two legs and arms and a large head, standing and helping itself to the bird food she'd just put out.

Rising slowly, Amanda raised the loaded shotgun to her eye, and pushed the stock back into her shoulder. Having decided it essential to know how to use a gun correctly in such a remote area surrounded by wildlife, she'd taken lessons at the local rifle range. She was a very good shot with her glasses on but without them, she was no Annie Oakley, but that didn't worry her. She didn't want to kill the bear, just frighten it off. As a precaution, she'd preloaded with cartridges filled with rock salt, producing a loud bang and a cloud of salt particles, just enough to scare any wild animal away without hurting them.

"Get out, you varmint," she screamed at the top of her voice. Continuing to help itself to the contents of the bird table, the bear then moved to a second table ten feet closer to the veranda.

"Damned cheek of it," she cursed and fired off the first round, shattering the idyllic sounds of the forest, which were replaced by the sounds of fleeing birds' wings.

Amanda realized the noise the bear made was very 'un-bear-like' after it stopped feeding. Had she heard right? Of course, it was just a growl. Bears don't speak, so she dismissed the idea that the bear had just sworn at her.

"I said, get out of my damned garden!" she screamed again. "You deaf or what?"

This time, there was no mistaking the bear's response.

"Bitch," it growled and charged on its hind legs.

Amanda knew the middle bird table was a fair distance away, but she would have to negotiate the table and several plant pots to reach the back door twelve feet behind her. It was an easy decision; she wouldn't get there quick enough. After witnessing bears running at full pelt in the past, she knew there was no way she would get to the porch door and safely into the cabin before it was upon her.

Putting pressure on the trigger, she braced her legs. The bear would have to get real close for the rock salt to have any physical effect on the beast, and it didn't seem fazed by the noise of the first discharge. She cursed herself for using rock salt cartridges and not getting her glasses earlier, vowing that if she got out of this situation alive, she would hang her glasses around her neck and keep the second chamber of the shotgun loaded with metal shot. As she watched the bear approach, everything slowed down as the adrenaline flowed, her senses on high alert. Had it called her a bitch? She threw that question aside as the bear thundered closer. She could feel the hairs on the back of her neck rise, and took a sharp breath and held it in, waiting for the very last moment to fire. Too soon and the rock salt would just be harmless dust; too late, and this enormous mass of muscle and fur would be upon her. She'd seen bear kills on the mountainside above the cabin, deer almost ripped apart by powerful jaws and huge razor-sharp claws, and knew if she mistimed the shot, she might end up in shreds herself. She could see better as it approached, and as it was almost up to the edge of the veranda, she saw the human traits in its face as it came into focus. It wasn't a bear!

"No!" it shouted. She stepped backward in shock, but with pressure already on the trigger, the involuntary jolt made her tense up, and the gun discharged at point-blank range.

FORTY-NINE

"Jeff, go see what's taking Jacy so long," said Herbie, pointing into the dense trees, "and make sure your safety catch is off just in case."

"I'll go with him," said Penny Walters, standing and unholstering her service weapon.

Herbie nodded and looked across at Ben. "What were you two discussing before he went to take a leak?"

"Just chit-chat."

"About what?"

"Taking samples, what to look out for. The usual stuff when you're searching for clues," said Ben, hoping he sounded convincing. The look in Herbie's eyes said otherwise.

"Sure that was all?"

"What are you getting at, Herbie?" Ben could feel Herbie's eyes almost burning into his skull.

"Seemed like you two were planning on doing something."

"We were. Planning what we needed to look out for."

Herbie nodded and looked away. The unsubtle accusation and the silence in the clearing made the next couple of minutes uncomfortable. Ben reflected on their long-distance investigation, which, after just a few days, was far from what he expected, having been misled, followed and spied upon. The main aspect of the investigation that puzzled him was the difference in the rate of spread. In London, it moved quickly through the food chain but thankfully had not crossed into the human population, apart from the sewer worker, which authorities had contained. The same had been present much longer in this corner of Nevada and California but without the rapid spread. Why? Climate, water quality, animal and human densities? Could it be something else he was missing, or maybe a combination of components? He needed more samples and raw data, but with Herbie and Vince King having their own agendas, it was like trying to read a book while people kept setting fire to the pages.

Twenty minutes passed before the two agents returned without Jacy. Herbie walked over to Ben after Penny Walters confirmed they could find no trace of him.

"Okay, Ben, time to let us into your conversation with Jacy just before he left us. And before you spin some cock-and-bull story, just remember I have been doing this for a long time and interrogated hundreds of suspects, and I know when someone is holding back."

"So now I'm a suspect?" said Ben.

"You know what I mean. Quit stalling and tell us where he went."

Ben knew he had no option and also felt troubled that something might have happened to Jacy. He was about to speak when Jeff Easter beat him to it. "Look!" he shouted, pointing into the trees and raising his rifle.

Jacy stepped out from the trees with his hands raised, followed by a huge hairy man, also with his hands held up.

"Lower your weapon," said Jacy. "He's unarmed and no threat." He stepped in front of the giant stranger, blocking any chance of a shot.

Herbie gestured to Jeff Easter, who nodded, then eased the rifle to his side.

Herbie assessed the strange man standing close to seven feet tall and built like a three-hundred-pound linebacker.

"Who's your friend, Jacy?" said Herbie.

"John Drake. As you can see, he's no bear."

They all looked at Drake, who stood expressionless, with piercing brown eyes fixed on Ben through a mass of coarse black hair with a blue sheen, covering almost every inch of facial skin. "You can help us?" said Drake in a low whisper.

"I'll try my best," said Ben, taking a step closer.

"Stay back, Dr. Sharman," warned Herbie, but Ben took no notice, moving forward, reducing the twenty-yard gap between himself and John Drake.

Herbie glanced sideways and nodded to one agent. In a split second, two things happened. John Drake grabbed Jacy, lifting him off his feet, and ran toward the trees. A shot rang out from the agent's rifle, and Drake dropped Jacy roughly to the ground, stumbled to his knees, pulled a tranquilizer dart out of his thigh, then rose quickly and ran off, crashing through branches and disappearing.

"After him," ordered Herbie. "He won't get far."

Three agents ran into the trees.

"You idiot!" shouted Jacy. "I told you not to shoot."

"He'll be okay, just a tranquilizer to knock him out," said Herbie, offering his hand to pull Jacy up out of the dirt.

Jacy ignored the gesture and sprang to his feet, fists clenched.

"He was no threat. He and the others need help."

"Others? What others?" said Herbie.

"There were two others with him. You've probably scared them off with your heavy-handed tactics."

"You should have thought of that before you snuck off," said Herbie, who tapped his throat mic. "Lomax to Edwards. Any sign of John Drake?"

"We're following his trail, but boy can he move. That dart should have taken him down or at least slowed him up, but he's way ahead. We'll keep following till he drops."

"Just be careful. There are two others with him. Keep me posted. I can track your location on the scanner. We'll make our way toward you. Lomax out."

"There's another problem," said Jacy. "There's been a shooting over at Rubicon Bay," Jacy said, "Involving another infected man."

"Explain?"

"If you hadn't gone Wild West on us, I was about to tell you."

"Well, you can tell me now. Stop wasting time."

"There are several living in the hills in this area. Some are just showing small signs of change. Some are well-developed with the infection. They're telepathic and are staying out of harm's way, or at least trying to. Someone just shot Brett Daniels over at Rubicon Bay. Not fatally, but enough to immobilize him for a while. The woman who shot him called for an ambulance."

"Shit, I need to stop that."

"What? He needs help. The man's been wounded."

Herbie pulled a phone out of his backpack. The conversation was rapid fire, with Herbie barking orders to someone. He put the phone in his pocket. "We need to move out now."

"I don't understand," said Ben. "What about John Drake?"

"Three of my agents in pursuit will take care of him. We need to get over to Rubicon Bay and get to this wounded man before this gets out."

"Is that all you're interested in? Keeping the lid on it, and for what?" said Ben.

Herbie snapped back. "So you can do your work without a plague of reporters buzzing around your arse. Now get back in the vehicle. We're leaving right now."

Claire strapped herself in as soon as she got in the back of the SUV and suffered an even rougher ride as the driver drove at breakneck speed down the deeply rutted track, even though she was squeezed between Ben and Penny Walters. She saw the smile on Jeff Easter's face; he seemed to revel in the roller coaster ride from hell.

The SUV reached the main road and tore off south toward

Rubicon Bay. Ben looked across at Claire and almost laughed. Her hair had somehow twisted across her face with the rocking and rolling of the cab along the nightmare ride from the forest high above the coastal road. She looked almost as hairy as the enormous man being hunted by Lomax's agents.

FIFTY

"You and Claire stay put," said Herbie, as the SUV screeched to a halt in front of Amanda Dooley's log cabin. Easter and Walters leaped out, weapons raised. Herbie signaled, and the two agents took opposite sides of the house and disappeared from view.

Ben watched through the dust-caked windshield as Herbie ran in a peculiar half-crouch to the edge of the porch and was amazed at how agile he was, considering he was such a big man.

Herbie approached the front porch and moved to the side of the half-open front door, flattening himself against the wall. He tapped his throat mic, whispered something into it, and then swung himself into the doorway, gun sweeping left and right as he entered.

"What the hell are we doing here?" Claire asked. "We're supposed to be on a scientific investigation, not part of a posse with Wyatt Earp and his deputies!"

Ben laughed. "The same thought crossed my mind," he said, his gaze fixed on the cabin door.

"I have to get out," Claire said. "That ride made me feel sick."

"Earp told us to stay put," Ben replied.

"I don't care what that idiot said. I'm getting out unless you want me to puke all over you." She stepped out, staggered a few steps, pressed both hands on her knees, and took several deep breaths.

"That bad, eh?" Ben asked, now standing beside her with his hand on her back.

"I'll be okay. Just need a minute and some fresh air."

Herbie appeared at the side of the house and beckoned them to follow him.

"There's nobody here. Looks like Brett Daniels took the woman," he said. They walked through a small wicket gate into a large garden open to the forest behind. A shotgun lay in the grass just off the wooden veranda, next to an open first aid kit.

"I believe she was trying to help him," Herbie said, crouching next to the shotgun.

Penny Walters stepped out of the kitchen door. "House is clear. No signs of any struggle inside, and there's a car in the garage."

Ben scanned the wooden veranda, noting a wet smear on the table. He moved closer, bent down, and sniffed. "Beer."

"Could have been knocked over in a struggle," offered Claire.

"I don't think so," Ben said, pointing at the puddle under the table surrounded by an army of red ants with a trail of them disappearing under the veranda. "They've been having a party for a while," he added, watching the ants marching back and forth to the spilled beer. His eyes trained across the wooden slatted surface and came to rest on the edge where it met the short, dry grass of the lawn.

"Fetch the field kit, Claire. I assume we still have it, or did we leave it behind?"

Claire shook her head. "Good thing one of us is switched on. I threw it in the back."

While Herbie and the two agents searched the garden and surrounding trees, Ben and Claire examined the area around the veranda.

"Someone has fallen and was bleeding here," Ben said, pointing at the grass next to the veranda. "I can see where the woman... what was her name, Claire?"

"Dooley. Amanda Dooley."

"Looks like she tried to bandage him up. See the scissors laid out and the end of the bandage roll is small? She used a fair amount on him."

"Could have been used for something else before," Claire suggested.

"No, look," he said, pulling a plastic wrapper wedged under the corner of the first aid box. "Freshly opened bandage. Label says six yards, and there's only a small roll left. She used most of this on him, and there's a reel of surgical tape opened here," he said, pointing into the box. "Conclusions, Miss Manson?"

"Not as much blood as I would have expected, which is strange for a shotgun."

"It depends on how far away he was when shot." From a distance, and it might just be a slight skin puncture. But you're right. If someone shot him at close quarters, then there would be massive trauma and blood everywhere.

Ben stood and looked down the garden at the bird tables. "She liked her feathered friends. Tables are loaded up for a birdie banquet." He walked toward the tables but kept to one side of the garden, looking for clues in the grass.

"I can see where she's been walking from the house to the tables to fill them up, and where she stood while she topped up each one. But the farthest one is interesting," he shouted to Claire, still crouched down by the veranda.

"Hang on, Ben, I'll be with you in a minute. I think I've found something."

He looked back and saw Claire shading her eyes and walking in a large circle around the shotgun. She walked toward him, turned, and looked back at the house.

"Notice anything strange about the grass?" she asked.

Ben looked back at the grass near the veranda again. "Nope. What can you see that I can't?"

"Perhaps it's a trick of the light, but I can see a trace of a lighter color. Fan-shaped, opening out from the veranda."

"Take some samples to be sure and we'll analyze them back at the lab. Now come here and look at this."

She stepped beside him and looked down at the rough wooden top of the bird table.

"See it?"

She bent her head forward. "Oh yes," she said, and teased out several black hairs with a blue sheen caught in a crack in the wood.

"Looks like our man-bear was having breakfast," Ben said. "This table is almost clear of seed and nuts, and you can see where something has entered the garden from the trees." He stepped back, revealing a flattened grass trail ending where the lawn met dry pine debris. "Okay. Let's assume Ms. Dooley saw our man-bear helping himself to the bird table she had just filled up. She takes a shot at him from the back of the house, which is a good distance, and wings him, breaking the skin but not doing serious damage."

"That doesn't add up, Ben."

"How so?"

"Lethal range depends on the type of shot and the gun itself."

"You think it should have done more damage?"

"That shotgun looks like a twelve-gauge, and even with a short-range cartridge, it would have done more damage."

Ben smiled. He always enjoyed watching Claire's brain whirring into action. "Go on, Miss Marple."

"If she fired from the farthest point from here," she said, stepping back to the kitchen door, "that's just shy of seventy yards. With some angle of spread as the shot traveled, it would have taken out the other two bird tables, and this one at the end of the garden should at least have some damage. Either he arrived with an injury, or that gun was loaded with something else, and I don't think it was metal shot."

"Okay, what if she discharged the shotgun but not at him? Perhaps to scare him off?"

"Then there would be damage to the trees and plants in the

garden, and to reach him, I think she would still have hit at least one of the other bird tables. I don't see any other damage. Do you?"

Ben scanned the garden once more and nodded. "So, what do you think the gun was loaded with?"

"It wasn't metal shot. I'll take some samples from the barrel and cartridges and better do it before the feds impound everything. I believe he was shot at short range nearer the house."

"Ben, Claire, we're on the move again," announced Herbie, appearing at the kitchen door.

"Not yet," said Ben. "We need to take more samples."

"Leave it. We're going. We've found a trail of blood and need to go after them. Can't leave you here unprotected."

Ben approached Herbie. "You go ahead and we'll take our chances." He explained their theory that the man had been shot at close range, but they needed to confirm the facts.

"I don't care. We can come back later. Now get moving," said Herbie.

Ben folded his arms. "No."

"I won't tell you again."

"We're not coming with you, and you're wasting time. Go find them without us. We'll only slow you down, anyway. Stop barking orders at us, Herbie Lomax."

Herbie glared at him, reached inside his jacket, pulled out a gun, and marched toward Ben.

"Whoa!" shouted Ben, raising his hands.

Herbie laughed and turned the pistol. "I shouldn't be doing this, but under the circumstances," he said, handing the pistol to Ben. "It's for your own protection in case that hairy guy comes back. Ever used one before?"

Ben shook his head.

"I have," said Claire, stepping forward with her hand out to Ben. "Spare magazine?"

Ben handed her the gun.

"There's enough in there," said Herbie. "Keep the throat mics and earpieces on, and we'll keep you updated. If the beast comes back, Claire, aim center mass, right at the ticker." He turned and left.

"Where did you learn to shoot a pistol?" Ben asked.

Claire smiled. "There's a lot you don't know about me, boss. Now let's get doing what we do best, and if Bigfoot turns up, don't get too close to him, as I'm not a brilliant shot!"

"Thought you just told Herbie you can use it. Have you actually fired one?" Ben asked, staring at the pistol in her hand.

"I've fired plenty of rounds, and that's why you need to stay out of the way. Trust me, I couldn't hit a barn door at ten paces."

FIFTY-ONE

"You hungry, Eddie?" asked Jimbo, lying on the floor under the window.

"No bro', just need a drink. It's bloody boiling in here."

"They shut off the water and I can't open any windows. Council locked every one of them."

"Man, I'm parched and sweating like a pig. It's so hot."

"I'll open the front door for a while. Let some air in. There's a drop of cider left. Here." He passed a large plastic bottle, got up and staggered through the living room door into the dark hallway, feeling for the door catch, then swore as a piece of splintered doorframe pierced his finger.

Jimbo turned the handle and pulled at the door that he'd pried open earlier with a crowbar. The empty flat was a lucky find as the council was usually quick to seal any vacated property with bolted metal panels over the doors and windows, keeping squatters out. With a groan, the door dragged on the filthy hallway carpet, requiring all his strength to pull it, but he only managed to get it half open. Stepping outside, the cooler air was a welcome relief but not fresh, laden with vented steam from the flat kitchen next door. Madras, he guessed, as he inhaled the heavily spiced air, making his stomach gripe, after eating nothing all day other than a half-eaten, stale sandwich scavenged from a garbage bin. He peered to his right along the concrete balcony, clear to the open concrete staircase, and leaned on the brick parapet wall, scanning the street two floors below where two teenagers kicked a ball around. Jimbo shook his head. Why the kids' parents let them play in the street in the early hours was beyond him, but nothing in London surprised him anymore, after spending the last two years living rough. He stepped back as an army patrol approached the lads. A short verbal exchange began as they ordered them off the street and a few expletives from the boys filled the air. The older soldier threatened to knock their parents up and the boys disappeared into the opposite block, leaving the two men standing under a street lamp chatting and smoking.

Jimbo spent an uneventful day with Eddie foraging for food, and a few hours begging for spare change from customers outside the local supermarket till the manager moved them on. Most customers ignored them or claimed they had cards and no cash. One man even suggested they should invest in a card reader, and had been perfectly serious. Jimbo laughed. What an idiot! At least they were given enough cash by a few benevolent souls for a fix. Eddie had been out of it for two hours after scoring and just woken up. He stepped back inside to see Eddie drinking the last drop of warm, flat cider.

"Cheers, Eddie, didn't wonder if I was thirsty?"

"Sorry, bro', I didn't think."

"No worries. I'll survive. There's probably water in the toilet cistern."

"Gross, man."

"Got a better idea?"

Eddie shook his head, tried to laugh, began coughing, and sat up so quickly that he fell forward, crashing into the ancient coffee table left by the evicted tenant, scattering used syringes and a full ashtray over the stained rug. He lay on his back, laughing hysterically, trying not to cough.

Jimbo looked on in amusement at his stoned companion on the floor.

"Get up, you idiot. It wasn't even funny," he said, then started laughing himself. "I'm going to get that drink unless some dickhead flushed the water away."

Eddie laughed even louder.

From the dark shadows of the block's concrete staircase, a black dog appeared as it reached the landing, stopped and raised its nose in the air. It turned and looked at a second dog a few steps behind and whined. The scent of food wafted across the landing and it turned left and trotted across the open balcony, arriving below the source, an extractor vent above the kitchen window on the last but one flat. It searched for an opening but found the front door and windows shut tight. It was about to turn tail when it heard a man laughing, the sound coming from a partly open door at the end of the balcony. It crept forward, and the second dog joined its side. They both moved through the half-open door into the hallway. The thick black fur, tinged with iridescent blue, rose on the lead dog's hackles, as its blood-red eyes focused on a thin, disheveled man lying next to a table, through the open living room door.

The attack began with each dog approaching from either end of the table. Eddie, with eyes screwed shut, laughing on his back, didn't feel the razor-sharp teeth of the lead dog tear his neck wide open, severing the carotid artery. They worked ferociously, tearing and ripping clothing off his body with ease and pulling away chunks of flesh, devouring the man while he was still alive. Eddie registered the huge fangs and glowing red eyes for a split second and then his life ebbed away as blood gushed and sprayed, consigning him to oblivion, spattering walls and the sparse furniture as the two dogs tore and gorged their way through exposed flesh.

"What's going on, Eddie?" shouted Jimbo from the toilet.

The dogs stopped dismembering the body and turned to the door, blood dripping from their muzzles. Jimbo was about to enter the living room and froze, not being able to process the scene or the two sets of red eyes glowering at him. The lead dog leaped, knocking him sideways through the front door onto the balcony. He hit the doorframe on his way out, toppling down on his knees with the weight of the animal on his back. The animal sank its fangs into his shoulder and Jimbo screamed but managed to reach out, gripping the parapet wall, and scrambled upright. The dog fell off his back, allowing Jimbo to stagger along the balcony a few steps. He shouted for help and tried to make a move toward the stairs, but the dogs were a formidable team and the second dog lunged forward and bit through the back of his ankle, severing his Achilles tendon. He staggered onto his knees once more with both dogs upon him.

A gunshot sounded from below and the two dogs stopped instantly, alert and erect. Jimbo crawled, still screaming, covered in his own blood, trailing his injured leg. The lead dog left the second dog to guard their prey and padded forward to the staircase landing as the two soldiers approached. It growled and hunkered down, ready to attack. The first soldier turned the last corner, and the dog leaped, hitting the man full in the chest, knocking him backward down the stairs, where he collided with the other soldier. The dog didn't stop to attack, but continued down the stairs and disappeared into the street.

"Okay, Sarge?" said the second soldier.

"Hit my arm, but I'll live," said the sergeant, examining a bloody scratch on the back of his hand. "What the hell was that?"

"Dog, I think. Went past in a blur."

They heard another cry for help above them. When they reached the balcony, the second dog began growling, and stepped over Jimbo, approaching the two soldiers. With the balcony lights illuminating the animal, was now clear to see in all its horrific glory. A heavily muscled black animal with a blue sheen to its thick coat and a head, barely recognizable as a dog, with heavy extended jowls, rows of huge razor-sharp teeth, and vivid red eyes stood ten feet away from them, lips curled back, giving a low guttural growl.

"What in God's name..." said the corporal.

"The bastard's about to charge us," said the sergeant. They

backed up and retreated to the staircase. It followed, snarling, baring the huge glistening white teeth, from its cavernous maw as blood-stained drool trailed from its lower jaw. The two men backed slowly down the stairs.

"Keep going. Take it nice and easy, Corporal. Need to keep its attention on us and away from the poor sod on the balcony."

The dog didn't take its eyes off them and followed, keeping up a step at a time. As they backed onto the balcony below, facing the stairs. The shadow of the beast appeared on the left-hand staircase wall just before it rounded the last corner and stopped.

"The bastard knows," said the corporal.

"Don't be daft, lad, it's just a dog."

They waited, but it didn't move.

"What the hell is it up to?"

"Beats me. I'm calling this in. Can't allow the other one to escape."

As he reached for his handheld radio, there was an unearthly growl from the stairs and the dog charged. The sergeant dropped the handheld and tried to raise his rifle but knew he wouldn't be quick enough and braced himself for a second impact with a horror dog. A shot rang out right next to his head, and the dog hit him, knocking both the sergeant and the corporal onto the balcony. The dog continued, clipped the top of the parapet wall, and cartwheeled over the edge.

They got up and peered over the wall. The monstrous dog lay dead on the pavement with a single bullet hole between its eyes.

"Nice shot, Corporal, but next time not so close to my bloody ear!" said the sergeant, tapping and rubbing the side of his head.

FIFTY-TWO

"You look cool in that leather bomber jacket. Where did you get it?"

Ron, wearing a false mustache, sideburns, and shades, could have stepped out of a time machine from the early '70s. He sipped his coffee and smiled across the table. "Retro's all the rage, so I thought why not? Got it a while back when I was working on another case for Ben."

"Had me fooled. You could have walked straight past me, and I wouldn't have had a clue it was you."

Ron tapped the pocket on the jacket. "Mind if I smoke?"

"It's not illegal to smoke outside a cafe," said Chris Williams. "That guy is," she whispered, pointing toward an old man smoking a pipe two tables away, "and it doesn't bother me."

"Cheers, Chris. I was gasping for one. Two hours on a train without a fix nearly killed me."

Ron pulled out a full packet of Marlboros and looked at it lovingly. He lit up and took a huge draw, leaned back, and blew a swirling cloud above, smiling as the commuter stress ebbed away.

Chris Williams sat while he devoured the first cigarette, stamped it out, and lit another.

"Better now?"

He nodded and eased back in the chair.

"Just remember not to smoke your ciggies right down to the filter like you usually do, or you'll burn your disguise."

Ron put his hand up to check the wispy mustache, then laughed.

"All squared up back home?"

"Yep. Sent my other half off for a short break out of harm's way and gave him my car. I won't be using it down here with those thugs looking for me."

Chris nodded. "Probably for the best. What about Ben? Is he okay with you being back in London?"

"He hasn't said a word."

"Blimey. I was convinced he'd object."

"He would if he knew I was here," said Ron, winking. "I haven't told him yet. This case is too important for me to be hiding away."

"You're either mad or extremely brave. I haven't made up my mind yet," she said.

"Just stupid," said Ron, grinning.

"Well, Mr. Logan, I've arranged twenty-four-hour protection for you, and it won't be a copper watching your back from a patrol car either. I'm talking about special forces-style security. They'll be sticking to you like glue, going everywhere with you, and you'll be sharing a room."

"What do you mean, sharing?"

"Like I said, they'll be sticking to you like glue. We don't want you disappearing again."

Ron knocked back the last of the coffee, leaving a line of froth on his new mustache. Chris passed him a napkin, pointing to her top lip.

"Just a couple of requests," said Ron, nearly wiping the mustache off his face.

"Anything, Ron."

"If you ever meet my other half, not a word about this," he said, drawing a finger across his lips. "I don't want him knowing I'm sharing a room with a stranger."

"And the other request?"

"Make sure this bodyguard's a hunk."

Chris sniggered. "I think you'll like Frankie Jones."

"Like I said, not a word to my other half. He gets jealous if I so much as look at another man."

Chris checked her watch. "I have to go. Stay put, Ron. Your hunk will arrive shortly. I'll catch up later."

Ron watched Chris disappear into the crowds of early morning workers and shoppers and considered how fortunate he was not to live in the ant nest that was the capital city. He was on his third Marlboro and musing about his new job prospects when a young woman sat at his table and waved to a waitress.

"Excuse me?" said Ron. "But that seat's taken."

She tilted her head, and two dazzling blue eyes looked over the top of her sunglasses. She took the glasses off and stretched out her hand.

"Frances Jones, Mr. Logan. You can call me Frankie."

Ron's jaw dropped with the remnants of a Marlboro still attached to his bottom lip. He shook her hand limply.

"You look disappointed, Mr. Logan?"

"No... It was just that... Sorry, Frankie. Please call me Ron."

While she ordered a latte, Ron studied his new bodyguard. Slim, frizzy shoulder-length red hair, and beautiful bone structure. Her smooth white skin was exquisite but marred with heavy makeup around her stunning blue eyes. He smiled to himself at the heavy beads around her slim neck and the cheesecloth, tie-dyed dress, and thigh-length leather boots. It complemented his retro theme, and he wondered what she looked like when not undercover. Alas, not a man, but very attractive.

"Ground rules, Ron. You will never be out of my sight while you're here. I've booked us an Airbnb close to Cricketers Bridge. A hotel would be too risky. I've already checked out the apartment and made precautions there for your protection. You're officially my partner. We're on holiday doing some family tree research, which will give us the perfect reason to go to the more non-touristy places. Not that anyone will ask why we're here, but just bear that in mind. Questions?"

"Loads. When you say I will never be out of your sight, do you mean that literally?"

She laughed. "Well, I won't be watching you take a pee or in the bath if that's what you're worried about, but yes, while you're in London, you'll never be more than six feet from a rat, as the saying goes, or me."

"What about sleeping arrangements?"

"The apartment has one bedroom, but it's a twin, so I won't be sharing a bed with you, just the room."

"Isn't this a bit over the top?"

"Someone would have murdered you if you hadn't been rescued from that lockup in Hackney. One man connected to this case has already died, and criminals have threatened you, your partner, and two of your colleagues. You are integral to the investigation, so if it means sleeping in a double bed with you and sitting on the loo watching you take a bath to keep you safe, I would do it."

"That's telling me then!"

She nodded.

They sat in silence for a minute while Ron mulled over this new phase of the investigation; disguised, with a beautiful bodyguard, and a potential murderer stalking him. The new job at Moreton Scientific Investigation certainly wasn't boring. He wondered how Ben and Claire would react if they knew he was back in London. He turned to Frankie.

"You seem to know all about me. What about you?"

Frankie removed the sunglasses and pulled her chair closer. Ron sat up and leaned in toward her.

"I'm twenty-nine, from the States. Single, unattached, and have been doing this job for eighteen months."

"Only eighteen months?"

"In this role, yes. I was an FBI agent for six years before that in LA."

Ron stared at her for a moment, wondering if this was a wind-up. He could see in her eyes she wasn't making this up to impress.

"So, what brought you all the way across the pond?"

"I love the UK, and an opening came up that suited me. There's some truth in the family tree research story. Most Yanks descended from early settlers have their roots in Europe. So, I came on a research mission, loved London, the job came up, so I stayed."

"What sort of opening?"

She shook her head. "Sorry, can't discuss that. Let's just say I do a similar job to the one I did back in LA, but without carrying a piece."

"Piece?"

She laughed again. "Sorry. Carrying a gun."

"So you're not armed?"

"Not normally, but for this assignment, yes," she said. Ron wondered where she was keeping the gun. "Anyway, enough chit-chat. You need to get down to business. Let me update you on what's been happening in the last twelve hours."

"More developments?"

She smiled and sipped her latte.

"The spread of the problem has moved up a gear during the night. Two dogs killed a man in a squat on the Minerva Estate, close to Regent's Canal. They ripped him apart, seriously injured another man, and would have attacked more people if an army patrol hadn't intervened. The patrol shot one dog dead at the scene. Unfortunately, the other got away. There's a search in progress to find it."

"Connected to our investigation, or was this a random attack? XL bullies?"

"No, this wasn't another banned dog mauling. These were Labradors, or what were Labradors until they became contaminated. You can see the body of the one they shot later. Labradors are not typically considered vicious, but these two morphed into the hounds from hell. More worryingly, there was an attack on an elderly man in

Tudor Road in Hackney, just a couple of streets away from Victoria Park. The man, who was walking his dog and had almost reached his house, was grabbed around the neck from behind. He said he was being strangled and thought he was going to die. Thankfully, his dog came to the rescue and bit the assailant."

"So, how is this significant?"

"The old man got a good look at the attacker and said the attacker didn't look human, describing him as extraordinary, with a horribly deformed chin, sharp teeth, and a face completely covered in black hair with a blue sheen. Sound familiar?"

Ron exhaled. "God. It's reached its destination at the top of the food chain. Not good. Not good at all. Any forensics?"

"Yes, plenty, but it will take time to analyze. I have duplicates for your lab, and I bet you can get results quicker."

"Yes, I'm sure our wheels at Moreton Scientific Investigation move faster than your local forensic lab."

Frankie sat back in the chair, drank the last of her latte, and stood. "Come on, partner, here's our ride. You have work to do."

The old man sitting two tables away looked over his newspaper as they climbed into the Uber, then turned to see the bald-headed man, who had been watching Frankie and Ron from the charity shop window opposite, get into a silver Range Rover and accelerate away in the same direction as the taxi.

FIFTY-THREE

"When you said the incident happened in a squat, I imagined this estate would be dilapidated," said Ron, as they stepped out of the Uber. "These flats look quite modern."

Rows of imposing four-story light gray blocks filled the tree-lined streets as far as the eye could see.

"Far from it, Ron. The estate was built just after the Second World War. Many of these blocks were built after large parts of London were flattened by the Luftwaffe, especially here in the East End. The Minerva Estate was the first London council estate to be completed after the war and it looks new because a refurbishment was done about twenty years ago.

"Which block is it?"

"Follow me," said Frankie. "The block we're going to is under siege by the press, so we'll approach from the back." They walked along a path linking the streets of the estate until they arrived at a police cordon at the rear of one of the blocks. Frankie showed her ID, and the police ushered them through. As they turned the last corner to the front, a hive of activity met them, with reporters standing with their backs to the block, giving live updates to the media. A bead of sweat trickled down Ron's forehead, and he instinctively felt for the bulge of the Marlboro packet in his jacket pocket, but stopped after realizing what he was doing. He was glad he had taken the trouble to wear the ridiculous disguise as he didn't want to be identified on national TV as there was a chance the Cambridge team's director would have spotted him working for their nearest rivals while on paid garden leave. He hoped Ben and Claire were too busy in the States to be watching TV because this would be a big deal and go global as the press caught up with the weird situation.

Chris Williams, deep in conversation with the scenes of crime officer at the entrance door, stopped talking when she saw Ron.

"Step inside," she said, and they entered the entrance lobby at the bottom of the stairs.

"The squat is on the top floor, right at the end of the balcony. The council had just cleared the flat a week ago and was about to move a new tenant in when a couple of homeless men took up residence. Unfortunately, legal issues prevented them from evicting them yesterday, resulting in a delay.

"Can we go up to the flat?" asked Ron.

She glanced up at the SOCO, who nodded and said, "We're just packing up, so yes, you can go in."

"Do you want us suited and booted?" asked Ron.

He shook his head. "No need for protective suits. We're done here. Have a good look around, but touch nothing. To be honest, the state they left the flat in, you won't want to touch anything. We've taken samples which are being couriered to the lab at Moreton and should be there soon."

The smell of rotting food in the entrance hallway of the flat made them both gag, and Ron pulled a handkerchief from his sleeve and balled it up under his nose. The living room, lit with the SOCOs' strong tungsten floodlights, was in chaos, strewn with empty takeout cartons, bottles, and every piece of drug paraphernalia Ron had ever encountered on a battered coffee table dotted with cigarette burns. Used syringes poked out of an empty lager can with the top ripped off, and a fringed, heavily-stained single lampshade, which had once been blush pink, hung at an angle from the ceiling above the table. He felt the back of his knees tingle as the metallic tang of blood breached the handkerchief.

"Jeez," he said, stepping back and almost knocking Frankie over.

With blood spattered across every wall and the ceiling, the room resembled an abattoir. The attack had been swift and violent, and Ron guessed that at least one major artery had been severed to turn the room into a crimson red abattoir, now going black in patches. It was a bloodbath, and whatever had attacked the man in this room was powerful and possessed.

"I don't understand people," said Ron, taking several photos of the filthy, blood-spattered scene on his phone. "Okay. Take drugs if you must, but why live in a shit-hole?"

Frankie shook her head. "They're as high as a kite or on a downer, and housework isn't high on the agenda."

Ron felt light-headed and fired off as many photos as he could while holding his breath. The bile rose in his throat and he couldn't stand it any longer.

"Can we get out of here?"

Frankie looked at him with astonishment. "Seriously?"

Ron didn't wait for an answer and pushed her out of the way and almost bolted for the door onto the balcony. She followed him out and found Ron leaning over the balcony wall, looking into space as white as a ghost.

"What's the matter, Ron?" she said, placing a hand on his shoulder.

"Blood," he croaked.

"You're kidding me?"

He turned away from the edge of the balcony, realizing reporters were looking up at him. The beads of sweat shimmered in the intense lighting coming through the living room window.

"Sorry. I just can't cope with blood and hospitals. Sets me off," he said, pulling a Marlboro to his lips.

"Is there anything I can do to help?" she asked.

"Like what?"

"Do you want me to video the whole flat on my phone?"

"Please," said Ron. The pallid skin on his face turned crimson as embarrassment set in, and his nose resembled a large bulbous strawberry.

"Will you be okay out here?"

He nodded, waving his hand for her to go back inside.

Frankie spent half an hour meticulously recording and taking pictures from every conceivable angle, but kept walking back onto the landing to make sure Ron was okay.

When she had everything she wanted from the flat, Frankie stepped out to find Ron laughing.

"Thought you weren't feeling too well. What's tickled you, Ron?"

"It's just bizarre when you think of it. A flat covered in blood and me, a so-called scientific investigator, scared of blood and dressed like some seventies rocker." She smiled and looked out over the balcony. The smile vanished, and she took a video of the crowds below and several still shots. She stepped back and reviewed the images.

"Recognize this man, Ron?" she said, pushing the screen at Ron and zooming in on a single face. Ron's eyebrows arched, and that was enough to set her moving for the stairs.

"Stay here, Ron, and don't move."

She ordered a constable to stay with him, ran down the stairs, then walked out, pushing through the police cordon into the crowded street. Ron glanced over the balcony. He could see the bald-headed man looking up at him through binoculars. He held the stare, and the man vanished. People around where the man had been stood were backing away, revealing the man face down with Frankie Jones sat on his back, holding him flat to the floor in an armlock.

FIFTY-FOUR

Wayne Fletcher saw the commotion from the lookout point on the top balcony of the opposite block. He was about to rush down and assist, but cursed, seeing more police move in and restrain the bald man below. Instead, he watched Zak Wilson being cuffed and bundled into a police van and knew it would be the end of the line for his partner on this assignment. Now, he'd have to complete it on his own.

Reflecting on the events so far, he wished the boss had ordered them to kill Ron Logan when they had the chance, as leaving him overnight in lockup so the boss could question him the next day proved disastrous. Alex Monroe should have interrogated Ron Logan as soon as they had him, instead of going off to some high society cocktail party for the evening. Wayne wondered who had identified Zak. Perhaps he was also in the sights of the local cops? He moved to an alcove, where he could watch from a shadowed section of the balcony next to a staircase where it would be difficult to be seen. He had to admit to himself that the woman cop in the weird plain clothes was good. Very good, as Zak Wilson was no pushover, and she'd taken him down without so much as a scratch. As the police van pulled away, he saw her disappear into the crowd of reporters. He switched his gaze to Ron Logan on the balcony opposite and laughed to himself. Did the idiot think he could fool them with that pathetic disguise?

After seeing him disappear into the toilet on the train and come out in a bomber jacket and false mustache, he had almost given himself away by laughing out loud behind his newspaper. Ron Logan transformed himself from an ugly-looking bloke into an ugly oldest-swinger-in-town. Wayne was thankful for Ron's attempt at disguising himself, as he was now even easier to spot in a crowd. The platforms and concourse were heavily monitored with surveillance cameras, making it impossible for him to take him down outside Paddington Station. Ron being met on the platform was something he hadn't anticipated, so he had to bide his time once again and would be going solo now that his partner was indisposed. He pulled the phone from his inside pocket and rang Monro to give him the bad news and receive further instructions.

Ron couldn't believe what he'd witnessed. The girl sent to look after him had wrestled one of the brutes that kidnapped him to the ground and cuffed his hands behind his back. Three police officers moved in and lifted the struggling man to his feet. She continued to put pressure on his arms, lifting them up and forcing his head down as he tried to kick out, but she was fast and pulled his arms higher, making him scream out. Once they had him in the back of the police van, Frankie vanished into the crowds and a minute later appeared on the balcony.

"That was impressive," said Ron, in awe of his new bodyguard.

She smiled. "I like to be efficient."

"How the hell did you spot him?"

"We obtained a photo from a customer's iPhone in the Grapes the night you were abducted, and captured clear images from CCTV that covered the bar where the two men were standing, ordering drinks. I have a good eye for faces, and once I spotted the little toe-rag, and you confirmed it, he had to be arrested."

"You made it look easy."

"Ron, I may look fragile, but let me assure you, it wasn't difficult. He wasn't expecting a woman to apprehend him. I have a very accurate kick which put him in a world of pain once I made contact with the right spot. Believe me, he went down easily. My concern is Wayne Fletcher's still out there."

"Wayne Fletcher?"

"Zak Wilson's partner in crime. Zak Wilson is the man you just watched me arrest." She scanned the street below.

"He would have legged it after seeing his mate carted off, surely?"

"No. My guess is he's still down there somewhere watching, but we won't find him now. It seems like they expected someone from your lab to show up, or they've already discovered your cover. Mine is definitely blown after that."

"Who are they, and why target me?"

"They're hired thugs. Both have a string of convictions, but why they're targeting you, we're not sure yet. They're obviously acting on behalf of someone who wants Moreton Scientific Investigation out of the picture. Maybe a business rival?"

"I can't see that. Our main competitor wouldn't stoop that low."

"You sure about that?"

"Absolutely. I just finished working for them, and I know they wouldn't do it."

"What could be the benefit of removing your team from this investigation?"

Ron stroked his chin. "The only thing I can think of is political gain. Hampering the investigation could lead to the spread of this contagious infection, which could take down the city with catastrophic consequences.

"We considered that, and it may be the case. Those two clowns have large families and have lived in the capital all their lives. I can't imagine them wanting to shit in their own backyard and have their families overrun with giant rats and killer dogs, can you?"

"That's if they understand the consequences of what they've been asked to do."

"Perhaps. Now, unless you have any further business here, shall we find somewhere for lunch?"

Wayne saw them leave and waited till they were out of sight before slipping away to his car a block away. The boss wanted him to lie low for a while, but that was not Wayne Fletcher's way. There was a score to settle.

Ben shut his phone down and sighed.

"What's happening?" said Claire, who was labeling samples they'd collected from Amanda Dooley's garden over the last two hours.

"Just spoke to Kath O'Brien. After she told me all her woes and ailments, she let it slip that Ron is back in London. Bloody maverick. I told him to stay away till the police sort out who's behind the kidnapping."

"Have you spoken to him?"

"No. He's not picking up. I'll give Chris Williams a call and see what he's up to."

"I can see why he's there," said Claire. "I'd do the same."

"What do you mean?"

"This investigation is so important that risks have to be taken. Every day he's not at the sharp end is a day lost to the spread of this contagious nightmare."

"But he could get himself hurt or worse."

"Stop thinking health and safety. This is far too important. Ron's a big boy, and I'm sure he'll be more vigilant."

Ben picked the phone back up and tried Ron again. He answered.

"Ron, why are you back in London?"

"Didn't take you long to find that out," said Ron.

"I told you to stay away."

"You did. But I didn't. Now can we move on? You'll be pleased to know that the police have one of the two kidnappers in custody and they have a name for the other, so stop worrying about me.

"Good. What are you doing now?"

"Having a light lunch in a pub in Hackney with a stunning blue-eyed bodyguard."

Ben laughed. "You have a bodyguard?"

"Yep. Chris Williams insisted."

"And is he your type?" quipped Ben.

"If I were straight, she'd be right up my street."

"She?"

"Yes, as in female."

Ben could hear a woman's laughter in the background.

"There've been developments in Bethnal Green. Two infected Labradors attacked and killed a squatter and badly injured another. Worse still, an old man's been attacked by someone we think has been infected. Looks like it's progressing here," said Ron.

"Same here," said Ben, and recounted their current investigation at Lake Tahoe. "The odd thing, Ron, is the difference in the rate of spread. If the meteor theory is correct, then it's been present over here at Pyramid Lake and Lake Tahoe for much longer than in London. But the spread has been far slower. That must be significant. Something has either increased the rate of spread in London or inhibited it over here in the States. It has to be key to solving this."

"I've been thinking the same. I've got Roger and the rest of the crew working and reworking all the samples again. We're going to rerun Claire's test with the meteor particles in water. You whisked her away before we could draw positive conclusions. There's also another factor."

"Oh?"

"Oxygen content in the air. Jen pointed out that Lake Tahoe is over six thousand feet above sea level while London's a mere seventy-eight feet, and probably lower than that at Limehouse Basin."

"Is the difference in oxygen levels significant?"

"Over four percent less oxygen content in air at Tahoe compared to London. I would call that significant. I'm not saying it would make any difference, but it is a difference between the two sites that's worth considering."

"Good thinking, Ron, and thank Jen for the information. Salt could be a key factor, as Pyramid Lake is one-sixth the salt content of the oceans with very little unnatural activity since the first sightings of those lights in the water, and the canal water back home is salt free. We want to do more tests over here, only we keep getting hijacked by King and Lomax. Lomax is investigating King's business dealings, although he won't admit to it. I just want to get back to the lab and work every piece of evidence we have."

"I'm about to examine another site where giant rats killed two people in an abandoned underground substation."

"That's terrible. Who were they?"

"Two homeless men using it as a night shelter. Looks like it was linked somehow to the sewer network quite close to Regents Canal."

"Okay, Ron, keep me updated, and for goodness' sake, keep your eyes peeled for anyone coming after you."

"If you'd seen my bodyguard take down the thug, you wouldn't be worrying about me in the slightest."

He hung up and turned to Frankie.

"Where's the body of the dog?"

"I just had a text from Chris Williams. It's on its way to your lab in Moreton. Should keep your team busy."

Ron's phone pinged with the same message and some photos of the rogue Labrador. Ron stared at the grotesque images. Elongated jaws with protruding razor-sharp teeth, more akin to a shark than a dog, and the telltale blood-red eye staring at whoever took the photo. It was 'Labrador-like' but not a pet you would want to stroke. The usual black fur covering bulging muscles now had the telltale glossy blue sheen. He thought about the unfortunate man who'd been torn apart by the lethal jaws and wondered where the other hound was hiding. The phone pinged again with another message.

Keep looking over your shoulder, Logan. I'm still here, and that pathetic disguise won't help you.

FIFTY-FIVE

Amanda Dooley sat on a large boulder at the dead end of the gully. The man's huge index finger was on his lips as approaching voices broke the silence. Millennia of flash floods carved the small gully into the hillside, and an uprooted tree, fallen from the ridge above concealed it. The tree landed upright with roots almost filling the entrance. It was a good hiding place but a trap if discovered, as the only other way out was up a twenty-foot wall of loose dirt, rocks, and roots. The man crouched beside her, watching for movement between the tangled mass of roots concealing them. Still breathing heavily from the fast half-mile ascent of the mountainous slope, Amanda tried to focus on getting her heart rate and breathing back to normal, thinking of the incredible turn of events.

When he charged at her in the garden, her gun went off but hadn't disabled him, and she was sure she was about to die. He lay stunned for a few seconds, half on, half off the back porch, then sat up and stared at her, rubbing his eyes. To her utter amazement, he apologized for scaring her in a deep voice, even though she had just shot at him. Thankfully, most of the rock salt charge instantly turned into harmless powder, and the larger pieces had missed all but the top of his immense chest, neck, and face up to his nose, which had been peppered. Blood poured down his chest, seeping into the remnants of a torn checked shirt. She leaned in and looked closely at the injuries. "Stay there," she said. "I'll get you something to cover the wounds."

She stepped into the kitchen, found her glasses, and pulled a first aid kit from a drawer, trying to open it with hands shaking so much she couldn't undo the clip. "Dooley, get a grip of yourself," she hissed. In her previous existence as a nurse, this would have been a simple task, but after just shooting a man she thought was a marauding bear, the adrenaline rush was over, and shock set in. The box snapped open, but there was little of use inside and he was losing a lot of blood. She picked up the phone and dialed 911 for an ambulance, and had almost finished the discussion with the operator when a huge hand pulled the phone away and switched it off.

"No," he said. "I have to leave. No ambulance, no cops. It will just cause more trouble."

"But you need to have treatment. You'll need more bandages and stitching up." She pointed at the blood trail he brought into the kitchen. Then, looking up into his dark eyes, just visible through the mass of matted black hair, she said, "You need help."

"No, I need to leave and find the others." He turned and walked out onto the veranda.

"Wait," she said. "I'll get my other first aid kit. I'm coming with you."

"Too dangerous. You stay here."

"Don't tell me what to do, you over-grown ape. I'm coming with you, so shut up and get moving."

The man laughed. "Okay, but you'll have to keep up. We need to get away from here before they come looking for me."

Amanda snapped out of her thoughts and heard the voices getting closer beyond the entrance to the gully. They were very close. She could see the huge man tense up. He stood and pulled her as far back into the gully as they could go, both flattened against the dirt wall. Sweat and crumbling soil ran down her neck, giving her an irresistible urge to step away, but he kept her pinned in place, unable to move.

"Here," said a man. "Blood. Must have gone this way, through that gully."

Amanda looked up the terrified man. She could feel the tension trembling in his massive forearm that kept her clamped in place and knew he was scared, even though she couldn't see any expression on his face through the thick, black hair.

"Wait," said the woman on the other side of the giant tree roots. "There's a smear of blood here. A couple of patches. He must have gone through."

"Keep still," whispered the man, "and listen. Safety catches off."

Amanda held her breath, praying they would move on.

"Hear anything?"

"Nothing."

"I can see something," said the woman.

"What? I can't see a damned thing."

"It's him. The other side of these roots, and he has a woman with him," she whispered.

The agents crouched down, peering through the tangle of roots.

"I see him. There's no way out of there." The agent stood with the gun trained on the big man inside the gully. "Come out with your hands in the air. We won't hurt you."

Amanda fell forward as the big man released his grip on her. He leaped upward, catching a thick root farther up the dirt wall, and clawed his way up the near-vertical gully wall. Dirt and stones showered down on Amanda, who crouched, covering her head with both hands as part of the wall collapsed. She couldn't see a thing as the shower of dirt and dust made it impossible to open her eyes or breathe, the cascade of soil beginning to bury her. As she tried to stand, a shot rang out and a fist-sized rock hit the top of her head. A wave of bright light flashed, and acute pain filled her head just before her world went black.

FIFTY-SIX

"Can you hear me, Amanda?"

Wincing at the bright sunlight as she opened one eye, Amanda cried out from the jolt of pain. She tried again, opening both eyes slowly, and a blurred woman came into focus. Amanda screwed her eyes shut again as another wave of pain throbbed through her head.

"Yes, I hear you," she whispered, clutching her dry throat. "Where am I?"

"In your bedroom. We're just waiting for the paramedics to arrive. You took a nasty bang on the head."

"Where's the big man? He was with me. I heard a gunshot."

"He got away. They're looking for him now."

Amanda opened her eyes again and looked up at the woman. "You're not American, are you?"

"No," said Claire. "I'm a Brit, like you."

Amanda tried to sit up but slumped back on the bed and moaned.

"Try to keep still. The medics will be here soon, and they'll give you some pain relief."

The injured woman settled back onto the bed, deciding any more movement would be too painful.

"Did he hurt you?"

"No, he didn't do this. I went with him to look after him."

"I thought so. They said you took a first aid kit with you."

"Yes. I have two. The one under the kitchen sink was useless for such a big guy, just small plasters and a the remnants of a roll of bandage. But I remembered I keep another in the pantry. He was bleeding badly. Is he going to be alright?"

Claire didn't want to upset Amanda, but she thought she would find out, anyway. "I'm sorry to say that your big man has been wounded, but nothing life threatening."

Amanda sat bolt upright and gasped with pain. "What the hell did they shoot him for? He wasn't going to harm anyone, unarmed and defenseless. What's wrong with them?"

"They were worried about your safety."

"The hell they were. They could see him trying to escape, then shot at him. He was trying to climb out of the gully when I heard the gunshot, and then something hit my head."

"A falling rock, where the big man was climbing above you. The whole gully wall was collapsing. You were lucky those guys pulled you out alive. Did he speak to you?"

"Of course. He's a man, not some freaking gorilla."

Claire nodded at Amanda, who she could see was seething, and tried a different approach. She reached out and held her hand. "I've spoken to another man who is in the same position."

Amanda looked at her, puzzled.

"You can meet him later. His name's Jacy. He lives on the other side of the lake and has recovered from an infection that caused the same transformation with all the hair and body changes."

"Infection?" said Amanda.

Claire gave her a brief outline of the investigation she and Ben were attempting to solve.

"Is it contagious?" Amanda asked, staring at her hands, looking for any signs where she had touched the big man.

"We're not sure. We think it moves up the food chain by consuming infected food. This man ate fish from the lake. Maybe an infected trout, but it seems to affect humans differently. Every other affected animal we have encountered gets more aggressive." Claire recounted the spaniel that lost its paw to an infected pike in Regent's Canal.

"That's awful," said Amanda. "So it's happening back home as well?"

"Yes, but we think we have it contained. What I've just told you needs to be kept under wraps for now. We don't want to cause mass panic. The press is onto it already, but they don't know the details and are best kept in the dark for as long as possible."

"Don't worry. I won't breathe a word. I'm just worried about that poor man. If this gets out, you'll have every hot-headed, gun-toting idiot scouring the hills, hunting him down."

Claire wondered if there were already men gathering a posse together. "We have to find him quickly and get him to safety."

Amanda began to cry.

"Don't worry, we'll find him," said Claire, sliding onto the bed next to her and putting her arm around her shoulder.

"It's all my fault. If I'd had my damned glasses on, I wouldn't have shot him. I could have blinded him."

There was a knock at the door, and two paramedics entered. Claire left them in the room and walked out onto the veranda.

"She okay?" said Ben.

"More shook up and upset about the man she shot."

"Brave lady."

"Ex-nurse. Looks as soft as soap on the outside but has a steely interior. She just wanted to make sure he wasn't going to bleed to death and didn't think about herself."

"Some good news, Claire. Jacy has tracked the others. John Drake is unconscious, but the other two with him have carried him to a log cabin high in the forest."

Claire shook her head. "Not such good news with Herbie and his crew on the warpath."

"No. Jacy gave them the slip. He contacted them through telepathy and is with them now."

"Tell Jacy to get them down here after I find out where Herbie and the lynch mob are," said Claire, beginning to dial Herbie's number.

Ben stopped her. "No need to call Herbie. They won't come here, and Jacy said he's taking them all to a place where not even Herbie will find them."

"I can't blame them. Did he say where or how long it would take?"

"Nope. Too risky to say where it is on the phone. He'll contact us when they get there."

They watched as the paramedics wheeled Amanda into the ambulance. Claire walked over and climbed in the back with her. She turned to the medic. "Can we have a moment?"

"Make it quick. We need to get her checked out."

"Where are you taking her?"

"Barton Memorial."

The paramedic stepped out, and Claire told Amanda that her man was on his way to meet Jacy and would be safe.

"Will you lock up for me?" said Amanda. "The spare key's under the flowerpot on the stoop."

"Stoop?"

"Sorry, the flower pot on the front door step. They call it a 'stoop' over here. It's a Dutch word."

Claire smiled. "Thanks for the lesson. I'll come and see you at the hospital and keep you updated."

"Thanks, but I have no intention of staying at Barton Memorial for any longer than I have to. I'll be back here."

Claire stepped out of the ambulance and stood next to Ben as the paramedic climbed in the back and pulled the door shut.

"Tough old bird," said Ben.

"She certainly is that," said Claire, admiring the woman's bravery and tenacity as the ambulance disappeared down the pine-covered slope.

FIFTY-SEVEN

The lab appeared empty after the long drive back from Egan's house. The search for the missing infected people was ongoing, and Herbie told Ben to get back and start making some inroads with the samples. When Ben asked about Vince King, all Herbie said was that he wouldn't have to worry about him anymore. He said it in such a way that it sounded final, which puzzled Ben and Claire.

After the short drive with Egan back to the jetty at Meeks Bay, and a forty-five-minute boat ride later, they docked at the end of Egan's garden at Zephyr Cove. Jacy, still missing in Herbie's eyes, kept in touch with Ben on his burner phone to update him that he and the others were safe, and Brett Daniels, had only a superficial wound on top of those inflicted by Amanda Dooley.

The confrontation they expected didn't materialize when they got back to Barngate Holdings.

"It's going to be nice working here without Vince throwing his weight about," said Claire.

"Enjoy it while it lasts," said Ben. "I bet he'll be back here sooner that we think,"

"I doubt it," said a voice behind them.

Ben and Claire turned to see Elsa Smyth grinning at them from the office door at the back of the lab.

"You missed all the fun."

"Missed what, Elsa?" asked Claire.

"Vince King and that sweaty little slug Kelvin. Both arrested by the feds about two hours ago."

Claire looked across at Ben, then back to Elsa.

"They asked me to leave the building while they made the arrests."

Ben stared at Elsa in disbelief. "What were they arrested for?"

"I didn't have a clue what was going on at the time. But now I know what they've been charged with."

"Herbie told you?"

"No, not his style. He just called me straight after the arrests and told me to carry on assisting you. I asked why they'd been arrested, but he wouldn't comment."

"Sure it was an arrest?" asked Claire.

Elsa snorted. "Both were handcuffed and read their rights. I think they were doing a bit more than helping with their inquiries."

"I thought you said Herbie sent you outside," said Ben. "How do you know what they've been charged with?"

"Same way as that scoundrel King has been watching and listening to you pair," she said, pointing to the dummy smoke detector above Claire's head. "I'll show you the arrest in the monitoring room. They've been charged on multiple counts. King has been blackmailing and bribing officials to get his holiday complex fully open."

Claire gave Ben a knowing look.

"So, I don't think we'll be seeing much of Mr. King or Kelvin Staples for a while," said Elsa, smiling."

"What's Staples' involvement? I thought he was just King's minion?" said Ben.

"He is, but he'll do anything for Vince. Literally anything. Honest, dishonest, and worse."

"What do you mean, worse?"

Ben could see that Elsa was enjoying the slow reveal.

"Kelvin was charged with murder, on two counts.

"Now I know you're winding me up," said Ben. "Murder? Come off it, Elsa!"

"I can assure you this is no wind-up,"

Ben laughed. "If you'd said Vince King, I might have believed you."

"You wouldn't think that little creep Staples was capable of it, would you?" she said. Her face was serious. "I'm not joking. King is jointly charged with one of the murders."

Ben realized it wasn't a wind-up and took a seat, stunned by the latest revelations. "Who's been murdered?"

"Two men in Vegas."

Elsa took them to the monitoring room, and they watched the arrest with Vince and Kelvin being led out to two black sedans outside the lab entrance and driven away.

Elsa held up the desk phone to Ben as she dialed a number. "Herbie wanted you to call him as soon as I briefed you on the arrests."

Herbie picked up immediately. "Ben?"

"Yes. We're back at the lab. Would you like to tell me what's been going on? Elsa says that King and Staples are under arrest for murder."

The line went silent for a few seconds. "How does she know that?" asked Herbie.

"CCTV. It's everywhere in this building, or had you forgotten? Elsa did a quick rewind of the surveillance video, and there it was. I just watched them being handcuffed myself."

"Ah, of course."

Ben could hear him breathing heavily. "Well?"

"I'll fill you in with the details when I get back. I'm on my way now, but I need you to keep the arrests under wraps. If this gets out now, it will just add to the media pressure. I'll explain everything soon. All I want you to do is to find a cure for this disease, infection, whatever the damned thing is. If you want more help, Elsa will get you as many lab techs as you need. If you want more equipment or outside resources, just ask her. You're in charge there now."

"Does that mean the death penalty if they're found guilty?"

"Depends on which state they're convicted. Nevada has the death penalty but hasn't carried one out since 2006. Look, I have to go. I'm halfway down a steep hill on my way to the car. I'll explain everything when I get back. Put Elsa back on."

Ben handed Elsa the phone and her eyes narrowed. Even with the phone close to her ear, they could hear Herbie shouting at her.

"He didn't sound happy," said Claire.

Elsa, whose cheeks were flushed, didn't answer and stormed out of the room into the lab.

"Must have torn a strip off her for telling us too much," said Claire. "Can you believe it? Kelvin a double murderer and King implicated on one!"

"If they're guilty, good riddance to both of them. Okay, Miss Manson. We have the green light to do what we should have been doing. Forget about those two clowns, take a seat and plan our priorities. Decide what kit we'll need, and I think a few additional lab techs are essential. We could do it all, but it'll be quicker with some help, and speed is of the essence.

"Get some coffee on the go and we can start planning."

Claire nodded, glad they were back on course.

"Elsa, can you join us?" said Ben when Claire returned. "We need to straighten out a few things before we get working on this." Elsa sat opposite Ben on the main lab desk, still smarting from the roasting Herbie had given her.

"Look, Elsa. Herbie's just doing his job. Nothing personal, and we all want the same thing, which has even more urgency if that were possible. I just had an update from Ron, and against my advice, he's back in London, but thankfully he now has a bodyguard. She's very good, apparently."

"So, what's happened to make things more urgent?" said Elsa.

"There have been several people killed, and a large area radiating a mile out from where the problem was first discovered at Regent's Canal in London is now under curfew. That may be stepped up to total lockdown if it can't be contained. The army has been drafted in, patrolling every street, watercourse, and all the parks." Ben told them about the dog attack on the Minerva Estate. "I think we have to focus on the differences in the environment between here and London."

"It's significant," said Claire, "and you're right. It must hold the key to this mystery, even if it's just to slow the spread down."

Elsa raised a hand. "You said several people were killed in London. Who were the others apart from the man attacked by the dog?"

"Another two homeless people sleeping rough, close to the canal. Attacked by rats as they slept. The police told Ron there wasn't much left of them to make an ID. He's going to the scene with his new bodyguard."

Claire shuddered. "God, I hate rats."

"The army has shot eight affected dogs and over twenty giant rats. Bait has been put in all subterranean waterways, but it doesn't seem to affect them. No poisoned dead rats have turned up."

"You haven't mentioned cats, squirrels, birds, or other wildlife," said Elsa. "There must be plenty in such a highly populated area."

"Cats haven't been affected so far," replied Ben. "I can only think that the giant rats are too big for them to tackle. There's been a report of a huge deformed urban fox that has been sighted several times."

Claire cupped her hands around the mug of coffee, staring out of the window at Pyramid Lake and the hills surrounding the shoreline. "What other wildlife do we have over here, Elsa?"

Elsa opened a drawer under the worktop and pulled out a file. "I have a complete flora and fauna list for the area you can look at. The most likely candidates would be coyote, cougar, snakes, and lizards. Plenty of snakes and lizards around here." She slid the file across to Claire.

"My God, the list is endless," muttered Claire, leafing through the pages. "Where the hell do we start?"

"We start by getting more people here to do the spadework. Testing, and researching specifics while we focus on brainstorming, trying to piece this together. Herbie said we could have more techs here if we needed them."

Elsa nodded. "How many do you want?"

"Half a dozen, for starters. Where's the money coming from to pay for all this now that Vince is locked up?"

"Herbie's arranged everything. You can have whatever you want. There's no budget limit on this."

"Great, can you arrange that for me? We need them as soon as you can get them here."

Elsa disappeared into the lab office as Ben's phone buzzed.

"Shit," he said, looking at the message. "They've just announced full lockdown in large areas of three London boroughs: Newham, Hackney, and Tower Hamlets. We better work fast on this."

FIFTY-EIGHT

The stone steps, covered with weeds and brambles, led down to a rusted iron door crisscrossed with police crime scene tape. Ron looked back at Frankie, who shook her head.

"Sorry, Ron, but there's no way I'm going in there. I'll keep a lookout up here while you do your job down there."

"Sure about that?" Ron laughed at his protector's phobia. Her fear of rats evened the score with his problem with blood and hospitals. "I'll squeak if I need help."

"Don't!" she said, pointing at him. "There's a cafe across the street. I'll get us some coffee."

"Sounds good to me. And a donut if they sell them."

Frankie smiled and gave him a thumbs-up from the top of the steps.

Ron pulled the police crime scene tape aside and pushed the door, which protested with a scraping metallic screech, setting his teeth on edge. He put his shoulder into the door, taking several attempts to get it open, with its heavily rusted hinges. Inside, the police SOCO halogen lamps were long gone, and all he had to illuminate the dark passage leading from the door was a small but powerful

LED torch attached to the front of his headband and a portable high-beam lamp.

The moist air inside the cool passage smelled of urine overpowered by the stench of damp and mold. Not the most desirable place to sleep, but for several people, this served as a night shelter until infected rats attacked, killed, and almost consumed two of them.

Shadows danced across the passage wall as Ron walked forward, head bent to avoid hitting the low, arched brick roof. Dusty old webs hanging from the ceiling, caught him in the face and clung to his hair. He brushed them away, rubbing the matted webs off his fingertips. The passage opened into a small chamber filled on one wall with redundant metal electrical cabinets, stripped of wiring and switchgear. The underground substation, disused for over thirty years, was now a nightly refuge from the cold and rain.

Ron scanned the space, placed his field kit on the slab floor, and pulled out a rechargeable lamp and extendable tripod. Once set up, the whole room took on a completely different feel. No longer a creepy, dank, dark space, but a well-lit, crumbling example of past subterranean services under the main roads of the capital city. He began taking photos and video, working first on the layout, shining the powerful halogen back up the entrance corridor, then around the space, and into a service tunnel that followed the street above for over half a mile. Ron, glad that the incident with the two victims happened close to the entrance and not deeper into the service tunnel, meant any problems, and he would be just a few steps from fresh air.

Two old mattresses lay next to the back wall, both ingrained with dirt and deeply stained with blood from the two victims, a meal for rats that were not part of the initial feast, resulting in the chewing away of much of the top surface of the mattress nearest the service tunnel.

Ron tried not to think of the scene, but couldn't help himself; being fast asleep and woken in the pitch dark by indescribable pain as the rodents bit and gnawed their way into flesh. He shuddered, imagining the two deceased men trying to defend themselves, not knowing what monsters were attacking, feeling warm, furry bodies and claws pinning them down. Nobody could have heard their screams, and their remains would still be here, decaying or totally consumed, if another homeless person hadn't discovered them.

He crouched to study the area around the mattresses. There wasn't a lot to see, as police and SOCOs had trampled over everything. Rat feces were everywhere, some normal size, but mostly from giant rats. Ron collected and bagged samples, and as he moved his head, the LED headband beam picked out a small trail of blood leading away from the mattresses and entering a second tunnel. With his head bent, he stood and followed the trail into the tunnel, which was twenty feet long. At the far end, gaps appeared at the top of a cinder block wall sealing off the tunnel. The thin trail of blood reached the wall and rose vertically to one of the larger holes. Ron moved closer, and saw rat footprints in blood on the blockwork. An injured rat, or a rat dripping with blood? His skin crawled, but he knew he had to see this out. As he lifted the high-beam torch up to the hole in the wall and shone it through, a wave of fear swept over him as he imagined what might be on the other side. A horde of the devilish creatures waiting to attack?

Before looking through the gap, he stopped breathing and listened. At first, nothing. But then the faintest sound of short gasps. What was it? Ron exhaled and drew in a large breath before peering through the hole. The tunnel on the other side continued until it disappeared into blackness. He listened again. The gasping sound was close. He moved the torch around, but all the beam picked out was floating dust particles, then as he lowered the beam, he jumped. A giant rat lay on its side, still alive but breathing erratically. Its red eyes stared at him but didn't seem to register his presence. The torch picked out the blue iridescent fur on its back as its haunches rose and fell with each labored breath. Blood around the extended jowls seeped between jagged teeth.

The wall needed to come down. If this rat had been injured or poisoned, there was a chance to capture it and get it back to Moreton, where they could examine a live infected animal—if it lived. The light from the chamber behind him flickered and went out. Ron cursed to himself for not recharging the halogen lamp he just set up. Still, he had the high beam and head torch, so it wasn't a problem.

As he took a photo of the immobilized rat, just in case it came around and disappeared before it could be caught, a noise caught his ear. He turned his head away from the hole and the distinct grating sound of the entrance door echoed around the tunnel as it opened, and squealed on the rusted hinges as it was pushed shut. Someone had just walked into the abandoned substation, and he was sure it wouldn't be Frankie.

"Hello, who's there?" called Ron. He waited. There was no answer.

"Hello," called Ron again.

He heard a low echoing chuckle, followed by a familiar voice. "You couldn't keep that big nose out of London, could you, Logan?"

Ron felt a shiver run across his shoulder blades, and sweat beaded like pins on his forehead. It was the same menacing voice he'd heard on the phone, and the three words in the text message kept coming back: `I'm still here`. He switched the high beam and his headband light off, hoping the man wouldn't see him in the dead-end tunnel. He knew it was futile; with the door shut, Frankie wouldn't hear him if he called out, and the man would find him.

"Did you think I would just forget about you, Logan?"

Ron remained silent, hoping the man would go into the service tunnel on the opposite side of the main chamber.

"Come out now. Let's make this quick. It's no use hiding, Logan. You know I'll find you."

Ron realized he was shaking, and his heart rate was off the scale. He focused on breathing, trying desperately to slow it down and not make a noise. Sweat trickled down the back of his neck.

The light grew stronger as the footsteps crunching on the debris-laden floor entered the main chamber.

Ron looked around for a weapon as the man's phone flashlight filtered into the passage, but all he had was the high-beam torch. Light danced around the passage walls, then away again. Ron prayed the man would try the open tunnel first, giving him a chance to bolt to the exit.

"Don't think you can hide, Logan." The man began laughing. Ron shuddered as the manic laughter bounced around the brickwork. The footsteps grew nearer, and Ron held his breath. If the man shone his torch into the tunnel, he'd be discovered.

Another distant noise seeped into the background, and the man's torch flashed into the end of the tunnel, then turned. He heard him move away and enter the service tunnel. Ron exhaled and wiped his brow with the back of his sleeve.

"Logan, I can hear you, and I'm right behind you," shouted the man, who moved down the service tunnel, his footsteps increasing in speed, receding into the distance.

Ron moved forward and peered into the chamber. He tried to remember where the access tunnel was in the room, which was now in almost complete darkness.

He stepped forward and tripped over the corner of a mattress, landing heavily on the floor. It was pointless being in the dark after making so much noise, so he got up, flicked on the high beam, and made for the exit.

He took a quick glance behind him, dropped the lamp, and stood rigid.

Wayne Fletcher stood ten feet away with a phone flashlight in one hand and a foot-long machete in the other. He grinned at Ron. "Nice try, Logan," he said, his gold teeth glinting.

Ron looked around at the access tunnel door, realizing that even if he reached it, Fletcher would be upon him before he could force it open.

The distant noise Ron heard earlier grew louder, coming from the service tunnel. A scurrying, scratching sound, building in momentum.

Wayne Fletcher heard it too, but didn't move, continuing to grin at Ron.

"I'm going to enjoy this," he said, raising the machete in his clenched fist and taking a step forward.

The sounds coming from the open tunnel were fast approaching and made Wayne pause. He only half-turned so he didn't have his back to Ron and shone the torch down the open tunnel.

He stared at the portion of the service tunnel that his flashlight lit up and gasped.

Ron saw a swarm of giant rats approaching, ears back, red eyes blazing, and without thinking, ran blindly along the access tunnel until he collided with the iron entrance door, almost knocking himself out, bouncing off it, backward onto the floor. Behind him, Wayne Fletcher cried out. There was a clatter as Wayne tripped over the high beam and fell face down, shouting for help, but there was no way Ron was going back. The high beam rolled, spun in a circle, and rested, pointing at Ron, now illuminated in its intense light, back on his feet, trying to yank the door open as Wayne Fletcher shrieked in the darkness beyond the light. Screams and the sounds of clothing and flesh ripping from the man's flailing body filled the access tunnel. Ron stood, unable to make the door open quickly. Using all his strength, it grated against the concrete floor, and light began to pinprick from outside through tiny gaps between the door and frame. With one almighty effort, he pulled the door, managing to move it a couple more inches, but not enough to get through and escape from the seething mass of giant rats, which would surely turn on him at any moment. He leaned backward, digging his heels into the floor, gritting his teeth, and pulling the door handle as hard as he could. The door squealed loudly as it moved an inch and he braced one leg against the frame, pulling with all his might. There was a loud crack, and Ron flew backward several feet, hitting his head hard on the floor. Dazed and confused, he lifted his arms and saw, in the harsh light beam, he was holding the door handle.

FIFTY-NINE

Ron tried to get up, stumbled, and fell back against the door. The pain in his head throbbed, and the large lump was solid where he'd hit the concrete floor. All he could see was the intense light of the high beam blocking any view of the carnage behind. The noise of feasting rats made his stomach roil, and the absence of any sound from Wayne Fletcher spoke volumes. He swallowed as the silhouette of a rat stepped into the beam of light, then another. Ron whimpered. This was it. He would not die from cigarettes or a heart attack. His last moments would be now, ripped to shreds. A meal for these vicious creatures. Two more rats stepped forward, noses and whiskers twitching, sniffing the air, their red fleshy tails flicking in eager anticipation. Ron reached into his pocket and pulled out his Zippo lighter. He knew animals feared naked flames and unclipped the lighter, thumbing the flint wheel, until a bright blue flame sparked into life and flickered, but the rats did not turn tail and run. They cautiously advanced. Ron counted seven as they moved, synchronized in a steady advance, joined by more behind. The pack of giant rats, only ten feet away, were too many to count.

"Ron," shouted Frankie from outside the door. "Your coffee's out here."

"Help! Get this door open!" he screamed.

"What's wrong?"

"Just get the bloody door open. NOW!"

He heard a thud as she tried to push the door.

"It's jammed."

"Get it open! I'm being attacked."

There was a louder thud as Frankie charged at the door, and it opened another few inches. Ron got his fingers around the edge of the door and pulled while she pushed. It opened another inch, then wouldn't budge. He looked around at a multitude of blood-red eyes staring at him, still advancing, just six feet away.

"Do something. There's a group of giant rats about to kill me," he sobbed, pushing his arm forward, waving the lighter, trying to ward them off, knowing there was no way she could get through the door. He gave up trying to scare them off and covered his eyes, waiting for the inevitable razor-sharp teeth piercing his flesh.

"Move to the hinge side of the door," she shouted through the gap.

"What?"

"Move to your right, against the wall. Do it now."

Ron shuffled across, not taking his eyes off the grotesque tribe in front of him.

He heard a slight metallic scrape and clatter, then a flash of light and a deafening blast. When he opened his eyes, every rat was gone.

"You okay, Ron?" she shouted as she pulled her pistol back through the opening in the door, but all Ron could hear was a high-pitched buzzing.

"I'm going to get help."

Ron sat with his head in his hands, shaking, waiting for the rats to return. It seemed an eternity before the door began to creak and scrape against the floor.

"Move away from the door, Ron," said Frankie.

Reluctantly, Ron shuffled forward a couple of feet nearer the light. Were they waiting for him just the other side of the high beam?

The door creaked, groaned, and then flew open. Ron felt strong arms grab him and pull him backward up the stone steps, then lift him upright. He fell into Frankie's arms and sobbed. She led him to a low brick wall and sat him down.

He looked up at two men staring down at him.

"You have these guys to thank for getting the door open."

Ron nodded and wiped tears away but couldn't speak.

"Are you hurt?" she said.

He pointed at the back of his head, and she leaned over to look.

"Big lump there, but I think you'll live. Now, what happened down there? I only left you alone for five minutes."

Ron lit a Marlboro and felt better. "Wayne Fletcher followed me in."

Frankie's eyes widened. "Oh shit, Ron, I'm so sorry. I should never have left you. Where is he now?"

"Still down there. Rats got him. He's probably dead."

Frankie crouched next to him. "Where is he down there?"

"Not far in. He was at the other end of the access tunnel from the entrance."

She pulled the headband lamp from him, walked back down the stone steps and shone the light into the tunnel. She held one hand out to shield the intense light coming from the high beam still shining at the entrance.

"Fletcher," she shouted. There was no response. Beyond the high beam, there was nothing she could see, and the head torch failed to illuminate anything past the end of the tunnel.

Despite her fear, she stepped inside a few feet and attentively listened, but there was complete silence. Moving ahead, she paused every few feet to listen, but all she heard was street noise from behind. When she reached the high-beam lamp, she picked it up and turned it into the chamber and gasped. Wayne Fletcher looked up at her from the floor through one lifeless eye. The other eye socket was empty, and his torso was a bloody mess of torn flesh, exposed entrails, and shredded clothing.

Suddenly, a distant scurrying came from the dark service tunnel ahead, just as she pulled out her phone to take photos. She turned and ran, taking the concrete steps up to the road above three at a time.

For several minutes, she sat next to Ron, breathing heavily, without speaking.

Ron broke the silence after lighting a second Marlboro. "There's a live rat lying injured on the other side of a block wall in a dead-end tunnel down there. We need to capture it for analysis. It's important."

Frankie nodded, stood, and began making calls. She asked the two men to take Ron across to the cafe while she waited for the cavalry to arrive. Half an hour later, the scene was swarming with police, army, and SOCOs.

After a quick briefing outside the cafe, the army broke through the dead-end tunnel and placed the injured rat in a secure container. They immediately couriered it to the lab at Moreton with a police escort on blues and twos.

"Fletcher's dead all right," said Frankie.

Ron nodded, taking another sip of coffee. He was still shaking.

"I have never been so shit scared in all my life," he said. "I can't say I'm sorry he's dead. He was about to carve me up with a machete. But, I wouldn't wish those rats on my worst enemy." He shuddered at the thought of what might have happened to him if Frankie hadn't fired the gun, scaring them off.

"I believe the threat to you has passed, Ron. One locked up and the other dead. We have Fletcher's phone, and the call register may give us the lead to the people behind this. I'll have our very best working on it this afternoon."

"Good," said Ron. "It's bad enough trying to solve the mystery without some dickhead trying to kill me. I still don't get why they would want to stop us from doing our job and preventing a bloody catastrophe."

"Fingers crossed. I should get some answers once we access the phone."

Ron tried to light a third Marlboro, but Frankie had to hold the Zippo as he was still shaking. "I'm hoping the injured rat will unlock the key. Something has affected it and it might help the investigation if we can find out what it was. It could be just a physical injury, but it gives us a chance to do more tests."

Frankie nodded and put a hand on his shoulder. "Ron, why don't you take a break from this investigation? Look at you." She lifted his hand, which was shaking so much that he struggled to keep hold of the cigarette. "I think Ben was right. You've been through a most traumatic experience. If I had been down there instead of you, I would have had a heart attack just looking at those bloody rats."

"No chance," said Ron. "I'm in this for the duration. Need to crack this before someone else gets killed."

"But what's to be gained? You've got plenty to go on back at the lab, including a live rat. Is there any point in staying in London?"

"Don't forget, there's still an infected man on the loose, and there's Bob French, the sewer worker."

"And?"

Ron was silent for a minute, contemplating the question. What could he do? Wouldn't it be better for him to help out in the lab? "I'll see what the boss wants me to do."

"Good call," said Frankie, "and for now, you're coming with me for a hospital checkup."

"No hospitals," protested Ron.

"Do you want to go of your own free will, or do I have to wrestle you to the ground and cuff you?" she said, giving him a dazzling smile.

Ron laughed and nodded. He knew she was right. "Come on, let's get it over and done with," he said and tried to stand, but the pain in his head was so intense that he sat straight back down.

"Come on, old man," she said, putting an arm around him and helping him to his feet. He rested his head on her shoulder and took in the scent of her perfume. "You'll have to let me know which brand you're wearing. Smells divine."

"Chanel Coromandel. Nice, isn't it? The boss bought it for my birthday."

"Smells expensive."

"Just over two hundred bucks a bottle. Thinking of buying one for your mother?"

"No, Graham actually. He doesn't do aftershave, and I really like this one."

"Lucky old Graham," she said as she helped him out of the cafe door and onto the pavement.

After a checkup confirming a mild concussion, and a conversation with Ben, Ron was ordered back to Moreton to recover. He tried to resist, but Chris Williams agreed with Ben, and he slept fitfully, dreaming of pitch-dark tunnels throughout the journey to the Cotswolds while Frankie drove.

SIXTY

"Well, if it isn't the devil himself," said Kath as Ron and Frankie walked into reception. "And who is this gorgeous young lady?"

Frankie smiled and offered a hand to Kath. Kath took it but didn't shake it. Instead, she reached out and took the other hand as well and looked down. "No wedding band? Ron, don't tell me you've decided to go on the straight and narrow?" She burst out laughing and started to cough. "Sorry, my love. Just joking. You must be Frankie? Heard a lot about you and much prettier than this eejit said you were."

"And you must be Kath. I've heard a so much about you."

"All good, I hope," she said, giving Ron her customary stare of death.

"Of course. He thinks you're wonderful," said Frankie, smiling sweetly at Ron, who shook his head.

"That's just what my Patrick says when he wants something. Just take last Friday. There I was clearing the dishes away when he tells me the same. He must think I was born yesterday. Friday night is darts night at the Black Bear and—"

While Kath talked at Frankie, Ron tiptoed up the stairs.

"Glad to see you back, mate," said Roger, as Ron strolled into the lab. "How's your head? Heard you gave it a crack."

"I'm okay. What have I missed while I've been away? Have you looked at that rat yet? Is it still alive?"

Moving to the front worktop, Roger pulled a sheet off the large cage that the rat was delivered in. Ron stepped back, feeling the same cold chill sweep across his shoulder blades. He composed himself and walked nearer to the cage.

"Well?"

"Well, what?" said Roger.

"Where is it?"

"Sleeping."

"Where?"

"What do you mean, where? Under the hay in the cage. Can't you see its tail sticking out?"

"You didn't receive this rat from London."

"It most definitely is the same rat."

"Stop messing around, Roger. The rat I found in that hellhole was about the size of a large cat."

"It was when it got here."

The hay in the cage moved, and a head poked out. Two dark eyes stared at the two men and retreated.

"Explain, Roger. Stop winding me up."

Roger stood next to him and scrolled through several photos on his phone. The first was of the giant rat lying in the cage on its side. The next was the same rat, but slightly smaller, and the bright red color had faded from its tail. As the dozen photos progressed, the rat reduced in size, and its gruesome features receded. Serrated teeth disappeared. Its extended jaws shrank, and the glossy blue sheen to its dark coat faded until it was back to a natural rat brown.

"Bloody amazing, don't you think?" said Roger, who flicked back and forth through the incredible sequence of images. "And it all took place in just a few hours in front of our eyes."

"How did you do it?"

"I didn't do anything. It just happened."

Ron stared at the cage and then smiled. "This rat has to be the key."

"I guessed that," said Roger, "and it makes a change for *us* to find out why rather than the boss and Claire."

"Have you told Ben yet?"

"No, I wanted you to see this first before we do a conference call and give him the good news. It needs more than a chat on the phone."

"Okay, set up the call. I'm going back downstairs to rescue Frankie from something far scarier than a giant rat."

Roger waited until it was after breakfast time in Nevada, and Ron and Frankie joined him in the conference room.

"Nice to see you again," said Ron, smiling at the huge plasma screen. "Some good news."

Ron retold the events of the last day and the discovery of an affected rat regressing to its normal condition.

"That is good news," said Ben. "Now the work begins. We need to test this rat to the nth degree to find out why it returned to its natural state. Any theories?"

"A few," said Roger.

"Such as?"

"Perhaps this mutant condition is only temporary, and reversal is part of the process, or the rat has eaten something to reverse the condition."

"I would go for the latter but without ruling out the 'temporary condition.' It just seems pointless for this process to take place then reverse of its own accord, but I'm not discounting it," said Ben. "What do you think, Ron?"

"I'm with you on this. It must be something it's eaten or maybe another disease or bacteria it' has picked up that has countered the extreme deformities."

"I'll arrange with Chris Williams to catch a few more to test any ideas coming out of the tests you do on your live specimen."

Ron shuddered. "Do I have to be here if they capture more?

Sorry, Ben, but after what happened, I don't think I could stomach it."

"No, you've been through enough trauma, and if it wasn't for your dogged determination, we wouldn't have found the 'cured' rat. Take a couple of days off if you like."

"Not a chance," said Ron. "I'll go back to London and keep my finger on the pulse, but this time I'm staying above ground!"

"Good idea, Ron. Frankie, thanks for looking after Ron. Can you make sure he does no more subterranean investigations?"

"Will do," she said, laughing.

"How's work going on the samples I sent over, Roger?" said Ben.

"Okay, but the blue fish they pulled out of Regent's Canal are far more interesting, especially the monster pike."

"Why?"

"Have you heard of fungal panspermia?"

Ben shook his head. "No, I don't think—" then he paused for a second, raised a finger, and nodded. "Hang on. It's ringing a distant bell. Is this the theory that fungal spores can travel through space and spread life?"

"You've got it. It's speculation with nothing concrete to back it up, which has been doing the rounds since Anaxagoras, a Greek philosopher, from the fifth century BCE, came up with the idea of 'seeds of life' throughout the cosmos."

"I remember now," said Ben, who was pacing around the conference room on the screen. "Where did you drag that obscure reference from, Roger? I didn't think Ancient Greek history was your forte."

"It's not. It was Kerry. She's been brilliant and researched it online. I'd like to take credit, but I'm just the messenger."

"Are you suggesting that the meteor shower at Teakettle Junction is connected to this theory?"

"It's a possibility. When we took the pike apart, we found evidence of a unique form of mycelium type structures attached to the spinal cord. Strands spread from the spine to the areas on the fish's body where there'd been the most drastic physical changes."

"That fits in with what Vince King told us when he came to London with Herbie Lomax," said Claire. "He had a theory that the lights in Pyramid Lake were alien beings that might be parasitic or having a symbiotic relationship with the host fish."

"Conclusion, Roger?" said Ben.

"I have no proof of this, but my gut is telling me that the meteor shower contained fungal spores from a distant galaxy with the ability to survive the extreme temperature variations during space travel and entry friction into Earth's atmosphere. The spores reacted with water in Lake Pyramid and Limehouse Basin, creating small aquatic life forms that can attach themselves to living organisms and transform their physical and mental status. Sounds farfetched, I know, but you don't believe in coincidences, and neither do I, especially when there have been so many. The meteor shower, its trajectory, the link with water, and the same mutations on different continents."

Ben gave the thumbs-up on the screen. "Well done, Roger. It sounds farfetched, but I believe you're on the right track. With a little more research and testing of the live affected rat, I think we can solve this and avert a global disaster."

The conference ended, and Frankie prodded Ron in the back.

"I'm pretty good at my job, apart from letting you nearly get eaten by an army of rats, but you lot just lost me. What was all that nonsense about fungal spores in space?"

"Do you know what mycelium is?"

"No, please enlighten me, and can we have some coffee? I need a boost," said Frankie.

"The coffee machine's on the blink, but there's a cafe in town that does fabulous coffee and cakes. My treat, I owe you."

"You do," she said and followed him out into Church Street. "I can see why you want to move here. Moreton's a lovely place," she said. "Much nicer than London or LA. It feels like... I can't quite put my finger on it?"

"Calm and stress-free?"

"Yes, and fresh air," she said, inhaling through her nose. "It smells fresh and natural. Not like a city. London air is clingy."

"Clingy?"

"Clinging, laced with tarmac and stale city air."

"Clingy?" said Ron. "I like that. Sounds perfect for London."

"Yes, it must be heaven to live here in Moreton."

"Nothing stopping you from moving from London," said Ron, lighting up a Marlboro.

"Bit of a commute every day, and there's no working from home in my line of business."

"Perhaps you could go freelance. Live where you like?"

"I considered doing just that, but the pay is far too good where I am."

"Money's not everything, Frankie. I jumped ship from a similar job and took a cut to be with Ben and his team, but my sanity's worth a damned sight more than money."

They crossed the main road, and Frankie stopped and turned full circle.

"It really is beautiful," she said, admiring the old sandstone buildings. "I could get used to this."

Inside Martha's cafe, they ordered cappuccinos and Danish pastries.

"You were going to explain space fungus?" she said, scraping the peaks of froth off her coffee and putting the spoon in her mouth. "Why do they always spoil it with chocolate on top?" she said, pulling a face.

"Search me," said Ron. "Mycelium is a series of fungal threads that grow underground and are vital for many plants and animals. They can travel a long way underground by subdividing, a bit like continually adding extensions to a house. Mushrooms, their reproductive mechanism, sprout from mycelium and send spores into the air to be carried by air currents to colonize elsewhere."

"Right. Mushrooms I know about."

"The spores are more resistant to temperature and other effects, and if the theories of space travel are true, they are the most likely organisms to survive the vast distances between planets and solar systems, transported in space dust and meteors."

"The meteor shower Roger was talking about could have brought spores to Earth?"

"Right. It appears that interacting with water has activated the spores, and the rest you know. Giant rats and people looking like bears."

"So, what's the answer to stop it spreading?"

"The rat I found in that underground substation has regressed into its natural physical state, and there must be a reason for that. We have to find out what caused it to turn back into a nice, cuddly rat from a monster."

"So, why are we going back to London when all the action's here?"

"A rat hunt for live ones to test. Except I won't be at the sharp end looking for them."

She shook her head. "Ron, I might be missing something here, and I'm not a scientist, but why go to all that trouble and put yourself in harm's way again when you don't need to?"

"What do you mean, I don't need to?"

"Get some rats from your lab suppliers, pet shop, or wherever you get lab rats from. Infect them with the spore thingies in the lab, then try out any antidotes you come up with."

Ron stared at her for a second and burst out laughing.

She blushed. "Have I said something stupid?"

He slapped the table. "Frankie, you're not just a pretty face." He rang Roger, stunned that the easy, safe, and obvious source of infected rats had crossed no one's mind, except for his very attractive bodyguard's.

SIXTY-ONE

Alex Munro poured his third glass of wine and sat back in the office chair, drumming his fingers on the desktop as he contemplated his next move. One of the two goons who was supposed to be watching his back was in custody. The other was not answering his phone and, if the rumors were true, was dead following an incident in a disused underground substation.

The biggest worry was Zak Wilson, who was in custody at Bethnal Green police station after being arrested on the Minerva Estate. Would he keep his mouth shut, especially after learning that Wayne was dead? He unlocked one of the desk drawers, pulled out a journal, and thumbed through the pages until he found the name and contact number. The call received an immediate answer.

"Mr. Munro. How nice to hear from you! What can I do for you this time?"

"Are you at work at the moment?"

"I am."

"Good. Do you still have Zak Wilson in custody?"

"Still here. He's being interviewed again later this morning."

"Has he said anything interesting since his arrest?"

"Nothing. It's 'no comment' all the way, so far."

"Have you heard anything about Wayne? Was it him?"

"Just found out he's dead, Mr. Munro. Half-eaten by rats, I heard."

Munro went silent.

"Are you still there?"

"Yes, sorry. That was shocking to hear, that's all. Does Zak Wilson know about Wayne yet?"

"No. I think the detective interviewing him this morning will drop that little bombshell into the interrogation to see if it loosens his tongue."

"I would like you to give a message to Wilson, and it has to be before the interview. Do you understand?"

"Of course, Mr. Munro. Will it be the usual fee?"

"That goes without saying," said Alex, annoyed by the mention of the money, "and don't include me when you tell him."

"Got it. And the message is?"

"Tell him Jonny Clarke asked, would you like to join him for a drink?"

"Jonny Clarke, you said?"

"Yes. Make sure he gets the message as soon as possible. It's really important."

"I'll be doing a routine check of the prisoners in about five minutes. He'll be the first cell I visit."

"Good man."

Alex cut the call and sat back, taking another large sip of wine. If Zak Wilson kept his mouth shut, there should be no comeback. He pursed his lips and tapped the speed dial. His other assistant would deal with Zak when he was released from custody, tidying up the remaining loose end.

SIXTY-TWO

The phone call from Chris Williams changed everything at the lab in Moreton-in-Marsh.

Three army trucks arrived in Church Street and took Roger and Jen, along with all their equipment and twelve live rats, to set up infection experiments at a secret location in nearby Oxfordshire. Chris Williams insisted on carrying out the task at a secure army facility thirty miles from Moreton-in-Marsh, away from any built-up area and within a secure military establishment.

Roger protested but was overruled by Chris Williams with solid logic. "We've already had an anonymous threat from someone claiming to be from an animal rights group, and the last thing we want is the lab being broken into and infected rats released into the wild," she said, before telling him he could argue all he liked but this directive had come from the very top.

The three-vehicle convoy, with a police escort, arrived at the secret base, which looked like a group of farm buildings at the end of a mile-long track, off a country lane. The similarity to a farm disappeared once they passed through twelve-foot-high double gates into a central concrete yard. Each farm building surrounding the yard was a facade, like a Wild West film set, topped with razor wire and with CCTV covering every conceivable angle. Roger pointed up at the cameras to Jen.

"Chris was right. We'd have been easy pickings for a break-in at Moreton. This place is like Fort Knox!"

"I feel like a bloody prisoner," she said. "Where do we go now?"

Soldiers were offloading the trucks and placing the boxes, bags, and crates around the double steel doors to a central brick, windowless outhouse in the center of the yard, no larger than a double domestic garage.

"They have to be kidding," said Roger. "We'll never get all this kit in there and have space to work."

The steel doors opened, and a man in a gray suit stepped out and shook hands with them both.

"Clive Johns, Home Office. Sorry to drag you out here, but I'm sure you understand. Follow me."

He turned, and when they entered the small building, the penny dropped. It was an entrance lobby to a lift.

"Welcome to our underground facility," he said as the lift doors parted and they stepped in. Roger saw there were just two call buttons in the lift. They descended for what seemed like an eternity before the lift smoothly came to a halt.

"Is the lift the only way in and out?" said Roger.

"Of course not. Don't panic; we have a remote exit for emergencies."

The lift opened into a long concrete corridor with several numbered doors on either side and a larger door at the end.

"Your personal bedrooms are in three and four," he said, pointing at two steel doors on the right. "They have en suites."

"Sorry, but we don't intend to be staying overnight," said Jen.

Clive Johns stopped abruptly and turned. "My apologies. Chris Williams obviously didn't inform you. You cannot leave this establishment while you are working here."

"You have to be kidding?" said Jen.

"Sorry, but I don't make the rules. Even I'm incarcerated here until you've completed your work. The powers that be are not expecting a nine-to-five day with nights off. They want this wrapped up as quickly as possible with no time wasted traveling back and forth."

"But I haven't brought spare clothes, toiletries, or anything else I might need."

"Don't worry, we'll provide everything you ask for."

"And if we refuse to cooperate?"

Roger put his hand on her shoulder. "Jen. Stop complaining. This is far too important, and he's right. We need to be working flat out on this with early starts and very late finishes. You won't feel like going home."

She glared at Roger and went quiet.

Clive Johns moved forward. "Room five is the kitchen diner, and eight is the consumables' store," he said, pointing to the left. "And here we have your temporary lab," he said, pushing the door open at the end of the corridor.

Roger stepped through the doorway and looked up, then around, taking in the vast space the size of a football pitch. It appeared to go on forever, with just a small area set out with benches and equipment.

"What is this place?" said Jen, her voice echoing as she stared at the concrete ceiling thirty feet above.

"It's been here since the Cold War began in 1947 and was mothballed in the early '90s when the Soviet Union collapsed. Ever since it's been maintained, but never used except for inter-military and government exercises."

"Interesting," said Roger. "Plenty of space to work in."

Clive Johns laughed. "It was originally designed for a lot more people. Take a look at the equipment we've already installed for you. It should match everything you have at your lab. We did a full inventory check when you had your previous alien encounter in Moreton-in-Marsh, so you should have everything you need, plus your latest additions, which the soldiers are bringing down now. Use the army lads and lasses to set everything up, not to waste time. I'll be in my office, room six." He smiled, turned sharply, and walked back into the corridor behind them.

"No wonder the country's going to the dogs when they're spending money on crap like this," said Roger.

"I'm not happy about this," said Jen. "I don't want to be staying in this concrete prison day and night. Who the hell do they think they are?"

Roger put his arm around her. "Cheer up, Jen. If we can crack this, we're out of here. Think of the overtime. I just hope there's a few beers in my room. I could do with a couple right now!"

She gave a weak smile. "I suppose I'll just have to grin and bear it. I'm going to look at my room before I do anything else, and it better be good, or I'll personally strangle Chris Williams."

SIXTY-THREE

Ben called it a day, late in the afternoon, after a short update meeting with Herbie Lomax, during which he asked probing questions about Jacy's whereabouts. It was an uncomfortable exchange, and even though they gave nothing away, Ben could tell that Herbie knew they were holding back.

They arrived at the diner, and the grin on Zinnia Charleston's face was as wide as ever, even though Ben had turned down her offer of a date.

"She doesn't give up easy," said Claire under her breath as they walked to the table that Zinnia gestured to.

"So nice to see you again, Dr. Sharman," she said, without mentioning Claire. "What can I get you?"

"Just coffees, please," said Ben, smiling back.

Claire had to check herself, as once again, she started to count the woman's teeth.

The coffees arrived at the same time Egan slid into the seat next to Ben.

"Everything okay?" said Ben.

"Fine. Jacy and the two guys have settled into the safehouse.

"I can't thank you enough for helping us," said Ben.

Egan shook his head and smiled. "You're doing your best to help everyone, and any little help I can give needs no gratitude."

"Are John Drake and the other guy in good shape?"

"Yes. John's not feeling too good from the after-effects of the tranquilizer, but that will pass, and Brett Daniels is doing fine."

"What about Brett's facial injuries from the shotgun?"

"Something I suspect will greatly interest you both."

"Oh?"

"I changed the bandages covering Brett's face and upper chest, and when they came off, the hair underneath came off with them."

"Pulled off by the bandages?"

"No. That's what I first thought. I assumed blood had dried into the hair and removing the bandages had yanked it out. But it wasn't like that. It's as if the hair around the injured areas just fell away. Like he molted."

"What about the skin?" asked Claire.

"That's the other strange thing. The gunshot had broken the skin, but now it's back to its normal color. The blue tint is gone."

"We need to see this firsthand," said Claire.

"Finish your coffees, leave your car here, and I'll take you to the safehouse. It's about twenty minutes away, just outside Nixon."

"It's no trouble. We'll follow you there," said Ben.

Claire laughed. "Ben, we're going in Egan's car."

"What?"

"Our car's bugged, remember? And unless you want to lead Herbie's posse to the two men, I suggest you listen to Egan."

After they finished their coffees Egan jangled his car keys. "Shall we?" he said, walking to the door.

The safehouse was actually a scrapped yellow school bus located at the back of a car wrecker's yard on the outskirts of Nixon. The bus, which hadn't carried schoolchildren on board for many a year, had all the seats ripped out and now functioned as the yard's office and a place to crash when the owner, a friend of Egan's, had a few too many beers and couldn't drive.

As they pulled into the yard, Egan stopped short of the bus and stared ahead.

"Something's not right," he said.

Ben squinted in the harsh sunlight at the battered old bus. "Problem?"

"There," said Egan, pointing at what looked like a large sleeping Doberman, lying in the dirt just outside the bus door, attached to a steel spike by a long metal chain.

"Sorry, what am I supposed to be looking at?"

"The dog would normally strain at the end of its chain, barking like hell."

Egan got out, opened the tailgate, and pulled out a rifle.

"Stay put," he said and walked over to the dog. He crouched next to it and lifted its paw before dropping it, and shook his head. The dog was not responsive.

Ben and Claire watched him step up through the open door into the bus, walk the full length with his rifle raised, then lower himself near the back.

"This place is giving me the creeps," said Claire, eyeing the huge piles of wrecked cars and trucks surrounding them. "Far too quiet."

Egan appeared on the steps of the bus shouting, "Bring my first aid kit from under the front passenger seat and hurry!"

Ben pulled the small box from under his seat and ran to the bus, with Claire right behind. As they stepped up, they could see that someone had turned the converted office upside down. A desk and two chairs were like matchwood, and the deck of the bus, strewn with scattered papers, files, and beer cans made it look as if a tornado had ripped through. At the far end, Egan crouched over a body at the back, talking on his phone.

"Pulson's Yard, Wishbone Road. Two casualties. Looks like they've been assaulted. Both are unconscious. One bleeding heavily from the shoulder. Yes, I am about to stem the bleeding. Okay, thanks, and ask them to hurry. I don't know how long ago this happened, and there's a lot of blood." He threw the phone aside and opened the first aid kit, ripping open cotton bandages, bunching them up, and forcing them into Jacy's shoulder, applying pressure to the wound. Lying next to Jacy was Brett Daniels, on his back, unconscious but breathing.

"What the hell happened here?" said Claire, helping Ben push the giant man onto his side and into the recovery position.

"Not sure," said Egan. "But there's no sign of John Drake. When I spoke to Jacy earlier, he said John had taken a turn for the worse and was getting really agitated. I just thought he was getting testy with the after-effects of the tranquilizer."

Jacy groaned and opened his eyes. He tried to sit up, but Egan stopped him. "Stay still, son. Help's on its way."

"Where's Brett? Is he alright?" said Jacy.

"Out cold, but he looks okay. I'm sure he'll be fine," said Egan. "Keep still, son, you're bleeding from the shoulder."

"John went crazy, started fighting with Brett. I tried to pull him off, but he threw me, and I must have hit something."

"We can talk later. Just lie still."

"His face changed. He looked like an animal."

"In what way?" said Ben.

"Wider, sharper features and a weird ridge on the top of his head. His entire head seemed to be changing shape," said Jacy, who pushed his father back, sat up, and cried out in pain.

"Listen to your father, Jacy, and lie down," said Claire, who held the back of his head, lowering it gently onto the floor.

At that moment, the bus shook as John Drake clambered up the steps, standing at the other end facing them. He held an iron bar in his huge, clenched fist and was about to advance on them when Egan stood and faced him with the rifle.

John seemed even taller, his head almost touching the roof of the bus. His eyes, now vivid red, glared at Egan. His lips curled back, revealing rows of serrated teeth, and the ridge of his nose now extended upward, creating a pointed crest to the top of his head. The hair that had covered his face was thinner, revealing rippling blue skin underneath.

"He's transforming into something else," whispered Claire. "There's no human being in there anymore."

Egan fired the rifle, deliberately missing, shattering the front windshield. Drake turned and ran off the bus, disappearing between rows of scrap engines, his thundering footsteps receding to the far side of the immense yard. They caught sight of him again above a pile of crushed cars as he scaled the perimeter fence with ease, dropping to the other side into scrubland.

"They know," said Jacy.

"What do you mean, 'they know?'" said Ben.

"They know you're trying to make them human again, and they're going to resist."

Ben was silent for a moment.

"Jacy," said Claire, "who are 'they?'"

"I don't know, but they're the ones controlling John Drake and the others, and they're beginning to change physically and mentally as they used to exist."

"What are you talking about, son?" said Egan.

"They are not of this Earth. They had to find a new home, and this was the only way."

Egan looked at Ben. "He's delirious."

"I don't think so," said Ben. "I think he's making perfect sense."

SIXTY-FOUR

An ambulance pulled into the wrecker's yard, and seconds later, two black SUVs came to a screeching halt close behind.

"Here we go," said Claire, seeing Herbie Lomax bearing down on them.

"What the hell do you think you were doing, Ben?" said Herbie, arms folded, staring at him. "This charade is exactly why you should have left this to us and stuck to being a scientist."

Claire pushed Ben aside. "How dare you talk to him like that? You were the ones acting like you were back in the Wild West, like a pack of irresponsible gunslingers—shoot first and ask questions later. Thank the Lord we don't allow guns in the UK." She continued to glare at him, her eyes blazing.

Herbie stared back, their eyes locked for over a minute before he began to laugh, without looking away.

"I have to give it to you, Ben," he said, still laughing. "You won't go far wrong with Claire watching your back."

"Can we discuss this in a civilized manner?" said Ben, stepping between them to end the visual joust. "You're right, Herbie. We are scientists, but we're also compassionate scientists, and we felt you'd harm these people, who are simply victims of some unworldly infection. They're not wild animals that can be shot without a second thought, but human beings. That's why we've put their welfare first."

"Okay, okay, I get it, but you have to see the bigger picture here. We can't have people wandering the streets with some extraterrestrial disease that could be highly contagious and deadly, and we'll take whatever means necessary to keep our citizens safe."

"I just think that your idea of 'any means possible' is too heavy-handed."

"Look, Ben, we both want the same thing, so let's not get into a pissing contest over this. So, what happened here?" he said, stepping onto the bus.

Ben went through the events leading up to Herbie's arrival.

"So, if one of them was trying to kill you, what's your scientific conclusion, Ben? Are these people safe to be left to their own devices?"

Ben desperately wanted to say that they were, but couldn't. Herbie was right. He had to think about the bigger picture.

"I believe that contaminated food allowed alien spores to enter their bodies, and their vascular systems then transported the spores around, infecting these people. The entities have attached themselves to the nervous system then spread, taking over the person's body. The latest events seem to have sped up the transition, and it could be because of your actions."

"What's that supposed to mean?" said Herbie, raising his voice.

"These entities are intelligent, and it doesn't take a rocket scientist to figure out they realize their softly-softly approach to taking over a person's body and mind needs to be taken up a gear. My guess is that they will try to infect more people to grow in number and accelerate the physical transformations into whatever they looked like when they existed in some far-off galaxy. In a nutshell, they're flying under the radar to take over very effectively."

"If you're right, then my so-called heavy-handed approach is the right way."

"Don't forget, Herbie, underneath their unworldly appearance, these are human beings, and I am sure the condition is reversible."

"All noted," said Herbie, impatiently. "Now I suggest you get back to the Barngate lab and find a cure for this damned space bug before it becomes a pandemic. I'll send Brett Daniels to the lab where you can run tests on him, but we have to find the rest of them." He stalked away, barking orders to the agents.

"Let's get out of here," said Egan. "You've said your piece. Now it's time to find a cure, and I need to see how my son is. I'll drop you back at your car at the diner."

As they stepped out of the bus, agents carried Brett Daniels to one of the SUVs, and paramedics loaded Jacy into an ambulance.

"I can see you're both upset with Herbie, but I can also see why he's so concerned," said Egan as they pulled out of the wrecker's yard.

"But you can see my point?" said Ben. "They're looking at these poor individuals as wild animals."

"They are, but just consider if this gets out of hand and we have a whole commune of them, turned into murderous monsters."

Ben remained silent until they arrived at the diner parking lot.

They got out, and Egan leaned out of the car window. "Focus on the cure and take your mind off Herbie. Clear head, Ben. Those poor folks depend on you. Just keep that firmly in mind. Herbie's just a distraction."

Ben nodded and climbed into the SUV.

Zinnia Charleston waved through the door of the diner as they pulled away.

Claire pointed at her. "See that look of disappointment, Ben? She hasn't given up yet."

"Shut it," snapped Ben.

"She'll get you in the end."

Ben pulled the car over, killed the engine, and gave her a long, hard, icy stare.

"Ben, I'm only winding you up. Don't get so touchy."

"I know you are, but pack it in. I'm not in a good place at the moment and could do without your constant jibes."

There was a long silence until Claire spoke.

"Okay, sorry, but what's eating you? It's not this case, is it?"

He shook his head.

"It's Amy, isn't it?"

He said nothing.

"It is Amy, isn't it? What's happened?"

He nodded, staring straight ahead.

"It's none of my business, but if you want to talk."

Ben looked back at her, the anger gone, his face softened. "She applied for a promotion, successfully passed the board, and was offered a position as a detective chief inspector."

"Wow, that's great, Ben. Good for her. It'll mean more money coming in."

"I wish it was that simple."

"Oh," said Claire, connecting the dots. "Where is this promotion taking her?"

"Newcastle, and she's given me an ultimatum."

"To move with her?"

"Yep, over two hundred miles from Moreton."

"And she's definitely going to accept the promotion?"

"Accepted, rubber-stamped, and starts a week from Monday."

"Ben, I'm so sorry."

"Thanks, but it's my problem, not yours. And don't worry, I have no intention of leaving Moreton-in-Marsh."

He started the engine, and they drove in silence all the way to Barngate Holdings.

Guilt filled Claire's thoughts during the journey. She had flirted and teased Ben, and all the time he had been wrestling with the dilemma of losing his career-seeking fiancée. Although she didn't really like Amy, she couldn't help wishing that she wasn't heading for a career change and leaving Ben. On the other hand, if her career was more important than Ben, then good riddance. He'd worked damned hard and put his life on the line to turn a small, local scientific business into an internationally recognized leader in scientific investigation. The guilt evaporated, and she nodded to herself. Good riddance, Amy, your loss, she thought.

SIXTY-FIVE

Jen shook Roger's shoulder. "Wake up. You need to see this."

Roger had fallen asleep at the bench next to the microscope he'd been working with for over two hours. He lifted his head, and she laughed at the imprints of fingers on his cheek where he'd been resting on them.

He rubbed his eyes and slid off the chair. "Must have nodded off. It's those bloody artificial lights," he said, pointing up at the huge strip lights thirty feet above. "They make me drowsy."

"It's not the lights, Roger. You're just knackered."

He stretched up on tiptoes, raising both arms above his head, and began scratching his hair. "What's so important?"

"Our rat. The one Ron found in the substation. It's perfectly normal."

"But we knew that already," he said, yawning.

"No, it just looked as if it had regressed back into a normal rat, but I've been running tests on it, and it's just a garden-variety rat. The only difference is it got injected with opioids. Probably heroin."

"How's that possible?"

"Think about it."

"I am, but I don't see how."

"You're a junkie just about to stick a needle in your arm, and suddenly you're attacked by a giant rat. You have a weapon in your hand and lash out to protect yourself."

"And the rat gets some of the fix? Come off it!"

"It had a needle wound on its back, and I tested the surrounding skin. The rat has been injected without a doubt. Blood tests prove it."

They walked over to the cage and looked for the rat, which was well hidden in a bundle of straw.

"I anesthetized it and scanned the whole body. The entity that attaches itself to the central nervous system has disintegrated. Just a residue left."

Roger considered the implications, still not quite believing that someone injected the rat with a syringe full of heroin. "How much heroin did the rat take from the needle?"

"Hard to say," said Jen. "Not the full dose, but enough to give it a decent trip. The point is that heroin, or some component of heroin, reverted this rat from a monster to a normal rodent, fully clear of any alien parasitic or symbiotic entity inside its body."

"Okay, I'll give Ben a call and let him know," said Roger, walking away.

"I ordered some heroin," said Jen.

He stopped and turned. "You know a local dealer?"

"Very funny. Chris Williams can get anything we want. She said it's from a stock of seized drugs from one of the UK ports. It's being transported by helicopter and will be here within the hour. As soon as it gets here, I'm testing it on the infected rats."

"The way I'm feeling at the moment, you can try it out on me," he said, yawning again. "And before I call Ben, how are the rats progressing?"

"Rapidly," she said, pulling a screen away from six large glass cages. Roger's eyes widened at the sight of six very large white rats with a slight blue sheen, whose blood-red eyes glared through the protective glazing, each bearing a formidable set of teeth and elongated jaws.

"How the hell do they bulk up so much?" he said. "It's not as if you've been feeding them for weeks." The rats, now the size of large cats, had lost their timidness and were right up to the glass with lips curled back. Blue spittle ran down the inside of the glass as they hissed and spat.

"Search me. Something we can look at later, but for now, I need to run the tests as soon as I get the delivery."

He was about to call Ben when his phone vibrated.

"What are you doing up at this hour, Ron?"

"Lots going on here, Roger. Do you want the good news or the bad?"

"Cheer me up first. Give me the good."

"I just took a call from Chris Williams. Bob French, the sewage worker who had to be isolated, has made a remarkable recovery, and it looks like it happened with no intervention from the medical staff. It's got them puzzled."

"Full recovery?"

"Yes. infection-free. They were lining up a whole load of varied treatments starting tomorrow, but Mr. French's immune system, or something else they haven't spotted, seems to have beaten them to it," said Ron.

"We need to get him here and run tests on him. The rat you discovered in that underground substation is the same. reverted to normal, and it looks like a dose of heroin did the trick."

"Heroin?"

"Yep. I think one of the junkies in that substation stabbed it with a syringe he was using and injected the rat."

"That's weird."

"I think we're almost there, Ron. Just need to identify the reason and we can stop the spread. Go on, hit me with the bad news."

"If you had the news on the TV, you'd know. There have been five deaths, shootings, and several other attacks in Hackney and

Bethnal Green, and it's not rats this time. It's infected people. The army shot dead two armed men who started firing at an army patrol close to Cricketers Bridge. The deceased were grotesque-looking, covered in black hair with the blue tinge. It's spreading into the human population, Roger."

"Is Ben aware of this yet? I was about to call him."

"I'd be amazed if he isn't; the news has gone global. There are bloody press helicopters filling the sky here."

"Can you get Bob French here soon? I can't leave this site, and we're up to our necks in tests."

"Chris Williams will sort it out. I'll ring her; you talk to Ben."

The lab at Barngate Holdings was like a beehive, even though it would normally be empty so late in the afternoon. The six technical staff drafted in took the grind and pressure away from Ben and Claire, allowing them more time to analyze results and think. Tests on Brett Daniels produced interesting results. The small particles of salt embedded in his lower face and chest from Amanda Dooley's shotgun appeared to clear the skin of its hair and blue pallor about an inch in circumference from every entry wound. After the discovery, they sprayed three test areas on his back, abdomen, and thigh, and after an hour, hair fell out, and his skin reverted to a normal, healthy color.

Ben's phone rang as he and Claire were preparing a bath full of salt water to immerse Brett Daniels.

"Roger, can I ring you back? Me and Claire are in the middle of something that might provide the answer."

"That's why I was ringing you. We think we have the answer as well," said Roger.

"Salt?" said Ben.

"Did you say salt?"

"Yes, as in sodium chloride."

"No, not salt. We think it could be morphine, or should I say heroin, which is morphine-based."

"Right, bring me up to speed. What have you found?"

Roger described the rapid reversal of the rat's condition with the injection of heroin and the destruction of the entity inside controlling its mind and body.

"We've got a batch of lab rats Jen has infected, and we're about to test them with heroin."

"That's brilliant!," said Ben. "Try immersing one in a strong saline solution and see what effect it has, not just on the general appearance but on the entity inside the body."

"The chap who was infected in London, Bob French, appears to have made a full recovery, and it seems he has achieved it with no medical help. I've asked Ron to have him brought here so we can have a good look at him."

"Things are looking up. Has Ron told you about the shootings in London?"

"I was just about to ask if you'd seen them over there."

"It's plastered all over every channel. We've made global news once again! I just hope we can get this sorted before mass panic sets in."

Ben finished the call and gestured to Brett Daniels, standing in the doorway in a pair of shorts, to step into the bath.

"Warm enough?" said Claire.

"Perfect," he said, kneeling down, then lying back. He just about fitted into the bathtub, and Claire was about to dip a large jug into the salt water, but he pushed the jug away and slid forward, immersing his hairy body and head under the water and staying under for a full minute. He remained in the tub for two hours before there were signs of a reaction. At first, a few floating hairs could be seen as he kept up the submerging routine. After three hours, with added warm water and a lot more salt, the hair was coming out in clumps.

By the time dusk arrived, Brett Daniels looked like a normal human being again.

"I think you'd better get out of the tub, Brett, before you turn into a wrinkled prune," said Ben. "Get yourself showered and dressed and come and have some food with us."

They stepped out of the bathroom and into the conference room, where an array of pizza cartons, just delivered, were waiting for them.

"Well, that proves it beyond doubt," said Ben, trying to speak while devouring an enormous slice of pepperoni. "Just need to scan him and see what effect it has had on the entity inside. I just find it odd that he's not developed further. What do you think?"

Claire wagged her finger, not wanting to speak while she was eating.

"Salt wounds," she suggested, after gulping back a large piece of pepperoni. "They cleared the area around each puncture of the skin. Perhaps the salt was more far-reaching than just the superficial reversal."

Ben nodded and looked around the room filled with lab techs and a couple of agents, all getting stuck into the dozen pizza boxes and beers they had ordered. He smiled to himself, feeling satisfied that at last they were making progress, and found it ironic how the key to unlocking this extraterrestrial problem was not some complex chemical formula but a simple compound called salt.

Brett Daniels suddenly burst into the room. "There's something going on outside," he shouted. "I can sense it."

The room went silent, and everyone turned toward the door.

"Sense what, Brett?" said Ben.

"They're coming here to stop you."

At that moment, gunshots rang out from outside.

Ben rushed into the corridor and peered through the side window overlooking the main car park, and a few seconds later dove on the floor.

SIXTY-SIX

"Everyone get down!" shouted Ben, just before the window he'd been looking out of shattered. Ben lay on the floor below the window, showered in tiny shards of glass. More shots rang out, and a huge hairy arm slumped down from the window, blood dripping from it onto Ben's forehead. An agent stepped forward, crouching next to Ben.

"You okay?"

Ben nodded.

The agent signaled to his partner, who called Herbie for reinforcements.

"They're on the way," he mouthed back after a quick conversation on his phone, giving the thumbs-up.

It had gone quiet outside. Too quiet. Ben saw at least half a dozen of the huge, infected men around the guard hut near the entrance. The security guard lay on his back in the middle of the car park, and even though the lighting was dim, Ben had seen the front of the man's shirt soaked with blood. He'd been shot and was presumed dead. One of the big men outside prodded him with his foot; the guard showed no sign of life. The light shone across the enormous man's face, and Ben observed the razor-sharp teeth, pronounced forehead, and the ridge extending from the nose to the top of the man's head. He was well on his way to developing into... what? As the man turned and ran toward him with a raised rifle, Ben reacted, diving for cover, below the window.

Ben looked back into the conference room where everyone crouched behind the oval table filled with pizza boxes and bottles. Claire's wide eyes stared at him from under the table. How did it come to this? thought Ben, wondering when the attack would restart. The huge arm hanging through the shattered window twitched, flexed, then disappeared back through the opening. Whoever it was must still be alive but wounded.

Silence prevailed. Had they reconsidered after one of their own had been shot? But Ben had the distinct feeling they were regrouping, planning, soon ready to make another assault. He considered the building's layout. Could they find a more secure place to take shelter until the cavalry arrived, or was it better to stay put?

Someone on all fours crawled out of the conference room. Brett Daniels crouched next to Ben.

"What do you sense, Brett?"

"Just a vague feeling. They're angry, and we're in trouble if we stay here. That salt bath must have taken a lot of the intuition away from me, but there's still something there."

"You think they'll attack again?"

"Yes, but not sure when. Sorry I can't be more definite. I think we should move from here. Too exposed."

The agent joined them, and Ben urged him to move everyone away from the conference room.

"There's a back room where the chemicals and equipment stores are kept," he whispered. "It's a secure metal door, and there are no windows they can attack from outside. The only thing is that the pass key is in my jacket in the lab, right next to a window overlooking the car park."

“Come with me to the lab door,” said the agent, “and keep your head down.”

Ben crawled forward and jerked his hand back. A glass shard protruded from his palm. He winced, pulled it out, and pressed his fingers on the wound to stem the blood. They moved forward along the corridor until they reached the lab door.

“Where are the light switches?”

“There are none,” said Ben. “All on sensors.”

“Shit, we’d be sitting ducks in there.”

Ben peered through the glass panel in the door. Every light was on in the lab. they would all go out in time, but as soon as they stepped through the door they would instantly come on again.

Any idea where the power shutoff is?”

“I haven’t a clue. Elsa might. She’s worked here for a while.”

Ben moved back along the corridor below window level and peered into the conference room.

“Elsa, come here,” he hissed.

She shook her head.

Ben saw the fear in her eyes and crept into the room, under the table, joining her at the back wall.

“How do I kill the lights in here?”

“What do you mean?” she said, ashen-faced.

“Elsa. We need to get into the lab with the lights off so they can’t see us from outside. The lights in the lab are on motion sensors, so we can’t switch them off. How do we isolate the power?”

She stared at him for a moment, then seemed to come out of a trance.

“Ben, I’m scared.”

Ben tried to calm himself. “We’re all scared, Elsa, but we need to think rationally. Now, how do I isolate the power to the lights in the lab?”

She continued to stare.

“Elsa.” She didn’t respond.

"Elsa. Where's the damned fuse box? Speak to me." Still no reaction. Ben backhanded her across the face.

"Sorry, Elsa," he said as she brought her hand up to her cheek, startled at being slapped.

"I... I'm not sure. I think the trip switches are in the cupboard behind the reception desk."

"Is the cupboard locked?"

"No, there's no key. It's always open." She started crying.

Ben rubbed her cheek and apologized again before crawling out into the corridor and signaling to the agent before turning toward the front of the building. This would be almost as dangerous as stepping into the lab, but the reception was partly shielded from the car park by a huge planter filled with four large yucca plants and vertical blinds in the main windows. It wasn't totally out of view from outside, but at least had some cover.

Ben crawled on his belly across the coarse carpet to reach the reception desk while the agent watched from a crouched position in the corridor, weapon raised. Cursing the sight of a photocopier wedged up against the cupboard door six feet behind the desk, Ben crawled to its side, braced himself against a corner wall, and, with both feet planted on one end, pushed it as hard as he could. It wouldn't budge. He tried again, straining with all his might, but the copier just lifted on one side, the other end caught on rucked carpet. He changed tack and pulled at the copier from the front, dragging it sideways, and this time it moved toward the desk where the carpet was flat.

The copier wheels squealed, and the agent hissed at him, putting one finger to his lips. With enough clearance, Ben pulled on the cupboard handle, and it began to open but jammed on the rucked carpet. With the cupboard door only open a foot, it was impossible to enter. Ben could feel his temper fraying and pulled again at the door, but it only gave another inch.

The agent waved frantically and mouthed something while pointing at the carpet.

Ben nodded, pushed the cupboard door shut, pulled and pressed the carpet as flat as he could, and pulled the door open enough to let him in. As he shut the door behind him, the front reception window exploded. Ben slammed into the corner of the cupboard as far from the door as possible as more gunfire erupted, and several bullets ripped through the cupboard door. Louder gunfire sounded as the agent returned fire, and a horrific scream pierced the air from outside. The gunfire ceased. The low moaning of someone in pain broke the silence.

In the dim glow of a panel light, Ben could make out the row of trip switches in a Perspex-fronted cabinet above him. One of the stray bullets had shattered the front panel of the cabinet, in line with the cupboard door. He didn't want to stand in front of the door, so he took a chance with the flashlight on his phone. With the inside of the cupboard illuminated, he saw the master switch and pulled it down, disconnecting all the power in the office suites and lab.

Ben turned the flashlight off and eased the door open with his foot, still wedging himself in the cupboard's corner. When there was enough of a gap for him to get out, he got on all fours. He inwardly prayed and made a bolt for it, almost colliding with the slewed photocopier.

A flash of gunfire in the car park sent him diving into the corridor, landing flat on his stomach, almost winding himself. The agent returned fire, and another scream rang out from outside.

Ben and the agent, now both with their backs to the outside wall of the corridor, listened for movement. There was a dragging sound, something heavy on gravel. A body being moved and more screaming.

"Let's go," whispered the agent.

They half-crouched, half-ran past the conference room to the lab door. Ben crawled through and negotiated the stools and benches until he reached the lab coat hanging over the back of a chair near the window. He pulled the coat off the chair back and found the keys.

As Ben bolted for the lab door, another burst of gunfire erupted, and shattered glass filled the room as several windows at the far end of the lab imploded.

Ben ushered the staff and agents into a rear corridor at the back of the conference room. Once they were all through the door, he closed it behind them and turned on his phone flashlight once more. "Follow me," he said, pushing through the crowd and leading them to a steel door at the end of the corridor. He unlocked the door, and they piled in, spread out among the racks of chemicals, glass bottles, and lab equipment, and once all inside, he locked the door.

"Where the hell is Herbie?" said Claire.

"Still ten minutes away," said an agent, holding up his phone .

"Don't worry," said Elsa, who seemed to have recovered from her bout of dumb terror. "This room is bombproof. Reinforced concrete, steel door, steel ceiling. It would take oxy-acetylene cutting gear to get in here."

"I hope you're right," said Claire, who had her ear to the door.

The room, now lit with several phones, was large enough for many more people, but with so many racks and large equipment stands, it felt claustrophobic. An eerie silence descended, and the minutes ticked away without a hint of sound from outside. The hired technicians began talking in hushed tones. One girl sobbed into the shoulder of another girl and was getting louder until Claire 'shushed' everyone into silence.

"Can you hear that?" she whispered to Ben.

The female technician began to cry again. Claire leaned across and put her hand over the girl's mouth with one hand and raised a finger to her lips with the other. The room fell silent, and Claire strained to hear.

Doors opening and low voices filled the corridor outside.

"What's going on out there?" whispered Ben.

Claire signaled for him to stop talking so she could hear, pressing one ear to the door and cupping her other ear with her hand. She suddenly jolted back and pointed at the door handle. It was turning. The door rattled several times as someone outside tried to push it open. Claire put her ear to the door once the door handle stopped moving, and then with a crash, it shuddered once, then twice as someone tried to barge it open. The door held solid. Several more muffled voices seemed to argue, then the door shook violently again but didn't yield.

The voices were getting more distant.

"I think they've gone," she whispered to Ben.

Ben pointed at the door. "Keep listening."

"Mr. Lomax is five minutes away," said the agent, now crouched next to Claire, studying the doorframe. "Holding up pretty good," he said. "You were right. It is bombproof."

The girl behind them began crying again.

"Somebody shut her up," hissed the agent.

Claire glared and shook her head at him, then signaled to Ben to swap places with her.

She moved to the girl and led her to the back of the storeroom.

"Don't worry," whispered Claire. "Help is on the way, and they'll be here soon."

The girl nodded and sniffled into Claire's shoulder.

Ben looked back at her and waved his arm to keep the noise down.

The voices were back in the corridor, and something hit the door from outside. A series of thuds and scraping sounds filled the store. Ben looked at the agent next to him and raised his palms. The agent shook his head, unable to identify what was going on outside. Then it went silent again for a minute.

An ear-piercing wail filled the room, along with a red flashing strobe light on the ceiling. Everyone had their hands over their ears.

"What the hell is that?" shouted Ben, then Elsa screamed, pointing at the floor.

Ben looked down at wisps of smoke curling around his feet, coming from under the metal door.

SIXTY-SEVEN

Puffs of smoke seeped through the gaps around the door and frame, forming a haze of acrid smoke above their heads, spreading to the back of the room, and beginning to descend.

Ben grabbed several lab coats from a shelf, ripped off the plastic wrapping, and stuffed them along the bottom of the door to prevent more smoke from entering. He considered their chances. If it was as bombproof as Elsa claimed, it should stop the flames from getting in and roasting them all, but the smoke might get them first.

Elsa sobbed, and Claire put an arm around her.

"Don't worry, we'll be okay. Help will be here soon enough," Ben yelled above the ear-piercing fire alarm.

Sweat beaded on Ben's forehead as the temperature rose and he wondered how long it would take for the fire service to arrive. Herbie and his men wouldn't be able to extinguish the fire on their own and rescue them. He looked around the room for inspiration and pulled a box from a top shelf, ripping it open. Rolls of duct tape bounced and rolled across the floor. Ben picked up two rolls and threw one to the agent, and they began sealing the gap between the metal door and its frame. The volume of smoke entering the store almost stopped, but the room was now a haze, difficult to see through, with everyone coughing.

"Get down as low as you can," Ben shouted.

The eleven occupants of the small storeroom were now lying flat on the cool concrete floor.

Over the crashing and crackling of the fire outside and the sound of the fire alarm came a distinct hissing sound, and the lab coats at the bottom of the door moved as clouds of steam forced their way into the room under the door.

"What the hell is that?" shouted the agent.

"Sprinklers," screamed Ben, above the ear-piercing sirens. "Thank God the building's got sprinklers."

He rammed the coats back into the bottom of the door and saw them soaking up water from the deluge of sprinklers in the corridor.

Distant gunshots added to the cacophony of noise.

"Sounds like the cavalry has arrived," said Ben.

The gunshots continued for a few minutes, then the fire alarm stopped and the only sound was the constant hissing of the activated sprinklers outside in the corridor.

"They've got everything under control," said the agent. "And they're coming in to get us out of here."

Less than thirty seconds later, someone was hammering on the door.

"You can open it, Ben," said the agent. "It's our guys."

The door swung open, and smoke and steam flooded in, making visibility virtually nonexistent. A man in black combat gear stepped in, dripping with water.

"Follow me quickly," he shouted. "I'll take you out the side exit. Hold your breath. There's still toxic smoke in the corridor," he shouted through the mask. "Watch out for the boxes out here," he said, kicking a stack of smoldering files sideways that had collapsed into the doorway.

They marched through the corridor like a giant caterpillar and, by the time they reached an exit at the side of the building and emerged into fresh air, they were all soaked to the skin. Several of the technicians lay on their backs on the ground, gasping and coughing with streaming eyes, in the floodlights illuminating the yard.

Ben saw flames spreading across the flat roof section of the office suites toward the main block of the Barngate building. He looked right and was relieved to see the lab unaffected by fire, and apart from several shot through windows, it looked virtually intact. Four bodies lay in a row near the gatehouse: the security guard and three infected men, all dead, with sheets covering their heads. Another five men and a woman sat on the ground with their hands on their heads, surrounded by armed men that Ben assumed were part of a SWAT team.

The six live captives displayed various stages of the infection, and Ben could see a male and a woman with the telltale ridge running up their pronounced foreheads, showing an advanced state.

A tall man dressed in full black combat gear walked toward Ben, lifted his mask, and smiled.

Ben smiled back. "I didn't think I would ever say this, Herbie, but am I glad to see you."

He reached out, and they shook hands.

"Is it safe to go back to the lab?" asked Ben.

"Not until the fire chief says so, and the fire service hasn't got here yet. Is there someone still in there?" said Herbie, suddenly concerned.

"No, we're all out."

"You were lucky. They set fire to plastic boxes and files from reception, piling them against the storeroom door to smoke you out."

"They'd have succeeded if the place didn't have sprinklers fitted. We'd have roasted in there."

Ben pointed across the car park. "What about casualties? I can see four bodies, and I know one of them's the security guard."

"The other three are part of the gang that was trying to kill you. Ben, we were left with no choice; they were shooting at us as soon as we arrived."

"I think I can help the six people you're guarding over there. We found a cure." They both ducked as a loud crash and an explosion behind them sent a small fireball into the night sky.

"The only problem is all our research and tests are in the lab. It's vital we don't lose it."

"Tell you what," said Herbie, placing his mask and helmet on the ground. "If I get some of my guys to set up a watch between the section on fire and the lab, and it looks okay, you can go in, and I'm coming with you."

"Great," said Ben, moving toward the entrance.

"Not so fast, Ben. Let me set this up first."

Ben watched him go and realized he was freezing cold, starting to shiver. It was a warm night, but the shock of the attack and being trapped inside a burning building was now coming out. Claire walked up behind him and slipped her arm around his waist.

"You know you made me second-in-command of Moreton Scientific Investigation," she said.

"Yes?" said Ben, wondering what was coming next.

"Do I get a pay raise and danger money?"

He laughed. "You might just do after this nightmare," he said, putting his arm around her shoulder.

"What a shit-show."

"That sums it up quite nicely, Miss Manson."

"You're shaking."

"Must be shock," said Ben. "I'm bloody freezing, and yet I know it's not cold. Adrenaline playing havoc."

"Might have something to do with us being soaking wet," she said. He looked down at her and laughed. Her normally pristine hair was now a soggy mess, plastered to her head.

Ben could see Herbie walking back toward them, and they stepped apart.

"Good to go, Ben."

"Where?" asked Claire.

"Into the lab, and before you ask—"

"Shut it, Ben. I'm coming as well. I can get some of my test stuff. Quit the chivalry and let's get on with it."

Ben didn't argue. Herbie raised an eyebrow and said nothing, knowing Claire was not to be tangled with.

They walked down the corridor and into the lab where, apart from shattered window glass at the far end, everything appeared intact.

"Ben, do American fire trucks carry equipment for making a water bath?" asked Claire.

Ben shrugged his shoulders. "Herbie?"

"If they haven't, then I'm sure they could improvise. Why are you asking?"

"Good call, Claire," said Ben. "If we can get one made large enough and immerse the six captives in it for a couple of hours in a strong salt solution, we can reverse the effect the alien infection has had on them."

"Salt?" said Herbie.

"Yes, and the ultimate cure is even more unbelievable. A fix of heroin."

"You have to be kidding me?"

"Nope. Our team back home has proven that heroin kills off the invading entity that attaches itself to the host's nervous system. The whole thing is reversible. Hang on, I'll prove it." Ben walked outside and returned with Brett Daniels.

"Remember this man?" said Ben.

Herbie glanced at him and shook his head. "Never met the guy before. Who is he?"

"Brett Daniels."

Herbie stepped in closer. "It can't be."

"Herbie, this is not the time or place for me to be having a laugh or joke. This is Brett Daniels, and a few hours ago, he looked just like one of the captives you have over there. We can do the same for them."

"It's no bullshit, Mr. Lomax," said Brett. "Can you help them?" he said, pointing to the six captives.

Herbie eyed Brett Daniels up and down for a few seconds. "Unbelievable! Salt! Who would've thought it?" Herbie leaned forward and stared at Brett's face in wonder.

Brett smiled and stoked his chin. "Best shave I ever had!"

Herbie slapped Brett on the back. "I'll have a word with the fire chief; by the sound of the approaching sirens, they'll be here in a minute. This I have to see," he said.

Two fire tenders rolled into the car park, and firefighters were quickly running hoses in all directions. Within minutes they brought the fire, which had almost reached the main building, under control, filling the car park with the high-pitched scream of the fire pumps and smoke-laden steam as the breeze from the hills above pushed the billowing plume downward.

Herbie spoke with the fire chief, outlining the unusual request for a large bath to fill with salt water. The chief agreed but said that if another call came in, they might have to go but would leave the temporary bath in place.

Ben realized he had a problem, as there would not be enough salt left in the lab to make an effective brine. The fire chief came to the rescue. "One of my men has a brother with a family business just outside town that cures fish. I'm pretty sure they could spare more than enough salt."

Within minutes, one of Herbie's black sedans screamed out of the gates, heading for Reno.

SIXTY-EIGHT

One fire crew continued damping down the hot spots at the back of the building, while the other set up an improvised bath using ladders and plastic sheeting. With the help of the staff and agents, they formed a chain, passing plastic drums, buckets, and kettles of warm water from the lab. It was full just as the salt arrived, and after dissolving several sacks of salt to create a strong brine, agents herded the six captives toward the bath and ordered them in at gunpoint.

With the fire extinguished, the first fire tender left the site, but the fire chief remained, not for any operational need but out of sheer fascination with the unfolding events.

"I've been to some strange incidents in my twenty years in the service," he said to Ben, "but this one tops the lot."

Ben laughed. "Pretty weird, isn't it?"

A disturbance at the bath made Ben rush forward. The largest male captive stood, leaped over the side, barged two firefighters to the ground, and bolted for the main exit from the parking lot with huge strides. One agent raised his weapon.

"No!" screamed Ben. A second agent rushed out of the guard-house and pointed a gun at the big man.

"One more step, buddy, and you're toast. Get back in the bath, nice and easy. Turn around."

The big man slowed but kept walking toward the gatehouse. The agent lifted his weapon and fired a round into the sky, making everyone jump.

"Last chance, buddy."

Ben saw the man in turmoil, considering his chances. But then his vast frame visibly shrank in defeat as he saw reason. He turned and walked slowly back to the bath.

Ben exhaled, feeling relieved that another life had not been lost. The man climbed back into the salt water and sat, head bowed in silence, with the other five.

"Wow, that was close," said the fire chief, watching his two firefighters stand and dust themselves off, unhurt by the fleeing man.

"Thought he was going to be shot," said Ben, amazed that the agent had given the man not one but two chances to comply.

"You're the scientist I read about in *National Geographic* a while back?" said the fire chief.

"Guilty as charged."

"It made me wonder. How did it make you feel when you discovered we aren't the only ones in the universe?"

"To be honest, I've always thought we weren't alone. The universe is infinite, as far as we know, and it would be arrogant to think we were the only beings in the whole shooting match."

"But it must have been amazing to actually meet something from another world?"

Ben thought back to the horrific experience of coming face to face with a being he was sure was going to kill him and Amy, his fiancée, on a previous investigation. The thought lingered.

"Sorry, have I spoken out of turn?" said the fire chief.

"Of course not. I would be more than curious if I were you. It was such a terrible situation. It's just that you transported me back to that underground cave with that monster."

"I'm so sorry, I—"

"No need to apologize. I expect you get asked about some of the terrible sights you see in your job?"

The man nodded. "Yes, but your experience eclipses anything I've ever witnessed or ever will."

"I have to agree with you there," said Ben quietly. "I wouldn't quite describe the meeting as amazing at the time. More terrifying."

"Excuse me a second," said the chief, who walked over to his crew.

"What was that ruckus?" said Claire, woken from her nap in the back of Herbie's SUV.

"Just one captive trying to make a run for it. All under control. No one's been shot."

"I don't know about you," said Claire, "but I'm starving. When can we go?"

Ben looked at his watch. It was half past three, just before dawn. She yawned, and it set him off as well.

"You'll have to wait a while," said Ben. "There's water damage from fire hoses in the canteen, and the power's off, so there's no chance of food here. We'll have to wait for our hairy friends to get back to some form of normality before we can go. Herbie's taking them into custody, and a patrol car's staying here after we leave. Shall we go straight to the diner? It opens early for truckers, so you can fill your face in a couple of hours."

Claire pulled a face. "But I'll never last that long."

"Grow up. You'll live. Think of those poor sods sitting in that salt bath for hours."

"You mean the poor sods that just murdered a security guard and tried to kill us?"

"You know as well as I do they weren't responsible for their actions."

Claire exhaled. "You're right. You know what I don't get?" said Claire. "How come Jacy managed to lose the blue hair stuff?"

Ben laughed. "And there was me thinking you were a scientific genius, Miss Manson."

"What do you mean?"

"Cast your mind back. Where did Jacy go after he developed the symptoms?"

She mulled it over and frowned. "He said he took a trip to Santa Catalina Island to go fishing."

"Correct. What type of fishing?"

"Deep sea and spearfishing on a charter. I still don't get what you're thinking."

"Spearfishing," said Ben, enjoying the fact that, for once, her brain cogs were going around the wrong way.

"I still don't get it."

"Spearfishing isn't chucking a spear from the boat at a passing whale; it's done in scuba gear, immersed in the largest volume of salt water on the planet."

Claire burst out laughing. "How stupid am I?"

Ben gave her a knowing look.

"Don't you dare," she said.

"Come on, let's sit in the guardhouse while we wait. My back's aching from standing here." Within minutes, they were both asleep until the fire chief banged on the window.

Claire sat bolt upright, leaned over, and shook Ben, lying on the floor behind her.

The fire chief laughed as Ben's head appeared, confused and disoriented from behind the desk.

"I think the group in the bath is showing signs of something. Come take a look at them."

Clumps of hair filled the bath, and the two with the most advanced features now displayed less pronounced jawlines.

"Look at the foreheads," whispered Claire in Ben's ear.

The distinct ridges and pronounced brows were gone, and the two looked human again, with not a serrated tooth in sight.

"I've never seen anything like this," said the fire chief.

"Hope I never will again," whispered Claire.

"Can somebody put some hot water in here before we die of hypothermia?" said the woman.

Ben leaned over to Herbie. "How long have they been in there?"

"Two hours and fifty minutes," said Herbie, without looking at his watch. "Another ten minutes? You said three hours."

"We'll let the four with less developed symptoms out first. Give the other two another twenty minutes, just to be on the safe side."

Herbie nodded. "Make it longer if you like. I don't care if we stay here till Thanksgiving, as long as it works."

"Don't worry. It will."

By six in the morning, all the captives were looking like normal human beings. All aggressiveness had vanished, and they were eager to cooperate. The fire chief left two of his men in a small rescue truck to keep watch for any further hot spot outbreaks in the collapsed section of the building, along with one patrol car.

Herbie took the six captives in a small convoy to Reno, and Ben agreed they would examine them later that day and discuss the next stage of their total cure.

Claire leaped into the SUV. "I don't care what I look like, I don't care how tired you are, I don't care that we absolutely stink to high heaven of smoke, I want food!"

"Let's hope the diner's open then," he said, pulling out onto the lakeside road.

As they pulled into the parking lot at Mary and Mo's, Ben's phone pinged.

"Roger wants me to call him. He's got some good news."

"Roger can wait. We're going in and ordering. I could eat a cow between two bread trucks."

Ben laughed, got out, and staggered. Standing in the Barngate parking lot for hours stiffened his legs. "You go in. I'll have the 'Walking Hungry' and a flat white. Tell Zinnia to throw in an extra caffeine shot before I doze off."

Claire was about to come back with a sarcastic remark about the waitress, then checked herself, remembering Ben's ultimatum from Amy, his promotion-hungry fiancée.

She stopped at the door when she saw a familiar smiling face. Jeff West, the *New York Times* reporter, waved from the other end of the diner and beckoned her across.

"Nice to see you again. What can I get you? It's on me," he said, with a broad grin.

"Up early, Jeff? You've come for the rest of the story, I take it?"

"Yep. I kept my part of the bargain. I'm here for yours."

"Before we discuss anything, Ben has to be here. He's just making a call outside, and I need food. Sorry, we both do." She ordered, and Jeff laughed when her stomach rumbled loud enough to hear. A waitress walked past with a plate stacked with pancakes, bacon, and maple syrup. The delicious aroma made her mouth water, and as attractive as Jeff West's face was, all she could think about was food.

The coffees arrived at the same time as Ben, who shook hands with Jeff and slid in next to Claire.

"To what do we owe this pleasure, Jeff, as if I didn't know?"

"Just collecting my part of our deal," he said, pulling out his recording device.

Claire moved a hand toward it and looked at Ben, who shook his head. "Let him record this. He's already proved he's on the level."

Jeff smiled at Claire and switched the recorder on.

"Before I say a word, Jeff, tell me what you know. I'll listen while we eat."

Claire was already attacking her 'Walking Hungry.' Her table manners had deserted her and Ben glanced sideways, starting to laugh, and almost choking on a mouthful of fries.

Jeff had limited knowledge of the events the previous night but was aware of a shooting, a fire, and the capture of several infected individuals. He accurately reported the events in London and that the team based at Moreton had relocated to an unknown destination. Most of the information gathered was already in the public domain.

"What I would like to know is the finer detail that only you,

Claire, and your team are aware of," said Jeff, poised with a pen and notepad in addition to the recorder.

Ben took a moment to consider the request and the extent to which he could disclose information that might contravene what Chris Williams had stipulated. The ground rules Chris had laid out were for the London part of the investigation.

"I won't comment about our involvement in London until I have contacted a representative from the Home Office back home," said Ben.

"Confidentiality issue?"

Ben nodded.

"Understood. So, could you let me know what happened last night and in the early hours of this morning at Barngate Holdings?"

Starting at the wrecker's yard just outside Nixon, Ben narrated the events up to the time they restored the six captives to their original human selves. He left out the discovery that heroin was also being investigated as being too controversial on top of what would cause tremendous interest, and it was still at the testing stage. At least they had tried salt, and it had proved a success.

"Where are the six being held?" said Jeff.

"Reno, but I haven't been told exactly where yet," said Ben.

"I need to speak to at least one of the six in custody."

"Why the ones in custody?"

"Because they've experienced going as far as possible in the transformation before you checked it with the salt bath. I bet they have insight into the alien life that started this all off."

"If they are smart, they'll consult with lawyers and refuse to engage in any discussions. I know Herbie Lomax won't allow it." Ben paused with a distant stare.

"Ben?" said Claire, but he didn't respond. "I think he's having one of his eureka moments," she whispered to Jeff.

"Give me a moment," said Ben, getting out of his seat. "I may have another way to get what you want." He started to walk outside to make a call.

"Ben, don't bother," said Jeff. "We need to get out of here."

"What do you mean?" said Ben.

Jeff gestured toward the front window overlooking the main road. Three vans and half a dozen SUVs pulled into the parking lot.

"The vultures have arrived," said Jeff. "Can we get out the back way?"

They barged into the kitchen where the owner and three kitchen staff were in conversation.

"We need to use your back door," said Ben.

Zinnia stepped forward and, before her boss could protest, unlocked the door at the back of the kitchen.

"What's the problem?" she said.

"The media are hounding us," said Claire. "They've just pulled into the parking lot."

Zinnia nodded. "Go," she said. "I'll keep them busy for a couple of minutes. You owe me, Dr. Sharman," she said with a mischievous smile.

SIXTY-NINE

Roger knocked on the door to room three. It took several minutes for the door to open, and Jen, in her pajamas, squinted into the harsh light of the corridor.

"What's up?" she said.

"Sorry, Jen, but I think I have the answer."

"Come in," she said, stepping aside. She sat heavily on the bed, rubbing her eyes, and lifted her watch off the side table. "What's so important at four in the morning? I'm absolutely knackered."

"Sorry, Jen. Look." He passed her his phone, displaying a text message.

"You read it," she said, yawning. "I can't focus."

"It's a list of medicines that doctors have administered to Bob French since they took him into isolation."

"And?"

"Codeine."

"What?"

"Codeine. They've been giving him codeine for headaches."

"So?"

"Come on, Jen. Codeine is an opioid pain reliever. I think this removed the alien symptoms from Bob French, and if it did, it's a simple cure."

"I just can't think at this time of day," she said, rolling sideways and pulling the bed cover over her. "Now get out of my room and let me sleep. We can't get hold of any codeine at this time of the morning to run tests, so sod off and let Ben know."

"Codeine?" said Claire.

"Yes, you heard correctly, and it makes sense. Codeine would act a lot slower than heroin, but fingers crossed, it's done the same job and destroyed the entity within the host's body. I've arranged with Herbie to bring two of the captives here for us to test after they've had full body scans at the medical center in Reno, which is happening as we speak. He'll arrange for the results to come straight to us here."

Clearing up the last fragments of glass from the far end of the lab were three of the six lab assistants who opted to stay, plus a new volunteer. The broken windows had been boarded up, and the power re-connected.

"Almost back to some form of normality," said Claire. "Apart from the stink of smoke."

"Just have to put up with that. It's not ideal to work in a contaminated environment. We'll examine the two who are arriving shortly, and then I think we're done here.

"Back to the UK?" said Claire.

"If the tests prove positive, then there's no reason for us to stay. We can't work in this place in a smoke contaminated lab."

"You better not set your heart on it until you've told Herbie."

"Already have, and he agrees. We can go home. We're better served working in the UK at the secure lab and using conference calls to collaborate."

The two arrived, a man and a woman, handcuffed, dressed in

boiler suits, and both looking shell-shocked.

"I think you can remove the cuffs, gentlemen," said Ben to the two police officers escorting the prisoners.

"Sorry, Dr. Sharman, but we have orders to keep them cuffed."

"I assume you removed the cuffs while they were being scanned at the medical center?"

"Yes, but..."

Ben stood upright, folded his arms, and frowned at the officer. "I can't conduct my medical examination and scientific tests with them trussed up like turkeys."

The officer looked at his partner, who nodded and uncuffed them.

"Okay, folks, take a seat. Can I have your names?"

"Miranda Cape," said the woman softly.

"And you, sir?"

"You don't recognize me?"

"John Drake?"

The man nodded. Ben studied the man's face. Native American, blue eyes, age around mid-forties, and nothing like the huge, hairy man he met before. He looked across at Claire, whose eyes were wide and her mouth hanging open.

"Yes," he said, "and I cannot express how sorry I am for what happened at the wrecker's yard and how grateful we all are that you saved us."

"No need for that. You had no control over your actions. Just hope the authorities see it that way."

Ben called over the new lab technician. "Can you interview John Drake in the conference room? I want to know every detail about his ordeal. Take down everything he says and record it."

The technician nodded.

"Claire, can you do the same for Miranda but stay here? I want the interviews to be independent of each other."

Ben turned to the officers. "Is that okay with you? While they're being interviewed, I'll be running tests and reviewing the full body scans you took them for before you got here." The officers agreed, and split, one to attend each interview.

Ben viewed the scans and, in both cases, discovered that the entity remained in place at the base of the skull, but all filaments extending from it had retracted. He groaned to himself. If the salt bath eradicated *every* trace, they could fly back to the UK. The images confirmed they would have to stay a little longer.

After interviewing both Miranda and John and conducting dozens of tests, the police officers handcuffed them and took them back to Reno. Each of them received a potent dose of codeine, which the other four prisoners would also take every four hours. The next day, they would undergo scans to monitor the effect of the codeine on the entity still inside their bodies.

Ben watched the patrol car pull out of the site onto the main road and entered the conference room with Claire.

"You can take your lab coat off after you copy every note you've taken on the photocopier. Did you get everything you needed to ask?"

"That was genius," said Jeff West. "I got a lot more than I bargained for. It's going to make one hell of a story."

"You actually looked the part. Perhaps you should change professions," said Claire, offering him back the lab coat.

"I think I'll stick to what I do best. I couldn't compete with you guys."

"Just remember our agreement," said Ben. "Not a clue in the report that you got this here. It's too close to the bone, and I might get into real trouble."

"My word is good," said Jeff. "It'll be an undisclosed source, and I'll word it so it looks like my source is someone outside your scientific circle."

"Good. Now you better copy your report for me and get out of here before Herbie or one of his men turns up and starts sniffing around."

"Thanks, Ben. That has to be the most fascinating interview I've ever done. He told me what it was like to feel and think like an alien species. All I can say is it was a good job you stopped the process before they fully changed, as I think we would have been in real trouble. They planned to speed up the process. Their development was in the early stages and only ramped up when Herbie Lomax went on a hunting expedition. You could have been looking at hundreds, maybe thousands, of infected folk."

"How?"

"If someone sabotaged the drinkable water supply by releasing spores, it wouldn't take long for thousands of people to get infected, and once the spores multiplied, it would become more difficult and maybe impossible to stop them.

"What about others that remain uncaptured?"

"He believes that all infected individuals here have been captured or are dead. You can read it in the report, and I'll get the recording transcribed for you."

"Let's hope he's right. There are still infected people in London who haven't been captured. I'm going to talk to our contact at the Home Office."

After Jeff West left, the lab conducted multiple tests on samples from Miranda Cape and John Drake, and the three genuine lab assistants went home for the day. Ben and Claire reviewed the interview that Jeff West had done with John Drake.

"He's very good," said Claire. "I wouldn't have known he was a reporter, would you?"

"Have to agree. Every question he's put to Drake has a plausible scientific angle. He wasn't joking when he said he was good. But there's one thing that bothers me, and it's not in the interview. These entities have a telepathic ability, but how far does that capability extend? A few hundred yards, miles, globally?"

"You're thinking they may have already contacted others in London? Surely that's a stretch? John Drake would have known."

"You could be right, but I just have a nagging doubt. We rely on facts, and where we don't have all the facts, we have to consider the worst."

SEVENTY

"What will happen to them?" asked Ben.

Herbie removed his sunglasses and took a sip of beer. "It has to go the usual route, I'm afraid. We can't bypass the system in any way. All six individuals face charges of murder, along with numerous other offenses, including the attempted murder of eleven people locked inside a storeroom. The six prisoners were involved in the murder of the security guard. Only one person shot him, but all six were there and implicated."

"But that's ridiculous. You know as well as I do they were not responsible for their actions."

"Of course, but it has to follow the law, and the law dictates they all have to be tried for murder."

"Isn't there any kind of intervention from the White House?"

"If you're thinking that the President would intervene and offer a pardon, then no. State law, not federal law, governs the crimes committed."

"So it comes down to evidence and expert witnesses?" said Claire.

Herbie drained the glass and handed it to Dorothy.

"You like more, Mr. Lomax?"

"Just one more, Dorothy. I think I've earned it. You are quite correct, Claire. It will be a trial carried out under Nevada state law, and the evidence is twofold. What they did, which isn't disputed, and why they did it, which is where you and Ben will be called as expert witnesses."

"When will this happen?" asked Ben.

"I can't answer that until a judge sets a trial date, but you'll know well in advance."

"From what I've seen, it all comes down to the skill of the lawyers," said Ben. "Let's be honest, who on a jury is going to believe that aliens are the actual murderers?"

Herbie shook his head. "You're forgetting something. Every jury member will have heard of you and the alien cases you've dealt with in the past. This latest alien encounter is global news, and unless any jury member has been living under a rock for the last week, they will know who you are, what you've done, and be thankful you prevented catastrophic outcomes that could have affected everyone on this planet. Do you think they'll not believe your expert evidence?"

Ben said nothing and looked at the scrubland beyond the garden fence. Two days had passed since the prisoners started receiving regular doses of codeine, and the results showed positive outcomes, completely eliminating the alien entities from their bodies. Although he and Claire had spent a relatively short time in Nevada, it seemed like a lifetime, and he was ready to go home.

The thought of Amy moving to her new job in Newcastle, over two hundred miles from Moreton-in-Marsh, had almost overshadowed the success of their investigation and troubled him for days since she gave him the ultimatum over the phone. He would talk to her face to face, and if she went through with the move, which looked certain, as she'd accepted the promotion, he'd decided he wasn't going with her, and if that meant the end of their relationship, then so be it. On the surface, this felt selfish and maybe a little spiteful, but deep down, he knew she was not the woman for him. He'd known for a long time but had just bumbled along with the relationship; familiar, comfortable, and boring. Yes, it was boring, and he'd finally admitted to himself that they were best going their separate ways.

"Calling Ben Sharman," said Claire, snapping her fingers in front of his eyes. "Is there anybody there?"

"Sorry," he said, turning back to face them. "Miles away."

"We need to pack. The flight's at midday tomorrow, and we have to be at the airport by nine, so an early start."

"Already done, Miss Manson," said Dorothy.

"Hang on, Dorothy. You don't know what I was going to wear on the plane."

"I guess," she said. "Hope you like. I wash all dirty clothes, dry, iron, and put in case."

Ben laughed. "Manson. You don't even know yourself what you were going to wear on the plane."

Claire laughed. "Thank you, Dorothy. You've been wonderful. We'll miss you."

The little woman gave a sad smile, bowed, and disappeared across the patio into the kitchen.

"The good news is that you won't be involved with Vince King's and Kelvin Staples' trial," said Herbie.

"I'd forgotten about those two. What's happening with them?"

"Both charged with first-degree murder. Both pleading not guilty and so far, 'no comment' from either of them. They've hired some of the best defense lawyers, as you would expect with King's considerable resources. Trial date's not set, but the prosecution team has enough on them to put at least Staples on death row."

"You must have solid evidence?"

"We have, but there were also some golden nuggets from a reporter at the *New York Times*, Jeff West."

Claire coughed and spluttered. "Sorry," she said. "Drink went down the wrong way."

"You okay?" said Herbie, patting her on the back. She nodded vigorously.

"Wasn't he the one who broke the story about the capture of our six?"

Herbie gave Ben a slow nod and a faint smile that spoke volumes. "The very same," he said, continuing to look at Ben with the same knowing smile. "He's been tracking Vince for over a year and supplied me with so many facts and figures about Vince's dealings that tied in with our investigations that it was almost watertight."

"Almost?" asked Claire, who had regained her composure.

"The best pieces of evidence came out of Vince's and Kelvin's mouths."

This puzzled Ben. "I thought you said they just provided 'no comment' interviews?"

"The problem with Vince King is he's no criminal mastermind. He forgot to wipe the video and audio recordings at Barngate Holdings that he used to eavesdrop on you two. What he should have done was delete them all after he listened.

"I don't get it. What did we say that incriminated him?"

"You didn't. He and Kelvin did. They had many discussions in various locations in the building about several corrupt meetings, and in one session in the canteen, they talked about the two murders in graphic detail. The problem with Vince is he's careless and lazy and only watched and listened to the sections where you and Claire were in the building. I'm not even sure he realized the recordings are voice-activated. He wasn't the brightest with technology. So we have him by the balls. The idiots gave a video-recorded account of what they'd done, and we didn't even have to ask a question. It'll be interesting to see how the defense lawyers react during disclosure when they get to see the video evidence."

Herbie downed his beer in one and stood. "Okay, folks, I'm going to take my leave. A car will pick you up in the morning and there's no rush to get to the airport. You're pre-booked and flying from Vegas, business class. This isn't goodbye. I'll come over to the UK to see you soon, and you'll be asked to return to give your evidence at the trial."

They walked him to his car and watched the black SUV drive off.

"Old Herbie's been a bit of a roller coaster," said Claire. "One minute I thought he was our enemy, then I liked him, disliked him, and now I like him again."

"Just doing his job, but I think he's alright. He could have been much more heavy-handed with everything, including us."

"Shall we have another drink as Dorothy has packed for us?" said Claire.

"Why not? I have a few things to discuss with you, anyway."

"Sounds ominous."

"Not really. I just want you to know something before we head home."

Claire sipped her final Harvey Wallbanger, leaning on the pool bar, while Ben told her about his decision with Amy.

"Isn't there any way you can save the relationship? It just seems sad that you've been with her for so long and it's over just because of distance?"

"It isn't just that. Things have been brewing even before this cop promotion thing came up. I've been questioning whether we were right for each other for a while, and I suspect Amy's been doing the same."

She drummed the bar top with her fingers. "You need to think long and hard before you end it. You don't want to regret it somewhere down the line."

Ben sighed. "Down the line is the problem. I've tried to imagine what it would be like living with her in the future, and I just don't see it working."

"Here's what I think. Do nothing. Let her move to Newcastle and see how it pans out. If it was meant to end, it will, but if there's still a spark, I think both of you will know and want to stay together. What's that saying about absence making the heart grow fonder?"

Ben shook his head. "No. My mind's made up, and life's too short."

Claire reached across and put her hand on his. "You might still be miserable without her."

"My problem. To be honest, I'm looking forward to being unattached."

"Pity I'm attached," she said without thinking, regretting it immediately. She removed her hand and closed her eyes, feeling the heat rising up her neck.

Ben didn't respond for a while. "Sorry I offloaded that on you," he said, with his head bent. "But I needed to talk to someone."

She reached her hand across again. "Anytime, Ben."

SEVENTY-ONE

"Kind of creepy looking," said Chris Williams, looking down the street from Cricketers Bridge. White dust coated every part of the tarmac, sidewalks, and greenery. They peered down the approach to the canal towpath, drenched in a strong saline solution that had evaporated, leaving salt deposits everywhere.

"Do you think it'll work, Ron?"

"You'll never stop all of it, but if it's kept on top of, then I can't see it getting out of hand again. My worry is that the government haven't treated a wide enough area, and if it travels beyond the decontamination zone, it'll start again."

"Yes, but at least we know how to deal with it."

Ron lit a Marlboro and took a long drag. "I thought I'd seen the strangest sights during Covid, with empty streets in London, but this comes pretty close. Gritters treating the roads when it's not winter and salt residue painting every surface, plant, and tree. You can almost taste it in the air."

"Did you hear about that animal rights group?"

"The ones moaning about rat testing?"

Chris nodded. "They tried to get an injunction to stop the salt decontamination."

"Really?"

"We live in a strange world. They had no problem getting a barrister, which sickens me. Money overrides everything."

"You said they tried?"

"It was a non-starter, thank goodness. The PM pulled the national security card on them, but they're appealing through the European judicial system."

"It makes me laugh. If someone has a gripe, no matter how absurd, they're able to get an injunction at the drop of a hat," said Ron, taking his sunglasses off and wiping his brow. "Can we get off the bridge, Chris? I'm bloody melting."

Chris drove to Limehouse Basin, where Ben and Claire were waiting for them in the Grapes.

"Nice to see you and Claire back in old Blighty," said Chris, pointing to a table at the back of the bar with a reserved sign on it. "I've ordered lunch for us all. The landlord was more than pleased to get the booking. Not many dining out around here since this thing started."

"Has any more human infection turned up since we last spoke?" said Ben.

"Thankfully, no," said Chris. "Roger and Jen have run tests on Bob French, and he's clear. Codeine tests on infected lab rats have proved a complete success, and we've continued with the rat extermination program and kept watch for any signs of other aquatic life that's been affected. I'm confident we can open Limehouse Basin and the canal network again, but we'll be keeping a close eye on everything."

"What about the old man attacked by an infected male?"

"Turned out to be a hoax. Well, not so much a hoax, as the elderly man was attacked, but the attacker was wearing a mask. CCTV picked up him taking the mask off in the next street and he's been identified and arrested. There are another seven people identified who had the infection. All apprehended and treated. Fingers crossed there are no more."

"Any more on the two thugs that kidnapped Ron and almost saw him off in the substation?"

"Interesting one, this. The National Crime Agency has been looking at a gang involved in fraud and money laundering and flagged up the two men as doing work for a person of interest, who has been recycling cash through a huge property scam. The person of interest has no bearing on your investigation, but the agency has flagged up Wayne Fletcher and Zak Wilson as employees of none other than the Museum of Alien Life, whom you dealt with when you interviewed the owner, Alex Munro.

"I just love coincidences," said Ben.

"This is where it gets mysterious. No one has seen Alex for two days. He's disappeared. Nobody at the museum knows where he is, and he hasn't used his phone, credit cards, or spoken to any known associates or family members during that time."

"So what's the score?" said Ben.

"We think he's gone to ground, worried that Zak Wilson, who's still in custody, has grassed him up. We believe Munro ordered the kidnapping."

"Sorry, I don't get it," said Ben. "Why would he be behind the threats, kidnapping, and attempted murder of Ron?"

"We're not sure yet."

"This is all supposition?"

"Strangely, Zak Wilson seemed to want to cooperate at one stage, but at his interview, he was tight-lipped. Not a word. The detective interviewing him observed a significant shift in attitude from the time of Wilson's arrest to his formal interview, as if someone had pressured him.

"So, do you think there's still a potential risk to Ron or anyone else who works for me?"

"I don't think so. That's the best I can offer. I believe Zak Wilson wouldn't dare do anything else, and of course, Wayne Fletcher's dead."

"Good. I think we can all return to Moreton. Chris, unless you need us for anything else, our work is done."

"We've set up a team to monitor any future outbreaks which mirrors what they're doing in the US, but I'm confident we've got the handle on this and there won't be any problem here. There's just one thing I need to clear up. This is for my superior; I didn't initiate this. They want to know how the *New York Times* managed to get such a comprehensive insight into the case."

Ben kept his eyed locked on Chris. "I read that report, and it was obviously an inside informant."

"It wouldn't have anything to do with you?" she said, staring at Ben. "Only the reporter supposedly had no access to John Drake, who's still locked up, awaiting trial. The only time Drake was not locked up was when he came to you for tests."

"I can assure you that I have discussed nothing about John Drake's experiences with any reporter."

"But you have spoken to the reporter concerned?"

"Yes, Jeff West approached me to comment on what happened the day of the attack and fire at Barngate Holdings. He already had most of the information at his disposal, and I merely told him the sequence of events from my perspective."

"You realize you weren't supposed to discuss the investigation with anyone without prior approval?"

"Of course, but I was only discussing events in the USA, most of which was already in the public domain. Everything he reported about the investigation in the UK he got from his own efforts, not me. I informed him at the time that I would not discuss the investigation in the UK without your approval."

"I was sat with Ben and Jeff West at the time and confirm that Ben flatly refused to discuss the UK investigation," said Claire.

"So I can tell my superiors that you only discussed events on the day of the attack and fire, refused to comment on the UK operation, and the *New York Times* did not interview you regarding John Drake?"

"That is exactly what you can tell them."

She smiled, and her entire face lit up. "In that case, I'll buy the next round," she said and downed a whole pint of lager before going to the bar to order.

"That was intense," said Ron. "She'd make a good interrogator."

"I just hope they believe what she tells them, as the payoff from this is unbelievable. I'd like to work for her again."

"Well, you weren't lying, were you?" said Claire. "Talking of payoffs, and I'm speaking for my mate Ron here as well..."

"God, you are so transparent, Manson. You're after a pay rise?"

"Correct."

"I'll give it some thought. You'll both get a one-off bonus for this work, and I'll pay you for your missed garden leave, Ron, and a bit more for the danger you've been put in. Some of it self-inflicted..."

Claire raised an eyebrow.

"Just joking," said Ben. "We'll have this last drink and head home. The Cotswolds and my bed are calling."

EPILOGUE

"Second time lucky," said Connor O'Hare, firing the diesel engine of the Pride of Skibbereen back to life after over a week of being moored at Limehouse Basin.

"And it can't come a moment too soon," said Mary. "I'm bloody sick of living in a hotel, even if we didn't have to pay for it. Full steam ahead, Captain," she ordered. "Let's go on holiday."

Connor smiled and pulled her in tight with his spare arm.

The boat glided across the mirror-finish of the basin before reaching the lock gates. Together, they passed through both sets of gates and entered Regent's Canal for the second time.

"Just take a quick look behind, Mary, and see if there are any blue bubbles following us," said Connor with a chuckle. Although she knew he was joking, she couldn't resist looking over her shoulder.

"Oh my God."

"Yeah, yeah, Mary. Nice try."

"No. Look. There's a body."

Connor swung his head around and could only see water, the towpath, and the lock gate fifty yards behind.

He started laughing. "Nearly had me there, Mary." He looked

across at her. Her hand was over her mouth, and her eyes were wide. He knew she wasn't joking and stopped the motor. The Pride of Skibbereen, drifted forward.

"Where?"

Mary said nothing, pointing at the reeds at the edge of the far bank near the lock gates.

Connor cupped his hand over his eyes and saw it. A man's head, face down in the water, with the neck and shoulders just above the surface. He pulled out his phone and began to dial the emergency services. Mary snatched the phone and shut it down.

"Not this time," she said. "Let someone else discover it and make the call. I'm not spending another minute here. If you call the police, we'll be stuck here for another day, at least."

"But, Mary..."

"O'Hare, start the engine. We haven't seen a thing. He's as dead as a doorpost, and there's nothing we can do for him now. Let someone else find him and get quizzed by the cops. It's not going to be us this time."

He looked into her eyes, bright, intense, and not yielding an inch. Connor nodded and put his hand out. She replaced the phone in his palm and pointed ahead. He stared at her, so she jabbed him in his ribs and pointed ahead again.

The diesel engine burst into life as she slipped her arm around his waist, kissed his neck, and rested her head on his shoulder. Above the steady chug of the engine, the only sounds were the occasional cries of moorhens from the reeds shrouded in mist, and the distant hum of traffic in the concrete sprawl surrounding the still water ahead. Without looking back, the O'Hares continued along Regent's Canal on the holiday they had been dreaming of for decades.

The wake behind drifted outward, hitting the bank and rocking back into the middle of the canal. Enough to dislodge the body, twisting it face up. Alex Munro gazed up at the early morning London sky with eyes that would never see again.

ACKNOWLEDGMENTS

I would like to thank the following people who were kind enough to help me with invaluable feedback:

Des Burns
Christine Williams
Amanda Griffiths
Lawrence James
Nigel Hall
Jen Willey
Alan Loewen
William Duthie
Richard 'Dickie' Davies

ALSO BY ROB NESBITT

BOOK 4 IN THE MORETON SCIENTIFIC INVESTIGATION SERIES

ROB NESBITT
EXCAVATION
MORETON SCIENTIFIC INVESTIGATION SERIES

BEFORE YOU CLOSE THE BOOK...

If you would like to read my other books, receive free short stories and other goodies please sign up to my author mailing list here at https://rnesbitt.com

Beneath

Requests to publish work from this book should be sent to
r.m.nesbittauthor@gmail.com

Cover Design by Rob Nesbitt

Editor Melanie Underwood

Written in American English

Printed in Dunstable, United Kingdom

78720385R00228